# T
# Creamsickle

## Rhiannon Argo

**2009**

*For Alexander*

# Acknowledgments

Thank you to Katherine V. Forrest for making a place for this book in the world. Huge thanks to Michelle Tea for all her generous encouragement and for creating ultrafun opportunities for broke queer artists to publish, perform and even get paid. Thanks to Nadia and Tiger for fueling my mania with theirs. Thanks to Jaye the little editing fairy that fell into my lap at the perfect moment, and to Ian Phillips who nicely donated editing aid. Thanks to Yes Alexander who makes music that is magical to write to, to Amos Mac for being such a cute and talented photographer and to Elisa Shea and Six Morsch for also taking hot photos of queers and Creamsickles. Thanks to my awesome Sister Spit tour mates, Cristy C. Road, Ali Liebegott, Robin Akimbo, Nicole J. Georges, Tamara Llosa Sandor, Tara Perkins and Eileen Myles. Thanks to Michael Nava, Nic W, Sasha Mace, Janette B, Malic Amalya, Whiskey, Whale, Kirk Read, Len Plass, Keiko, Kerri Valentine, my Las Chicas, Mesa High, The Lambda Literary Writers Retreat, Peter Moore, and tons of thanks to my mom who lent me a room to write in.

# Chapter 1

I don't want to tell you her real name because right now it feels like sandpaper on my tongue to even try to say it. That's how mad I am about the fact that I fell in love with her. I guess I'll call her Hurricane. My roommates hate me right now because I recommended Hurricane as a good potential roommate after I met her at a coffee shop and started crushing on her. But when I'd first hooked up with her, a month after she moved in at the beginning of summer, I swear she hadn't been such a mess. I admit the house drama is partially my fault. Everyone knows the number one rule to maintaining a happy home is *Never fuck your roommate*. The other day, when I was trying to sneak out the door to meet up with my skate crew, our other roommates cornered me with a list of complaints.

"The neighbors all hate her," Jeremiah said. He was right. One night we came home and the woman who lives in the house in front of ours poked her head out her front door and stopped us. "On Tuesday night there was way too much noise," she said, glaring at Hurricane who kept walking down the narrow path to our front door, pretending not to hear her. The noise, the neighbor informed me was not music it was "other things." She said "other things" in a low, hushed voice. I blushed when I figured out what she meant—that since Hurricane was the newest addition to my house the loud sex noise was all her. But

I was partially to blame. We fucked loud with the windows wide open to let in the midsummer night.

"All her druggie friends are always over here watching movies and we're going to get robbed," Jeremiah continued.

"I think she's turning tricks. And she better not do it out of this house!" Leonora pursed her thin lips. "We want to kick her out and change the locks. We're having a house meeting Friday to figure this shit out. And you better be home."

My friends hate Hurricane too. For days and days I had to hide the fact that I'd started fucking her but Cruzer soon caught on. She's known me since I was fifteen so it's especially hard to hide shit from her. The reason it even took her as long as it did was because she was consumed by this intense crush she'd developed on our friend Dixie and all she could do lately was talk about it. I didn't even have to bother with lying about my situation because Cruzer was so distracted. But, then I started doing Oxycontin. That's when I lost all control over anything as slippery as secrets. One day Cruzer cornered me, demanding answers, and the details of my hot and frenzied affair leaked right out of my overly relaxed mouth.

"What the fuck!" Cruzer shouted. We were standing on the street and people started looking over at us like we were going to fight and they felt sorry for me since Cruzer was so much bigger and tougher looking.

"What? You and Soda are doing hella pills," I protested. It didn't seem fair that she could be such a hypocrite about things that she'd been swallowing that were simply different colors.

"That's *so* different. You're practically a fucking junkie doing that sort of pill, *and* what's worse is that you are fucking a junkie!"

"It's not like that. It's just Oxy and she's not a junkie anymore."

"I don't fucking care what she is! *She* is going to ruin your life!"

After that sidewalk showdown Cruzer and our newest skate buddy Soda started taking turns checking up on me. They'd say stuff like, *I was just skating by* after they'd incessantly rung the annoyingly loud and impossible to ignore doorbell buzzer, but really they wanted to make sure I wasn't simultaneously on drugs and fucking Hurricane. Most of the time I'm not doing this but just pathetically watching Hurricane slouching around the house in all her gloriously destructive beauty. It doesn't matter though because whenever Cruzer and Soda stop by the house they get ultraparanoid about *whatever* I'm doing. *What the hell are you doing watching tripped out movies holed up in The Cave all day when it's sunny outside?* People like to refer to my house as *The Cave* because it's practically underground. To even get to the front door you have to go down a series of concrete paths and stairs that descend into damp basement darkness. During these visits Cruzer might even shove my skate shoes on my feet, grab my board and pull me outside, all while glaring at Hurricane who was usually slumped on the couch, too out of it to care.

Cruzer and I would skate away from The Cave, the bright day sun hurting my bat eyes, and all the noise of the outside world bursting in my ears like firecrackers. Skating is incredibly fun on pills. The closest thing I'll ever get to flying. I've attempted flying other ways but those methods have resulted in broken, bruised or sprained limbs. I started attempting to fly really young. I have a scar between my eyes from when I hurled my body down some stairs at three years old. I broke my arm for the first time when I was seven and Cameron Jones told all the other kids racing in the dirt at this construction site that I couldn't ride my bike off the biggest of the dirt mountains. When I was twelve I fell off a roof and came home with a black eye from a tree branch smacking my face on the way down. Then when I was fifteen I came home with my first skateboard. My mother screamed about it for a week. She told me I had to give it back to the boy who gave it to me. She threatened to use it for firewood. She said if she had to pay another one of my hospital bills it would put us all out of house and home. I hid the skateboard in my backyard in the row of bushes underneath my bedroom window. When I did stuff like rolling my ankle or tearing half the skin off my shin, I would come home and hide myself in my room. Around that time was when she graduated night school and got a job that had her traveling all over the country so she stopped noticing what I did anyways.

The messed up thing about my Bois checking up on me is that it heightens this feeling that I'm having a sneaky affair. Everyone knows taboo sex is way hotter than an average hookup so maybe that explains why dykes are always fucking their friend's exes? Can you really blame it all on the zero degree of separation in queer communities? Naw. It's because sneaky sex is hot. Like when I'm fucking Hurricane in this frenzied fast way and I keep thinking any second the goddamn doorbell will ring, or there will be a rat-tat-tat on my windowpane, or my friends will bust in my bedroom door and flip out, or my roommates will come home early from work and accuse me of making the house more desirable for our awfully undesirable roommate, or that the neighbors will call the cops about the fact that Hurricane sounds like a screeching train whistle when she's coming.

Of course all these worries also work to stress me out during the time that I'm *not* actually having sex with Hurricane. The good thing is that she's got pockets full of colors that make everything okay for about four hours.

I'm pretty sure right this second my happy four-hour high has completely worn off because I'm starting to think too much. It's this watermelon rain kind of evening. The kind of rain that's a cool slap of mist that leaves spider web droplets in your hair. I'm lying in my bed and watching it fog up my bedroom windows and thinking neurotically about how I should start looking for a new place to live, like right this second to get out of this mess. Hurricane is lying next to me in a post-fuck daze staring at the ceiling and lighting up a new cigarette every ten minutes. I can't believe I keep letting her smoke in my bed. I can't believe I recommended her as a good potential roommate to my other roommates when she really is a total disaster. I can't believe I just made her come three times using these new tricks Cruzer told me about last week while we were skating the downtown Bridge Blocks.

My cell phone rings and Hurricane trembles beside me like

the noise has just shaken her out of a bad dream. It's Cruzer calling. I put my finger to my lips and give Hurricane a look and she rolls her eyes at me. She hates Cruzer. "I'm coming by your house to get you in fifteen minutes. I'm throwing an enchilada party for Dixie," Cruzer says. The Enchilada Party is all part of Cruzer's scheme to prove to our friend Dixie that she's special so she will put out. Dixie always just rolls her big brown doe eyes and laughs when Cruzer kneels in front of her and offers presents like her favorite liquor Alizé and V's. She's smart and she's making Cruzer work for it. They've been friends long enough that she knows firsthand what a jerk Cruzer can be to girls she sleeps with. Plus Cruzer's all-consuming crush came so out of the blue that no one believes it. "Is she really serious about all this?" Dixie asked me, confused when Cruzer first confessed her love, and I had to say yeah because she hadn't shut up all week about wanting to fuck Dixie, even though her talking about our friend like that completely grossed me out. She'd never even mentioned thinking Dixie was hot before and then one morning at breakfast at our favorite diner it was all she could talk about. She said she fell in love based on Dixie's new hairstyle, which she described as all bleached golden bottle blond and blunt cut like Nico. A few days later I saw Dixie and Cruzer was right, she'd undergone a serious transformation. Her long dirty blond hair was chopped off, and she no longer looked like the sweet girl with the Southern drawl that doodled horses on the bottom of my skateboard when she stole my Sharpie out of my backpack at the park.

Cruzer calling is the perfect excuse to jump out of my bed and get away from Hurricane who is looking super hot naked lying next to me. The smell of her skin alone is a toxic rush. I pull my jeans on. "That really was the last time," I say, like I do every time we *accidentally* have sex. "I can't wait till your boyfriend catches us and kicks my ass."

"He's not my boyfriend."

"Oh I forgot. I mean your drug dealer."

Hurricane dials a cab to take her to some punk show where most likely her "boyfriend" is. Why do I have to like her? Why do I have to be addicted to the frenzied this-really-will-be-the-last-time kind of sex we have? The explosive, crazy, leave-the-planet kind of sex we have? Hurricane slides her naked body out from underneath my covers and out of the bed. "Why's it so cold? Fuck summer in San Francisco," she whines. I lace up my shoes and look at her hard nipples and think about how I want to have sex with her again. I'm even trying to calculate in my head how long it will take for Cruzer to skate to my house.

Hurricane peers into my mirror to fix her sex-hair. She rats her poppy-red curls with a comb making them bigger, and shoots on some hairspray like she's pretending the mess is on purpose. "Do you think I could be one of those sexy girls who sell cigarettes and candy at bars?" She's asking because our boss at the coffee shop where I got her a job when she first moved to the city and became my roommate, is about to fire her since it's hard to be a good employee and a drug addict at the same time.

"Sure. Why not?" I'm annoyed that Hurricane is about to get removed from yet a second situation I recommended her to. I lean into the mirror next to her. I need a haircut. It's curling, all wild out from under my railroad cap. I hate when my hair gets too long because I start looking girly. It's an easy thing for me—some boyish-girls, like Cruzer or Soda, can get away with growing their hair shaggy and still look like boys–but I walk a fine line. I especially hate my lips, how they have this way of turning bright red the morning after a night of drinking, and it looks like I'm wearing lipstick. Makes all my girlfriends jealous but I hate them, also my rosy cheeks and how they soften my face when looking like a tough boy is my objective.

"You're a day-walker," Soda said the other night when a bunch of kids were playing spin-the-bottle in Dolores Park and after Soda spun the bottle it shuddered to a stop with the neck pointed directly at my shoe. Typically Soda would skip over a Bro and wait for the bottle to land on a femme but for me she just shrugged and cocked her hat to one side so our hats wouldn't knock off when we made out. Secretly, I love making out with Soda but I would never admit to that.

I put product in my shaggy hair since I can't find my hat in my mess of a room. I usually keep my room clean but the last month of fucking my roommate has been extremely distracting for my home life. "That really was the last time," I mutter at Hurricane's reflection in the mirror. She's so pale she looks like a porcelain doll with eyes that glow wild like electric orange marbles catching light. My weakness: *Punk rock girls with death-wish eyes.*

"Why are you so dramatic Georgie?" she huffs. She's trying to shove all her big hoop earrings back in. She wears these big, black ones with the paint chipping off the edges, circular earrings that look like mini warped records, that she doubles up with even bigger silver hoops.

"Because I'm falling in love with you and you won't stop doing insane amounts of drugs, or fucking around with that dude."

"I can't date someone I love."

The word love falling from her mouth makes me feel dizzy for a second.

"Naw. You can't break up with your hook-up." I slam my skate down on the hardwood floor a couple of times, harder than I need to in order to get the water off the wheels from when I skated to the store earlier to get Hurricane the candy she wanted. Man. I'm so nice to her. Hurricane purses her lips. She looks disappointed like maybe she really believes we will never have sex again.

"That really was the last time," I say again, like I'm reassuring myself and not her. She opens her mouth to try to agree or protest and her lip stalls a bit on her tooth. I have this urge to run my hand across her pretty lips in a way that is way too sweet, but then three honks come in a row from outside and she jumps up. Her cab is here.

By the time Cruzer comes into my room to stash her skateboard all evidence of Hurricane is gone. I've even opened up the windows to air out all the smoke even though the drizzle starts coming in.

"What's up, Bro?" Cruzer taps her hand cupped in an upside down C against my outstretched fist so our matching horseshoe rings click together. When we started our skate crew at the beginning of summer with Soda, we all bought the rings at this bling shop on Market Street to represent the C for The Crew. Whenever any of us meet up we cup our hands in upside down C's and tap our rings together.

Cruzer's huge floppy mess of dark curls that usually stick straight up are wet and flopping weakly to one side. Cruzer has some of the biggest hair around, she even gives the rocker chicks with the razor sharp Mohawks that hang out in front of *Mission Records* a run for their money. Cruzer's many talents involve hiding stuff in her hair. The other day she stopped by my house and parted a mass of curls to reveal a white bird with wire claws twisted around a chunk of curls. *Meet Twilly, Sadie found her for me at a sidewalk sale.* When we were teenagers I often witnessed her using her hair for shoplifting and sneaking stuff past her grandma.  Her grandma would be sitting watching TV, and Cruzer would walk by with an entire pack of her grandpa's Pall Malls shoved into her hair, and smile at me waiting on the doorstep with my skate under my arm as her grandma hollered after her, *Maricruz you better not be going to that skate park! Your mom said no skate park!*

Cruzer wipes the water off the bottom of her deck with her hand. "We gotta stop by the corner office. I told The Doc I'd skate by like a half hour ago but then the fog got all crazy on me."

Since a waterlogged deck sucks we leave our skates and walk fast down Capp Street. Cruzer calls The Doc. "I'm headed to your office." The location of "The Doctor's office" varies but it's usually on the corner of 16th and Mission on a square of sidewalk between the front of a fruit stand awning and a corner store market. Sometimes when we walk up, or drive up and park really quick in the bus lane (Soda calls that Drive Thru Doc) The Doc's sitting there waiting but most of the time he just comes all zippy around the corner in his mechanical wheelchair. Today when we get to the corner he's already there, parked in the awning-covered spot with a plastic rain cape on with his arms poking out the sides and folded together in his lap as he stares into space. He looks like an innocent old man sitting in his wheelchair and contemplating the rain. Really, the wheelchair is just a smart cover for his pill hustling enterprises.

The Doc is the pill supplier to half of the neighborhood's hipster kids, but to get in with him you have to be introduced by a special person who is already a good customer. Of course the special person who introduced my friends to the cheap high of street pharmaceuticals is Hurricane. She referred them months ago when she got annoyed that they kept calling her for stuff. "I'm giving you the name of my Doctor, so you jerks will leave me alone." Soda had laughed because she thought she was joking. *Huh. Your doctor?* Hurricane also taught them the ways The Doc liked to be treated to get the best deal. Like whenever she met him Cruzer always leaned down and kissed him on both of his cheeks because that's the kind of hello he liked. Hurricane knows a lot of tricks about 16th and Mission. One time she pointed out this guy leaning against his truck who coughed in his hand and then shook this scrawny kid's hand in front of him, that he was actually spitting the heroin that was wrapped in a plastic capsule from the inside of his cheek into his customer's palm. "They're squirrels," she'd said, "but with cheeks full of tar instead of nuts."

The wheelchair makes The Doc look sweet but his true colors come out when people walk by and holler at him. Like a guy might walk up and ask him for change and The Doc will scream, "Fuck off! Move on down the line! Can't you see I'm busy?" One time this lady kicked his wheelchair while we were talking to him and said all flirty, *You gotta license for that thing?* And The Doc glared at her so menacingly that he had the lady shuffling away growling insults at him over her shoulder, *Eh, what's up Doc? You better get off that high horse. Bitch ass.* Sometimes The Doc gets real mad and loses it. Like the time we found out he didn't need his wheelchair because he got up and chased this guy down the street. He ran okay too, for an old man, not even limping or anything.

"Hey, we need extra pills tonight 'cause we have sexy enchilada dinner dates," Cruzer tells The Doc.

"Shoot," he sighs. "I wish I was your type."

Cruzer pockets what he gives her and we duck into the corner store a few feet from his office so she can buy some Mexican sweet rolls that she shoves into her mouth as we walk towards her house. She doesn't want to swallow her pills on an empty stomach but she wants to make them disappear before Soda guilt trips her into sharing any extras. Ever since my friends got crazy about pills they're all real sneaky.

Now that we're not in a hurry to catch The Doc, the rest of the way to Cruzer's house she stops every few minutes to do some romantic street propaganda. In front of a street sign she pulls a roll of masking tape out of her hoody pocket. "Rip this," she instructs me as she hands me the fat roll of tape. She needs my help because she has a cast on her hand from falling off her skateboard last week while bombing down Dolores Hill. She tried to blame me for the accident since right before skating to the top of the hill she'd stopped by my house to check up on me but I hadn't answered the door. Cruzer claimed all her worrying made her skate wobble which made her bail. On the two-by-two squares of tape that I rip off for Cruzer, she writes *I love Dixie* with an electric blue paint pen that glows neonish against the glossy black tape. She has several different colors of tape in her bag along with assorted paint pens so she can mix up the styles when she instantly makes the *I love Dixie* stickers that she has been slapping down on Mission bar tables, bathroom walls, street signs, bus seats, or people's sleeves lately.

"Masking tape is a lifesaver," Cruzer likes to say. Ever since I've known her she always has some on hand in her backpack, or in her pocket. Once, when we were like sixteen, my board got run over by a car but it didn't bust all the way so she taped it up heavy duty and I was able to at least skate the deck home before throwing it away. Another time when we had first moved to the city and were looking for jobs, this big guy on the 22 Fillmore bus sat on my big style headphones, crunching them in two and Cruzer fixed them up for me. This other time Cruzer didn't have her tape with her and she dropped her cell phone and broke the battery when we were walking down some street in the Castro. She had to have her phone work because she was on call for a job she was very, very close to being fired from. "Shit, we *need* duct tape," she said. We went into the closest bar, where she taped up her phone successfully. Then we looked up and saw we were in a Bear bar with a fantastic seventies disco ambience. We ended up staying for hours, distracted by Bears and two-for-one-beer specials until Cruzer's ghetto-rigged cell phone lit up with her job's number. By then she was drunk, but she did that job better drunk, so it was okay. She climbed up on the bar and shouted at our new Bear friends and me. "See how duct tape just stopped me from starving on Ramen noodles?" That was when she delivered her Duct Tape Manifesto, and the crowd was so drunk they cheered her on. They didn't care what she was talking about because they were so easily riled up. They were celebrating some sort of new gay book, or movie, or store, or Web site, or politician, or game, or clothing line.

Now duct tape is a key staple in Cruzer's grand plan to seduce Dixie, who is still playing coy. The latest seduction attempt is The Enchilada Party. Cruzer is going to make Dixie's favorite dish, enchiladas. Cruzer is going to use her Grandma Lola's recipe, *real* Mexican enchiladas that she says will trump any that Dixie has ever tasted.

"There's no way Dixie won't hook up with me tonight," Cruzer says as we turn down 20th Street. "Walking to my house she will see how the neighborhood is a goddamn canvas for my adoration of her. And then she will arrive at my house where I've got the kind of pills she loves, booze, romantic watermelon rain, and authentic enchiladas." She beams a wide proud smile. *Smack*. She slaps down another *I love Dixie* sticker on the seat of a bike that's strapped to a telephone pole and we continue on our way.

# Chapter 2

Cruzer is lifting small dumbbells with a *Buffy* episode flickering in the background on silent. "You see, girls look at your arms. It's what we got to show. It's like in the hetero world how guys have their packages. Good arm muscles are our packages," she's saying like she's teaching a class on butch aesthetic. She passes the dumbbells to Tiny who's such a little scrap of a thing that it looks like she's having trouble even holding them both in her hands. Tiny is this little Jewish kid with big brown eyes that she recently started hiding behind these nerdy looking black square-framed glasses. At first Cruzer and I thought she'd started wearing the glasses so girls would think she was smart and indie but apparently she'd always been halfway blind and just couldn't afford glasses till now. That explained why she was such an awful skater, the reason Cruzer wouldn't let her *officially* be a member of our skate Crew.

"Check it out." Cruzer flexes her upper arms at me. It does look like they're getting more defined but I know she's like me and she never remembers to lift the weights. They usually stay under her living room couch and whenever a garbage truck or a bus drives by that shakes the house they magically roll out into the center of the room. That's because The Creamsickle is sinking into itself. It seems crazy that the third story of a house could be drooping off its frame at a concave, but we tested it out one day by throwing skateboards down on at various corners of the living room and watching how they rolled towards an imaginary spot in the center of the room. Also at parties everyone always seemed to end up puddled into a pile in the center of the room even if there were tons of other places to hang out in. They got drunk and gave in to gravity.

Everyone calls Cruzer and Soda's house The Creamsickle because it looks like an orange popsicle that has been dropped in the dirt a few times, since it's painted a splotchy orange with a white trim that's splattered with pigeon shit. Cruzer insists that the house especially deserves the *cream* part of the name because of its long-standing reputation as a queer bachelor pad. The house has been passed around and handed down like a good dirty joke. Revolutionaries trampled its floors for twenty years, a slew of hippie fags and fairies lived there in the late eighties, and the grunge lesbians overran it all through the nineties. There's a wall in the kitchen that's scribbled over with the memories of it all, messages and old disconnected phone numbers of touring bands, notes, love letters and ranting poems from drifters, party kids and all the artists who had stayed there. So many people have come through the house that all the fingertips on the walls left the paint a dull coat of gray.

"I gotta check on the enchiladas. You help Tiny. She needs to be buff by next month's Jell-O wrestling match," Cruzer says. Tiny is going a little crazy with the dumbbells shadow boxing, kicking her feet up and down.

"Let's have a pull-up contest," I challenge her. I go first and do two pull-ups and then when I almost have my chin over the top for my third, someone comes up behind me and starts tickling my sides. I start laughing and lose my grip and turn around knowing already that it's Soda. I tackle her into a bear hug knocking off her black and gold fitted ball cap. She smells like tomato sauce and dishwater since she's been at work all day at this fancy Italian restaurant in the Marina.

"Soda, check it out I'm gonna get muscles and get hella chicks." Tiny starts to demonstrate her weight-lifting skills.

"Keep at it kid." Everyone always makes fun of Tiny because she has zero game.

Soda picks up her cap from the floor. "Man, have I told you guys about the hot ass maitre d' at my work?"

"Like ten million times." Cruzer walks back into the room.

"Well, Tiny doesn't know." Soda peers into the mirrored doors of the marbled cabinet case and adjusts her cap. "God she's so mean to me. I swear she wants to fuck me." She walks to the kitchen and comes back with a can of Hamms that she pops open. "Fuck, that place is working me like a dog. I'm going to party all weekend. I haven't been out all week. When are those girls coming over?"

After the enchiladas I tell everyone I'm leaving because all I can think about is going home to hang out with Hurricane, but when I try to go Soda blocks the living room door. "We're staging an intervention. That girl has ruined your whole summer. You're staying here until you're over it." I lunge at Soda and tackle her to the floor. I almost get her pinned because she's so busy talking shit to me and trying to smack my face even though I'm about to make her eat the dust off the dirty-ass floor, but then she gets serious and comes back at me, flips me back and pins me down fast.

"One. Two," Tiny counts down while pounding on the wood floor that my arms are pinned to, "Three."

Soda jumps up, sweaty and victorious.

"You two wrestling is hot," Dixie's friend Amanda says. She has this sparkling blue top on, the kind that becomes a bunch of folds of fabric when it falls into the girl's boobs and from my position on the floor with her leaning over the card table, I'm getting an eyeful.

I contemplate my defeat. I guess it's a good idea if I don't go home since there's a good chance Hurricane will be wrecked anyways, like she is so much lately, which is super depressing. "Okay I'll stay." I laugh and everyone cheers.

The next night I'm sitting in a hotel room at The Phoenix hotel unfortunately witnessing Cruzer and Dixie finally making out for the first time. It pretty much makes me want to throw up. I'm starting to feel like a true hostage, being sensually harassed like this. All night I've had to hear Cruzer trying to sweet-talk Dixie, stuff like, *C'mon you say all the time how chubby butch girls are your type. Your dream boi's right in front of ya, chubby and hella Butch*! *Dayum*. And Dixie saying *But you're my friend. Ew!* And *But you're an asshole. Grrrr.*

I'm impressed that Cruzer has been putting so much effort into something, especially courting a girl. She's also doing a super diligent job of kidnapping me. When I got off work earlier she and Soda were waiting out front in her truck. I'd been bummed out all shift about my house situation but when I saw them they immediately put me in a better mood. They were making me laugh, telling me about how they spent all afternoon preparing what they called a Hotel Seduction Bag for the evening. Apparently the bag was full of romantic movies, candles, and shit like that. Soda got the hotel as an end of summer celebration, and because she wanted to swim at a hotel pool legally instead of sneaking in like we usually did. Cruzer pitched in because she thought a hotel room would help with the Dixie seduction plan.

After scooping me they drive to Cala Foods and load up on hotel snacks like chips and dip, Pabst, Bud and ice. "And the bitches will bring the Alizé," Cruzer says.

"You should call the girls babes instead of bitches," Soda tells her.

"Why?"

"Because that's what Corey Haim and Corey Feldman called their ladies in the movie *License To Drive*," Soda says. The lady ringing up our groceries shakes her head and laughs at Soda's logic.

"You guys are embarrassing," I say.

Later at the hotel they discover The Hotel Seduction Bag didn't make it into the truck from their house and get in a fight about it. "I can't believe you forgot to grab it! That was your one responsibility!" Cruzer yells.

"Can I call Melanie?" I interrupt the fight. They both turn to me. Cruzer is smiling like a lightbulb is going to explode behind her big white teeth. They are both so happy that I want to hang out with a girl that isn't Hurricane. Melanie is this tall femme

I used to hook up with but I stopped calling her a few months ago when I started fucking Hurricane. She is pretty snotty with me when I call her from the hotel. She's probably heard things through the queer grapevine and knows why we haven't hung out in months. I describe our luxury accommodations, party supplies and the pool. "Okay. I'll come," she says. "But I'm not coming to hang out with you. I haven't seen Amanda and Dixie in a while so I want to hang out with them."

It starts to sprinkle again but everyone still ends up in the pool because it's heated and the raindrops create a steamy mist. Amanda even takes her top off and slingshots it at Soda's head in an act of flirtation that's beneficial eye candy to everyone else, because Amanda looks like a curvaceous version of Parker Posey. People start making out but when I try to kiss Melanie she says, "Everyone knows you're fucking your junkie ass roommate." *Shit.* But what sucks more than Hurricane ruining my reputation is that secretly I don't care so much about making out with Melanie because when I close my eyes floating on my back in the turquoise glow of the misty pool with the rain splattering my face, all I can see is the image of Hurricane swirling like cotton candy off my fingertips the last time we had sex, and how her fierce orange eyes pierced mine like they could slice me open, right down the middle.

The next day I get off work at the coffee shop and Cruzer is sitting on her skate on the sidewalk out front. "Man, you're still playing kidnap? Get a job!" I groan. Cruzer is smiling huge. I can tell it's her I-just-got-laid smile. "You fucked Dixie!" I high-five her. "Soooo. Deets?"

"Let's just say that I can get down even with this stupid cast on. She was all thinking I was going to let her fuck me since I had the cast but I was like hell no. That's why I always say you gotta practice being ambidextrous early on, for times like that."

Cruzer and I always share all the details of our hook ups with each other. I've learned a lot of crazy stuff from her. Ever since she moved into The Creamsickle she's always got some wild girl-related adventure up her sleeve. She's girl obsessed.

Might be cause she waited so long to come out, didn't admit she liked girls till she was eighteen even though I was one of her best friends and I'd been hooking up with girls since like fourteen. I think Cruzer was trapped in the closet because she didn't want to weird out her family with their traditional Mexican-Catholic values, and her stepdad who promised to pay for her to go to art school for photography if she stayed out of trouble. Not to mention how much teasing she got growing up from all her cousins, the Gonzales girls, a pack of mean chicas who went to my high school and liked to make fun of my ruffian style. One time Sonia Gonzales came up to me in the hall at school and glared at me. "You and my cousin are fucking lezzies right? That's why she begs my aunt to let her come down here every summer? You guys lez out together right?"

"Cruz is just my friend," I insisted. "She likes dudes I swear." I was scared of the Gonzales girls. One time I saw them slam this girl Cat's head into a locker.

But I knew Cruzer didn't like dudes. We just never talked about it. That was why she was my best skate friend ever. She wasn't like other girls I'd tried to skate with who just went to the skate park with their boards to try to hook up with guys. Cruzer didn't notice the dudes, except to try and make friends with them so they would take us to their exclusive backyard ramps and secret skate spots. Being down with these dudes and being part of the skate scene that was fiercely homophobic and hetero was more important to us than discussing our sexuality.

When Cruzer finally told me she was dating a girl she was eighteen and had been living on her own in L.A. for a while. She wanted me to come live with her in L.A. but I was stuck at this awful office job to afford living on my own, which I had been doing since seventeen. I didn't have the money to move. Then one day Cruzer said I wouldn't have to pay rent. She'd forgot to mention that before. People with money forget that other people don't have it. *Come here dude, we can skate all summer. You won't even have to pay rent, my stepdad is paying for my place 'cause I told him I wanted to take a semester off before I go to school to live a little and work on my portfolio.*

So I went to L.A. There wasn't anything keeping me in

Petaluma. The girls were lame. Riding the local skate park was as familiar as breathing. I needed new terrain. I wasn't going to the college nearby like some of my friends. I'd barely got through high school and had barely scraped up enough money to move out of my mom's house. How could I afford school? And where would I go with my diploma from the alternative school that didn't even issue grades? Cruzer was going to school, an expensive art school in Chicago, but that was because her stepdad was loaded.

In L.A. I worked at a sneakers store and skated all the rest of the time. There was a bunch of girl skaters there. In my little town it had just been me and one other girl, who actually took skating seriously, and she got pregnant, and pregnant girls can't skate. I was having so much fun I would have stayed there if Cruzer hadn't begged me to go to Chicago with her at the end of summer. *I'm paying for the U-Haul. C'mon have an adventure.* Cruzer begged me to leave behind the cute skater girls and endless summer days in Silver Lake. It was true I would have an adventure, but Cruzer was going to school and she would be the only person I knew out there. Lame. But then these other girls we hung out and skated with said they wanted to come too, that we could road trip out there and stop at all the skate parks along the way, and that we could all get a flat together in Chicago. That sounded awesome.

We only lasted a year in Chicago. We were California girls and couldn't handle the bone-chilling winter. "We need to go to San Francisco. The ultimate queer fly trap," I told Cruzer. I didn't know how much longer I could stay in Chicago, especially since this girl there was recklessly trampling on my heart. But I couldn't imagine leaving Cruzer. It was like she was my only family. I didn't talk to my sisters, we had nothing to relate on, they were focused on getting married and having babies, One liked to lecture me on "family values," one was a model who'd been saving up for fake boobs since like forever, and I barely even talked to my mom because we were always fighting about something or other, like how I wasn't going to school, or how come I couldn't have a nice boyfriend.

Our first month in San Francisco Cruzer fell in love with

this girl in her La Raza Arts class. The girl moved in with us. We were sharing a studio near the Tenderloin because rent was ten times more in SF. It was hell when Cruzer's girlfriend moved in, especially since she was such a bitchy girl. She hated me because Cruzer and I were so close and she was jealous. Luckily, I met Jeremiah while trying to weasel drinks off old men at a gay bar with Cruzer one night. Jeremiah wasn't an old man, he was a cute twink, and he had a room for rent in his house.

It was lucky I moved out when I did because a few months later Cruzer and her girlfriend started getting in crazy fights that involved televisions being thrown out the window. They stayed together for a while but eventually one day all of Cruzer's stuff was thrown into the street and she didn't argue because she'd got caught cheating. Later, she found out that her girlfriend had been cheating too, but she didn't care by that point. She had up and moved into The Creamsickle where her friend Shelby lived and life was good. She was spending most of her time chasing girls, taking pictures of them for her school art projects and final exhibition, falling in love with each new muse.

That's why now Cruzer's hard to keep up with and I'm the one trailing behind. Sometimes I provide the good deets though. Like when we first moved to San Francisco and I was the first one to figure out how to make a girl ejaculate. We were at this super cheap breakfast diner called The Triple P when I tell Cruzer all about Marie squirting down my arm the night before. "Draw it for me," Cruzer huffed. The expression on her face looked like when we were fifteen and I landed a kick flip before her even though she practiced way longer than me. She pulled a pen out of the front pocket of her cutoff jean jacket and shoved a napkin over the table at me.

We're always discussing sex at the Triple P because we're there the morning after whatever craziness we'd got into the night before. That meant whatever guy sitting next to us on his lunch break wolfing down the business lunch special got a real earful. Most of the time we are sitting at the same table as the business dudes since the place is always busy so they sit you cafeteria style, sandwiched between two strangers. When I was drawing Cruzer the napkin diagram I could feel Mr. Man with the tacky tie to the left of me slyly trying to glance over. Maybe that would have annoyed me but at the same time I bet he was thinking, *Goddamn how do those little rugrats looking like fourteen-year-old boys get ten times more pussy than I ever do?* Butches, Bois, Boyish Girls, BG's whatever you call us, we get enough shit in this world so a little pervy lurker is probably the least of my concerns.

My favorite thing to talk about with Cruzer at the Triple P is bad sex with girls because she makes me laugh so hard that once I almost snorted orange juice out my nose. I used to only associate bad sex with boys, and my limited experience of sleeping with them, like back when I was fifteen. But now, I *get* to have all different kinds of bad sex with girls, and it's waaaaay more fun. I mean, I wouldn't even call it bad sex, more like interesting sex.

"So where are we going?" I ask Cruzer as we walk away from my work. I'm bummed that I'm still a hostage because all through my shift I'd been dreaming of getting a cheap tattoo from my friend Manno who is training at this shop down the street. I've got a wad of tip money that I've been saving all week in the secret inside pocket of my jacket.

"I dunno. Whatever."

"It's up to me? I thought I was still a hostage and about to end up in a hotel room or some other crazy seduction situation."

Cruzer just shrugs. I guess now that the Dixie chase is over she'll have to find a new hobby.

"Okay then I was thinking 'bout going to get a breakup tattoo from Manno."

"Dude. Hurricane wasn't even your girlfriend. She so doesn't deserve that tradition."

"I know but I need this one," I whine.

"Fine. I'll go with you but not if you're gonna get some pathetic broken heart or some shit."

"Hell no. You'll like it. I'm going to get a scary dragon-looking slash flaming-haired Medusa girl."

After the tattoo we head to The Vine, which is this legendary lesbian dive bar where queers either start their nights, or end them or both. Monday evenings you can always find The Crew at The Vine, it's our favorite night because there's dollar Pabsts and free pool. Plus, the hottest bartender, Mikala, is on duty and she has this crush on Soda, so she never even needs the dollar. I spend a lot of other nights at The Vine too. I'm still excited about the fact that I don't have to try and sneak in anymore even though I've been drinking age for at least a year now. I guess I'm not sick of it yet. Plus The Cave house where I live doesn't even have a living room so I can just as well consider The Vine my living room: there are soft barstools, a TV, pictures on the walls, music, and the smell of booze and girls. *Mmmm.* All the comforts of home.

After The Vine we go to Cupcakes for My Cunts in the Castro. Melanie has obviously had one too many Jaeger bombs because she starts grinding up on me on the dance floor in this amazingly tight outfit like she's forgotten she hates me. Then later after she leaves, she drunk dials me from her house. "Come over." The breakup tattoo is already working its magic!

"I'm gonna go get some booty," I tell The Crew when I find them on the dance floor with Dixie and Amanda, and they agree to let me out of captivity for such an exciting breakthrough.

I hop on my board and start the long skate to Bernal Heights where Melanie lives. She's a professional lesbian but don't think that means she isn't hot as fuck. She carries a briefcase and wears pencil skirts. *Yum.* Cruzer taught me that girls who look all serious are the ones who get the dirtiest in bed. This was back when she was eighteen and started fucking older Hollywood power dykes who would come and pick her up at the skate park in their Mercedes. Cruzer also loves older women because they always buy her breakfast in the morning and since she never has a job, that's a nice perk.

I get to skate right in the middle of Folsom Street because it's so late that there are no cars. I sip off the beer that I smuggled out in my jacket from the club and look up at the two rows of majestic trees that rustle above me. They remind me of the wide suburban streets I grew up skating. Sometimes I crave those streets. Don't get me wrong. I'm so glad I don't live in the Boringville suburbs anymore, but the one good thing about it was the lazy days of huge concrete skate parks and wide, smooth streets made for skate wheels. The deserted street makes everything achingly quiet. Unlike Cruzer, I can appreciate a little silence. I think the world is too loud. It rings in my ears all day long. That's one reason why I love skating so much, because of how everything fades out and I can only hear the sound of my wheels that roll over the asphalt. The sound hypnotizes me and chills me out. Some people do yoga, or take a hot bath, and I bomb a crazy steep hill on a roughly seven-by-thirty-inch piece of compressed wood. I even carry my board under my arm sometimes in the same way those hot girls in yoga pants do with their rolled yoga mats, as they walk around my neighborhood, but most of the time I'd rather be skating by them, so I can get a nice eyeful of some yoga booty.

But, back to the silence.

It goes like this: first the people on the street go quiet, their footsteps, kids yelling and all the conversations. Then the cars fade out, the engines, wheels and guys that may try to holler from car widows. Then at some point you don't even hear the wind anymore, although there's a lot of wind in this city. Then lastly, the best part is when even your head goes quiet and all those crazy jumbling thoughts just fly right out your ears.

*Bam*.

And then I hit the sidewalk. This yapping squashed-face French bulldog comes running out of nowhere after my skate as I'm spacing out. Dogs think skateboards are their mortal enemies. The jump off my board sends my cell phone flying out of my hoody pocket, skidding across the sidewalk till it finally comes to a stop in the gutter. I search the leaves in the gutter for my phone and shit it's busted. Man, I think I would have rather my body hit the ground instead, because I don't mind some bloody palms or a nasty hip bruise, a battle scar or two, but not having a cell phone is a complete pain in the ass.

The next morning I wake up in Melanie's nice comfy bed. She's curled up with her arms hugging the pillow between us. I think she tried to spoon me before we passed out, the way she's doing the pillow, but I entangled myself. I sit up and rub my choppy hair around on my head because I know it's probably sticking up all crazy. There's a bunch of black and blue swirly stains on Melanie's white sheets that are from the fresh tattoo ink that oozed from my arm in the night. I feel bad for a second, but I did warn her last night right before we started fooling around and I saw how nice, clean, and so white everything was on her bed, "I'm gonna stain your sheets," I told her, but she had whispered something like, *I don't care what you stain* right into my ear.

I want to smoke a morning cigarette out on the back porch and call Cruzer, but then I remember my cell phone is busted. I ask Melanie if I can use her phone. I sit on her bed and pick at the crusty flakes of red ink on the edges of her top sheet, stains the color of the crazy Medusa chick's hair. I know Cruzer's number by heart because I've called her nearly every morning for years. Melanie is frowning at the stains on her sheets, like she's having second thoughts about being so generous towards my messy lifestyle last night, as she puts on this hot business-type suit with pinstripes and sexy shoes, getting all professional lesbian styled out for work. I think she's also annoyed that we didn't even have sex last night. Embarrassingly, I passed out. I couldn't get into it. She was so annoyed and kept trying to shove me awake till she finally gave up.

I tell Cruzer to meet me at The Triple P, apologize to Melanie again about her sheets, and grab my hoody and skate off her floor. I don't kiss her 'bye. She's putting on that bright red lipstick that I hate 'cause it gets all over my face. I figure it's okay not to kiss her. She's the kind of girl that I don't want to act like girlfriends with, or anything, because she always tries to get serious quick-style. The next thing I know *her* sheets could be *my* sheets and other crazy stuff like that.

I have to split up with Cruzer after breakfast since she'll probably be going off on some crazy adventure, causing ruckus somewhere, a guaranteed distraction from me getting my shit together and buying a new phone before work. I skate to the phone store on Mission, the one with the huge blow-up cartoon phone on the sidewalk out front that has a mechanical fan inside of it, so the weird arms on the side flap up and down like a penguin having a psychotic episode. I hate that blow-up thing because it takes up the whole sidewalk when I want to skate by, and those flapping arms try to whack my head off. But, I have to go to that store, because it's the only place you can get a cheap phone with no credit.

I roll home after I've got the new phone, listening to my missed messages. My roommate, Lenora called. She's talking fast and yelling about something. I've got to hop off my board and hit replay just so I can hear her. *Where the hell are you? Your girlfriend tried to burn the house down!* There are more messages, all from the night before, Hurricane crying in one. What the fuck, did Hurricane really catch the house on fire! *Shit*. Lenora is going to think I was ignoring her by not calling her back! Dude I so don't want to come home to all that drama. I just want to go home. My legs are tired from a night of not fucking and a morning of skating. I want a nap and it's been three days since I've even had a shower. I skate so slow to my house I'm practically at standstill. I change my mind, turn around and skate fast in the direction of The Creamsickle, turning my phone off, so I can pretend to Lenora that it's still broken, that I didn't get her message. Shoot, I'm finally allowed to go home and I'm going the other direction.

I don't go home till later that night after I'm kind of tipsy. At my house I do a kick flip off the banked driveway. The super slanted concrete slope is the best thing about my house, perfect for some minor bank skating. A bunch of the neighborhood kids recently discovered this and have been attacking the driveway with roughed up hand-me-down boards. I always high-five them when I come home from work, but my roommates and neighbors are jerks and send them scattering. The neighbor who complained about the loud sex thinks she's extra clever because she yells at them using the Spanish phrases she learned in college. The boys laugh at her before they skate away and call her bad words that weren't on her pop quizzes so she just smiles and waves. It's a good thing for my roommates that our front stairs are back and hidden from the street, because if the kids discovered them they would figure out how you could get speed off the side path and then Bomb Drop off of the three stair, which then sends you slamming into the hard wood of my front door. This body-slamming thud is Cruzer's calling card when she stops by to visit me.

Skating my driveway, drunk in the dark, I eventually bail. I sit on the sidewalk for a minute after, scrape off the pieces of gravel that are pressed into my palms. Down the street there's this stumbling shadow. Hurricane? I get up and skate over to her even though now my ass hurts. The shadow turns into Hurricane, who barely blinks at me when my board slaps up from the street with a pop into my hand. She's obviously out of it. I try to tug her home by the waist of her faded black pants that have started to fall off her ass lately since she barely eats, thinking about how I'd rather yank her by those big silver hoop earrings, make her actually feel something. She's still not moving very far even with me helping her stumble, so I plop her and her dirty white sequined purse on my board and push her towards the house. I wish I could drop her in a puddle at my feet like everyone else has, but I can't seem to let go of her.

# Chapter 3

I'm skating hard down Capp Street, Hurricane's orangey eyes spinning in front of my face like a slot machine going haywire. I skate harder, faster, so the wind makes me blink away the image.

When I'm sad or pissed off I skate it out. When I have anxiety I grab my board and let the sidewalk absorb the friction of my clashing thoughts. I put on my headphones and cruise down the city streets. My head empties as I watch the yellow lines of the street slide by underneath my wheels. I have my neighborhood streets memorized. I know the smooth patches and how the strips of asphalt on the left side are level all the way through. I don't even think about where I'm going. It's the movement I understand. I used to leave the fucked-upness of my mom's house this way. When my sisters were yelling at me and my mom was mom yelling at me, there was always my skate beside my bedroom door, waiting there ready to take me away from it and into the night. My mom would yell after me from the porch as I shot out the door and down the street. *If you're not back in fifteen minutes, I'm locking the fucking door!*

A few hours ago I pretty much got kicked out of my house because of Hurricane.

"Look. Why don't you start looking for a new place too?"

My roommate Lenora stood in our kitchen with her hands crossed over her chest and glared at me. We were fighting about Hurricane passing out on drugs in a room full of burning candles that eventually caught a curtain on fire, which woke her up and she beat the flames with a wet towel. It was the climax to all the bad things Hurricane had done as the worst roommate ever.

"I can't even tell whose side you are on," Jeremiah said, which was so not true since I had been trying to get Hurricane to move out, too. The last few days since Hurricane almost burned the house down I'd been trying my hardest to smooth things over and even attempting to talk Hurricane into moving. Lenora and Jeremiah had been giving me the silent treatment. When I came home that night and tried to explain to Lenora why I missed her calls she accused me of being irresponsible. Ever since Soda stopped calling Lenora back after they slept together, she's been holding a grudge against me. The messed up thing is that she's the only one on the lease. "We're showing Hurricane's room next week, and if we find more than one person who wants to move in then we want you to move out," Lenora said.

After that stupid meeting I charged out of the house and went searching the entire town for Hurricane. I wanted to wring her neck for tossing every way I hooked her up in the city back in my face. I stopped by the bar where her drug dealer boyfriend worked. I stopped by his house. I stopped by a dozen more bars. Still no Hurricane. I stopped at The Vine and got drunk and started spilling all my problems to the bartender, Jo, who always gives the best advice. "You better move out. Even if they don't make you move out they are never going to be cool with you like before."

Halfway through my third beer, Hurricane finally called me back.

"Lenora wants us both to move," I told her.

"Fine, so what then. Fuck those bitches. I'm going train hopping with Kevin."

I was glad Hurricane wasn't saying this to my face because then she would see me looking like I was going to cry as I choked on my anger. Hurricane and I had been plotting traveling adventures in our heads all summer. I was the one she wanted to hit the road with, not that scumbag Kevin. Damn, my mind was reaching its boiling point. I grabbed my board, hollered 'bye to Jo and left the bar.

I've been skating a few hours now and my head still hasn't cleared. All I can think about is how screwed I am. I'd spent all my savings on that stupid tattoo and a new cell phone. I don't have money for a new place especially something more expensive than the crummy Cave.

I finally come to a stop in front of the splotchy orange doorstep of The Creamsickle that I've already passed earlier since I'm pretty much skating loops around the neighborhood. This time, I slap up my board and go up the wide dirty marble steps to the front door. It's unlocked so I trudge up the long flight of stairs. Soda is in the living room watching TV, eyes glazed over, the way people's eyes look when they have absorbed hours and hours of flashing images. I ask her where Cruzer is and she points like a zombie towards the back porch. Cruzer is spray-painting stencils on white T-shirts to sell at this huge queer festival she wants to go to in Olympia. Her plan is to sell the T-shirts for food and beer money while she is up there. The other day I was helping her think up catchy queer-centric slogans while we were lying in the park.

I hop up on the porch railing and look out at the insane view. Whenever people first come over to The Creamsickle they always trip out on the crazy view that you can see out of the huge wraparound windows in the wood-paneled living room. On a clear day you can see all of the city, three bridges, Coit Tower, Treasure Island, the Mint, and all the way to the East Bay, since the house is on a small hill in a building that's a high slumping tower.

"What's wrong with Soda?"

"Hmm? Oh, I think she's on a lot of V's."

I sigh heavily. That's another good reason to hate Hurricane, the fact she introduced my friends to her stupid Doc.

"That hot mom is wearing that seventies short-shorts set again," I say as I look down at the endless zigzag of porches and windows. Cruzer is busy trying to make the stencils straight so she doesn't even look up, even though she loves the hot mom's lime-green velour ass. She props up a piece of board that her shirt is taped onto and starts to set out the stencil. "I think I found an early ride to Olympia in the morning. Starla hooked it up for me with like eight other kids in an RV." When we'd first heard about the festival, we were supposed to find a ride together, but the whole Hurricane thing had got me so distracted that I hadn't got my shit together to get the time off work, and plan my trip.

"I guess Soda and I will try to figure something out," I say, even though I doubted we would, especially when I think of Soda all slumped on the couch in the other room. I don't think she's even left the city once since she moved here two years ago. She got an anchor tattoo the second day she came to town after drifting city to city for so long and then she latched right onto The Creamsickle couch.

I update Cruzer on all my house drama. All about how I don't have money to move, and Lenora's betrayal, and how Hurricane says she's leaving, and how I worry about what's gonna happen to her, and finally about how I wish I could take off and chase the dust of America with her. "I know you want to travel," Cruzer says, "but that girl's not the one to go with. You just feel stuck. You should sign up for school with Soda next week. She's starting that sound engineering program, or whatever."

Cruzer's spray paint can makes a swish-swishing noise for a few minutes. I watch the telephone wires swing back and forth above and garbage blow across the empty basketball court far below.

"I think it's time you moved in here." Cruzer looks up at me.

I've avoided living in The Creamsickle this long because the last run-down house I lived in with Cruzer was bulldozed. I think of the cold Creamsickle winters. I hate the cold. I think about the dirt-cheap rent and how Indian summer would probably start soon, since the heat comes late in this city. It would be the one good time to live there, like just for the fall. I can jump ship before winter comes. "Take the key," Cruzer says as she finishes up stenciling *It ain't gonna lick itself* across the front of a white wife beater. "Just stay in my room or the back room while I'm gone and figure it out."

There's a key that hangs on a hook at the top of The Creamsickle stairs, booty calls tend to use it to let themselves out in the morning, locking the door behind them and slipping it back through the mail slot in the door, so that when I come over I often see it on top of the pile of unclaimed mail. I go and get it, put it on the Carabiner hanging from my belt hoop and I instantly feel a little better about life.

I stop by my house the next day to get some things and new potential roommates who are Lenora's friends are swarming all over the place to look at the room. They have bright smiling faces and they say, "Hmmmm, I'll definitely have to paint," as they scratch at the Bruce Springsteen lyrics Hurricane had carved into the painted wood of the loft bed. They look uptight like Lenora, and I sure as hell don't want to live with them.

The next week when I come home after work I can't even get in the house because apparently the locks were changed, and Lenora and Jeremiah didn't even bother to call and tell me. I call Lenora at her work. "We can't trust that her druggie friends won't come back and rob us. I'll get you a key later," she says all bitchy. I'm so annoyed that I'm sitting on the steps locked out of my own house when all I want to do is go inside and wash off my coffee stink. Plus, the little neighborhood boys are skating the driveway and I can't even get inside to grab my skate and kill some time with them. "Don't bother." I tell her. "I found a new place. How soon can that friend of yours who wants my room move in?"

"Whenever."

After I get off the phone I recruit some of the skater kids to shimmy under the front gate and then through the tiny bathroom window in the backyard. I give them the old decks I've got lying around my room as a reward. Then I show them the secret three stair in front of the front door so now it's guaranteed they will bug Lenora ten times as much. I start to pack up my stuff. I don't have much. Most of my furniture I found on the street so I can just put it back there. The Creamsickle is already full of stuff former roommates have abandoned over the years.

I call Soda to see if Cruzer left the keys to her truck since I don't know when she will be back from Olympia. Shit, I can't believe I'm going to live at The Creamsickle.

"Finally," Soda says when she comes to pick me up.

# Chapter 4

I wake up in the scroungy back room of The Creamsickle and I feel majorly disappointed in myself. The transient-friendly room is usually left empty. It's a lost and found, a nucleus of junk, a museum of abandoned furnishings that the house has collected over the years. The room was once a pantry. It has a sliding door that emerges magically from inside of the wall but doesn't actually close all the way, and rows and rows of pantry-type shelves lining the back wall. Over the years the shelves have become a vagabond's library. *Take a book leave a book*, a handwritten sign says. There are books dedicated to fighting the man, books about homeopathic medicine, books about Jewish history, old zines from our neighborhood a decade before, and books of feminist rhetoric. Once I found an old mini cereal box-sized Eileen Myles chapbook tucked behind the shelves in the dust. After reading it I put it back in the hidden spot, like a treasure that I could check back on. The rest are transient books, similar to the people who have temporarily slept in the pantry room, couch surfers, wanderers, people in between things, or on their way somewhere else.

I'm not on my way anywhere. I'm here waking up feeling depressed and stuck. Hurricane sure as hell is on her way somewhere though. She is flying through the air in the dead of night wearing all black so she blends into the gray grimy walls of rust-colored train cars. She is sleeping under the stars. She is spitting her stories into tin cans to heat up later. What if I had gone with her? If she had ditched the boy at the last minute and called me up from an old-school pay phone, whispered fast and frenzied into the receiver, *Oh Georgie, I'm waiting for my ride, but I'm telling ya, I could easily ditch him, and wait for you.*

*Where are you?* I would ask frantically listening to her soft panicked breathing, imagining her standing there in her tattered gold heels. When I close my eyes I can even imagine fucking her in old train yards, holding her hand as we run to catch the tail of huge moving things, feeling her palms get clammy and my heart beat faster with the thrill of it all. But then the edges of my fantasy start to get tainted with the thought of me having to regulate every exchange she might have with lurkers, questioning whether she is buying drugs and policing whatever she puts in her mouth, or nose.

So, I'm stuck in this house where the only motion is the old wood of the floors shifting in their instability. *Fuck you Hurricane*, I groan up at the ceiling before rolling out of bed. I have to part an avalanche of junk from the floor with my bare feet just to get to the door. In a few months Shelby, one of The Creamsickle roommates, might move to New York for a while and then I can have her room, or maybe I could fix up the pantry and build a loft.

Soda is asleep on the funky couch that's equally saggy as the floor, her head back, pressed into a pillow that's wedged in between the top of the couch and the huge bay windows, her dog Napoleon curled up on her feet. Cruzer told me that Soda never sleeps in her own bed more than two nights in a row. She's restless. I look above her at the city, how it glows with the morning sun. It's going to be pretty fantastic seeing The Creamsickle view every day. Maybe this situation isn't all that bad. I'll get to have my friends right here all the time, a cozy queer family.

I nudge Soda awake. "Let's go skate the Armory Building!" I'm excited that the sweet spot is just a smooth skate ride down hill from my house now.

"Man. I was dreaming about mermaids." Soda grins.

Soda is a pirate. When she first moved to the city, back before she even got the nickname Soda, she used to bug me because she hooked up with everyone and freeloaded off the ladies. Cruzer was the one who wanted to be friends with her. At the beginning of summer we were sitting on the sidewalk in front of The Triple P and Cruzer was reading the horoscopes out loud from the free weekly when she stopped right in the middle of mine and left me hanging on my weekly destiny. She was looking over my shoulder, squinting down the block. "Hey, there's that Soda kid. I wanna make friends with her."

"Naw, she sucks," I groaned.

"I think she's cool, dude. The other night she was standing by the jukebox at The Vine with that sleepy look on her—"

"What, her I-just-sniffed-glue-look?" I laughed.

"Whatever, I like how all these girls try to dance up on her and she just hangs out in the corner all night, like *so what*."

"Yeah, like she is thinking big thoughts or something."

"You're just mad 'cause she was fucking Melanie right before you."

"No. I just think she's sleazy. Believe me, lotsa girls share this opinion, including Melanie." The conversation was annoying me.

When Soda walked up to us I picked up the free weekly from where it was lying open on the ground and shuffled the paper looking for the sex advice column, then pretended to be super absorbed. Just because Cruzer suddenly decided she needed a new best friend didn't mean I had to play along. I glanced up for a second when Soda's husky voice came out from underneath her hoody's dark blue hood, which was pulled up over her trademark mesh cap with three rusty bolts screwed into the side of the bill. Soda kneeled down next to Cruzer. "What's sup, LezBros?" She laughed. "Last night was crazy, man."

Cruzer said, "You went to The Yoni Club, huh? I wanted to go to that for a millisecond, but then we ended up at Cozy's."

I zoned out their conversation for a minute, because I had started reading about a man who was scared to ask his wife to pee on him. I checked back in when I heard Cruzer say, "Dude, you just got your outfit scoped on and a nod of fashion approval from a ten-year-old." Her voice dripped with jealousy. I looked up and saw this kid who must have had a hipster mom. He was a little skater kid with shaggy hair and real clean clothes, and he was definitely checking Soda out, her fashion at least, he looked her up and down until his eyes ended up frozen on her skate shoes: white and black with skulls and crossbones patterned on the sides and laced up with thick baby blue laces. Then he trudged along on his way.

"Sweet, I checked him out too. He had light brown shoes with pink laces. That looks dope," Soda said.

"And your shoes are all clean and poser like his," I pointed out. Soda knew I bad vibed her but she always pretended like she didn't notice.

"That's 'cause you still haven't taught me how to skate, dude." Soda grinned.

That Soda was a real grinner, a sloppy grinner, who mostly seemed to grin for no particular reason. It was like she constantly had a can of paint thinner held under her nose, or maybe it was in a vial on a rope hanging around her neck. There must have been something that made her so grin-happy. Just last week, Melanie had said about Soda, "You can never trust a grinner, especially if she leans over after some hot sex and says, 'I love you,' and then a week later doesn't even return your phone calls. The grin curling up around the corners of her mouth takes the seriousness up and right off her lips."

I guess I had promised to teach Soda how to skate, back when she was dating this one girl, Knockout Nicki, but I didn't see the point in teaching her now. She would still ask me though when I ran into her at The Vine. "Hey Georgie," she would say, "when you gonna teach me how to ride, huh?" Soda worked the door of The Vine all spring so it was so easy for her to nag me whenever I went outside to smoke. Since Cruzer had rolled her eyes at my skate shoes comment, she was onto a new subject trying to bro down with Soda. "The other day that kid Marty and I got kids rate at the movie theater." She was bragging about the pros of passing as a fourteen-year-old boy.

"I still get carded for cigarettes," Soda said. "Oh, and you know that chick Tia? Yo, she took me to Vegas last month—"

"Blond Tia, or andro Tia?" Cruzer interrupted.

"Uh, the hot, rich, older one."

"Riiiight." Cruzer nodded and then smiled. She was probably recalling some sort of sex-related memory since she had dated that Tia for a while.

"Yeah, so the stewardess on the plane tells me I can't sit in the exit row, like I'm not old enough. You have to be fourteen or some shit to rescue everyone. I was like arguing with her for like ten minutes and then she even sends this other stewardess lady back a few minutes later who was all like, 'Are you sure you are fourteen sweetie?' And I'm all, 'Yeah, lady, I'll show you my ID when I order a drink later.'"

This story got me laughing. I couldn't help it. I was imagining Soda arguing with the stewardess with high femme Tia sitting next to her, probably looking more like her mom than her date.

"After we got back, Tia was like, 'I'm never taking you to Vegas ever again.' I got carded like every ten minutes when we were trying to chill and play slot machines. They wouldn't leave us alone. Vegas was tight though. She bought us matching tattoos from some crazy motherfucker off the Strip."

Soda rolled up her sweatshirt sleeve to show us the crusty clover on her forearm. "Don't matter though. I still have the worst luck." She shrugged.

"I have the best luck in the universe," Cruzer bragged, which was totally true. "I always win scratch-off lotto tickets. Hang around me and maybe some of it will rub off on you."

"Hell yeah. Well, I gotta go meet up with Cello. I was just talking to her the other day about helping me hem up my new work pants. I got this new restaurant job and they want me to dress nice." Soda slapped both our hands. "Call me about skating," she hollered as she trudged away, holding onto her belt loop since her pants were hanging off her ass, way below the colored band of her little boy's underwear.

"Man she's rad," Cruzer said. "The other night at Cat-fight we figured out we have almost the same birthday. We were totally meant to be best friends, Double Rammin' Aries action. Hey, that would be a good club name. I should talk to her about throwing a joint birthday party next month! Damn, Georgie we need to take her skating."

"You teach her," I suggested, wondering why that hadn't happened already.

"You know I suck at street.   It would be embarrassing," Cruzer whined.

That was true. Lately Cruzer would rather cruise around on her long board with a Pabst in her hand than keep up her skills. She just did Acid Drops off high curbs and three stairs, and she liked to fuck around on her old-school Powell Peralta board. She'd had that old-school board forever. It was pretty sick, red and black, with KISS carved into the grip tape. On the bottom there was this painting of Max from *Where the Wild Things Are*, a Sound-Garden sticker she'd stuck on in high school, and on the tail there was some girl's phone number that she'd met one day when we were sitting in the park.

Hmm, maybe teaching Soda to skate would be a good idea, I thought. It might give me a new skate buddy, even if Melanie would probably bitch me out about it.

A few weeks later there was this April Fool's Day barbecue at this girl Starla's house. I saw Soda out on the side porch. She was pinching rolling tobacco out of a bag she was holding in one hand and spreading it into the paper she'd cupped in the other. She looked like she had good technique. "Okay, you teach me how to roll rollies quick like and I'll teach you how to skate," I told her.

She grinned.

Of course she did.

Cruzer and I met up with Soda in the Cala Foods parking lot, late at night when the store was already closed so there weren't any cars. She only wanted to ride at night because she was embarrassed to have anyone in the neighborhood see her looking super awkward on the board. It turned out it wasn't so hard to teach Soda to skate. Some girls never really got it, like they would always look sort of unnatural on a board no matter what, but she got it right away. She mostly just had to get over being scared of the board. She said when she was fifteen she had stood on her brother's board for like half a second, and then it flew to the side, and she ended up breaking her wrist. That was why she never tried to ride a board again, even though she was obsessed with everything that had wheels. "Damn wrist is jacked for life," she complained and shook her wrist out. "All because of a skateboard." Soda kicked the bottom of the board I was lending to her.

"Hey *love* your board." I petted the worn-out grip tape of her new hand-me-down ride. I explained that the reason she fell was because she wasn't moving. To demonstrate I picked up a pebble from the street and set it in front of my board. I skated slowly forward so when the wheels hit the pebble it jolted backward throwing my foot off the board. Then I showed Soda how speed was your friend, how you could glide right over anything if you were going fast: pebbles, sidewalk cracks, maybe even the glass from a smashed bottle that was scattered along the edges of the parking lot. "See, the faster you go the less you trip on. Just get comfortable, balance and go fast, and that's all."

"Yeah right. That's all," Soda said skeptically.

We met up in the parking lot almost every night for the next few weeks after that. It was almost summer so there were some fluke hot days that ended in cool breezy nights, warm enough that after skating for an hour we would roll up the sleeves on our sweaty T-shirts.

One night I was goofing around on the small curb by the bike racks, practicing some Smiths Grinds, and Soda plopped down on the asphalt and took a break. "Georgie skates switch better than she does regular," Cruzer told her.

"I guess," I shrugged.

"Well you landed switch three-sixty flips before you landed them regular."

"What's switch?" Soda asked. "Like Switch-Hitter?" She was talking about switch-hitting in terms of sex.

"Well it's like *the way* you skate, regular or goofy-footed, depending on which foot goes first. Ya know like how people are either right or left-handed or whatever, like if your left foot's in front and your other foot is pushing, and goofy if your right foot is in front." Cruzer demonstrates this all on her board.

"And riding switch is doing tricks and stuff the opposite of what you learned, like playing guitar with your left hand when you're right, but you make it look normal if you're a badass."

"I dunno which way feels right 'cause I just started," Soda whined.

Cruzer shoved Soda hard from behind and she caught herself before hitting the asphalt. "What the fuck?" She turned around and swung at Cruzer but she ducked so Soda's punch landed in the huge pillow of her poofy hair.

"You just used your left foot to catch yourself from falling so you're goofy." Cruzer laughed.

"I can skate both cool," I bragged. "Probably 'cause I get hurt so much I always had to learn to skate the other way, like whenever I roll my ankle, or practically bust my knee. Plus, I think I have more pop when I skate switch."

"Did you teach Cruzer how to skate?"

"Ha. Yeah right. I learned from my cousin's friend Marcos in L.A.," Cruzer answered. "Before I met Georgie, I never skated with girls, but then we had a skate posse in Petaluma one summer and kinda when we lived in L.A., before we moved to Chicago."

"Girls didn't skate in Missouri. Not a single one. Heck maybe some do now, but five years ago when I tried out my brother's skate, they for sure didn't."

Back before Cruzer showed up in Petaluma when I was fifteen I only knew one other skater girl and she was kind of a poser. That was why I was so stoked when Cruzer showed up out of the blue and saved me from having the worst summer ever. It had so much potential to be a horrible summer since it was the year my mom divorced my second asshole stepdad, plus I got arrested for the first time for tagging and my mom started practicing Tough Love so she would lock me out of the house most nights, or just plain ignore me, and my sister got extra evil that year, oh and I'd run away for the second time, and I'd discovered drugs and was miserable at high school because I hadn't been saved from it by the accepting alternative school yet. So basically I hated my family, all the rednecks and asshole jocks at my school and my town in general, and the only thing I cared about was skateboarding.

Cruzer shared this life philosophy. At first she was pissed off about her mom ditching her at her grandparents for the summer, but that was before I showed her the skate park that Petaluma was famous for in skate mags. Cruzer's mom had just got married to the lawyer she was clerking for and moved them from their tiny apartment into his sprawling house in the hills. Right after the wedding Cruzer's mom sent her to Petaluma. "You're too spoiled in L.A.," she'd said. "You don't even know how to speak Spanish. You need to hang out with your Mexican family more."

"My mom sent me here so she could bang her new husband all summer long," Cruzer told me while we chomped on Jelly Belly's at the skate park.

"Well that's cool 'cause now you can be my partner in crime," I said.

After that Cruzer wanted to come back every summer. Her mom wondered why her Spanish never got any better. It was because Cruzer spent all her time with me, jumping fences, skinning knees, dropping acid in the woods behind the skate park and basically getting into whatever mischief was possible in a sleepy suburban town.

Monday night we were sitting at the end of the bar. "Hey guys, I was thinking. We should get a skate posse going," Soda said. "We'll get Tiny, Parker and Manno to get in on it. We could be called The Crew?" Soda suggested. "Like a ship crew!"

Cruzer and I loved that idea. We toasted Soda with our near empty beer cans.

Mikala set another free beer in front of Soda. "She keeps putting them down," Soda says about our empty Pabsts cans forming a triangle on the bar top.

"Well, we're celebrating what a shredder you are now," Cruzer said. Soda really was getting to be a good skater after those late-night sessions in the parking lot and after practicing balance on the smooth kitchen floor of the girl she was staying with.

"I'm a real skater. My shoes are all scuffed 'n shit," she'd said excitedly to me the other day on the phone. She had even looked like an old pro earlier when she'd come rolling up to The Vine's doorstep in the dusky light of happy hour, and cruised over the cracks of the wood floor practically skidding to a stop right at the bar counter. She also had this little bulldoggish puppy flopping behind her, chasing after her skate. "That girl I'm crashing with bought us a dog." She shrugged. The girl she was crashing with was actually sort of Soda's girlfriend, although my friend Cello told me the other night that she started hitting it with Soda. It's hard to keep track of shit around here.

We clicked our cans to our new name. Soda had some weed and she wanted to smoke us out, but Cruzer had a drug test upcoming for some new job she was trying to get, so she stayed sitting at the bar with Dixie. Soda left the pup with a group of cooing girls and we went outside and took a walk down what people call Vine Alley, which runs like a crooked creek along the side of the bar. A few houses down from the bar there was a small stairwell that led to someone's garage door, the perfect small step for huddling on. "Fuck, so I've been needing to talk to you," Soda said as she packed her bowl. "That girl I'm staying with is driving me nuts-o. I hate going home to her after work 'cause she's always nagging me. I'm glad I got into skating 'cause it feels like the only peace I have. I tell her I'm out practicing and she can't argue with that."

I'm sure Soda was practicing skating—all the way over to Cello's house.

"Man, and now she bought that puppy like she wants to have a happy family or something. I gots to get outta the situation. It's been like four months of me kicking it with her so you know that's pushing it."

Soda was the ultimate subletter of hearts. She hadn't lived in the city very long and never actually got a real house or room of her own and had mastered the art of bed surfing, which is very similar to couch surfing. But Soda didn't just stay a few weeks, fuck, and then move on; she stole the girl's heart for a few months. She told me later, one night as she filled me in on her life philosophies, that her general rule during the heart surfing was three months max. "That's when things always start to get shitty." But the first three months Soda was the best live-in lover a girl could possibly have. She usually didn't have a job so whatever girl she was currently fucking became her part-time employment. Girls would try to promote her to full time or permanent status, but she made sure to keep herself at entry level. Typically, she would sleep till the afternoon, cruise around the neighborhood on her BMX until evening, and then make sure to be back when the girl came home from school, work or whatever. Then she would help them carry their bikes up narrow flights of stairs, light all their cigarettes, and maybe cook a mean steak dinner. She would also do things like wake up at seven a.m. and drop them off at work every morning in their car, quiz a girl on her homework, look cute for the roommates, and most importantly she was an always-ready-to-fuck sort of top who could fuck them plenty, and fuck them right. Occasionally she even did yard work, fixed a broken doorknob, changed oil in a car and replaced lightbulbs around the house. There were times that Soda would fuck up, but she usually never got herself thrown out though—just a short-lived bout of resentment in the early morning hours when the girl had to go to work, when she was all tired and hung over from drinking and fucking all night. The girls would glare at Soda snuggled warm in their bed. That was when she did things like come home drunk the night before and wake up all the girl's roommates, ringing the bell at four a.m., or spend the only money she had on new sex toys so the girl had to pay for her food the rest of the week. But these offenses were easily excused when Soda fucked them and melted right through their bitterness, grinning up from between their legs with a charmingly cute face to back up all her bullshit. All she needed to do was smile her cute grin—lips playfully parted, cheeks rosy, her hair curling up from underneath her cap, and in return the girl would willingly buy her smokes, coffee, a club stamp and booze. That was all she needed. "It's like a puppy tore up their apartment all day while they were at work. Could they really stay mad at that adorable puppy that long?" That was the way Soda put it.

Soda did this for a year or so and it gave her a nasty reputation. Girls would shoot glares at her all the time from across the bar. That was because without fail a girl would come home one evening and lug her bike up the stairs by herself. She would look around the room and all that was left of the romance was traces of sex on the sheets. She would see Soda a week later with some new girl, holding hands with her at a club, huddled together at the neighborhood coffee shop sharing a coffee, and riding bikes home wobbling and drunk together from The Vine.

The puppy came flopping out the open double doors of The Vine, and ran up the street right to Soda's lap. "Are you meeting future ex-girlfriends for me in there?" Soda asked the pup.

That night we walked from The Vine up to the top of one of the steepest hills by Dolores Park. We were going to teach Soda how to power slide, our favorite late-night activity. While we were skating the puppy kept barking at our skateboards like dogs do. I sat on the curb and shoved it in my sweatshirt because we were in a quiet neighborhood at three a.m., but the dog still barked a muffled little puppy bark. "Napoleon, shut up," Soda hissed over at the shape of the dog covered in sweatshirt.

"Wha?' Cruzer said. "You're calling the puppy Napoleon?" She had been about to bomb down the hill but now she was doubled over with laughter.

Soda looked super serious. "He has a little man complex." She boxed the puppy's ears.

Cruzer just shook her head and pushed her foot back so she started to fly down the hill. She liked to go real fast on her cruiser board and carve circles down the slanting streets around the sides of the lot. Riding her board was like surfing concrete waves, how it was all bouncy and springy in the middle. I sat down on the curb next to Soda as she handed me a freshly rolled cigarette. I glanced at the huge anchor tattoo on her forearm. "Is that for your pirate ship?"

"Naw, I got that when I first moved here," Soda said. "To try to keep me from roaming."

"Roaming cities or girls?"

"Both. But this city has got me good. The first thing I did when I moved here and got off the Greyhound was go to the pier and check out the boats and the cruddy water that spoons around all the curvy sides of the peninsula. Every day for weeks I took the Muni to the beach, or the bay. Now I'm stoked about this new busing job at Fisherman's Wharf. I can see the ships come in. When I grow up I wanna work on a fishing liner like that."

For a while, Soda's new job kept her there late at night and she couldn't come skate as much. She would still meet us every Monday night at The Vine. She would bring Napoleon, who bewildered the drunk regulars with his mouthful of a name, so everyone just started calling him Nappy. The puppy didn't know it yet but he would also be a Vine regular. Lots of dogs grew up in The Vine. They were bar dogs from early on—cute little balls of fur that were passed around to cuddle in the breasts of cooing girls until they became old and jaded, dodging everyone's outstretched hands before flopping down on the wood floor and curling their paws inward to protect them from all the drunk feet. Whenever Soda saw us she would say, "My Crew!" and give us her toothy grin, flash our Crew sign: double opposing C's stacked on top of each other. Or when she was drunk, which she usually was, she would lunge at me with these extra long hugs that sometimes came with a sloppy smacky kiss at a slipshod angle on the cheek. It was her famous Soda hug. She made you want to hug her harder than all the rest.

Towards the end of that month, Cruzer's high fetish femme roommate decided to hop in a car going south for an impromptu summer road trip that would eventually end at Camp Trans, and she was vague about if she would even come back. She'd told Cruzer she didn't care what happened to her room. That was how it was at the ramshackle Creamsickle: roommates were often leaving suddenly, like they wanted to jump off the caved-in ship before it sank.

Cruzer called up Soda to see if she could move in pronto.

"Aw fuck yeah. I'm trying to get outta this girl's house. Hell but can I bring the pup with me?"

"That's cool," Cruzer said. They could have dogs at her house. They could do whatever the hell she wanted at her house. When Cruzer hung up she announced proudly to everyone hanging out in The Creamsickle living room that her new best friend was moving in with her.

"Don't be surprised if she tries to fuck you to pay her rent," I said because I was jealous.

"Hmm well, I'm not a fag," Cruzer said.

"You can pass that my way anytime," Amanda said and her eyes became wide with thoughts of romance.

"And anyways, even a freeloader like Soda could make the rent here," Cruzer pointed out.

Rent at The Creamsickle is dirt-cheap, because one of the people who were on the original lease in the late Eighties still lives there. Well...sort of. He uses the room as a commuter room so he's hardly ever there. He is a wino who Cruzer calls Potter because he always wears a brown wizard coat, thick round glasses and has short curly brown hair like Harry Potter. For an old guy Potter is pretty cool. He doesn't care what goes down at the house, but he can be a real downer because he has a cloud of sadness lurking around him. No one is quite sure where all the sadness comes from, and why for some reason Potter hangs on tight to the lease of the house, even after his parents died and left him a different house outside of the city. He has to hold on very tightly because in the last five years almost all the houses on the street have been gutted, fixed up and re-rented for much higher rents. Even the two bottom flats have recently been renovated and fixed up. The Creamsickle is like a historical monument, drooping gorgeously at the top of the block. Cruzer says that Potter is so obsessed with keeping the flat that everytime the landlord tries to talk him into moving he offers to buy the place from her, and even has gone as far as trying to hand her cash. Potter even pays part of the rent and bills even though he's never around. He comes over and fixes things, like the guardrail on the stairs that wobbled, or the glass doorknobs that were always falling off the doors. Preserving The Creamsickle is his bizarre hobby.

When Cruzer had first moved in she'd been incredibly

skeptical of Potter's niceness. She was convinced his subletting cheap rooms to young queers had some ulterior motive. When I would come over she would tell me all her new theories. Other people would get in on it too, mostly because when a bunch of people are drinking together sometimes they just need to invent some detective work so they have a purpose. "Maybe he's a CIA operative," Tiny once suggested. "And this ghetto house is his front so the enemy doesn't stake out his real pad."

"Maybe he has cameras rigged up all over the rooms and he is broadcasting y'all live on a lezzy sex Web site," Dixie once suggested, which sent everyone into a frenzy, scouring every nook and cranny for tiny cameras. Cruzer got obsessed with a hole that was in the wood paneling and for a long time whenever someone said or did something particularly dirty in the living room Cruzer would say, "Smile for the camera," and point at the hole just to freak people out. Then one night when she was on drugs she tried to take a hammer to the hole and truly investigate the camera theory but Shelby, the only practical person at The Creamsickle, talked her out of it.

Shelby is so sweet, she felt genuinely sorry for Potter and whenever he came by she would cook her Vegan specialties for him and chat with him while he polished off several bottles of corner store wine and told rambling stories about the Orange House. Funny because Shelby rarely talks very long with anyone else, she's a hermit roommate, hiding in her room and listening to records the rare times she's home from working long hours at a nonprofit, and when she does emerge she has big black DJ headphones on and her eyes have this faraway look like you don't want to disturb her because she's dancing on Mars. I used to have a crush on Shelby because she was so elusive, hiding behind her big bangs and thick mane of mousy brown hair, but I got over it when Cruzer told me she was more into guys than girls. I've been burned enough by girls who are wishy-washy about pussy.

When Soda moved in Cruzer and Shelby forgot to tell her about Potter. The night Soda found out it was hilarious because she freaked out. There's this club called Daisy Dukes that happens every other Friday Night at the Cat Fight Club. There was this club-after-party at The Creamsickle. That was also the night that I first hooked up with Melanie. I just remember following her red heels down the street after dancing, drinking tons of whiskey and making out in the smoking alley. In the middle of the party, while everyone was in the living room playing this card game called Ring of Fire that involves a lot of debaucheries truth or dares, I Never, and pounding booze, Soda screamed so loud from the kitchen that everyone ran to find out what was wrong. Soda was shaking and staring white-faced at the doorknob near the back porch door.

"What?" I shouted.

Soda couldn't talk. She was backed up against the farthest wall and pointing a shaky finger at the door. "Dead man! Dead man! In there!" she finally stuttered.

Cruzer stepped forward and stared at the door of the back room. Soda had only been living in the house a few weeks. "Did you not tell her about Potter?" Shelby shouted from beneath her curtain of bangs. All the girls were squealing and huddling at the edge of the kitchen behind Soda.

"Who is Potter?" Soda shouted, but no one answered.

I could tell Cruzer was scared because she thought maybe Potter really was dead, but she was acting tough for the ladies so she slowly crept to the door. "Oh my God. Oh my God," Dixie and Amanda chanted over and over.

"Don't do it!" Soda yelled. "Let's just call the cops!"

Cruzer sucked in a huge breath and turned the doorknob. The light from the kitchen flooded over the room, which I had never seen. Melanie was digging her nails into my arm. The first thing I noticed was how the room was for sure the best one in the house. There was a huge Victorian fireplace against the front wall and huge bay windows covered in thick dusty red curtains that when open would have an awesome view looking over the city. Then I looked at the foldout couch bed against the back wall and I sucked in my breath because there was Potter lying there in his usual outfit, mouth hanging half open and stained purple around the edges.

"Is he dead?" everyone shouted.

"Potter," Cruzer hissed.

Potter didn't respond. I looked closer at his limp figure and saw that he had earplugs shoved into his pointy elf ears. "He's not dead." Cruzer turned and announced to the room, "I can see him breathing. He just guzzles wine until he passes out."

"What?" Soda screeched. "Is this your friend? Did you, like, invite him, or something?"

"Yeah, she met him at the wizard convention." Dixie doubled over with laughter. Now everyone was either laughing at the situation or wandering back into the living room to continue flipping cards and making out with each other. Cruzer went into Potter's room. How brave of her. Dixie started to explain to Soda who Potter was and why there was a secret bedroom.

Soda glared at Cruzer. "Umm, can you explain why you're okay with a dead-looking guy hiding in a secret room in our house?"

Cruzer looked kind of stuck and looked at me for help. She was bad at confrontation and could not handle anyone being in her face. "Let's have a cigarette," I said to Soda.

Cruzer looked completely relieved to be let off the hook. Soda started to follow me to the back porch but stuck to the farthest edge of the kitchen so she could stay as far away as possible from the now shut door to Potter's room.

On a clear night, the back porch can feel like you are in the cage of a construction crane dangling over the city, hanging high over the arch of the Mission streets that run smack dab into the jagged edges of downtown, and the bridges like faded spotlights jut out along the side. When the view was that clear it looked fake. Other nights, for weeks even, it was just a gray mess of fog, the only thing visible were the things that glowed red, like the Safeway sign on the left, and the Coca-Cola billboard on the right. "Look, you can see when people turn on the office buildings' lights, each window one by one. It's probably the nighttime cleaning crews," I said looking out at the city sparkling beneath us.

Then I told Soda the whole story about Potter.

"I can't believe I nearly had a fucking heart attack." Soda chuckled. "But I am glad there isn't really a dead man living in my first real house here."

After that night Soda would mess with Cruzer. Sometimes she would say, "Remember when you tricked me into moving in with you and your old wizard boyfriend?" And Cruzer would come back with, "Remember when you totally screamed like a girl?" But really they would laugh about it. Also that girl Amanda distracted Soda from thinking about Potter anymore because while we were outside she'd told Cruzer to please use her next turn to dare her at Truth or Dare to give Soda a lap dance.

By the time the sun was coming up I looked up from making out with Melanie and the room had totally cleared out. Cruzer was sitting beside two girls on the couch, who were also making out. There was thumping coming from the kitchen, and giggles on the back porch. "Where's Soda?" Cruzer stared up at the ceiling and exhaled a long stream of smoke.

"I dunno. Where's Amanda?"

We giggled and tiptoed down the creaking hallway and put our ear to Soda's door. Silence. Where are they? We checked the bathrooms and the closets. "Cruzer, your room is locked," I yelled from down the hall.

"Dude, you have your own room!" Cruzer shouted at her shut door. She was laughing though. "That kid is so weird how she likes to sleep in every bed in the house," Cruzer whispered to me. I thought about what Soda had said about the anchor tattoo not working. "She also likes to sleep on the couch a lot. She's a funny one. It's like she can't stay still, has to bed surf to keep sane. That's probably why she opened Potter's door! She was looking for a new bed! Ha ha."

"Don't make me laugh or I'm gonna pee my pants!" I yelled to Cruzer, running down the hall, back to the living room to see if Melanie wanted me to walk her home.

# Chapter 5

With Cruzer gone Soda and I've been hanging out all the time. One night we come home drunk from The Vine and she says, "You've got to sleep in my new bed. It rules." I nearly panic for a second. I so do not want to sleep with a roommate ever again, plus Cruzer would freak on me if I fagged out with a member of our Crew. Then I realize Soda doesn't mean it like that.

I drunkenly scramble up onto Soda's high bed while Napoleon backs up to get a running start just to jump up on it because the bed is like six feet high.

"Your silly bed. You're gonna roll off it drunk in the night," Cruzer laughed at Soda after they finished building it. Soda hadn't started sleeping in her own room at night until she built herself a crazy pirate bed, almost a month after living at The Creamsickle. She got the idea to make the bed because she was over at a friend's house who lived with a woman who made queer porn movies, and she saw her bed, a big wooden thing with four high wooden posts and hooks with ropes along the side. Soda liked the ropes on the sides. The porn director used them to tie up her dates, but Soda was thinking more along the lines of pirate ship rope.

I guess she hasn't finished tightening the screws and bolts because the bed is still really rickety. It swings back and forth whenever I move, like a rope bridge. I imagine that there are other ships circling the bed. The shadows on Soda's white walls look like ships that will circle the bed all night like hungry sharks. When the bed sways, it feels like the entire house is swaying. Probably I just have the drunk spins. "This is your rickety, rocky pirate bed," I say.

"Beds should stay unstable, like ships," Soda mumbles, falling asleep.

For the next week somehow every night I end up sleeping in Soda's bed. I'm having withdrawals from my old room, and Hurricane. Some nights we stay up all night talking. We tell each other all the stories from growing up, dreams of the future and a few of our deepest secrets. Soda tells me that her ultimate dream is to learn how to build ships. I tell her that if I didn't have to work all the time to pay the bills in this expensive city I'd go back to school to be an English teacher because that was my favorite teacher at the alternative high school I went to, the only reason I bothered to come to school and get credits to graduate. Soda tells me about her dad hitting her across the face when he found out she was a dyke, when she came home with a shaved head. I tell her about my dad sneaking off to the local titty bar when he was supposed to be babysitting my sisters and me when we were toddlers, and how one day he left with all the cash my parents had saved to move out of the basement room they were living in and we never heard from him again. She tells me about how when she was a teenager her dad used to steal stuff from big hardware stores and make her go in and return it for cash and one time she got caught and had to do community service. We joke about how everyone we know seems to have their own "deadbeat dad" stories and at least ours are kinda so insanely fucked-up that they're funny.

Soda tells me she tried to pee like a boy so much as a kid that her mom used to scream at her dad because she thought he was the one "missing" the toilet seat and that her jeans legs would sometimes smell like pee due to her relentless practicing. I tell her about how I used to jack off to Jodie Foster movies. She tells me she used to suck a lot of her older brother's friends' dicks

when she was a teenager so they would let her drive around and buy her beer, and because she was obsessed with how their parts worked. I tell her about how my sisters completely ignored me at school because they were pretty and popular, one was even a cheerleader, and they were embarrassed that their sister was so "weird." She tells me she used to go deer hunting with her brother and dad just so she could bond with them, but she still feels awful about it. I tell her about the first girl I ever fucked, this pilled-out preppie girl I met in a one-night-stay group home. She tells me she hasn't let anyone fuck her since she was nineteen. I tell her about the time Cruzer's first girlfriend tried to seduce me and that it's my only secret from Cruzer. She tells me about how she fucked her brother's best friend's girlfriend right before she left town for good.

I like Soda's stories. Her hometown seems so much more romantic than the cookie-cutter suburbs I was confined to. She grew up in the driest landlocked town but she was obsessed with the ocean. As a kid she played with ships in the tub, and loaded little toy plastic docks up on her bedroom floor all day long. But there were no real ships in her town, just a looming paper mill that blocked out the sun and smelled like rotting apples and a few hundred grazing cows. Lying in the pirate bed I imagine Soda's hometown like this stifling armpit with a hazy cloud of fumes and the only ships were paper boats floating in a sludgy sea of paper pulp.

One night Soda asks, "What's your real name?" A faux pas question for most bois but since it's Soda I don't mind.

"Georgette," I tell her, laughing as it rolls awkwardly out of my mouth. "It was my grandmother's name on my dad's side. I never met her and my mom hates my dad so much that she won't give me her address to even try to contact her."

Soda tells me her birth name even though I don't care what it is. She makes me swear ten times never to repeat it. Then she says it again, the crazy long country girl name and we laugh hysterically about it for five minutes, at least.

Soda.

The City had named her. Some girl she'd kissed at a party her first week in town had mumbled, *Mmmm you taste like grape*

*soda*, and then called her that the rest of the night. The nickname stuck to her like gum on the bottom of a shoe. She didn't mind. She had needed a new name. She had needed a new life. That was why she had run away from that small Midwest town in the first place.

The pirate bed is lodged up against the two corner windows. All night long the fog laps against the windowpanes like small waves of water.

When Cruzer finally comes home I stop sleeping in Soda's bed. She would think it was weird like we were fooling around or something. That night I go to bed back in my pantry room and miss the rocking of the pirate ship. In the morning I wake up early and want to crawl into Soda's bed and laugh with her for a while. I go down the hall to her room but Soda isn't alone, Amanda's dark bobbed hair is peeking out of her covers. I feel a small, stupid pang of jealousy.

"Georgie!" Amanda squeals when I come into the room. She hops a bit out of the covers and grabs my hand. She isn't wearing a shirt, small metal barbells glint off each of her nipples. She pulls me into the bed between her and Soda. "I'm so excited you live here now!" she says with her morning-after smoker's voice. "I heard that crazy girl tried to burn your house down."

"I don't think she did it on purpose," I mumble but Amanda isn't listening.

"I never liked that bitch. She and that coke dealer boy she hung around with swiped my cocktail once."

I just laugh.

"Hurricane stole Georgie's heart so she won't talk bad about her," Soda informs Amanda.

"Whatever." Amanda says, "My friend Lorrie thinks you're cute. You should make out with her. She is nice. She won't cut you, or try to burn your house up."

"Sounds good," I say even though I can't imagine hooking up with anyone. Actually the most action I've gotten lately is one morning last week when I woke up in Soda's bed all tangled up in her limbs in the dark. In the morning though we were both on separate sides of the bed so maybe I imagined it.

A few weeks later I wake up in the middle of the night and I still feel drunk. There's this cute blonde and pink-haired Australian girl sleeping next to me. I should be fucking her, I guess, but instead I'm lying here stiffly staring at the ceiling and feeling incredibly lonely. I think Hurricane permanently ruined my sex drive. It's been weeks and weeks since she left but it doesn't matter who I make out with. It's like my five senses have been shut off and girls feel, smell and taste like nothing. The irony is that I've just moved into one of the most notorious bachelor pads and I don't even care about getting laid, but I promise I've been trying, I really have.

There's a little system that Cruzer has described to me countless times, before I moved into The Creamsickle, that I now have unlimited opportunities to put into action. The system is called *The Three Step Plan*. Wow, it sounds like a diet fad or something. But actually it's Cruzer's foolproof plan to get a girl into bed. All you have to do is find a cute young thing at The Vine and invite her over, or whatever, and then you implement the steps. Here is exactly how the steps are written down in Cruzer's scrap journal in Soda's handwriting, with some things crossed out and re-scribbled in unrecognizable handwriting and in a different color pen. It's titled, *Booty Call Steps*.

Step 1. Take her for a beer and smoke on the back porch. Say something like "Oh want to see the view?" = romance. That's when you first kiss her. ~~Play some Marvin Gaye~~.

Step 2. Go in the living room (never go straight to the bedroom after the first kiss) have another beer and a smoke on the couch and JUST talk. You can put your hand on her leg or some shit, but don't make out. This will make her want it more. Believe me. She *wants* to talk.

Step 3. Now, take her to your room. ~~MAKE LOVE~~. Fuck.

Okay, so this formula looks sleazy on paper but a lot of Soda and Cruzer's list making is just jokes. The reason the list came about is because Cruzer realized one day that she always did the same thing whenever she brought a girl home, and then she swore that it worked every time, so Soda tried it out. I think there was even a bet waged between her and Cruzer on the foolproofness of it. And then I move in and I'm the only one who ever fails to make it to the finish line. The whole process is so boring, by the time I follow the imaginary diagram around the house, when it comes to the fucking part I end up nearly yawning into some girl's mouth.

The last few times I brought a girl home, I found myself opening one of my poetry books that I just started reading for school, or one of Hurricane's favorite books she left behind, and reading them to my dates until they eventually fall asleep, probably out of pure boredom. "You are so fucking gay!" Cruzer shouted at me when she heard I still hadn't fucked Amanda's friend Lorrie, but had gotten halfway through Mina Loy's *Lunar Baedeker*. "Cross out Step Three = Fuck, and write in, *Read Her Poetry* instead," Cruzer instructed Soda. "Georgie has moved in and it looks like she's making some amendments to *The Constitution of Booty Call*."

"Georgie is just a romantic," Dixie told her. "You should have heard the other night how she explained to Amanda about why Soda has a pirate bed. She told her this whole story about a town full of paper boats, but no ocean."

"I like when you do that," Soda said. "Turn my smelly old hometown into something worthy of a movie."

*The Three-Step Plan*, according to Soda, is pretty much foolproof on out-of-town visitors, or girls who just moved to town, because the view of the city works extra special on them. Every fantasy they might have had about San Francisco in whatever homophobic or stuffy town they came from hits them, right then, smack-dab in the face, when the huge, sparkling Queer Fuck of a city rolls out like a carpet at their feet. So, I had had an easy lay with the visiting Australian but I'd read her Michelle Tea poems instead. Now, I think about waking her up by kissing her, or starting something hotter, like a short sweet kind of fuck in the middle of the night while the whole world sleeps, but instead I want something familiar. I get up and tiptoe into Soda's room.

The pirate bed creaks when I climb in. Soda wakes up, but she's used to me crawling into her bed so she doesn't freak out.

"Hey, how's your cutie Aussie?"

"I dunno. I'm just not into it."

At dawn the light comes in Soda's blinds. I remember there's a girl in my bed so I should get back in it. Crawling back into my bed I wake her up, and make out for a while, but then right when I start unbuttoning her pants, she says *I've got my period* in this tone that sounds like, "My dog just died." *Shit.* Finally I'm ready to fuck the first girl since Hurricane and then code red.

We both stare awkwardly at the ceiling. I can feel her wondering if I want to be fucked, wondering if she touches me if I will push her hand away or let her put it down my pants. Or maybe she isn't wondering any of that and she thinks I want it but she's just nervous. Who knows? Neither of us says anything. Usually, I will totally bottom out whenever. I don't play how Cruzer plays, like how as a rule she never bottoms out till the third date, or Soda who never bottoms out, ever. I like to get fucked. But at this particular moment I'm not in the right place to get fucked by a stranger, to be that intimate. I could fuck her, but if she fucked me I was scared I might lose it or cry or something terrible like that.

I tug the Australian girl over and pull her on top of me so strands of pink bubblegum hair fall in my face. She's only wearing these sheer blue panties. I lift her up a little and put my hands down my boxers and she slides her hand between her own legs. She moves up and down like she is riding me. Soda once told me this is the only bottoming out she ever does. Topping from the bottom, she calls it. Thinking of Soda gets me even hotter, and I come when the girl leans down, her hair falling like a dark curtain in my face and runs her tongue in circles around mine.

I wake up hours later to shouting and doors banging in the hall. I get up to get a glass of water and see Cruzer is trying to rewire the TV in the living room that apparently has all the cords messed up from Soda and her friend Ed playing video games last night. "Soda fix this!" Cruzer is hollering, "The soap is almost on!" Any day now the soap opera lesbians are actually going to have a sex scene. It is a huge ordeal. Soda comes in from the back porch where she usually smokes her morning cigarette.

"Turn it on. Turn it on," Cruzer shouts down the hall at her as I duck in the bathroom to piss.

"Dude chill, it's not even noon yet!" Soda yells back.

My head pounds.

The lesbians may never fuck. It's been ages since they first kissed. On soap time everything goes in slow motion, plus whenever the lesbians try, something happens.    People are constantly sabotaging them, their ex-boyfriends, parents, and kids, causing the two to have Lesbian Bed Death before they ever even get dirty. A few days ago when we were all watching one particularly frustrating buildup and they *still* didn't have sex, Cruzer compared it to my sex life. "Okay next they're gonna start reading Emily Dickinson, I betcha."

In the living room Cruzer hands me half a bagel from her coffee shop hook up around the corner. Cruzer gets a gay mafia hook up just about everywhere in the neighborhood, free coffee from Cello, free sandwiches if Jen's boss isn't there, free pizza from Freddy's, film developing from Dina, and so on. Cruzer's always been like that. When she wants something she just points at it and it usually ends up in her hand. When we were younger and this didn't work for me I just got really good at stealing to keep up with her freebie luck.

Soda is already sitting on the couch ready for soap time, her face sleepy under the shag of her messy hair, and she's still wearing her boxers, with a black bandanna around her neck, and a blue-striped collared prep boy shirt that Cruzer had spray painted *Rammin Aries* across the front, from when they threw a party in April for their joint 22nd birthday. She has her gray heather fleece blanket scrunched up around her feet because no matter what, even if the morning sun is streaking through the cracked window above Soda's head, The Creamsickle is always cold. Cruzer has her own matching blanket that she usually keeps on the other couch. Soda's friend Ed had bought them the matching blankets after he'd come over to play *Tony Hawk Pro Skater* with them one afternoon on a particularly cold day and couldn't believe that he could see his breath since there wasn't any sort of heater in the house. That probably explained why they had so many parties, because they were freezing and they wanted people over simply so they could steal all the body warmth.

The Australian girl comes into the living room and I get worried. Soda and Cruzer have strict rules about no overnight guests staying during soap time, since during the commercial breaks they dish about girls, mostly details from whatever adventure happened the night before. There are all these strange rules at The Creamsickle that I've been trying to get used to. Luckily the girl is going to Golden Gate Park for the day with her friend. She asks if I want to go but I tell her it's a really important day on the soap, embarrassed that I'm probably confirming her stereotypes on Americans by revealing my addiction to a daytime TV show. I want to explain that we'd only gotten hooked on the soap because of the lesbians. For the last month, every day at noon since Cruzer and Soda had started watching that soap, they would rush home every morning if they woke up somewhere else. Sometimes they even courtesy-called like, "Hey friend I'm at Stephanie's. Uh yeah more on that later, but I'm walking now, I'm two blocks away." For Cruzer, the soap opera time requirement is the closest thing she's had to holding a real job.

Soda starts to recap the show to try to convey the importance of today's episode to the Australian girl. She is speaking in fragments between gulps of coffee and bites of her bagel. "There is this chick Bianca who came out as a lesbian...the first lesbian ever on daytime TV...she turned this chick named Maggie out...Maggie has this abusive boyfriend...Get this! The brother of the abusive boyfriend is this guy that once raped Bianca, which later resulted in Bianca having his baby!"

"Bianca is the daughter of Erica, you know, Susan Lucci? The absolute queen of daytime television? Yup, her TV daughter is totally gay!" Cruzer adds.

"They're for sure gonna fuck today. I know it." Soda says excitedly and hops up a bit so that the old couch groans underneath her.

The Australian girl looks officially weirded out by us, which is probably a good thing, and she leaves.

On the first commercial Cruzer is going on and on about sex with some girl she met at her art opening last night. "What did she sound like?" Soda asks, which means, "What did she sound like when she came?" Hanging around Cruzer and Soda has made me a secondhand aficionado on the way most of the femme girls we know sound like in bed, down to the smallest sounds they made. Soda would be like, "You know that girl Dasha, well it's just like this series of small short screams, like an opera always ending on the same fourth scream." The result is that I'm forever stuck into hearing these noises in the back of my head randomly, like when I wave to a girl on the street, or when that hot femme bartender hands me my drink, like this girl Hillary who we call *Hillary The Hisser* because she hisses like an angry cat in bed, according to Soda. Hillary is Soda's favorite submission into *The Orgasm Imitation Files*. Soda is super good at doing the imitations, like when she does Hillary she even makes this small whistling noise between her teeth. Cruzer isn't usually as good at it, all hers tend to sound the same, but she still always tries.

By the middle of the soap we're all completely frustrated, because it is obvious the lesbians are still never going to fuck. Cruzer keeps screaming at the TV. The last scene, Soda throws an old beer can at the set. I feel shitty from drinking too much last night and they are making my head hurt worse.

I go lie down on my bed but I can't deal with how much it smells like the girl's perfume so I go into Soda's room and once again, climb on her pirate bed. I curl up and look out the window at the way the telephone wires dance on the wind. The cold will be coming soon. You can see it in the thin layer of morning fog, cold wind and dark clouds that are lurking in the distance, ready to spread out over the city.

I look down at the mess of Soda's room and see something familiar lying on her floor. I get up and tug it from a pile of rumpled clothes. It looks like this hoody I thought I lost a few years ago. I put it on and remember how it fit me perfectly. As I walk down the hall, I notice it is even better now, softer with a few years worth of fade and new holes worn into the right places. I go back into the living room wearing the hoody. "Whoa that hoody is old school." Cruzer squints at me and feels the fabric. "I remember when you practically tore the sleeve off at that ramp party in Petaluma."

"Where'd you get this?" I ask Soda.

"Huh?" She peels her eyes from the soap to glance over. "Oh, that uh, I think from Amanda, or no, I think…umm, oh yeah, Coby had it one day and I was cold so she let me borrow it."

"Well it's mine, but Hurricane stole it from me forever ago."

"Wait, does this mean you're taking it back? Aw c'mon it's my favorite."

"It's mine too." I smell the collar for traces of Hurricane. "So does that mean she fucked Coby and left it at her house?" I ask Soda or Cruzer, but may as well be talking to the wall because neither of them answers. Soda just looks at me with her typically toothy mouth closed in a straight line. It dawns on me that Hurricane could have been fucking other girls when I thought she had been with that boyfriend. The fact she may have been fucking other girls while we had been fucking makes me ten times more jealous than I was of that silly boy. I consider girls to be different, more important. Or maybe Coby got the hoody some other way. Who knew how many girls and beds my long lost hoody had passed through before it came back to me.

Soda breaks the silence. "You can have the hoody back."

I must look pretty pathetic sitting there smelling the frayed sleeve edges and the soft folds of the collar. I toss the hoody onto the floor. "I'm not attached to it," I announce.

We all turn our attention back to watching the soap.

"The Australian girl sounded like this when she came." I demonstrate at the next commercial break. It's my first time contributing to the sex sound game in a long time. Soda is so excited that she jumps up to hug me. She loves any sign that I'm moving on from terrible Hurricane. Cruzer tries to imitate my new submission to *The Orgasm Files* but ends up sounding like a drowning cat and we all start laughing hysterically.

The end music for the soap opera starts to play all dramatically and the previews for what is coming up the next day come on so we all turn back to the TV. In one scene, one of the lesbians announces she's moving to France. "What! Moving to France!" Soda screeches. "They are never going to do it!"

That mess of gray clouds I saw earlier out Soda's window spreads over the morning sun that had been peeking through the duct tape-lined windows above Soda's head. The slouchy living room feels sad for a moment. Soap time is over and now Soda and I have to get ready for work and Cruzer has to pretend to go look for work, and what the fuck, the lesbians were moving to France to raise the baby!

"Fuck, daytime TV, I'm protesting! I'm sticking to Buffy," Soda huffs as she kicks her gray fleece blanket off with her tube-socked feet.

After Soda leaves for work Amanda comes by all gussied up in a low-cut vintage slip dress. "Where's Soda?" she wants to know. "I've been calling her for days and she is not calling me back. I mean, is she okay?" Amanda adds that Soda had not returned her calls all week. She takes a mix tape out of her purse that she made for Soda. "Is she playing me?" she asks us. She slams the tape on the coffee table, hard. We shrug.

When Amanda turns around, Cruzer and I look at each other helplessly. Why did we answer the goddamn door? We are both scared that we might have to witness Soda actually causing a real meltdown in a girl. I have heard about such things. I have heard stories about girls leaving broken glass around the edges of Soda's locked up bike. I have heard of bathroom graffiti that was so obscene The Vine bartenders had to paint over it right away. We both know Soda isn't going to call Amanda back, even if they had fucked for two weeks straight or even if the mix tape is so amazing that it makes Soda's jaw drop. Soda still won't call. Sometimes I'm not sure Soda even knows what a cell phone is, the way hers sits on the coffee table, lost in piles of stuff and vibrates all day long while her eyes don't move from the TV.

One day, I'm doing my homework in the living room, and halfway through my reading for English class. I hear a soft thud down the hall. I wonder if Soda left work early, but then Mr. Potter comes stumbling into the room. At first I think it's the slanted floor that is making him walk crooked until I see his purple cracked lips and teeth and realize he has probably just guzzled a few bottles of wine for breakfast. Probably before driving across the bridge from Marin too.

"Tim?" Mr. Potter squints at me.

I notice he isn't wearing his usual big round thick glasses, the ones that seriously need to be cleaned because they always have fingerprints all over them. When Mr. Potter says, "Tim," I look behind me where Napoleon is curled up in a black ball of dog, sleeping on the couch. I wonder if that is Potter's nickname for Naps.

"Tim?" Potter mumbles again as he walks closer. Then I realize he is talking to me. *Okay, I guess he thinks I'm a boy.* It's nice to occasionally dupe someone with my gender. Usually it's more likely to happen when I leave the city where people aren't used to gender queer.

"Uh, no I'm Georgie," I correct Potter. I know Potter is used to having new roommates in the ever-revolving-door rooms of The Creamsickle, but it seems strange that he has already forgotten me, especially since before moving in I have been hanging around the place for a few years.

"Oh," Potter says looking terribly disappointed. He comes and sits down next to me, which instantly makes me feel like I need to sneeze. I'm allergic to dust and his seventies style brown corduroy jacket has a gray film of it on the shoulders. Or maybe he is a ghost and it's his dusty ghost aura. I feel a little scared being alone in the house with him. If he is a ghost, did anyone else know him outside of The Creamsickle? It's not like we ever ran into him walking down Valencia, or buying food at the corner store. He could be dead like Soda had originally thought!

Potter sighs long and hard. His breath smells like a wine cellar. I decide that ghosts can't have booze breath so he must be human. "Tim will come someday," Potter says firmly.

"Who is Tim?" I ask after my next, almost-needing-to-sneeze feeling passes.

"Tim is my husband. We moved in here together fifteen years ago. We were revolutionaries. We were escapists! We were in love!" Potter is sort of queeny, he throws his hands around, fingers covered in thick gold rings. My first thought is that Potter has invented this person, like he is some sort of blow-up doll. "Tim is in Canada, but he is coming back."

"Uh, when is he coming back, man?"

"I have been waiting ten years." Potter sighs one long whistling sigh. "He will be back though. He had to take care of some things back home," he says with assurance. Potter looks so sad and yet so sure of himself at the same time that I now feel bad for my joking attitude. My stomach churns because I haven't eaten all day except a bagel and with the realization that Potter isn't messing with me, that this Tim person is his great love and he has still not gotten over it, after ten years.

"No one remembers him around here anymore because everyone is dead. All our friends are dead. They all died of AIDS, and I'm the only one left so no one remembers anything, anything at all, but me," Potter says, this part stated in a steady, matter-of fact way, much like a dramatic monologue, something I recently learned about in my English class. I feel like the entire house suddenly drops down an extra two feet.

All I can do is stare at Potter's misty eyes and purple mouth. I want to hug him but I don't know if he is that kind of person, and also that would probably give me a sneezing fit. All the hypothesizing about why Potter held onto The Creamsickle so tight has been wrong. He isn't a CIA agent, or the proprietor of a lesbian Internet porn ring, he's a poor sad man, getting drunk off nostalgia. It makes sense now, what Cruzer once told me about a weird conversation with him when she asked if they could trade rooms, since he was never home and his room was the best in the house. She said that Potter's eyes grew wide with shock and he said, "No! That room is extremely important to me. I don't want anything about it to change." She wanted to ask why, but Potter seemed so offended that she had even asked, and he practically flew out the door, his ghost feet barely tapping the stairs.

"It is so wacky!" Cruzer said. "Why is he so attached to a

room he never even sleeps in?"

Now I know that the room is a museum to a love affair, a shrine to a time that is never going to exist again. Potter's life of revolutionary love with Tim is over, but he is stuck in that decade, a carefree time before AIDS, before all his friends went away. I can't even imagine losing my queer family.

Potter is staring bleary-eyed down the hall, his head swaying slightly. His teeth are so yellow and purple that they look like the third day of a good bruise. I pat him on the back awkwardly and a puff of dust comes off his jacket. I close my English book and get up to change the record to something more upbeat. I put on some Joy Division for him since he likes the Eighties and I can tell he likes it because he smiles and starts wobbling back and forth to the beat. I pour myself a glass of his red wine and end up spending the next three hours listening to him tell dozens of amazing stories about what he refers to as "the glory days of The Orange House."

Later, Potter goes to pass out in his room and leaves me feeling so sad. I call Dixie to meet me at The Vine. It looks like it's going to rain so I can't skate. On the walk, I call Cruzer. She's hanging her photos for a show at an art gallery in SOMA. "I know why Potter won't let you have his room," I tell her and relate the whole story.

"No shit. That's so sad." She groans. "I can't believe he hasn't put a curse on the whole house. But jeez, it's like the exact opposite. The Creamsickle is a pussy goldmine!"

"I think we should give him a makeover and take him out in the Castro. I'm for sure going thrifting this week and finding him a new jacket that isn't covered in dust."

"Totally. We could attack him in the hall like they do on that reality show. We'll hide behind my door and get him right when he walks up the stairs. We could tie him up with that rope hanging off Soda's pirate bed, then pin him down and give him a stylely pompadour," Cruzer plots.

At The Vine I usually play certain songs on the jukebox that remind me of Hurricane, like this one song I heard for the first time right after we fucked and were all sweaty, tangled up in each other, lying on the bed, high off multiple orgasms and fun shit like that. But if I had learned anything this afternoon from Potter, it is that it's time to stop that pathetic bullshit. I don't even go near the jukebox this time. I play a few games of pinball while I wait for Dixie and check out every new girl who walks into the bar.

For the next few months I concentrate on school and fixing up my room. Shelby changes her mind about moving to New York so I revamp the pantry. A lot of nights I sleep in Soda's room if she doesn't have a girl over, or if Soda feels like drifting she sleeps in my bed. Sometimes when she does have a girl over, the kind that leaves in the middle of the night, she'll come get me. *Tap, tap* at three in the morning, on the pantry door. "Georgie, pirate ship. Crew meeting."

One night lying in the pirate ship she says, "Feel my face." And after I do she grins. "Could you feel my beard?"

"No."

She looks disappointed. "Are you sure?"

She nuzzles her cheek against my face. I squint my eyes at her chin looking for her beard, searching for something on her pale cheeks that glow white with the light from the city skyline beneath her window.

"I shaved my face," she says with a smile that makes her look like she's a small child confessing she has just stolen candy. "I want my 'stache to grow back darker and thicker. I want a pirate beard!"

"Let me feel again." I run my hands across her face again and I can maybe feel something there, a sort of tingling of hair follicles under my fingertips. It's electric underneath Soda's baby cheeks.

"Okay. Maybe I did feel something. Yeah. There's definitely something there."

# Chapter 6

Thanksgiving eve, I'm sitting shotgun in Cruzer's truck, with Soda, Dixie and Tiny in the back cab, driving south down the freeway. Soda is so excited. She's been a non-stop grin all day long, because we are on our way to a town by the sea. She's jumping around the back of the cab, like Nappy.

This morning we were sitting around the house, bored, the city dead quiet with most of our friends away for the holidays. We are the leftover queer orphans, celebrating together, so we decide to go on an impromptu gay-cation. We wanted to take over a small town, to bombard the local gay bar and rile up the dance floor. We wanted to flirt with new girls, and Soda had an old fuck she wanted to revisit. Less than twenty minutes after we decided on a destination we were piling into the truck, dragging sleeping bags and skateboards behind us.

After the disco-style small town gay bar calls last call, one of the smallest little queers hops up and down in front of Dixie and jangles some keys in front of her face. "Let's go party at the diner." The local kids tell us that tonight is the only day of the year that the all-night diner where all the queers in town work is actually closed. It's even open on Christmas Eve. But tonight it closed early for the first time in years.

The girls unlock the double bolted back doors and we all

rush in, about fifteen drunk queer kids. We're hushed at first but quickly get rowdy, putting money in the jukebox, slumping into the empty booths, dancing on the checkered floor. One girl even starts dancing on the countertop. We have plastic bags full of bottles of booze that we mix with Coke straight from the pop fountain. I'm sitting at the diner counter, watching the crazy girl in combat boots and a tie-dyed skirt dancing on the counter and then I look over to see this super hot girl that I would much rather be watching tabletop dancing. The girl is sitting back coolly against the wall of one of the red booth seats. She's got a matchstick of a body, with a jet black tip of hair falling like a jagged line of spilled black paint over her eyes, which are darting lines of mascara-clumped slits. I catch her eye for a second, and it makes me feel nervous. I turn back around and suck hard on my sixteen ouncer of pop and whiskey.

A little bit later, the girl comes over with her friend and they sit down on a diner seat next to me. "Your friend Cruzer just told us you once ollied off a roof to impress a girl and broke your ankle," the hot girl says as she swivels in the diner seat.

"Jeez." I try to brush it off but can feel the back of my ears turning red. *Damn, Cruzer is such a punk.* "There were tons of bushes below so I didn't think it was that dangerous, but then I err, missed the bushes, I guess…"

Cruzer walks up behind me, "Girls, meet Georgie, we like to call her our li'l romantic," she says, patting me on the back.

"I'm Mia," the hot girl says. "I work here. I could make you a milk shake." I shake my head no. I'm having trouble talking to her, there is something hypnotic about her gravelly voice. "OK, then come smoke with me." She nods to the outside patio through the double glass swinging diner doors.

Bunches of kids are outside, sitting on the enclosed patio, huddling and smoking, with their jacket hoods up over their heads blocking the cold ocean mist. Everyone is talking about John Waters, and passing around the tail end of a blunt. Dixie is sitting by Mia, and I'm sitting by Dixie. The sky is threatening to light up with morning.

When Mia is distracted and talking to Dixie I glare at Cruzer. "What? She asked about you," Cruzer leans over and whispers in my ear. "You should be thanking me. Girls love that romantic shit. I'm helping you get some."

"She asked about me?"

Cruzer nods. "Play it cool."

I see Mia glance over at us. I smoke and pretend I don't want to spend the entire dawn checking her out. "I'm moving to the city soon. For my music," I hear her tell Dixie before we all head back inside. Daylight is coming quick, so we have to scramble to leave the diner before light exposes our illegal party hub. I start putting our leftover bottles of beer in my backpack. Mia walks by me and tugs the shirttail of my plaid button-up shirt and then continues walking. *Is she teasing?* She's headed towards the hall that leads to the bathroom, the opposite direction of the back door that leads to the parking lot where everyone else is headed.

Mia looks back at me. I'm standing in the middle of the empty diner and the jukebox is playing Dolly. I follow her.

I wake up to cold hard metal digging into my back. It's the ridges of the truck cab poking me, even though I'm lying on a pile of blankets that are soft, but smell like dog. Mia is asleep next to me. Curled into a pile of dog hair-covered blankets. Her short black hair is stuck to her face with damp sweat, because the air is hot and thick in the truck with the morning sun beating into the windows. She has the longest eyelashes I have ever seen, falling like stray wishes onto her cheeks.

Napoleon is whining. That's what woke me up. He's staring at the back cab window, and then looking pleadingly back at me. I unlatch the window and poke my head out. We are parked in a gravel alley, with a sleepy stretch of suburban homes on each side of us, and huge trees swaying overhead. I can smell the ocean. Nappy jumps out and the whole truck shakes.

Mia wakes up and smiles shyly across the truck at me. Even half asleep she looks fierce, with sultry black-eyeliner-lined eyes squinting against the sun. She looks like the kind of girl that probably has a switchblade in the back pocket of her tight black pants. She is still wearing black fingerless mittens, and a red hanky tied around her neck. She starts to look around the truck for her T-shirt. She doesn't have any tattoos except for a name scrawled on her tit. "My first band when I was sixteen," she told me last night when she was sitting on the sink counter in the empty diner bathroom with her T-shirt lying on the bathroom floor. There are marks on my arms where her fingers pressed while our mouths were smashed together.

Mia crawls over on her hands and knees and pops her head outside with me, "Oh how did we get here? That's my ex-girlfriend's house we're in front of," she mumbles. *Ha*, I guess her city's scene is just as small as mine. We hop out the back of the truck and shake Nappy's hair and sawdust from our clothes. Mia's black clothes are so tight that I would help her clean them off anytime. "Nappy take me to Soda," I say when the dog comes running back up to us.

The dog runs straight up to the door of the house that we're parked across from. Mia knows how to get into the house through the side door, being that her ex lives there. Inside, we find Soda asleep on the couch. We wake her up and she tells us Cruzer is upstairs with the girl who lives here. "Ya, my ex." Mia rolls her eyes. When Soda and I look at her to see if she is upset about it, she quickly adds, "Oh no drama, it's an old ex. We're cool."

"Let's leave Cruzer here. I want to see the ocean," Soda says.

We walk to the beach. Napoleon, who is the only one who's not a little hungover, runs straight into the icy cold ocean. "Man, I want to go in too!" Soda whines. "You're so lucky you live here."

"Soda is a pirate. She wants to live in a shack by the sea," I explain to Mia.

"You can have my house," Mia says. "I'm over it here. I want to move to the city soon."

We sit on a big scrap of timber and take our shoes off, even though it's freezing. We sink our feet into the cold, damp sand. "Where are you from?" I ask her.

She draws a makeshift map in the sand using pieces of driftwood. "Me and my guitar went like this." She draws a zigzag in the sand with her fingers connecting a dried-out flat piece of wood that she says is New Jersey to a piece of prickly pine that she says is California. "I stopped and played songs for change along the way."

Mia tells me a few random travel adventures about her migration west. She's only twenty but she's been living on her own for a real long time. It's true that her eyes are those of a girl who has *really* lived.

"What are you?" I ask her. I know my words came out sounding weird but she gets what I mean, since I'm staring at her eyes. Plus, she probably gets asked about her ethnicity a lot. I feel lame about being so typical.

"My dad is Italian. My mom is half Native American."

Soda walks up to us. "Everyone is eating turkey with their families in their fancy ocean houses." She's looking behind us at the houses on the cliffs.

"My mom doesn't celebrate Thanksgiving," Mia says. "We usually go to Plymouth for the National Day of Mourning with her Native American activist friends. This year I wanted to go home but I couldn't afford a plane ticket. My grandma died this year and she usually goes with my mom, so I wanted to be there for her because she is all alone in this big ole empty house. It's depressing."

I don't tell Mia that my family lives only a few hours away, and I could afford to take the bus there but the reason I don't go home for Thanksgiving is because I'm always fighting with them over something stupid and I can't handle it, and going there makes me feel shitty about myself because I can't relate to them, and they make snarky comments about my lifestyle. I don't tell her that my mom didn't even invite me this year because I haven't bothered to pick up her every-other-month phone call to check if I'm alive. I feel guilty, since Mia seems so sweet, like she's the kind of person that would try harder to have a good relationship with her family and not be so *whatever* like me, like how she really does want to be home for the holidays but just can't.

Soda, who I thought hadn't been listening because she was running zigzags while tossing rocks for Nappy to chase into the water, saves the silence. "When I was little, every Thanksgiving my dad would take me and my brother to different hotels to sneak into, and then we would steal the holiday buffet food, and after that we would swim in the indoor pool for the rest of the afternoon. Or we would go to Sizzler and since they were so busy for the holidays, it was the perfect time to dine and ditch."

"Jeez, you can get away with so much when you have little kids to act as your buffer!" Mia says. "That's probably why so many people have 'em."

Soda tosses a rock far down the beach. "Now, my parents won't even talk to me 'cause I dropped out of school and moved to the big city to be a homo." Soda runs after Nappy, who has started to follow some kids down the boardwalk. "What can ya do? Fuck 'em!" she hollers back at us, the last end of her sentence sing-songing into the wind.

I look out at the dark clouds over the windy ocean, and then up at the super nice houses that hang over the ocean cliffs. It's almost afternoon on Thanksgiving Day and by now the families in those houses are sitting down to eat. "I hate the holidays, but today is cool." I smile at the sight of Soda's limbs flailing down the beach after Nappy. Mia nods in agreement. She tosses the twigs that had just represented her hometowns at the small sandhills in front of us.

We drive back home, passing around some good weed that the Santa Cruz hippie kids gave us for the trip. We keep the music turned down so we can all hear Cruzer describing the trashiest details of the girl she hooked up with the night before, while Dixie makes her usual hilarious and sarcastic observations. "Oh yeah she said 'look into my eyes when you do it.' I like it when a girl looks in my eyes," Cruzer says.

"Really?" Dixie asks. "She said that? So, did you take your sunglasses off for her, or what? *Tom Cruz–er*!"

We're all giggling at Cruzer and Dixie's banter. They don't fuck anymore but they're still friends, which everyone was relieved about since having drama in the friend group is so annoying. Soda is still smiling the widest about spending the morning at the ocean, Nappy's ears are flopping out the window with the same contentment.

Back in the city we stop at Cala Foods and pick up five pies to bring to The Creamscicle where Shelby is throwing a vegan potluck. Shelby makes us keep them on a table in Soda's room so's not to offend her vegan guests. We start calling Soda's room Pie Central, which seems like an appropriate nickname for her lifestyle. Mia calls to tell me she accidentally cooked the turkey upside down at the queer dinner she's at and that everyone made fun of her. Her voice sounds amazing on the phone.

Later I curl up on the couch, super stuffed with pies and brandy. Cruzer is shuffling the card deck on the rickety coffee table and I can hear Dixie and Soda in the kitchen, trying to one-up each other on who had the most white trash childhood dinners.

"Macaroni and cheese with little hot dog wieners," Soda shouts.

"Spam and canned peas," Dixie shouts.

"Tuna casserole with potato chip crust."

"KFC bucket of chicken."

I love my queer family. I feel good cuddling with Naps. I'm still having flashbacks about the night before. Mia had fucked me first. We tossed each other around for a while before she had me pinned to the jutting metal truck cab, yanking off my pants. I'm sure the truck must have been rocking in the gravel. And then I just let her, gave in. A girl had never tried to top me that persistently on the first fuck. It was the first time I had been fucked in ages, I guess since Hurricane. I was glad it was completely dark in the back of the truck so she couldn't see my face. She fucked me way better than Hurricane ever had, in the few times she had. I never wanted it from her though, because she never knew what she was doing or cared, or was too drunk and high to care. Hurricane had fucked to bruise. So I was cool just being a top.

Mia fucked me and I disappeared from everything for a minute. I completely forgot where I was, what town, what truck, what world. Her hands were rough in the back of that truck. They felt cold and chapped. They were music player's hands. They were the hands of a girl who had just made her way with her guitar strapped to her back across America. When

I fell asleep in the back of the truck, she had been drumming a rhythm out of her head onto my hipbones.

# Chapter 7

At The Creamsickle's New Year's Eve party, at one in the morning, Soda's date, a Roller Derby girl named Natasha Nun Chucks comes up to me and Cruzer and asks if it's okay if all of her teammates come over. Nun Chucks says that her teammates are mostly straight girls but they're known to wrestle down and suck face with each other, especially when they've got tons of holiday brandy and eggnog pumping through their veins.

Twenty minutes later, the house is like the Invasion of the Roller Derby Girls. They swarm all over the house like it's a roller rink, two dozen tatted up, loud mouthed Roller Derby girls wearing turquoise cut-off Dickies jumpers with frayed edges that end right underneath their asses and curled up at their shoulders. The jumpers have patches sewn all over them with stenciled letterings of their names on the backs, *Molly-tov Cocktail, Taxi Trash, Viva Vendetta, Betty BoneCrusher, A Kate Forty-Seven, Farrah Felony*.

In the morning the house is trashed and rumor has it that one Roller Derby girl went home with a bloody nose. The Invasion of the The Roller Derby Girls had actually started on Christmas Eve, when Soda had brought home Natasha Nun Chucks from the all-you-can-eat Chinese food buffet and karaoke at The Silver Room. Soda and Tiny were tearing up the karaoke mic and I guess their skills got the attention of some holiday-orphaned Roller Derby girls. Tiny said she thought for sure Soda was going to go for the derby girl called A. Pocalypse since Soda had an obsession with the soon approaching end of the world, but instead she brought home Natasha Nun Chucks. Natasha Nun Chucks gave Soda a black eye for Christmas when they were fooling around on the back porch.

Natasha Nun Chucks' team has a match against Oakland. We all sit in front drunk off the shots of whiskey in small plastic cups, and holler at the girls flying by, skating so fast, bent over with cleavage whizzing at you. The San Francisco girls have the best outfits, these little camouflage mini dress things, but they still get their asses kicked by the other team. Outside everyone smokes near the water, Alcatraz glowing through the fog so close. Cruzer is trying to get this Roller Derby girl to let her into the back dressing room. I'm not trying to flirt with any of the girls because lately my head is just filled with thoughts of Mia. I want to go home just so I can call her up.

The next morning I wake up way too early to the noise of slamming doors coming from the hall. When I get up later I see there's a pair of roller skates in front of Cruzer's shut door. I guess Cruzer had scored her own rollergirl. "Her name is Viva Vendetta," Soda says, out on the back porch while we are sucking down some coffee and cigarettes. "And she's fucking crazy."

That night I call Mia and tell her about Viva Vendetta because she had been at the party. Since I met her, we'd spent more than a few nights talking till dawn and we even had phone sex one night when we were drunk. Nearly every other weekend, she'd come up with her friends to go to Cat Fight Club and dance with me, then come crash at The Creamsickle. On the phone Mia says, "Oh yeah, that was that wild roller chick who was showing off how she could do the splits on her roller skates, then tried to skate off the coffee table and almost broke her face so I had to pin her down and perform a Roller Skate Intervention! Tiny even had to help me pull the skates off of her!"

I get the full story from Soda. Super early that morning, Viva Vendetta had showed up at The Creamsickle and told Cruzer that she refused to go to work. Instead, she spent all day in Cruzer's big spray-painted gold bed painting her nails and talking on her cell phone. Cruzer didn't mind much because Viva was hot, tall and tattooed, just how she liked them, and it gave her motivation to stay in her room and finish her scrap art project as she listened to the girl yap on her cell phone. "Fuck, Slap Shot Suzy!" Viva yelled. "She side butted me for no fuckin' reason!" Viva had sprained her wrist during the last game so she was out for the rest of the season. It was obvious that Cruzer caught Viva as she was hitting the second to last rung on a serious downward spiral. Viva was having Roller Derby withdrawals and she was so pissed about not being able to compete that she was acting out and trying to get herself fired from her job. What a terrible time to meet Cruzer.

Viva doesn't leave Cruzer's bed all week. One night, they're up till dawn taking a bath in the fancy tub that stands perched on a platform in the corner of our bathroom, gold and white with a marble tray on the side that's crusted over with candle wax and soap scum. The bathtub is the rundown house's shining glory, with its elegant claw feet resting boldly on the exposed and cracked concrete floor that is splotchy with mold at the corners. I go to pee in the middle of the night and Cruzer and Viva are *still* splashing in the bubble bath, holding a bottle of cheap champagne and smoking cigarettes. Viva keeps forgetting about the bright electric blue cast on her arm, nearly dropping it in the water repeatedly. She gets me to take a picture of her washing Cruzer's hair with a big sudsy mess of bubbles, her cast resting on Cruzer's forehead. Their brown legs are slung over the side of the bathtub, toes all shriveled from being in the water for like fifty hours.

Viva comes out drinking with us one night and no one can handle her 'cause she gets explosively loud and drunk. She also lies all the time, these terribly fabulous lies that Cruzer totally falls for. "Today, Viva told me about her pet pony back home in L.A." Or even better, "Today, Viva said she is an heiress, and she went to an all-girl boarding school where she shared a room with lesbian twins." By Friday, I can't deal with Viva's screeching voice in the morning anymore so I borrow Cruzer's truck and go to the seaside to hang out with Mia.

When I come home after the weekend, Viva is *still* lounging around The Creamsickle, still drinking champagne from a bottle in the living room, and now she even has a tiny white fluffy dog. She's adjusting some gold chains from a pile on the floor into dog-sized necklaces and wrapping them around his neck. Napoleon is snarling at the white fluffy wiggling ball. "What is that?" I grumble from the doorway. *A Chinese Crested Powder Puff.* "A what?" I look to Soda for an explanation. "Where did this girl come from?" I ask her with my eyes. She can only shrug. "And now the dog too?"

Who knows where Viva came from. Before she met Cruzer she was maybe straight, she has tattoos everywhere her clothes aren't but they are the kind of tattoos that tell no secrets, the kind that came off the wall of a tattoo shop with no thought process at all. And who even knows how she got that little dog. She says her ex bought her two very expensive dogs but apparently only this one was left. On the third day of Viva's downward spiral, during which the spray-painted gold bed was headquarters, she got fired from her retail job, and hadn't left the house since.

After another week of Cruzer having a handful of that terrible mess of a girl and spending all her time taking care of her, I come home from work and she's holding the tiny dog in one hand and a Dear John letter in the other. She'd come home earlier after leaving Viva in her bed while she went to get them coffee, a pick-me-up since Viva had been in a particularly down mood, and when she came back, no Viva. Only a note on the bedside table scribbled on the back of Cruzer's film scanner installation guide that had been lying on the floor. The thick black pen scribbled all over the guide made it so Cruzer would never be able to read the instructions.

*Thanks for being an awesome person and helping me see the world in a different light. I just had a nervous breakdown sitting on your toilet and then I called my mom. I'm going back to L.A. to check into rehab. Thanks for letting me crash. P.S. I left you the dog.*

Underneath that there was an arrow pointing to the right,

*P.S.S. I left you the rest of my weed :)* ---------⊠

And then Cruzer walked into the living room and there's the tiny fluff of a dog sitting on the sagging Creamsickle couch looking sad and abandoned.

Cruzer lets the dog stay a few days but it's terribly high maintenance and she can't handle it and Viva won't pick up her phone. I suggest that Cruzer give the dog to Dixie. It's a genius idea since Cruzer still has a weakness for her. *Romantic!* she shouts. She goes out on the porch and spray paints red hearts all over a box, puts the dog in it, and then puts the box in her bike basket. We ride our bikes over to Dixie's.

Dixie starts jumping up and down with excitement after she opens the box. Cruzer looks terribly proud of herself for making Dixie so happy. "A late Christmas gift. The mama is in rehab and I'm not sure if she is even fit to be a very sane dog mother. She didn't even leave it any food!" she explains.

Dixie takes the dog to get a sophisticated haircut, buys him more gold chains and cute little outfits. She keeps the dog tucked into her jacket and takes him with her wherever she goes. Everyone starts calling the dog diffcrent names than Fluffy. They call it Misfit, or Orphan, The Mafia Boss, or Roller Derby Spawn.

# Chapter 8

The city is marrying gay people. The other day we were skating by City Hall and there were long lines of couples waiting to be wed. Seeing the crowds of people was so exciting. I like the buzz of things happening. It reminds me of a few years before, during the anti-war protests when everyone shut down the city. All the different ways all week that people were protesting, like this girl who I was dating at the time set up a knitting circle and knit for peace, like a knit-in-sit-in. Now everyone is saying, *Let's get married*, even queers that have only been in love for a few weeks. Just to do it, because it feels exciting.

In The Creamsickle living room, everyone who has been hanging around all winter smoking cigarettes and shooting the shit on a revolving basis, Dixie, Tiny and other kids like Coby this BMX brat who lives around the corner, Patch, this freckled-faced traveling boi who is just passing through, Cello, this art school girl with musical instruments tattooed on the undersides of her arms (we used to hook up and I'd leave her hickeys on her trombone), Darling Nicki who Soda used to date so now they hate each other and who is this femme fox with a choppy mess of dyed black hair and red lipstick lips, and Zeena who looks like a Blythe doll with her perma-bugged out eyes and tiny limbs, are now arguing with each other all the time about gay marriage.

"Marriage supports the oppressive, patriarchal institutions of religious bullshit!" Patch yells.

"I love weddings," Dixie says.

"Who gives a fuck about marriage? Why would I get married? So my parents can buy me a toaster oven?" Tiny says.

"I want to get married in a white leather minidress with a heart cut-out on the chest, and gold necklaces," Knockout Nicki says.

"Gavin is just trying to get attention, what an attention-whore!" Cello says.

"I want my cake to be pink and shaped like a vagina," Knockout Nicki giggles.

"Why do we need straight privilege? I miss five years ago when being gay was actually a statement against the system!" Coby shouts.

"I think it's a perfect moment to celebrate LOVE!" Zeena shouts.

"Love, love, love," Soda chants. "Blah."

"Hater," Dixie says.

"But I love all of you!" Soda yells.

Soda isn't in love of course, but she did recently break up with Natasha Nun Chucks and is now dating a yoga instructor that she is pretty into. "I need a girl who is less accident prone," she'd told me.

I'm still hanging out with Mia. She is still salting my bed with our sticky love affair. She comes to visit for the weekend and we fuck for forty-eight hours until she has to catch the Cal Train back home. The distance is drawing things out in a good way.

We all watch the people getting married on the evening news. They are only six blocks away from us, lines and lines of them, famous people flying to our city and smiling on the TV. "They don't even get cake! What a shame," Nicki says.

"She should bring them some cake," Soda tells me, but loud enough for Nicki to hear. Whenever the two are forced to be in the same room they make passive-aggressive comments about each other.

"Throw the cake at those Gay Traitors," Patch shouts.

"Will you marry me?" Cruzer suddenly proposes to Dixie.

Dixie promptly answers, "Yes," which shocks everyone into silence for a minute, like we're all wondering what kind of strange love potion the city has put in the water. Or maybe Cruzer may have finally won Dixie over with the dream dog gift.

Then Zeena jumps up and shouts, "Let's all get married to each other!"

Everyone starts laughing because Zeena is so loopy that people call her Zany Zeena and this evening she seems to be on a particularly manic high. Zeena has been practically living at the house lately. She sleeps on the couch some nights, or she stays at this rocker hotel. Soda likes this because she likes to stay at the rocker hotel too, when Zeena is there. Everyone else likes Zeena because she always brings over drugs. She is somehow both very rich *and* very paranoid which can be a bad combination. Plus, Zeena completely messes with the energy of the house, because everyone else takes downers, but she's constantly popping little pink speed pills and white powders. She talks incredibly fast and gets super excited about the littlest things, but everyone puts up with it because she also cleans the shit out of the house every time she comes over. "I can't believe you guys live in this dump!" she shouts as she empties all the ashtrays, throws away the leftover food containers on the coffee table, and stacks up the scattered cards from recent games of *Ring Of Fire*. She even tackles the beer can recycling if she's in a particularly good and high mood.

"I'm going to plan the wedding!" Zeena shouts.

Patch groans and gets up from the floor and walks out of the room. The front door slams loudly from downstairs.

Cruzer is trying to fashion an origami ring for Dixie out of a Budweiser beer label that she has just pulled off her beer bottle.

"A huge wedding!" Zeena jumps up.

Dixie smiles and claps her hands. She's such a Southern girl that she really likes the idea of a big wedding. "I'm going to wear gold. Those aren't my colors," she tells Cruzer about the red and black origami ring.

"Don't you worry, everything is going to be color coordinated," Zeena says. She has this crazy look in her eyes. It's similar to the one when she decided to scrub The Creamsickle bathtub last week. She grabs a pad of paper from the black briefcase she always carries around with her and starts to write down what she says is everyone's characters. "Cello is bridesmaid Number one Tiny is the best man. Georgie you will be marrying me."

*Eeeeerrk.* The mental record player in my head screeches to a halt. Did Zeena just say I was marrying her!?

"Oh yeah?" Cruzer raises her eyebrows. "Go Georgie! We get to have a double wedding."

"I'm unavailable," I say. Cruzer glares at me because until this moment, I have not verbally confirmed to any of my friends that Mia is my girlfriend. They all know that ever since we went to Santa Cruz she has come to stay in the city every weekend, spending most of the time in my bed, but calling myself unavailable has not come into the picture.

"Georgie *can* marry you," Cruzer tells Zeena. "Her girlfriend is long distance. They only talk on the Internet. None of us are even sure she exists."

"Shut up!" I tell Cruzer. "What about Soda?" I ask Zeena.

Zeena purses her lips at me and taps her pen neurotically on her yellow legal notepad. Everyone knows that one night Zeena and Soda fucked when they were on a lot of drugs at the rocker hotel, and now they hate each other except when they are high.

"I will not marry *that*."

"I love everybody!" Soda yells. She's super stoned so she's mostly glued to the footage of Rosie O'Donnell marrying her girlfriend on the news, making her the only one in the room not getting wrapped up in Zeena's manic role as the wedding planner. She's also completely oblivious to the fact I have just been pawned off into an arranged marriage to a crazy person.

"You'll need a white tux," Zeena instructs me as she jots something down on her pad.

"Do I have any say in this?" I stomp my foot and almost squash Dixie's new kitten/dog. Napoleon is the only one in the room who looks at me with any sort of sympathy. Everyone else shouts "*No*" in unison, and then Zeena moves on to color coordinating the roles and outfits.

"Can Roller Derby Spawn be in the wedding?" Dixie asks.

"We can have the wedding at The Stud," Cruzer suggests. That's the bar where Cruzer and Soda recently started their own club night.

I call Mia later when I'm in bed. I call her a lot when I'm falling asleep because her voice is so hot. She also talks real dirty and lately we have been having a lot of phone sex. I never thought I'd be all into phone sex but we'll sometimes stay up all night taking turns inventing dirty things to do to each other. I wait till we've already had phone sex to tell Mia that I'm getting married. I don't want to piss her off before she gets me off.

"Huh?" she says. We'd recently had that talk about how we weren't interested in fucking anyone but each other and that if we did start sleeping with someone else, we would tell each other. I quickly try to explain in one long rambling breath, "Well, there's this girl Zeena and she's been staying in the back room for a minute, and well she's planning this huge performance piece type wedding in honor of the gay marriage shit. And Cruzer thinks if she marries her to Dixie, then Dixie will finally fall in love with her and Zeena is making me marry her at the same time, and there's going to be protesters who think gay marriage is bad that are also our friends, like Patch probably, and there's gonna be cake and champagne, and we get to dress up, and the small dog is wearing a gold bow-tie! It's like a performance piece about a wedding party. Errr, I think. It's political. I think? But, I'm not sure how it's political but Zeena says it is, but well it just sounds like a party."

"Weird," Mia mumbles.

"I know. Very."

"So can I be your date to your wedding?" she asks.

"Yeah," I say. I think about how Zeena will hate that and I feel a little scared.

For the next few weeks, every day, The Creamsickle living

room is over taken over by Zeena with her papers, flyers and generally insane wedding planner mania. She calls the zines and pamphlets the Wedding Propaganda. I pick them up and read them.  Each one is different, with small type, in lowercase on a typewriter and other parts in all CAPS that say all kinds of stuff about celebrations, partnerships, friendship, a statement against forced monogamy and heteronormativity, in support of civil unions and domestic partnerships, and how the wedding will basically be a huge party. Zeena has so much energy, staying up all night in her hotel with a typewriter and a laptop, making all this stuff.  Sometimes we're sitting around The Creamsickle and Zeena comes by with more and more stacks of flyers, letters and scripts.

"She's our little Valerie Solanas," Cruzer says admiringly.

Dixie likes to read the invitations aloud, super enunciating the capital letter parts. *"Come LOVE EVERYBODY at our wedding!"* In the beginning we hadn't known what we were getting into. We just never said no to a party, but Zeena is trying to make us actually work, she wants a cast, scripts and even dress rehearsals.

Patch and Tiny come by one night and announce that they are going to create a picket line in front of the wedding. "And take me off the list, I'm going to go mental if I get one more email about the wedding party! Is it just me? I feel like I'm under attack, with like fifty emails a day!" Tiny says.

Cruzer and I both suck in our breath at the same time. We'd just watched Zeena pop her pink speed pills all afternoon as she cut out hundreds of wedding invitation-style flyers to plaster the town with, and we knew any show of ingratitude might send her over the edge.

"PROTEST!" Zeena screams at Patch and Tiny with her head bouncing back and forth like a Bobblehead Doll. "The more the merrier! By the way, it is about all of us LOVING each other Tiny! It is about the entire lesbian community marrying EACH OTHER because we all LOVE each other."

Patch and Tiny go scrambling down the stairs to work on their picket signs and gather up an army. "We don't really all love each other," Dixie mutters, "I mean, my flower girl stole my last girlfriend and I hate that Nicki is my bridesmaid."

"I am not going to photocopy the script again!" Zeena screams. Her eyes are really bugging so Dixie clamps her mouth shut. She just likes to see if she can rile Zeena, like the other day when she tried to get her to be less controlling about the color schemes. Zeena was drilling everyone so hard that she almost made sweet Cello cry, her short blond corkscrew curls trembled on her head as Zeena shouted orders at her like an angry soccer coach. Everyone is so paranoid and on edge about the Wedding Takeover this month at our house that the usual people don't even come over to hang out anymore. They avoid The Creamsickle like it's been taken over by a wedding dictator.

"I can't wait till my wedding is over," Dixie sighs.

"Let's get this over with and cut to the honeymoon," Cruzer says.

There are so many drugs at the wedding that no one even follows the script. Zeena runs around the whole time flinging her tiny arms up like she is throwing rice, but actually she's just trying to make people stand where they're supposed to. All Cruzer and I have to do is walk down the aisle, and then I have to make out with Zeena, and Cruzer makes out with Dixie. Dixie is wearing her prom dress that she spray-painted gold in her backyard after work, right before the wedding. There's a gospel singer and a poet, a rocker minister and a wedding band, and a ton of champagne and cake. The Sisters of Perpetual Indulgence are all dressed up in their nun habits, and there is a reporter taking pictures for the gay newspaper. Outside there is a crazy picket line. There's a rumor going around that Zeena herself actually paid random people on the street, like even homeless guys, to protest the wedding.

Cruzer keeps trying to get a bridesmaid into the back room. Actually, she is working on two bridesmaids. There's a bunch of people who think Zeena and I are a real couple in love, coming up and congratulating me. I watch Mia coolly watching all this from where she is leaning against the back wall. Zeena goes to cut the three-tier wedding cake that this queer ally who works at a pastry shop hooked up. Zeena starts passing out slices. She looks extra wild residing over the cake, and yelling, "Let them eat cake! Let them eat cake!"

I sneak over to Mia. "Your friends are so crazy!" she says as Zeena shoves cake into people's laps and screams, "LOVE EVERYONE!" Mia grabs me and tries to get me into the small black bathroom where so many fags have had sex but there is a long line. Instead we both walk towards the back entrance of The Stud, where there isn't a picket line. It feels so naughty sneaking away from my own wedding and manic bride. I follow Mia with her tangled hair and mischievous smile like she is an evil husband stealer. I can't wait to get her home. Just when we are sneaking out the door, I see Zeena headed towards us, her wedding dress hitched up so she can run through the crowd. Outside, we run towards the nearest cab down the block as she comes flying out the door.

In the cab we are both gasping for breath. I think I hear Zeena screaming about love before the door slams shut. Mia starts saying things like, "Naughty boy, leaving your lezzy wedding for the bridegroom," in her phone sex voice. The cab driver nearly gets us in an accident because he's so busy glancing at us in the rearview mirror.

Since we snuck out of the wedding early, no one will be home at The Creamsickle for a while, especially since Zeena's having a wedding after-party at her rocker hotel set up and everyone's going.

I fuck Mia in the living room, she's sitting on top of the back part of the couch, her ass halfway on the window ledge, her back pressed to the dirty glass windows that look out over the city.

"I feel like I'm falling," she whispers.

The city flickers outside the windowpane that's pressed into her back. I look over her shoulder for a second. Something is different about the skyline.

Later we open the window wide and the cold night dries the post-sex sweat in our hair. We share a cigarette. The city view is so clear it looks like a tourist's snow globe. When Mia ashes her cigarette I look down at how the ash falls over the city and it looks like the powdery snow that falls over the globe when you shake it.

Mia is half naked, the yellowy city lights flickering across her tawny skin, freckled moles on her neck and small handful of perfect tits. I hold my hand on the small of her back as her hair dangles over the ledge. Her mouth is like a fishhook luring me over the edge. I don't want to fall in love with her because falling in love totally fucks shit up. I've still got that snow globe image stuck in my head so all I can equate love to in this moment is how calm instantly turns into a wild storm inside a snow globe. That's what love is.

Messy.

I look out the window. I think I've figured out what is different. The glowing dome on top of the City Hall building, six blocks away where the gays are getting married, usually glows white, like the same color of the office buildings all along the cityscape, but on special occasions the city changes the colored lights that light up the dome, like on St. Patty's day it's green, and on the Fourth of July it's red, white and blue, and now, it glows red as a throbbing heart.

Even a week after the wedding, people would still scream stuff from the pamphlets that were scattered around The Creamsickle. Soda likes to yell "*We All Love Each Other Now!*" in the morning to wake everyone up. Mia laughs when we wake up to Soda yelling. She rolls over and smiles at me, looking so beautiful in the morning, with her choppy jet-black hair and dark brown eyes, the lids fringed with those inch-long eyelashes, and the light shining on the freckles scattering on her caramel cheeks that you can only see when you are real close to her and she isn't wearing any makeup.

Mia has started calling in sick all the time to her job at the diner down by the seaside because she doesn't want to leave the city, or me. She had been saving her money to move, but then she had a fiery trail of bad luck, her car was stolen one morning when it was parked in front of The Creamsickle, and was found later all trashed up by Ocean Beach, strange coded words keyed into the side doors as if it had been abducted by aliens and marked with carvings that resembled crop circles. The whole thing got Soda excited, preaching to us all about the apocalyptic messages she saw in the cryptic carvings, while Cruzer scoffed, "Yeah right, someone just had too much crack for breakfast and wanted to fuck shit up." Meanwhile Mia had pouted and shelled over the money to get the car out of the tow yard, and had to further dip into her Move-To-The-City savings to fix the damage.

When she's finally fired from her job she gets a new job offer from a girl she met in the city. Her other friend says she can stay on her couch while she looks for a place. So, even though she doesn't have any money, Mia moves.

I leave my house to go to work one Friday evening, a few weeks after Mia has moved to town, three days before Valentine's Day, and Mia on a bike screeches to a stop in front of me on Mission Street. It still shocks me that she lives in my city now and that she can just pop up anywhere. She's on her way to Critical Mass, the monthly mass bike ride through the city that disrupts downtown traffic for hours. She's so excited about it, stopped in the street with her tight black leggings and Frye harness boots, perched on her bike like the hottest thing ever. I lean over her handlebars and kiss her, tasting the salty sweat on her lip. The dizzy smell of her. I'm so falling in love. It's sneaking up on me like the February rainy season.

"Look, why don't you just stay with me?" The sentence pops out of my mouth before I even think about it. All I know is that it's cold and rainy and I want to come home from work tonight and find her in my bed.

"Okay." Her smile is explosive.

That's how I end up with a live-in girlfriend.

# Chapter 9

The night air is cool with the first days of spring as it comes in the open window to where I'm lying on my bed watching Mia sitting on the windowsill with her fingers plucking the strings of her guitar. All day at work I was stressed out thinking about money, since Mia got fired from yet another job, the second this month, but right this second I don't care. I just want to watch Mia with the glow of the city making an orange halo around the black line of her body. Mia mostly wears the same stretchy black jeans, with a gray patch over one knee, and tight black T-shirts that she sews to fit snug around her shoulders, and tits. You can always see the top of her well-worn leopard print bra that peeks out from the frayed hems of her low-cut T-shirts. Mia plays her songs in the window all night long sometimes, serenading the sleeping bums in the doorways on the street below. They never complain, or throw rocks at her, like I thought they would when she first started the ritual. They must want her voice as much as I do, with its husky hollowness, mixed with sweet and terrible sounds that always send chills up my spine.

Mia just started a new band with this boy she met at this job where she'd made pizzas for a month. Every job Mia has had so far has each lasted almost a month. She has washed dishes in dark Chinese restaurants, tagged sensors on clothes at trendy clothing stores, made juice at a juice bar, and fixed bikes at the bike shop around the corner, but because playing music is more important than paying her bills, she never keeps the jobs long. Like if she has to play a show and can't get the night off then she's guaranteed to be unemployed the next day. That's why she has been living with me so long. The girl can't save a single dime to put towards her own room, and even when she has money she puts it towards stuff for her new band, a new guitar or rent on the practice space. So far, no one has cared *that* much around The Creamsickle. Shelby even took the back room and gave me the bigger front room because she wanted to save money so she can spend the summer traveling. Last month Mia and I fixed up the room, painting and buying curtains and thrifting for furniture.

Mia named her band after our love affair. She only ever sings about love and heartbreak. A few weeks ago she played her first show that a bandmate hooked up at this grungy metal bar. The crowd was one-half big sweaty hairy dudes and one-half skinny tattooed slouchy dykes who swayed back and forth in the front row, trying to make their faces stay screwed up in their toughest looks possible. Then when Mia started shaking and howling on the stage the entire rowdy room went dead silent. With every song she played, she dug deeper into her chest and pulled out more of her heart. The mouths in the crowd got soft. People forgot to swallow. They watched Mia's heart fall onto the stage and flop around like a fish, wet and bleeding. The dykes started to throw their arms around each other's waists. The dudes stayed quiet and solemn, intimidated by all the emotion on display. They chewed their bottom lips and tried to keep their gazes fixated on Mia's tits so they didn't have to see how her pretty face was leaking all her most intimate secrets. I pushed through a wall of dudes and stood up front, a bunch of my friend's hands grabbed me and held me up with their rocking bodies. Soda kissed the side of my mouth. *I love you, man.* Cruzer was also saying she loved us. Mia had melted my hard-ass friends, stripped right through their leather jacket armor. Everyone was suddenly being so nice to each other, all the girls. It was like everyone in the room had just shared a huge bag of coke together and loved everyone in their false high, *I love you and I'm not just saying that because I'm on drugs!* But the high was natural. They were high off Mia's voice. I was convinced it was why Cruzer and Soda let her stay at The Creamsickle for free month after month. They didn't want the music coming from my windowsill to stop.

Mia has a song that is for her dead grandmother, when she sings it she screams her name so loud that her small bird lips crack right down the middle torn open with it. She would come home from the practice space with her lips and throat raw. And she never stopped writing her sloppy and beautiful love songs. All day while washing dishes, or spraying perfume on old ladies, or slapping cream cheese on someone's bagel, she would be writing the songs in her head, coming home to jot them down in little black books. A lot of times she couldn't find the books so the words would be written on her hand or whatever she saw in front of her, scraps of paper, or in random places around my room, once on a lampshade, and once on the bill of my favorite mesh cap.

The only thing we've fought about so far is money, the lack of cash for bills, rent and food. I work extra shifts some weeks just to cover everything. But I believe in Mia's dream, her passion to someday make money on her music even though everyone knew it was the hardest thing to do. Whenever we walked by this powder blue Cadillac that is always parked around the corner from our house, she would say, *George Baby, when I'm a rich rock star I'm gonna buy that car and drive us around town in it,* and then I think about all the ways I will fuck her in that Cadillac when it's ours. Mia likes to call me George because she says it sounds like an old grandpa name, and she says she wants to sit on rocking chairs on the porch of an old house in Tennessee with me someday. That she likes to close her eyes while scrubbing dishes at work and imagine us living in this magical old house at the end of a long dirt road. *The kind of house you have to drive a truck to, with dogs, lots and lots of dogs.* Sometimes she uses an old lady voice and teases me. *Hey George pass me over one of them cigars.*

Tonight as Mia practices in the window she competes with the noises of an after-party in the living room. I can hear the spin of the bottle when it rattles on the floor. *Soda you fucking cheater!*

a girl's voice shouts. The music gets turned up. It's weird how months and months can fly by so quickly when you are so busy just looking at someone. Nights and nights spent watching Mia sitting in my windowsill. Nights and nights spent lying on my bed for hours, with legs and hands intertwined, staring at each other's faces. Outside on the street below my window the whole world is happening. Outside my door The Creamsickle is still a zoo of foot traffic, rowdy, gossiping girls and parties. A dozen people could go by my door, banging and hollering at it or on it, but Mia and I were too busy looking at each other to come out. Me, tracing the constellation of tiny moles that started behind her ear and fell like tiny circles of mahogany-colored confetti down her neck, and even a few below her shoulder blade. Her, slipping her thumb underneath the waistline of my little boy's underwear and keeping it there like she had me on a hook.

Mia turns now from the window and smiles at me. "I am going to jump on you any second now." She's looking at me with eyes and lips that could just eat me alive and then she leaps onto the bed. Mia straddles me. Her dark hair is growing out. A lot of femmes grow their hair out in the city like they don't need it chopped short anymore in order to be visibly queer, how they did in whatever small town they moved from. It's falling from its clip and into my face. I swirl my tongue around hers, my hands all over her body, slipping under her clothes, fingertips encircling her nipples, trailing down her waist to her hips and grabbing a handful of her ass. She presses into me, harder. I pull her shirt up, slipping her tits out of her bra. Mia has the greatest tits. I reach around her back and unsnap her bra with one hand and her copper penny nipples slip into my mouth. I can hear some party kids arguing loudly about the hanky code and whether left means bottom or right means top or left means top or right means bottom, outside my bedroom door. The bathroom is next door to my room so people stand in front of the door in a line to wait for it. I suck hard on Mia's nipple and she moans loudly, which makes the conversation stall for a second, then become giggles. I yank off Mia's black stretchy pants, lick and kiss her thighs, and then slip my fingers into her pussy. She has the most beautiful pussy I have ever seen. I told

Cruzer that one morning and she wanted me to draw it for her but I couldn't do it. *That's too personal.* I lick Mia and slip more fingers in and she starts to thrust harder into my hand. She yanks the pillow over her head to muffle the loud noises she is making that are probably entertaining the hallway bathroom line. I grab a handful of Mia's ass, and pull her closer to the edge of the bed. When she comes I always watch her, legs quivering, eyes rolled up to the ceiling, like she is desperately searching above for something more than the three minutes in which everything in her world just disappeared. I don't stop fucking her until I find the right spot in her pussy that makes her body shake like it's being electro-shocked, and she squirts all over the bed, wet as fuck, into my hand. Mia says that my hands are the right key that fit her lock, that my hands are the ones that hit the perfect spot, just like that. She says, it's funny how so many hands could just not fit, and then there's one pair that always feel like heaven between your legs.

Then Mia is back in the window. The city behind her moving in time lapse, offices in the highrises finally shut their lights out, entire buildings go to sleep for the night. Mornings come and go, afternoons sharp and bitter and then night again. Days and months and days and more months pass like this. Mia's silhouette seems permanent, like a gargoyle with a guitar in the window, both of us smoking and humming, all the way to summer.

# Chapter 10

I stare up at the palm trees above my head, lying in Dolores Park on a hot day in June. Cruzer and Soda are playing this game that Cruzer and I invented a few summers ago. How it works is that Cruzer opens a blank page in her legendary scrapbook and writes at the top, *Girls to Send Postcards to This Summer*. The title is "in code" because our friends sometimes flip through Cruzer's scrapbooks if they are lying around The Creamsickle and we don't want anyone to know that the list really means *Girls I Want to Fuck This Summer*.

I used to play this game with Cruzer and she always won. The prize was that every time you hooked up with a girl on your list and you checked the little box by her name, then the loser would have to take the winner out to breakfast at The Triple P the morning after the hook up and hear all the details over a greasy breakfast. The result was that Cruzer, who was never employed very long, got a lot of free breakfasts, which I didn't care so much about because they only put me out less than five bucks. Obviously she was much better at the contest than I so I'm glad that this summer Soda is around to actually challenge her.

"Georgie, I know you are not playing 'cause you are all married and shit but how 'bout you make a hypothetical list for the fun of it?"

"I just like Mia."

After a while of listening to Soda and Cruzer make their lists I start to feel left out. That's always half the fun, choosing the girls, saying, "How 'bout so and so…"

"Fine. Make me one but I'm not doing the ten, I only want like five."

"Are you sure? So many hot new girls have come out of winter hibernation," Cruzer says as she writes down, *Georgie's Girls to Send Postcards To* next to their lists on the page.

"Knockout Nicki," I say for my first one because she is crazy and so fine. We call her Knockout Nicki because rumor has it she once either knocked herself out, or knocked someone else out, in some sort of public sex escapade that caused sirens to come wailing over to the party. There's lots of versions of that rumor, involving windowpanes or windshields, staircases or Stair Masters, and even a version I've heard that involves either monkey bars or monkey suits, but Nicki never confirms any details. If you ask her about the nickname she just smirks and goes, *Sometimes things get wild.* Knockout Nicki has other nicknames like Naughty Nicki or Nasty Nicki. She's got a bad reputation. Most of the bois think she's a cold-hearted vixen. It's even written huge on the bathroom wall at The Vine, part of the ongoing dyke drama graffiti poem that you can't help memorizing while pissing. *Knockout Nicki's heart is a vacant lot*, and on another wall in an angrier looking black Sharpie scrawl, *Nasty Nicki is a homewrecker.*

"I can't believe you haven't fucked Naughty Nicki yet," Soda says with disbelief.

"How's that possible?" Cruzer asks.

"She gave up on me, long ago."

"She did not. She never gives up. Remember right before you shacked up with Mia she tried to stick your hand in her skirt under the card table at Heather's party?" Cruzer says.

"I don't think she knew whose hand it was." I laugh.

"That girl is the biggest tease, ever," Soda says. "I remember before I got with her she drew it out for so long. She used to not wear panties at the park and I'd be lying there drinking my beer and looking at the clouds drift by and she would casually smile at me, and step right over my head in those cotton, short, stripy skirt things she used to wear. Then she would walk away, right down the hill. Drove me wild."

Back when Nicki and Soda used to fuck they nearly destroyed each other. It was love on a short fuse. That was the first time I ever saw Soda. She'd started hooking up with Nicki a month after she moved to town and her BMX bike was permanently strapped to the pole outside the girl bar every night as she explored the new terrain and new girls. Nicki was the self-proclaimed Mayor of the Girl Scene. You had to pass through her gates to be initiated into it. I remember this one day Cruzer called me when I was getting off work and said, "Meet us at the park," and when I rolled up, I found everyone sitting on one edge of Nicki's pink polka-dot blanket. Nicki's ultra long legs were shooting out from under a very short flouncy skirt, and she didn't care about the wind, so whenever it blew her skirt up she flashed her panties, which was working well at holding everyone's attention. She was perched in the middle of two bottles of champagne, one empty and one full, with a box of strawberries, Cruzer, Soda, and this kid, Coby, scattered all around her. When I first met Nicki she had her naturally strawberry blond hair but now she dyes her hair black so her clear green eyes pop from her pale face bright as a tiger's.

"Have you heard my new plan?" Nicki turned her pouty snarl on me when I plopped down on a corner of her blanket. "I'm gonna rent bois out. My company is going to be called *Naughty Nicki's Bois for Hire*. So now you guys won't ever have to get jobs. You'll just get calls to come fix a window, or rake a yard, or scrape up some dog shit. But you will have to wear cute boy outfits with tool belts."

Nicki patted my leg with her hot pink nails. "Georgie, you can work there too."

She always put her hand on your thigh, or leaned into you when she talked. I rolled my eyes at Cruzer. "She's being really offensive," I said, loud enough for Nicki to hear. I was half-joking, half-serious because I knew she was making fun of Soda. Plus, "You guys are being really offensive" was exactly something Nicki or Dixie would say when they tried to call Cruzer, Tiny, or me sexist or something when we were talking about girls.

"Honey, I think that is just my point." Nicki smiled and tried to feed me a strawberry, but I backed off and grabbed it with my own hand. I was the only one on the blanket who hadn't slept with her yet, so she played a lot of games with me. "I see an open market and I pounce," Nicki laughed. She turned her green cat eyes on Soda. "What do you think?"

Soda just shrugged. You could tell she wasn't quite sure how to handle Nicki, who was so stellar hot she intimidated even the cockiest bois. "Oh!" Nicki said with faked surprise. "That would give you major competition, huh? You might be out of a career? You would be working for me!" Nicki flapped her manicured hand at her face like it was an old-fashioned fan and smiled.

A few days later Cruzer, Dixie and I went to visit Nicki at her work, this trendy vintage store on Sixteenth. Nicki had dressed Soda up in new clothes. She let her rummage through the bins of mesh caps that said things like, SAM'S SHRIMP SHOP, and ED'S KNIFE STORE, trucker-style hats that Soda would never have worn back home in Kansas City but now, in this new city, they were a fashion statement. Soda went for the ones printed with shipping logos or dock companies. Nicki was showing off her new hot accessory, "Soda POP," she called her. Under the yellowy store light you could see the shadow of Soda's dirt 'stache, the one that made her look like a teenage boy. Paired with her slight country way of talking, it was enough to make her Nicki's wet dream. When her lipstick lips nuzzled into Soda's dirty gas station style jacket, her face emerged looking high off girl sweat.

We went outside to smoke, leaving Soda to try on stuff with Dixie. Cruzer and I stood outside, smoking in the drizzle when Nicki came out for a drag. "That kid is driving me wild." She glanced back into the store to make sure Soda wasn't coming out or listening. "She's got trashy truck stops in her eyes."

I smoked and watched the rain. The blotchy bruises on Nicki's thighs slowly gathered goose bumps.

A month after that Soda and Nicki broke up. Even though Nicki tried to hide it, a little tiny piece of her stone cold heart chipped off. Ever since then, her eyes always looked a little crazier. "Nicki doesn't have a heart," Cruzer had always insisted about the stone fox femme. But I had witnessed the opposite, days after their break up, when I was hanging out at Dixie's where Nicki used to live before Dixie and her roommates voted her off the island, so to speak. Nicki was all messed up over Soda and she was downing a bottle of chilled white wine, pretending she wasn't getting misty-eyed.

"I woulda ran away with that kid. I loved her I really did," she said.

I was eating popcorn and my mouth sort of fell open. I had never heard Nicki talk like that about anyone. She acted like she was unattached to all the sex she flung around like piñata prizes. I was convinced she was a cold-hearted femme player, but my opinion sure changed that night.

"Lucia," I say for the next name on my list. Lucia is this hot Brazilian art school student that Cruzer and I met at the Sunday Morning Vegan Breakfast in the spring.

"I can't think of anyone for the third." I shrug.

"Talia, A.J., Diana, Heather, Bird, Griselda, Jenny." Cruzer and Soda keep suggesting names and I shake my head for every one.

"How 'bout put Soda down," I say.

"Yeah," Soda grins.

"Nooooooo, I refuse," Cruzer howls.

Soda grabs her pen and scrawls her name in. "Whatever. She gots a wife. She's not playing anyways." And she winks at me.

A few minutes later Dixie, Cello, and the small fluffy dog, walk up so Cruzer snaps her scrapbook closed. Dixie tells us this story about how this old guy came up to them just now at the bottom of the park and showed them two different fully laminated Kinko's style photo books of all these young girls, most of them our friends and people we knew, making out at Dyke March and Folsom Street Fair. "All these topless girls making out!" Dixie says. "It was like a yearbook, of us. I was like, hey, there's Soda kissing Nasty Nicki. There's Coby and Amanda. There's Lucia topless! So then he asks to take our picture and we're like, no way! Then Cello asks for a copy of the book, and he says no, he doesn't have the rights to sell it! He just has them for his own personal collection!"

"Creepy," Cruzer hisses. "I hate that I want the money to make photo books about us but instead we've got rich lurker dudes documenting us like we are in a zoo. Fuck that dude and his pervy pictures." Cruzer is about to go off again on the same tangent but her phone rings. "Viva Vendetta!" she shrieks. Dixie groans but Cruzer is excited because she has been trying to track Viva down for months. Viva has been sober and hiding out. She doesn't call anyone, or at least she doesn't call any drunks, so that definitely excludes Cruzer. Tiny was the one who discovered that Viva was even back in town, because she started coming into the video store where she worked. Apparently, since Viva was trying to stay away from booze she had distracted herself and had become addicted to *Six Feet Under* and *The Sopranos* on DVD. Every night, she didn't go out to the bars and went to Tiny's video store for her fix instead. "I'm so proud of her each time she comes back so I give her a Gay Mafia Sobriety discount," Tiny had said. "But I'm getting nervous about what will happen when she runs out of show episodes? Will she run to the nearest liquor store and down a bottle of Jameson?"

When Dixie heard that Viva was back, she got nervous about things other than Viva's sobriety, she was afraid Viva would want the dog back that she'd fallen so in love with. She barely let the dog out of the house after she found out Viva was in town because she knew if she ran into her on the street then she would for sure lose in an encounter with the crazy Amazon roller derby girl. It was all enough to give Dixie an anxiety attack and now she actually needed the anti-anxieties that she usually just took for fun.

Cruzer kept trying to get a hold of Viva though. She claimed it was because she wanted her vintage Ferrari sunglasses back that Viva had been wearing that memorable day she escaped The Creamsickle and headed straight to rehab. I was convinced that Cruzer just wanted to see Viva again, and didn't care so much about the sunglasses. She had an entire wall display of vintage sunglasses in her room, so what was one pair?

On the phone, Viva tells Cruzer that if she wants to meet up, it's now or never because she is roller-skating in the neighborhood and can possibly take a quick break. She refuses to meet at any bar Cruzer suggests so they arrange to meet at a coffee shop. "She's crazy so it's better if it's still somewhere public," Cruzer says after she hangs up. Then she says, "Georgie, you *have* to come with me."

"No! I can't stand that girl. Soda you go!" I plead.

"Viva hates Soda because she dumped Natasha Nun Chucks. Viva always loved you, because everyone loves *Sweet Georgie*," Cruzer says. "You will charm her crazy nerves."

"Okay, fine I will go if you blow me up that picture of Mia dancing at Cat-Fight. Huge."

"Deal."

We meet up with Viva at this coffee shop. At first it's fun because Viva immediately pulls all these photos out of her fake Gucci purse of herself in rehab with her face bloated up like a balloon. It doesn't even look like her.

"This is me in detox," she says. "Alcohol bloats you up."

I think she is trying to work some kind of intervention on us, in a low-key way, but it has the opposite effect on Cruzer, "Whoa, that is what you look like when you quit drinking?" She whispers to me, "Let's never, never quit."

Viva also brought Cruzer an article about a shark attack. I guess they used to get into enormous fights during that week of lying in the gold bed about Cruzer claiming you could save your life if a shark attacked you by punching it in the nose and Viva arguing that it is impossible to punch a shark underwater. The fight is for sure a tense issue between them because it starts up again right there in the coffee shop. They both start shouting about whether or not the article proved either of them right or wrong.

To make matters worse Viva chooses that moment to bring up the dog. She seemed to have forgotten it altogether, hadn't even mentioned it until this point, but then she got pissed about the shark article. "You know, I really miss that fucking dog." Viva crosses her arms over her chest.

They sit there a minute and glare at each other. Then Viva puts the Ferrari glasses back on. "See how they look better on me?" she says smugly.

Cruzer grabs them off her face and turns to me. "Uh no way. They look best on me right?"

I refuse to answer. I can't believe I'm stuck between my best friend and a mean-looking newly sober girl, with two inches of wing-tipped eyeliner on, a permanently bent finger from a roller derby fight, and a gi-normous chip on her shoulder about a "stolen" dog. I think Cruzer probably could trade the sunglasses for the dog, if she truly wanted to settle the issue once and for all, but she seems intent on looking better in the glasses, having them stay glued to her face.

Viva sits back and pouts. "I really miss that fucking dog!" She keeps saying the phrase louder and louder in the quiet coffee shop. I start telling Viva how happy the dog is and she cuts me off. "I could sell that dog on Craigslist for nine-hundred bucks."

"Dixie even gives the dog cute little haircuts," I say. With that, Viva's face starts to turn the colors of her red and black color combo fashion outfit. She clenches her fist tight around the shark attack article. Any second now she might charge at Cruzer like a mad bull on roller skates. There's a flicker of fear in Cruzer's eyes, like when I try to peer pressure her into dropping into a vert ramp on her board.

Cruzer suddenly smiles. "You're right! They look so much better on you." I let out a sigh of relief as she whips the sunglasses off her face. "It's actually kind of nice how they hide your eyes," she throws in.

Viva ignores the extra jab. She snatches up the Ferrari sunglasses and doesn't say a single word again about the dog. She sips the last of her latte, says, "See ya," and rollerskates out the door.

"Remind me to tell Tiny not to give that girl the Gay Mafia Sympathy Discount anymore," Cruzer says.

"Remind me to tell Dixie that you traded your old Ferrari sunglasses for her thousand dollar dog."

"What can I say? I'm a sucker for Dixie."

I butt fists with Cruzer. Then skate over to the bus stop to catch the 22 to Mia's house in the lower Haight.

She'd finally gotten a place of her own a few months before. I hadn't minded living with Mia, drinking a lot and stumbling home together, laughing and taking hours to get home because we had to make out on every staircase, but in the end the money stuff stressed me out, so when she finally got her own place I was stoked to finally sleep alone again.

At Mia's house, I try to fool around but she's stressing out about her Summer Love Tour, which she's leaving for in a few weeks. She's busy and tired trying to get ready to take off. She plays music at her practice space late into the night after work every day and she comes home to pass out. She puts everything in each song until she is so exhausted she doesn't even have the energy to fuck. It bums me out. I hope it isn't Lesbian Bed Death. I've spent countless hours with The Crew sitting around and proving all the ways that the entire concept of LBD is a myth, a queer urban legend that we refuse to accept. But, now, could it be happening to me?

I slip my hand under Mia's shirt and she sighs, "I can't. I'm too fucking exhausted. Oh can you take care of my cat while I'm gone?"

Damn it. She did not just say that.

At a party on the Fourth of July, we are all on the roof watching the last of the fireworks over the Bay and I see Shelby making out with some boy who looks familiar. They start walking towards us, up the row of people who are sitting on the piping. "Who's that kid with Shelby?" I ask Cruzer because she knows everyone.

"That's that English kid Lucy, remember? He's a boy now, so you have to call him 'he' and also his name is Luc."

Luc sits down next to us on the ledge and takes out a Marlboro. "Hey guys." He smiles. Soda turns around and puts one leg on the other side of the piping so she's facing him. "You're on T?"

Luc takes a drag off his cigarette. "Yeah, for a year now. I started up in Portland, which was cool because I didn't have to worry about people getting confused with my boy name, ya know back when I still kind of looked like a Lucy."

One time at this party I heard this girl say, "We're losing all our butches to T," and this other girl said, "That's fine with me. A tranny boy gets my panties wet."

Shelby and Luc start dating so he's always at The Creamsickle. Soda is sort of obsessed with Luc. She likes to follow him around the house, which annoys Shelby. She also asks Shelby every detail about their hook-ups. That doesn't annoy Shelby as much because she's so crushed out that she wants to gush about it.

"Is he stone? He never lets you touch him, right?" Soda asks.

"In the beginning I didn't know what to do with him," Shelby says, chewing a big chunk of her hair like she's a nervous schoolgirl. "Like, the first time we fucked, I waited for him to make the first move. I nearly had to sit on my hands to keep from touching him! I mean he didn't say anything, like no, but you could tell he wanted complete control. We were at this hotel downtown and he kept all his clothes on."

"Was he packing? Does he all of the time?" Soda interrupts. Her eyes aren't even glued to the morning TV like they usually are. She listens intently to Shelby's every word.

"Yeah, totally, it was so hot. He has this cock that has wire in it so he can bend it into his pants, or pull it out and make it straight and fuckable. Like, the first time he put my hand on the bulge in his jeans, I was completely transported back to my teenage years of jacking guys off. *Hot.* Plus, we can fuck anywhere, all over town. He just whips it out. We fucked in the Box at The Minxy Peepshow. I sucked him off the other night in Vine Alley. We fucked in the back of his friend's car after a show…"

"Why are you so obsessed with Luc?" I ask Soda one day. I guess I'm a little jealous or something.

"We are both pirates," is all Soda replies.

A few days later, I'm out skating with The Crew and we stop by Walgreens in the Castro because that's where Luc told Soda he got his binder. The binders are actually backbraces, but bois are starting to use them to press their tits down. Soda usually layered, or she used a cream-colored elastic bandage, wrapped around and around a bunch of times with a half a dozen safety pins pinned up along one side. You could see how this process would get annoying. The new binders are much easier, some just Velcro in the back, or some stretch out and then suction around your ribs. We all try them on over our T-shirts while standing in the Walgreens' aisle, with all our skateboards perched against a vitamin display. Cruzer says she wants one too, after she looks at Soda and sees how incredibly flat her T-shirt is. Never again would a guy on the street look to see if we had boobs while we were skating, because they just aren't there. I see how good Cruzer and Soda look and I want one too, even though I usually hide my B cups fine under a sports bra, layered with a few T-shirts.

We leave Walgreens with our new chests. I nearly can't breathe, for a second skating up the next hill because the thing is so tight it squeezes all the air out of my body. I'll have to get used to this.

The next day Tiny and Coby go buy the binders too. They tell a bunch of other kids, and then all the bois in the neighborhood collectively put all the Walgreens out of stock. Kids started calling and asking them to order more. I look around The Vine one Monday night, and I notice that just about every boi in the bar has a flat-as-a-board chest. The binder is an integral part of boyish-girl style, now that it's so easy to get. Cruzer and Soda wear theirs every day, but I stop wearing mine after a while because it makes me feel like I have asthma.

Lying in my bed one night Soda says, "This new binder, I can already feel it making my life easier. I don't mind walking down the street, because no dudes say, 'Hey lady,' or try to check out my tits to judge *what* I am. It's like so amazing passing, or not even that, I guess, but just not being *looked* at like a girl, ya know? It's like, it hurts my ribs sometimes, and makes me sweat more when I skate, but I'll put up with it 'cause it's better than some drunk type of fucker sitting on the street yelling after me. Or some dude whispering to his friend loud enough for me to hear, 'Is that a boy or a girl,' and then, 'Hell, well gots tits. I think it's a girl.'"

"Fuck that shit," I growl. I remember the time this dumb street lurker guy yelled that exact thing at Soda when she was walking down Mission Street with Dixie.

"You know when I get out of the shower I never even look in those huge mirrors we have in the bathroom. I just pretend like they don't exist. I get my clothes on as quick as possible and that's the only body I know, the one that's my clothes. Hey if I start going by 'he' pronouns, would you call me that?"

"For sure," I say. I don't know what else to say. I have no reference point to what Soda is talking about, but I know she doesn't need me to say anything or have any answers. It's just good for her to talk about stuff in general because she keeps so much bottled up inside. When she gets mad or sad she promptly gets stoned and leaves the planet. She's good at checking out, and has been doing it consistently since she was thirteen. I'm the only one Soda ever talks to about this stuff. Cruzer is too sarcastic to have a heart-to-heart with. So I'm actually glad Luc is hanging around lately, and Soda can talk to someone who knows about this shit.

"Does it have to be one way or the other?" Soda says later when I'm falling asleep.

"What?" I mumble.

"Gender."

"Like couldn't we all just stay in-between?"

"Yeah. Like we could we all be called pirates or monkeys instead of girls or boys."

# Chapter 11

There's a rumor that Hurricane is coming back into town. I hear it was told to Cello's ex, Tobia, who lives in New York, who then told Cello's friend Tash, who then told Nicki, who then told Tiny, who then told Cruzer, who then told me. When I hear the news while Cruzer and I are skating the bridge blocks I immediately roll my eyes to the sky for signs of a storm brewing. Then I keep trying to land this trick and instead I kick my skateboard into the wall. *Dammit.* Just when she is so far gone out of my mind, why does she have to pop back up?

"Don't make it easy for her to hang out with you," Cruzer advises.

"Don't even go *near* her," Soda says. He even grabs my phone and tries to look if her name is in it so he can delete her.

"It doesn't matter if I've got her number or not," I sigh. "She'll find me."

I want to see Hurricane, but I don't want to fuck things up with Mia. She's already super jealous at any mention of Hurricane.

For the rest of the week, I'm wary every time I walk the neighborhood. Before I skate down a street I scan up and down to know what I'm getting into. Hurricane would recognize the rattle of my wheels like a calling card.

Then, one day I'm in the park with Mia, her last day before leaving on tour, and I'm having so much fun just kicking back with her, lying in the grass and eating fancy chocolates from the gourmet food store around the corner.  Plus, I know that since she's leaving in the morning and doesn't have a million things to do for the tour anymore that we are for sure gonna fuck all night long.  I can't wait. Man, Mia is cuter than ever this summer.  Her hair is growing out and she puts the tangles of it up in these ratty haphazard pigtails.  They poke my cheeks with their hairspray crunchy ends when she kisses my face.  She is wearing a red halter-top and I like to dot my hands over the light freckles scattered over her caramel back, up the constellation of tiny freckle-like moles that are on her neck, usually hidden by her hair.

*I want to see you.* I get a text message from an unknown number. I'm convinced Hurricane has been trying to call me. Earlier, a weird number called me twice while Mia was giggling underneath my fingertips in my bed.  I had to press the 'ignore' button with my free hand.

"Who was that?" Mia asks.

"It's nuthin'," I say and go back to kissing her neck.

The Crew goes on a mad drinking and skating binge during the warm end of summer, the week right after Mia leaves on tour. Soda and Cruzer are neck and neck in the *Girls to Send Postcards To* game so they're being extra funny and slutty when they go out.

"Soda is fucking cheating," Cruzer claims. "He's completely lowering his standards in insane ways. And the other day I caught him trying to alter the names on his original list, like I wouldn't notice!"

I'm having fun going out every night but I'm still on guard from any sneak attack from Hurricane. All week since the text message, every time I swing open the double doors of The Vine my heart thumps hard and the hairs on my arm tingle, imagining Hurricane might be lurking over a beer at one of the shadowy corner tables.

One drunk night after I've almost forgotten about that

fickle rumor, Soda, Cruzer and I slam through The Vine doors just before last call, and there's Hurricane. Luckily, the insane amount of whiskey I've drunk has made me numb and I don't puke all over her gold heels when she's suddenly standing in front of me. A year of traveling and she looks even more intriguing, if you can believe it. Her face has hardened like every part of it has fallen right into place, to stay. It's no longer half-puffy-half -thin, how the drugs had made it so instantly collapsible. Her eyes are bigger and wider, brimming with all her adventures. Her hair is dull reddish brown and dirty, the curls pinned back with a bunch of black bobby pins. She throws her arms around my neck to hug me.

"Didjya miss me?" she says. Oh, that old familiar flirtation of a voice.

Standing in Vine Alley later, Hurricane tells me she thought of me often. When I skate home I wonder if it was me, or the city that had marked her mind.

A few days later I'm riding my bike to work and I hear a click-click-click noise following me down the street. I pull over and see how the corners of a cardboard paper have been woven in between the spokes of my back wheel. I pull the folded paper out and see a faded print of a roaring lion face and know immediately who it's from. *Fucking Leo Hurricane.* Over the image is the black scrawl of her handwriting that I know from all the letters she sent me when she first left town, before they stopped abruptly after a month.

*Georgie,*

*The thing is that I'm only here two more nights. The thing is that I'm sorry for everything and I love you. Meet me?*

I call the number scribbled onto the flip side of the paper.

Later that night I'm riding my bike back home and my hands are shaking, not because it's chilly but because I just left Hurricane, where I was making out with her. She met me after my shift and we found a rooftop of a building under construction around the corner from my work. She said I smelled so familiar, like coffee beans and *home.* "Where you going now?" I asked her.

"New York," she laughed.

"But I thought that was where you went!"

"Believe me I went *everywhere* but there."

After scrambling up some scaffolding and after only three swigs of whiskey we fell right back into each other's mouths. I had my hands under her clothes when the whiskey started to burn in a guilty way instead of a good way.

"I love you," Hurricane yelled after me when I scrambled to leave, shimmying down the side of the building and away from her.


Mia comes home a few weeks later from tour. Cruzer and Soda advised me countless times not to tell her about the make out. "Lesbians don't consider kissing cheating," Soda insists. And in contradiction Cruzer says, "She will just be paranoid about you if you bring it up." I was planning to tell her anyways but I don't because she has to go back to a shitty job instead of getting to play music.

"Tour is like a taste of freedom," she says. "Playing music all day and traveling, to think that could be your life..." She's so glum that it's easy to get distracted by things infused with more passion. Like Hurricane's letters. She starts sending them all the time. I get a letter from her through the mail slot in The Creamsickle door every single day. It's so predictable, obsessed with me when she can't have me. But, she writes me the most beautiful letters. She sends a Polaroid of her in one letter and she has rosy dirt-smudged cheeks, her orange hair poking out like straw from under my old railroad cap that I gave her as a goodbye gift. After I have read the letters enough times, I put them in a shoebox that contains everything she has ever written me and stash it on the top shelf of my closet.

Then Mia is flipping through Cruzer's scrapbook one day and sees the *Girls to Send Postcards To* list. She figures out the nature of the game pretty easily. She starts yelling at me, stuff like *How could you want to fuck Nicki? She's such a skank*! And later she gets all crazy that Soda's name is on there. She gets super paranoid and demanding, like that afternoon I want to go

skating with Soda the way I usually do and she says I always want
to hang out with him rather than her. She even says I can't sleep
in his bed anymore. That night we go to Cat Fight Club and
she says I can't dance with Nicki or even look in her direction.
It's too much! We start shouting at each other in front of the
club and everyone stares at us like they know our relationship is
about to dead end.

On Sunday I'm sitting at The Vine venting to Dixie about
all my relationship drama. Dixie calls Sundays "Bloody Mary
Sundays" because she likes to have Bloody Marys every Sunday
afternoon. Sometimes she goes to bars where they have a make
your own Bloody Mary Bar. On her last birthday, in the morning,
The Crew took her on a tour of all the Bloody Mary bars in the
neighborhood. Dixie is so comforting to talk to. She rotates
from petting the fluffy dog's head that's nestled in her lap, to
petting my beanie-clad head. "I always thought that girl was way
too young," she says about Mia, even though she is only a few
years younger than us. "She apparently doesn't know how to
communicate and work out *trust* issues," Dixie drawls on. "You
gotta let her grow up."

Just let her grow up. Yeah, like it's that easy. Friends always
act like breaking up with someone is so simple. *Just break up* they
say, but they aren't in love with the person so it's easy for them
to say. I chomp on a cold green bean infused with vodka from
my second amazingly comforting Bloody Mary. The bartender,
Katie, comes over to us with her hand over the speaker of the
bar's portable phone. "Hey some girl is asking if you are here.
Are you?" she asks Dixie. Her eyebrows raised and her mouth
is trying to trap in a giggle.

"NO!" Dixie shout-whispers. She grabs her small dog off
her lap and tucks him quick as hell into her oversized purse so
only his little ears peek out.

"No. Haven't seen her in weeks," Katie says into the phone.
She ducks into the back room to hang up the receiver and comes
back. "That girl is *still* after that dog!"

"Viva has a Vendetta," I say, which is a joke we say all the
time at The Creamsickle so it's pretty played out, but Katie

hasn't heard it yet. And, man, do I love to make Katie laugh. Mostly, well okay, *only*, because when she laughs her awesome tits that are usually three-fourths of the way out of her shirt bounce in the most hypnotic manner.

I watch Katie laugh as Dixie fills her in on the recent developments as to why Viva is once again obsessed with getting her dog back. Viva got this new sober girlfriend and they moved in together and Viva had an actual real house for the first time since she had abandoned the dog. So now she wanted the dog back. But, it was way too late. The little dog was so happy with Dixie, they were completely codependent and in love. And now Viva has been calling The Vine to see if she can catch Dixie there, so she can come looking for her. Dixie has been highstrung about it. "It's messing up my summer and my relaxing Bloody Mary Sundays! I have to always watch my back!" Dixie whines and because Katie is such an attentive bartender, she starts to make her a new drink.

"I heard you had to hide in the basement from her last week!" Katie says.

"Yeah, for like an hour," Dixie moans, "I was down there staring at the tequila bottles and feeling incredibly thirsty, till Mikala came down and told me that she left!"

"You need to get a secret back exit to this place," I tell Katie. "It would solve a lot of problems."

"No shit," Katie says before walking away to tend the bar.

I'm mainly thinking of how possibly breaking up with Mia soon will mean I have to avoid all my favorite places where the little alcoholic likes to lurk, and how a back entrance to The Vine could serve as a rotating door so when she walked in I could sneak out, without my heart breaking when I saw her cute fucking smile.

"I think it might be time I move to Portland where jaded lesbians retire," Dixie says, again stroking the fluffy dog's head. "I mean, am I going to look behind my back for the rest of my life in this city? Not knowing if someone is going to snatch my baby?"

"No! You're not moving!" I holler. I can never handle the thought of any of my friends moving.

Just then, Mia walks in with her friends.  She's holding a basketball and she's all sweaty.  She looks so hot.  I want to take her home and have some amazing make-up sex.

"See? A back door, that's all we need," Dixie whispers in my ear.

Mia's basketball rolls back and forth when the bed rattles the floor while we're fucking, until it finally stalls on the crumpled pile of her jeans. We both have our hands in each other, fucking each other, and rocking the bed. Suddenly she grabs my face with her hands right under my chin and holds me in place, making sure I'm looking at her. Sometimes I can even feel myself check out. I feel my eyes go blank. I'm not sure where exactly my mind goes but it strays. Either way, Mia definitely notices. I see the scared look in her eyes the moment she catches me slipping away.

# Chapter 12

"Fuck you. You lying bastard. You're just like your sleazeball friends. I thought you were different," Mia screams at me. She's standing on the sidewalk in front of The Creamsickle. I'm up on the steps holding the door open with my foot and trying to get her to come inside. It's four in the morning and we've been out all night. We went to this girl Starla's birthday party that was on a rented party bus, the kind that are painted all wild. The bus drove around the city all night long, to the very top of the highest hilltop views, to Treasure Island, over bridges and to the ocean, all wet and misty. At each stop the driver would park for ten minutes and everyone would get out and dance in the street, or pee between cars, or behind the big beach rocks, do key bumps, or just look at the view. I'd had a bottle of whiskey in my back pocket that Mia kept grabbing, so she really drank most of it. Then, of course, we started fighting about every little thing, which is the way things go lately.

Standing under the yellowy street lamps on the sidewalk, Mia is crying. When she cries her gorgeous dark eyes get all squinty and the thick mascara and liquid eyeliner gets extra ultra black and smeary. I want to take a picture of her. Once Cruzer had this photo show where the entire show was this series of pictures she took in art school of her first girlfriend crying. The crying happened in all these different places, in bed, naked on the toilet, on the street. Sometimes you couldn't even tell she was crying, but anyone who knew her could tell. Well, for sure the crying girl's new girlfriend who came to the art show knew. She had glared at Cruzer extra hard.

That's what I want to do with Mia's eyes right now, blow them up huge like one of those photographs. Cruzer's photos are so big, she prints them on huge strips, so one photo is made up of five or six diagonal strips as big as half a wall. Mia's eyes would be luminous with the wet clumps of her eyelashes looking like zebra stripes against the pale powder of her cheeks. She has a bunch of makeup on because she got all dressed up for the party. But damn, I shouldn't be thinking about taking her picture right now. The situation is actually pretty serious. Mia is pissed at me once again.

Everything exploded this morning when she found a letter from Hurricane in my drawer. She was pissed about the kind of things Hurricane wrote me and I was pissed she went through my stuff. Mia thought the letter was proof that I wasn't into her anymore. She waved the letter in my face, pieces of napkins with little cactuses patterned along the edges that Hurricane had scribbled on from a diner somewhere in the Southwest, lines of blue ink covering them.

"I just don't trust you," Mia cries on the sidewalk.

"I only kissed her and then I took off!"

I'm bummed that she found that note because I was thinking things were getting better between us. We wore these matching themed outfits for Halloween and next week it was our ONE year anniversary of meeting in the diner. The other day I bought her a new leather jacket that I found at a secondhand store. But now she's once again screaming about our sex life and the usual homeless lurkers on the corner in front of my house are getting a dyke drama earful. She is so drunk that it makes her extra angry and sloppy. She kicks the edges of the stairs with her dirty boots.

"Just come upstairs and sleep it off," I beg her, for the tenth time.

"I'm never walking up your fucking stairs again," she shouts.

'C'mon, it's late. You can't walk home."

Mia finally lets me take her upstairs and I tuck her drunk ass into bed.

In the morning, I have to get up early for work so I kiss her goodbye and tell her she should lie all day in my bed and sleep off her hangover, and when I come home from work at three I will bring her cookies from the cafe. She nods and looks at me sadly with puffy-smeared raccoon makeup eyes.

When I come home from work Mia is gone.

The evening is gray and the curtains are pulled closed so the room is dark. Before I even switch on the light I can feel that something is different. For one thing it smells like sage. Did she sage my room? *Weird.* Then I see that she has taken all her stuff. I look through the CDs by my bed and she took hers. I open the drawers and she took her underwear and T-shirts. I look on the walls and she took a painting we bought together at a thrift store. *Goddamn* she even took all the photo booth pictures of us from my mirror.

Mia doesn't pick up her phone. For three days, I go out and look for her but she is never at any of her usual haunts. I take the bus all the way over to her practice space one day after work and she looks really sad when she lifts her eyelashes up from the microphone and sees me standing in the doorway. Oh Mia. What an achingly beautiful face. I watch her play a new song, but she stops halfway through.

We smoke a cigarette outside. "You shouldn't have come here," she says. "I'm working on this new stuff and I have to really stay focused. I'll call you soon." When Mia kisses me goodbye her lips taste like sweat and salt. I can still taste her on my heavyhearted bus ride home, and I wonder if it will be the last time.

When Mia finally calls me her voice is stiff.

"Look. I just want to concentrate on my music."

"So, we're just on a break?" I ask hopefully. "'Cause, I really miss you. 'Cause, I really love you."

"I gotta go," she says sadly.

When I leave for work the next morning there is a scribbled note under The Creamsickle doormat.

*Georgie,*

*I can't get you off my mind. I lay in bed awake all night thinking about how scared I am of you hurting me. I can't handle it. I can't date you right now. I just wrote an entire album of songs about how you broke my heart.*

*Love, Mia*

I read the note over and over until I have it memorized and then I repeat it in my head all night at work. I can imagine Mia leaving the note on my doorstep in the middle of the night, probably drunk after bar closing time with her blue cruiser bike leaning against her hip as she bent down to shove the note between the mat and the cream-colored marble steps.

I'm so pissed that she's writing a new album. It makes me convinced that she broke up with me to fuel her music. She'd told me countless times that whenever she was in relationships her song writing hit a wall. There's this piece of paper taped up in her room above her mirror that reads: *You did it for the Music.* Now, she was probably looking at that sign a hundred times a day to justify breaking up with me.

I show Cruzer the letter. "I don't get it. I broke *her* heart?"

"You got dumped right before winter hibernation. Harsh."

She's referring to how much it sucks to not have a girl in your bed before The Creamsickle gets cold and all the queers in the neighborhood pair off and settle in for the winter, which makes it super hard for someone who missed mating season to get laid. Cruzer even has a steady date so she's all set for winter. She hangs out with her a lot, this girl named Topsy. She was one of Cruzer's *Girls to Send Postcards To* over summer, but somehow she is still sending her postcards far into winter. *Shit.* I'm about to be single and Cruzer isn't even excited about it because she is so busy with Topsy. "So, Mia broke up with you because she thinks you're not over your ex? That, by the way, is some Textbook Lesbian Shit." Cruzer enunciates each word slowly and shakes her head.

"I know. She is being such a hard-ass about it. Over nothing! A silly game and a fucking letter to an ex-lover. It's probably just an excuse for her to fuck other people. She hasn't done her rounds in this town yet, and she has all these little crushes that I bet she wants to fuck."

"Hmmm maybe. She didn't seem like that though. She was so all about you. Are you sure you didn't call her Hurricane or something when you were fucking her?"

"No!"

"Okay, Okay." Cruzer grabs the note off the table and stares at it for a few minutes like it's in some secret code she is trying to decipher. "But maybe she is right? Huh? Maybe you still think Hurricane is gonna come back and you still want you to run away with her so you keep one foot jammed in the door, ya know, keeping it open?"

I shake my head. "No no. I'm over that fucked-up girl!"

"Well how come you still wear her T-shirt all the time and you *never* wash it?"

God, Cruzer is such an asshole lately. I mean, she has always been an asshole, but lately she has been taking it to a new level.

"I don't need to hear your bullshit right now." I jump up and snatch my letter out of her hand. "Get a fucking sensitive side or something." I stomp down the hall and slam my bedroom door. I flop onto my bed and sink into the comforting covers. Where's Soda? I want to smoke a cigarette out on the back porch with him and talk shit about Mia and Cruzer.

Soda has been pissed at Cruzer too. First it was because after she got all hung up on Topsy she stopped showing up at the club she threw with Soda. For the last two clubs she no-showed, claiming she was busy having sex, but the third time, she said there was a new, cooler club that started up somewhere else and Topsy wanted to go there instead. Cruzer had become completely disinterested in her own club, even if she got free beer for throwing it. She hadn't even been helping Soda promote. The other day I went with him to the paper store where they get the *Gay Mafia* hook up for the shiny gold paper they like to print the flyers on. We took Cruzer's truck and Soda was bitching the whole drive about how this would be the last club he threw if he had to do all the promoting work himself, and Cruzer wasn't even going to show up.

We hadn't even seen Cruzer all week. After I tried to call her for the hundredth time she finally picked up. *Hellooow?* She had a sleepy voice even though it was mid-afternoon. "We're coming to get you." She tried to argue but I hung up on her.

We double parked in front of Topsy's house and waited like paparazzi. Eventually Cruzer emerged with her reflective sunglasses and her jacket hood over her head. She squished in next to me in the front seat and smiled dreamily like her head was in some magical place. *"Te amo muchachos,"* she said with a huge lolling smile. I rolled my eyes. Next we swung by my work to get my paycheck. When I hopped back in the truck, sad that I was so broke since I called in sick twice the week Mia broke up with me, Soda said, "Georgie, listen to this shit! Cruzer thinks she is in love. That girl gave her some E and now she thinks she's in fuckin' love!"

Cruzer was quiet.

"You know Topsy did that on purpose right?" Soda yelled and shook his head.

Cruzer shrugged. "I don't care."

Soda pulled over in the bus lane on Sixteenth Street a few minutes later to make a drive-by pill pick up. He had to lean down out window to reach The Doc in his wheelchair.

Cruzer turned to me and grinned "That girl put two hits of E on my tongue and then when I was coming down I thought *Whoa I love her.*"

"Well everyone knows that's how Zeena got Katie D." Soda popped his head back in the window for a second and yelled back at us. "Yeah that's how their fucking relationship started and now look at them! Zeena is craaaazy!"

"No, no. It's not like that. I love her 'cause I love her stories." Cruzer sighed, like she was still on ecstasy.

"You weren't saying that last week," I said.

"Oh, but last night I was telling her how my favorite fruits are nectarines and lemons, and check it out, she was like 'Oh whoa, I've always wanted to get a nectarines and lemons tattoo because they are totally my favorite fruits!'"

"What!" Soda smacked his hands on the steering wheel, "Georgie! Help me out here!"

I couldn't say much because I couldn't stop laughing, imagining Cruzer and that girl on drugs, staring deep into each other's eyes and realizing how cosmically connected they were.

"Her pussy tastes like a cupcake," Cruzer said.

"Shut up," Soda said.

"Like a vanilla, peanut butter cupcake."

"You sound ridiculous!" I said between choking on laughter.

"She cares about the environment too. She's so sexy. I want to bottle her come. It's so good. I would definitely put it in a bottle and spray it on my body."

"Ahhhhhhhhh!" Soda had his hands over his ears. The Doc was craning his neck to try and see into the truck at what all the commotion was about. Maybe the commotion would get him to ditch the wheelchair guise for a minute.

"Man, you are so getting tricked by that broad," Soda said.

"Yeah, I do feel confused." Cruzer sighed. "But maybe that is what love feels like."

*Fuck girls. Fuck love*, I think while lying on my bed. Love is stealing my best friend. Love is making it feel like there is a hot knife stabbing deep into my chest. Why do people even get to know each other, fall in love and get close to each other if it hurts this fucking bad every time? Why did I even date anyone after Hurricane broke my heart? How many times can a heart break? All these questions jumble in my head till it starts to pound.

I wipe the start of angry tears from my eyes. I refuse to cry over a girl. It takes a lot for me to cry. I usually swallow back the salt and spit it to the ground before I will let it sneak out of my eyes. Or I punch the wall above my bed so there's now a row of indents on the wall, from all the tears that have been diverted into clenched fists.

I need to get out of my room, with Mia's song lyrics inked on the wall above my bed, the pictures of her, and the postcards she sent me when she was on tour tacked above my record player. I grab my board, and skate down the hall to the stairs. I can hear Cruzer holler something that's maybe a sarcastic comment, or maybe some sort of apology from the living room, but I don't stop to find out which it is. I run down the stairs, do an Acid Drop off the porch steps and take off fast down the hill.

I skate with no destination. It takes an hour of cruising for my head to stop pounding. Then I start to skate towards Soda's work, this bar called The Clubhouse that she has been working the sound for lately. On the way there I see Darling Nicki walking down South Van Ness. *Damn*, she is so fine. She is wearing tight-ass black pants, and rattlesnake print heels. She smiles when I skate up. "Hi honey." She looks tired. She says she has had a hard day. Do I want to get a beer? I tell her I only want to go to The Clubhouse, because I'm poor from calling in sick so much lately and Soda will probably hook me up with free beer.

"Do you think he's cool with me, yet?" Nicki asks.

"He's been really relaxed lately." I laugh thinking about the pile of pills The Doc gave him last week.

Soda is busy working so he doesn't even see us come in. We go straight upstairs to the balcony where you can shoot free pool and look out over the stage. No one else is in the huge club except for the bartender, Soda, and a guy in the band doing a sound check. I go get Nicki and me some beers. When I come back she is leaning over the balcony with her chin on her hands watching Soda work on the stage down below. "He looks so good setting up," she says.

I look down across the huge empty wooden dance floor, at the stage. Soda has on a sideways cap and skater-saggy jeans. He looks small down below but also so cute and tough, moving the equipment around, and telling the beefy band dude what wires to plug in while he turns knobs on the sound switchboard.

I hand Nicki her beer. "You know I always remember the last time Soda fucked me," she says. "I think I will remember it for the rest of my life. We were at The Shotgun after I was closing down the bar and he was helping me restock the beer fridges, and then we started fucking right up on the bar top with this case of beer rattling next to us."

I start to imagine Nicki in a short skirt sitting on top on the bar where she works. Nice. Down below, Soda starts to drag an amp across the stage.

"I should go," Nicki mumbles. "Seeing Soda makes me crazy. Crazier than I already am, makes me mad as a wet cat dropped into a tub that I can't have him."

"No!" I tell her to stop watching him. I try to distract her. "Let's play pool."

Nicki stays looking over the balcony as I rack the balls on the pool table behind us. "You know why Mia ran off on you, right?" She finally turns away from the railing. She takes another sip off her beer and swallows the last of it. I make a mental note to go get her a shot of whiskey. "'Cause people get scared when someone makes 'em that kind of crazy. It's always easier to run. Look at that kid, he's been doing it his whole life and he never cares about nothing."

I look over at my phone sitting on the tabletop near the pool table. I want to call Mia so bad all the time. I gulp my beer and try not to imagine her with someone else, a horrible mental image that has been running through my head all week. At the same time, I don't want to call her, because what if she turns the phone call into the stuff-exchange conversation, the true signal that it's the official termination of our relationship, the divvying up of the sex toys. I pick up the phone. I almost call Mia but then I call Tiny instead and tell her to meet us at The Clubhouse.

By the time Soda gets off work, Nicki, Tiny and I are all wasted off all the free booze. Because they're drunk, Nicki and Soda are being cool with each other. We all go back to The Creamsickle, making a quick detour to get a bag of drugs from Nicki's dealer on the way.

At the house, Soda announces that it's game night. I forgot about game night because we hadn't done it in months, ever since Cruzer stopped coming home. It had been a sort of boy's club night where we played poker and dominoes. "Where has Cruzer been anyways?" Nicki asks.

"Basically once that girl, Topsy, stops pumping her full of hallucinogens she will come back to us," Soda answers.

"Hmm, Topsy. I dunno. I hear she likes to wife a girl!"

"Shut up!" Soda says and I think for a second that he and Nicki are going to start fighting as usual, but instead his hand squeezes her thigh. *Whoa.* I wonder if they will hook up. Soda seems so vulnerable lately, upset about Cruzer ditching out and depressed about stuff he doesn't talk about.

I must have passed out on the couch because the next thing you know, Nicki is shaking me and saying she's going to put me in my bed. Soda is standing behind her. I tell them both, *Leave me alone I hate my bed.* The way it still smells like Mia. The way I wake up in the middle of the night lately and reach for her but find nothing there.

The first time I ever fisted Mia, she cried. Her eyes crumpled up and her hand flew in front of her mouth to cover up her quivering lip. I nuzzled her salty neck and felt her pussy clench tight around my fist. Sometimes the most stable thing in the world is your hand in a girl's pussy. Your entire fist swallowed. Your life will shake and rock around you but it may be the only thing that will keep you in one place.

# Chapter 13

I wake up on the couch a week and a half later. Or probably it's been more than a week and a half but I don't remember because I've been on such a bender. I haven't been sleeping that much. Apparently when I do sleep, it's on the couch.

The morning light is streaming through the bare living room windows. I squint at Nicki, who is sitting on the couch across the room. Cruzer's couch, but she hasn't been home in so long that I've forgotten what she looks like on it, sitting there like she used to, scrapping her new photos into her scrapbook and talking shit. She did stop by once, real quick last week, to grab a handful of boxers. She poked her head into the living room and found us playing *Tony Hawk's Underground*, which we had basically been doing for three days straight. "Aw, man you guys got THUG," she said about our new game.

"Yeah you can do Wall Plants and even get off your board and walk around. I just won Slam City Jam and turned Pro!" I bragged.

"I wanna try!" Cruzer tried to sit down next to us.

Soda and I clutched tightly to our controllers. We didn't feel like Cruzer could just bust in and hang out with us whenever her *girlfriend* was at work, or whatever. "You were just supposed to send a postcard, not move in with her," Soda said bitterly.

"I can't handle the cold here anymore," Cruzer bullshitted.

Soda and I could handle the cold because lately we got so fucked up we couldn't feel our bodies. We curled up in the gray flannel blankets and fought over who got to spoon Napoleon, or sometimes just curled up around each other. But mostly we tried not to leave the house. One day when it was raining super-duper hard Soda ordered delivery from the Chinese place that is owned by one of The Doc's friends. He joked about having The Doc put a pill order in with the take-out and to his excitement there was a little envelope from The Doc next to the fortune cookies. *I got the pills delivered with the Chinese*, Soda bragged for weeks to whoever would listen.

Nicki has a big pair of scissors and she is cutting the neck off a black Harley T-shirt that looks like one Soda was wearing the other day. Nicki loves to cut up other people's T-shirts. Once I saw her scissor-happy hands holding one of my Anti-Hero shirts, and I nearly put her on restriction from The Creamsickle. After that, she stuck to only stealing T-shirts from people she was sleeping with, because people who are sleeping with Nicki let her do whatever she wants. She cuts the T-shirts because she doesn't have any new outfits since she hasn't been home in over a week. She just grabs a skate shirt and slices off the neck, and maybe the sleeves, and then cuts a harp of slats in the back that she ties up tight with her pointy white teeth. Then she piles her gold chains and bracelets back on that are scattered all over the house, slips on her crocodile print heels, puts on some red lipstick and she's ready for whatever adventure.

Nicki notices I'm awake and comes over and sits on the couch next to me. "You all right sweetie?"

I nod. Even though I feel like I was run over by a truck. I drank way too much last night, did way too many drugs and stayed up way too late. Nicki pets my head. I like her being around. She kind of takes care of me. She has her sweet moments. Mostly when no one else is around, like Soda, who she talks to all sassy with a razor-blade tongue.

Nicki takes off yesterday's shirt, and puts on the newly altered one. The collar is cut deep, and it's super loose so it falls off one shoulder and hangs almost to her nipple. "Will you pin this up?"

She scoots her back to me, handing me some safety pins. I sit up and bunch the shirt together. I know she wants it to be as tight as a second layer of skin. I start to feel better, watching the light dance over Nicki's back. She has amazing skin. She doesn't have any tattoos, skin blank as rice paper, feels like velvet and smells like coconut butter. "Okay, I'm off to get us coffee and doughnuts," Nicki chirps and hops off the couch after I'm done pinning her. God, she is for sure still on drugs. She probably hasn't even slept yet. The last thing I had heard last night before I passed out was that she'd wanted to watch the sunrise on the back porch with Soda. Not only have they been fucking since that night at The Clubhouse, they've also been watching a lot of sunrises together. Either Soda is suddenly into the romance or he's just on a sleepless drug binge. It's hard to tell.

I turn on the TV and watch *Oprah* until Soda wakes up and comes into the living room. He sits next to me. "Last night Knockout told me she's breaking up with me!"

"What? That's a first!" I'm bummed because I like having Nicki around the house. Life seems less depressing when I watch her prancing around.

"She told me she has a hot date with a femme girl tonight. And she said she's not gonna fall for my lines just so I can kick her to the curb all over again in three months."

"Hmmm, smart girl."

"But, I'm into her. We keep staying up till dawn talking about everything. I even talked to her about my gender stuff! And now she's going and dating a femme 'cause she knows it will make me feel awful. She's trying to get back at me! Everybody knows she doesn't fuck femmes. She's the queen of..." Soda trails off because we hear the downstairs door slam, the sound of Nicki's heels clicking up the stairs.

"I heard you're into the ladies?" I say later as I chomp into one of the doughnuts Nicki brought us.

"Yeah hella." Soda rolls his eyes.

"Oh Soda you think everything is about *you*, huh? Like I'm just fucking femmes now to fuck with you, huh? Jeez, you're so conceited, it's disgusting!"

*Uh oh*. They are so going to have it out. Man, two weeks go by and no fighting, and now *ka-bam*.

"Give me my fuckin' Harley shirt back," Soda growls.

"Fine!" Nicki pulls off the T-shirt. "I'm sure my date will like this outfit better." She is now wearing a tiny thin white see-through camisole that clings to her ribs and tits. She tosses the Harley T-shirt right into Soda's face, then grabs her purse and clicks back down the hall and down the stairs.

A few minutes later while I'm listening to Soda bitch about her I think about how I want more doughnuts, but damn Nicki took them. When I'm looking on the coffee table I see that, insanely, she left her bag of drugs instead. I quickly sneak the drugs into my pocket to hide them from Soda. The drugs have been adding to his mania lately. Snorting has been exchanged for sleeping and his tired eyes only sleep in the seconds when he blinks. He has been upset about so much shit and now to top it off The Doc disappeared last week right when, as he puts it, when "we both totally need him!" Nearly every day the last few weeks, Soda goes to look for The Doc, but he isn't at his "office." He also doesn't answer his cell phone. "What kind of drug dealer doesn't answer their cell phone?" Soda groans. Usually he tries to get me to go with him to look for The Doc, but I don't like to leave the house anymore, unless I have to go to work. It's been raining for weeks and I can't skate so what's the point? I don't even know how to handle it when my head gets all crazy and I can't skate. And I can't even go dancing either; because the last time I had to watch every boi in town dance up on Mia like she's fresh meat. Everyone wanted to dance with her; she had a rhythm in her hips that made my crotch hurt just watching her. And she won't even talk to me anymore because her friend told me she thinks I'm fucking Nicki. So when I did try to go out I just ended up getting super sloppy just so I could make the pain in my chest go away for a minute.

It's better to stay inside, with Soda and Nicki. Or just with Soda, smoking weed and trying to beat *THUG*. People come visit us. I think our friends are worried they are gonna find us both frozen cold and blue one day, stiff in front of the TV, so there's always someone buzzing the buzzer and making us argue over who has to emerge from their thick cave of blankets and run down the long flight of stairs to unlock the door. Usually, Soda has to do it because I have the advantage of not caring so much about my dwindling supply of pills, so I bribe him with them. "Let Dixie and Tiny in and I will give you my last V," I say and Soda reluctantly trudges down the hall.

While we're playing *THUG*, Soda gets a call from her ex-girl Tiffany who tells him she recently sold her car to The Doc, for cheap, with a huge supply of drugs included in the price. This leads us to decide that maybe The Doc's just on a road trip and will be back soon. "I don't get it. Why wouldn't he call and say goodbye," Soda says sadly. I think most of her depression lately is directly linked to the disappearance of her Doc.

That night, of course, Soda wants to go to The Vine, there's some benefit for a queer music video there, but I know he really just wants to go spy on Nicki. We're only there five minutes when Manno comes up to us and says, "Holy shit, Nicki is making out with a femme and it's the hottest thing ever." We look over and sure enough Nicki is pressed tight against a tall sultry girl who looks like she could be her twin sister. A bunch of bois are standing around just watching the two slippery femmes with the same long black shags fall into each other's mouths between sips off their cocktails.

Soda stiffens. "Let's go," he grumbles to me. We push through the crowd to the door and Tiny intercepts us. "Hey guys do a shot with me for Casey's birthday."

"Soda, Georgie howdy. I can't believe y'all left the house!" Dixie comes over, and kisses our cheeks. In that same minute I catch a glance of Mia in a far corner, and it makes me want to puke. Soda and I look at each other.

"Ugh, let's go somewhere new!" Soda groans.

Dixie whispers to me, "Is Soda bent up over Nicki? Geez-Louise, I hate that bitch. What the fuck does she do to 'em? Is it something simple? The way she fucks 'em. What's her trick?"

I shake my head and try to get away from all my friends crowding around. All I'm thinking about is how I hope Mia sees Nicki on her date, so she can see how it's obvious that I'm not sleeping with her. Soda pulls the sleeve of my leather jacket through the sea of lesbians to the door, and the next thing I know we're in a cab headed towards this hipster-straight bar in SOMA.

I wake up in my bed for the first time in what feels like forever and all I can think of is how happy I am that it doesn't smell like Mia. Instead it smells like the straight girl I fucked last night. Man, sometimes I forget how straight girls are a fantastic form of therapy if you're feeling lame about yourself. I mean, they love to get fucked all night long and it's all dangerously new, exciting territory to them since they've fantasized about girls for long enough, so when it's actually happening they're completely thrilled.

Still, rebound sex for me is like a flashlight being turned off and on in my face. I barely blink. It just fills the emptiness with something. I had to concentrate real hard to not miss Mia's fuck-me face when the straight girl was lying on my pillows with her mouth parted into a half moan. Then when she had her legs spread over my face, doing a pussy sunset into my mouth and riding my hand I got this terrible aching feeling by the way she grabbed the curtains that Mia and I had bought together, the ones that hang like fuck-me-harder-support-ropes right above the bed. My mind drifted off to that day when we bought them at that basement-level discount fabric store on Mission. How I'd pressed Mia against the piles of leopard print rugs and kissed her bow-lipped mouth.

See how I'm so easily distracted?

But it's good that straight girls never want to fuck you back. I don't even want to be fucked by a stranger right now. What's the point? So they can fuck me too soft, fuck me too slow, fuck me too quick, or fuck me too hard? I'll take the lonely cigarettes over that any day.

After the girl and her friend leave, I go in the kitchen to make coffee. Soda is up. He says, "I usta love fucking straight girls. You know, making them see the light and never having to have the what's-off-limits conversation with them, and knowing they aren't gonna call and bug you 'cause they probably have a boyfriend tucked away somewhere.  But last night was so boring. She was such a dead fish. I'd rather hump a pillow then fuck another straight girl."

"That's 'cause you are hung up on Nicki!" I say. "It's a miracle. Everyone is growing up around here and suddenly capable of love."

"Naw," Soda says.

But later, while I'm eating breakfast I catch him staring sadly at Cruzer's huge blown up picture of Nicki that hangs on the kitchen wall.

I run across the street to catch the Mission bus and the asshole driver pulls away from the curb even though I know he saw me coming. One time Cruzer and I were complaining about how many bus drivers passed us in the rain in San Francisco, and Dixie and Cello were all, "Bus drivers always stop for me."

*Duh.* That is because you're hot chicks.

I curse the bus and try to walk/run to work. The rain totally hampers my wheeled transportation devices. I know I'm going to be late, which will be bad news if my boss is there because he is already mad at me since I called in sick twice already.

I'm ten minutes late and just like that I'm fired.

I try to argue with my boss but he says I've called in sick three times, which is untrue because one of the days was a day off I requested because Cello's best friend Goldy got killed on her bike by a hit-and-run driver and I wanted to go to her memorial at Ocean Beach. I even brought in the newspaper article about poor Goldy, showed it to my boss with red puffy eyes. Explained how she'd just kissed her girlfriend goodbye at the karaoke bar before strapping her Helmut on and riding down Polk only to get struck by a big black SUV running an intersection. It was all so terribly sad, making this the saddest winter in existence.

But, my boss is such a prick. He doesn't care about queer girls dying. He says there are no excuses for my sick days. I'm fired. I want to argue it more but I'm feeling so fucking numb. I'm tired and my pants are soaking wet from the rain and I'm about to cry. I leave before my asshole boss sees any tears.

When I walk home, even though it's raining, I detour by the corners in hopes that The Doc has reappeared. At first I think I see his wheelchair through the mist, but it's just a mirage. I walk closer and he totally isn't there. My world has been hanging by a thin thread and now everything is really crashing down. I head back home and pull off my nasty-ass work jeans, with the bottom cuffs permanently caked with coffee grounds and mop water. I've been wearing them to work for over a year. I hate them. I would love to never see them again. I toss them overhand basketball style into my trashcan but then I realize I can still smell them, so I go outside in my boxers and put them in the basement trashcan. It feels liberating for a second but then it feels sickeningly scary.

I go back upstairs, take some sleeping pills and crawl back to bed.

I wake up in a panic, with my heart beating hard in my chest. I had a dream that The Creamsickle was falling down, like huge chunks of it were crumbling, like when The Nothing attacks in *The Neverending Story*.

*Fuck!* I remember how I was fired earlier this morning. *Fucking shit*. I evaluate my situation. I have rent covered, miraculously because rent is so cheap, but after that I'm pretty screwed because I didn't work enough this month to have any sort of savings. I could borrow some money from Soda. He always has cash since he makes good money at all the new sound gigs lately. I'm definitely not allowed to spend money on booze or drugs. I figure I can stretch the cash I have for at least a few weeks while I scrounge for a new job.

Soda wakes me up to watch the sunrise on the back porch with him. He gets so excited about it every morning as if he never knew it happened on the daily. I think it sort of started with hearing about Goldy dying. The next morning Soda shook me awake and said, "Life is too short to miss the sunrise!" He sounded like my crazy bio-dad, who I only hung out with a few times, but both those times we went camping and he would wake me and my sisters up at super early hours and say things like, "Let's climb the mountain!" Both times when he dropped us off at my mom's house at the end of the weekend I was surprised that we were still alive after the wilderness adventures. That was before he disappeared into thin air.

I'm always surprised at how quiet the back porch is, like The Creamsickle is so high up that the noises of people really living don't come in our windows. There's no neighboring house walls sandwiching us, there's just a locked up basketball court and a vacated apartment that creepily emits no sounds except creaking. At sunrise the back porch is the most eerie sort of quiet, like the clouds might bring up a snatch of a conversation ten blocks away or the muted sound of sirens.

The skyline is oozing colors like the result of three different flavors of 7-Eleven slushy mixing together in a Big Gulp cup, cherry, root beer and blueberry. This city is so beautiful. That's why even when it gets me down, I still can't leave. I watch the houses on the hills that begin to get lit by sunlight, row by row. I think I can even see the café I worked at for nearly two years that I got fired from this morning. Even though I didn't make that much money, and I had to work so much that I didn't have time to take classes anymore at City College, I'm convinced it'll be hard to find a better job, one that lets me listen to my own music and doesn't care about my crazy hairstyles.

"I feel like I can't handle finding another job! I can't survive in this city!" I whine for the millionth time to Soda.

"If you leave me like Cruzer then I will kill you Georgie," Soda says in the saddest voice. He is looking at me with red-rimmed eyes, and a face as splotchy as the colors of the sunrise. When Soda gets cold his lips turn violet, his cheeks get splotches of pink like he's just been slapped, and his eyes get clear blue as a cloudless sky. "Everyone in my life has left sooner or later, mothers, sisters, brothers, friends, girls…"

"You're the one who is always leaving!" Soda is talking crazy. He's been up for three weeks straight, possibly. All night tonight he was up, talking about the apocalypse with some cokehead girls.

"You're not going anywhere. We'll go look for a new job for you tomorrow. I got your rent if you need it. I've got your back for whatever, bro."

I feel better. I take a deep breath of the chilly, foggy air and watch the purple ooze into the red of the skyline.

This girl Tiny brought over says to her, "What's wrong with your friend?"

"She's heartbroken."

"Still? Over that Mia girl, right?"

"Yup."

"I heard Mia is fucking Katie D."

"Shhhhh."

It's three a.m. and I've spent most of the night lying on the couch and pretending to be passed out because I'm still depressed, and the girls Tiny brought over are bugging me. And why does everyone know about my love life? That bugs me too. Is my heart splattered red and bloody all over the girl bar bathroom wall for everyone to see? *Probably.* All night people have been in and out of The Creamsickle. They pat my head. They sit on my legs, because I'm taking up the whole couch. They hand me drags of their cigarettes.

Cruzer is here. She's been hanging out the last few days, because her girlfriend is in Philadelphia looking at grad schools. After the Cat Fight Club got out, a whole slew of people came back to the house with her, including Nicki, who knows Soda is at work so she can come by. Soda is still mad at her for toying with him.

Nicki pulls her drugs out of her purse. It's going to be a late night. I know I should be good and go to bed and get up early to job search, but it's gonna be so loud all night anyways so why should I try to sleep? Plus, nowhere is hiring! I have blanketed the neighborhood with my resume, but I never get any calls back.

Cruzer is talking about how they still can't find the hit-and-run driver who killed Goldy. The first thing Cruzer did when she came home was set up a Día de los Muertos shrine for Goldy in the living room. Nicki takes a drag off her cigarette as she stares at it, her eyes teary. "Darling, there are a million sad, sad things. There are so many bad, bad things," she says to no one in particular. Nicki looks beautiful when she is high. Her clear cat eyes get as wide as the moon. She starts talking about *The Gossip* show on Friday. I can't afford to go. "I need a job," I groan.

"I wish they were hiring right now at The Dildo Factory," Tiny says.

"How 'bout you come work at the Minxy?" Nicki suggests with a giggle. She's referring to the strip club where she works, this peepshow where she says a bunch of rocker chicks and dykes work. I had heard her suggest this stripper business before to Dixie. I bet Nicki gets money or something for recruiting new girls since she's always so eager to lasso them in. She used to make Dixie drool by telling her how much money she could make, but in the end Dixie always backed down because she pretends she's a good Southern girl, too sweet for that sort of work.

"That would be so cute if we worked together," Nicki squeals.

"Georgie a stripper? *Ha ha*, yeah right." Cruzer starts laughing hysterically, which pisses me off.

"What, you don't think I can be a stripper?" I throw my hands up in the air toward her. She's sitting on the other side of the room.

"You can't even walk in heels. Remember last year when your sister got married and you nearly ate it like ten times? You have like zero balance and you're completely accident prone," Cruzer points out.

"Yeah right. Georgie can skate better than any girl I know," Dixie says.

"That's 'cause she's a daredevil, but check it out, she crashes just as many tricks as she lands."

I groan. Why are they talking about me like I'm not in the room? "Dude! How fucking hard could it be? Harder than mopping up junkie blood piss from the cafe floor?"

Nicki starts talking about how I don't even have to be all femmed-out to work with her. "There was this tough andro girl who just worked there for a bit. Man, I was hot for her but I think she took off to South America with her girlfriend. *Mmmm*, Charlie was her name. Had all the dancing girls lusting after her."

Cello, who I used to fuck, says, "I know you have a banging

body under all those baggy clothes."

"Yeah, you can't hide that ass," Dixie says.

"I don't know where it came from," I say referring to the ass that came out of nowhere on my angular body in the last year.

"It must be that God is trying to tell you something, either you just got them curves to make some babies or you got 'em to make some ass-shakin' money," Dixie says. Her southern accent sometimes makes her sentences sound like country songs.

"I'll take the bills please," I say.

"I have some old stripper shoes. I'm gonna bring them over here and you can practice in them," Nicki says.

"Ha! Do you ladies even know how Georgie got her name?" Cruzer asks.

*"Georgie Porgie puddin' pie, kissed the girls and made them cry,"* Nicki sings and runs her hand along my leg till it comes to a stop in my lap.

"Nah, Nah," Cruzer says. "None of that shit. That's a song for a chubby kid, like me. The real shit is that when little Georgette was a kid, her sister got this book from the library called *Georgie Grub* about this kid who refused to take a shower so his mom threw him out of the house, so her sisters started to call her that all the time. They would sing to her, *"Georgie Grub won't get in the tub."*

"No way," Nicki says. "That's so cute."

"It's not true." I glare at Cruzer. "My family started calling me Georgie when I was, like, three because I had a mullet and refused to wear dresses."

"Ima gonna find that book and show you guys." Cruzer grins, licking the edge of the joint she's rolling, "Anyways, you babes are not turning Georgie into a girl. She's my best friend because she doesn't cry or whine like girls do," Cruzer says. "She doesn't give a fuck, like me."

"Fuck you! You're such a misogynist, Cruzer," Dixie shouts. "You wonder why Soda gets *way* more ass than you. Well, she has charm and chivalry."

Cruzer shrugs.

"Spoiled trust fund brat," Dixie calls her. She knows Cruzer hates that.

"Dog kidnapper," Cruzer shoots back.

"You fuckin' gave me that dog!" Dixie hisses. "You stole it from your cracked out girlfriend who went to rehab, remember? The only kind of girl who will date you!"

"Oh wow, you guys have so much sexual tension," Nicki sighs.

Dixie stands up. "Cello let's go."

"I should go, too, before Soda gets here," Nicki says. She searches the couch cushions for her small gold purse.

"Too much drama lately," I groan. I find a direct link to the amount of coke everyone is doing to how dramatic they all are being. I need a job so I can get away from this bullshit.

Cruzer smiles after the girls have left. "More for us." She passes me the freshly rolled joint. It's three thirty in the morning, time to chill out. After we're stoned, Cruzer starts going off on this crazy tangent about nail polish. "Georgie, whatever you do don't let those babes paint your nails. Dixie was always trying to practice that shit on me when she was in beauty school and I personally think it's very rude to fuck a girl with a nail polished hand. I mean, that stuff could chip off inside someone or something."

She's making me laugh hysterically. "Where do you come up with this shit?"

By the time Soda comes home from work I'm so relieved because Cruzer has been talking about Topsy for twenty minutes while I stare off into space, bored and stoned. Hopefully, Soda will shut her up. But instead, after Cruzer tells Soda about how "all the babes had drama," she announces, "If Topsy moves to Philadelphia I'm gonna have to go with her."

"I can't handle your shit anymore!" Soda stalks off and slams the door to his room.

"You're really clearing the room tonight Cruz-y." I pull myself up from the couch to get ready for bed.

In the bathroom, after brushing my teeth I stand in front of the full-length mirror for way too long. I'm probably just stoned. I lift up my small men's undershirt and check out my body. I suck in and puff out my chest. I try a hip sway. I start to laugh, trying to imagine *Georgie Grub*, a stripper.

# Chapter 14

I'm anxiously waiting for the clock to turn to midnight because at that precise moment my food stamps card will be activated and Soda is going to drive me to Cala Foods so we can get pork chops. I'd wanted to get steaks because that seemed more celebratory but Soda invited The Doc who is finally back in town. The Doc has an arsenal of witty one-liners but one of Soda's favorites is, *Life is just a bowl of pork chops.* The Doc used that one just the other day when we stopped by the corners. He told us a long rambling story, explaining where he'd been, all about this woman who he described as a *wild gypsy witch* who kidnapped him and made him marry her in Vegas. *Put a spell on me!* he hissed as he shook an orange bottle of pills at us, making a noise like a rattlesnake tail.

This girl Kimi is also coming to the pork chops party. I've been forcing myself to have a crush on her, to distract me from thinking about Mia. I met Kimi a few weeks ago when I had a sugar high, because I had just wrestled Soda in a huge swimming pool of cherry Jell-O at a Queer Jell-O Wrestling contest. Soda won, he body slammed me pretty quick into the match, probably because I'm so poor lately that I'm malnourished. Everyone thought I won though because this kid Coby was the referee and she was so stoned that she got confused on the winner, and raised my hand after the match instead of Soda's, so even though the crowd was confused they still cheered me. Then I met Kimi. She was trying to say something to me about the match and then the crowd shoved me at her, and her white shirt got splattered in red splotches. *Shit. Sorry.* I felt bad so I took her into the bathroom to dunk the side of her shirt in the sink. She was super cute, wearing this outfit that was so coordinated and tiny that it looked like she stole it off a doll. I felt extra bad for ruining it. *It's okay I make all my own clothes. I never wear the same outfit twice*, she insisted. But, then out on the patio we bonded over how poor and jobless we both were. She had just finished fashion school and was stubbornly refusing to accept that the only job she could get was in retail. We pinky-swore that we would go to the food stamps office together. I had been looking so hard for a job every day that I kept on not getting my shit together to go there.

Cruzer told me to go get food stamps back when I first lost my job. At first I argued with her. "You told me yourself you got those so easy that time 'cause you're brown!"

"You could at least try! I mean you have no money to eat!"

My stomach growled in response.

Kimi was good motivation. At the wrestling event we promised each other we would bike there at eight a.m. on Monday and sure enough she was ringing my buzzer way too early in the morning, and I was cursing myself that I made any promises.

At the food stamps building on Mission and Third she let me listen on one of her headphones as we sat in those little plastic chairs for hours and hours and waited for our names to be called. I kept hearing everyone's full names read over the loud speaker and felt embarrassed that they were going to call my long girly name in front of Kimi.

We both had to come back the next day to bring back additional paperwork, bank statements that read, *I'm broke*, and proof of bills. "How 'bout I just sleep over at your house so that we both wake up in time for the appointments? Since your house is closer?" Kimi suggested.

By the third date I had to consider breaking it off with Kimi since I got food stamps, but she got denied. I mean, I was that broke. I didn't even want to invite her to the pork chops party, but then we stopped by happy hour at The Vine and there she was, sipping on a Guinness like people do when they are having beer for dinner.

I felt guilty. But could I be a nice person when I was starving? It wasn't my fault that Kimi didn't qualify. I had been sure she would since the Cruzer "cause I'm brown they practically handed me SSI" theory, and Kimi was Asian, didn't that give her a lead over me? I guess not because she was still considered a student, which made her not qualify. How weird. Students had to starve. What a deterrent to going back to school.

Smoking with Dixie outside of The Vine, she lectured me, said that going through the whole process with Kimi was similar to buying a lottery ticket with someone and there was mandatory prize sharing involved if I was a good person. So, I couldn't break up with her. Instead, I went back inside and invited her over for pork chops at midnight. "That's when the card gets activated. Soda is taking me to Cala so we can buy a feast."

After eating the delicious dinner Soda and I cooked Kimi leaves because she has a job interview early in the morning, but I wonder if The Doc was creeping her out. He kept joking with her about sitting on his lap. When I come back in the living room from walking her downstairs Soda laughs at me. "Yo, that girl just played you, she ate your pork chops and then took off before putting out."

I shrug. "I should break it off with her, huh? I'm so not even ready to date someone."

"Watch out she might be a gypsy witch," The Doc says in complete seriousness.

I max out the food stamps card real quick and decide it's partially Kimi's fault. And also, whenever I buy a bunch of groceries, all the scrounges who regularly hang around The Creamsickle just eat them all. Tiny stays over a lot and I let her eat my food because she makes us breakfast every morning. I miss Cruzer making breakfast. It was her specialty to make the whole house eggs, beans and tortillas that she got for cheap at the corner market. Or on special mornings she would make us huevos rancheros or chilaquiles.

Crazy Tiny only eats the bacon when she makes us breakfast. She never eats real food. The other day I watched her scarf down two pieces of bacon and guzzle a Sparks for breakfast and I asked her where she gets her protein and she said, "What's protein?" I couldn't tell if she was joking. She also never drinks water, just Sparks, and other bright and toxically colored energy drinks. As a result, she always has a perma orange mouth like she's a puppet on *The Muppet Show*. But, it's okay with me to feed Tiny because we hang out all day since she's jobless too. We skate around and stop at Internet cafes to see if anyone has emailed us about jobs. No one ever has. What makes me real mad is that Topsy and Soda's stupid dates eat my food. Like tonight, I go in the kitchen and see Nicki, who is so off and on with Soda it's hard to keep track, standing in the kitchen in lacy underwear and heels in front of the open fridge munching on my cheese slices.

I bitch at her and she says, "What you get it for free anyways. What? You mean we can't *all* get hooked up by the government?"

"I had to wait in line for like two days for those cheese slices," I say.

She ignores me and grabs some extra slices before clicking out of the kitchen.

"I don't have a job!" I yell at her hot ass bouncing back down the hall to Soda's room.

"You could have one! Call the Peepshow, duh!" she yells back at me. I hear her giggle as she shuts Soda's door.

A few nights later I'm bummed because everyone is at *The Gossip* show except me because I'm too broke. Even Kimi went because she caved in and realized she wasn't going to become a famous designer overnight and was now folding T-shirts at a trendy clothing store. Perfect timing now that she already had helped eat all my government aid.

I try to play video games by myself and get bored. Not having a job gets so boring after a while. My stomach growls. I take another sip off my beer. I'm living off beer calories. I finish that beer and then decide to drink Nicki's expensive white wine that she left in the fridge. Sweet revenge.

I sit on the couch and stare at Napoleon who stares at me back until we both get bored with staring at each other. The house is so quiet it's kind of scary. I should turn on a *Gossip* CD load and have a private dance party. No, that would just be more depressing.

I look over at Nicki's stripper shoes that have been sitting in the corner of the living room for nearly a month. They're half under the couch so they're about to disappear permanently, to the place where the elusive gold dumbbells hide. I've been eying the shoes a lot lately, checking them out. I'll be trying to beat *Grand Theft Auto* and I'll suddenly notice how they're sitting there, taunting me, like they're flashing slot machine money signs in my face.

I decide it's time to take the shoes on a romantic stroll around the coffee table. I pick them up and study them. They look like big plastic glowing spaceships, with four inches of clear glittery platform and a long pointy thing jutting off the back that looks like a mini stripper pole. It looks like an extra little stripper pole for a Barbie doll or something. I plop down on the floor, tug off my red scroungy skate shoes, and twist the sparkly straps of the moon shoes up and around my ankles. When I hook the strap tight I feel secure in the foot-high shoes. I feel so confident that I stand straight up and put all my weight onto them.

*Bam*, my ankle snaps down onto the hard wood floor.

*Ouch.*

Apparently the flimsy straps are not very supportive! It's easy to sway right off the slippery suckers. And how *loud* the crazy shoes are. *Clack, clack, clack* they chatter on as I walk in circles around the table with stiff robot steps that can't possibly look sexy. Napoleon watches me with his ears cocked to one side.

"Don't judge, Naps, if I can do tricks on a board then I can walk in these stupid heels!"

For real though, I feel like I'm riding Switch, doing the opposite of what comes natural, but trying to make it look like cake.

When Tiny and Soda come home from the show later I put the shoes back on so I can show them my new moves. I'm doing fine till I get a little carried away twirling around, and I guess Tiny threw her knit cap on the floor when she walked in, because it gets caught on Barbie's li'l stripper pole, and I lose my balance.

Soda tries to catch my arm before I fall, but I'm all wine and platform shoes, so I hit the floor so hard The Creamsickle shakes. I lie on my back and stare at the cracking plaster ceiling. Soda stands over me grinning. "Now we can confirm to Nicki that you're not stripper material."

"Yeah," I moan. "It's official."

"That's good because I was worried that I would be attracted to you as a femme, and that would be weird."

"Don't lie. You would love that." I grin up at him. I sit up and rub the spot on my ass that I know will soon be a huge bruise.

The next morning I wake up in my bed with all my clothes on. Soda is sleeping in his boxers and binder next to me. He stayed up super late doing drugs with Tiny and then crawled into bed when the light started coming through the window shade slats and mumbled, "Sleep," and I helped him tug off his pants. Then he curled back into the covers.

I've got my period.

I hate life. I get up and search the house for a tampon because I have no money to buy some and then resort to collecting change from under the couch cushions, so maybe I can at least start saving up. The house is so dirty with spilled beer, leftover drugs, and weed on the table. Tiny is passed out on Cruzer's couch. I figure she might have a tampon but she doesn't wake up, even when I throw pennies at her head from across the room.

I realize I may need the pennies for my tampon mission so I go over and collect them back from her hair. I lean over her and turn on the stereo. I turn it up way loud, but Tiny still doesn't wake up. I look out the window that teeters over the entire city. There's a fluke sun in the wintriness, a bizarre glow in the blue-sky breeze that blows the curtains back from the window. I should get out of the house. There are the drugs still on the table that I don't want to reach for. I could see myself resorting to doing drugs for breakfast, because I'm that bored and depressed. I call Kimi and see if she wants to go to the park. Mostly I just want to go by her house, try and bum a tampon off her, or her roommates.

It's hot for January, a baking-on-the-Mission-sidewalk kind of day, that makes me strip off my layers of hoody and thermal. I'm dizzy and there's a hill to Kimi's house, so by the time I get halfway up it, I feel like dying, hung-over, with blood probably trickling down my leg. Shit, I think of how pathetic I have become. I think about how money could solve at least a fraction of my problems. I sit down on Kimi's porch, my ass hurting from my crash landing last night.

I call up Knockout Nicki. "Hey babes, what exactly do I have to do to learn how to strip?"

"Look, why don't you just go there and check it out. See what it's about. Just don't come when I'm working because all your hard work of pretending like you don't want to fuck me for all these years will be ruined."

A few nights later Soda and I are at a bar drinking away Valentine's Day. We're both depressed about the holiday so we decided to have a hater date. I keep thinking about how one year ago I was fucking Mia in the windowsill of The Creamsickle, with both our hearts about to fall over the ledge. *Fuck girls*. Mia is probably on a romantic date with some new lover. Kimi has to work since she works at a fancy restaurant with a Valentine's event, and Nicki told Soda at the last minute that she was hanging out with her femme date. "It makes sense that Nasty Nicki would date that girl. She totally looks like her twin sister or something and Nicki is so vain that she probably feels like she's fucking herself," Soda grumbles.

"For sure," I agree. But is it wrong that I would give up my vintage skate deck collection to watch those two fuck?

It dawns on me that Nicki is on a date so she's not at work. We can go to her club! A perfect anti-Valentine's mission: strip clubs and a bottle of whiskey. I suggest this to Soda and less than five minutes later we're out on the street hailing down a cab to take us to North Beach.

The window slides up in the small booth Soda and I squeezed into and three seconds later my face is pressed up to the glass like a cat staring into a fishbowl. I see a cure for my lovesick heart. She's across the stage. She's stunning, wearing nothing but a black pageboy wig, and an old-school studded belt hanging around her waist. Three other naked girls all crawl or shimmy over cooing at us and all I think is that they're blocking me from looking at my future ex-wife. All I can see is *her*. "Only one guy to a booth," says a redheaded stripper who has been smiling into our window.

"Hot they think were real guys," Soda whispers excitedly.

"Are you two even old enough to be in here?"

We both nod. Yes. Yes. Promise.

"Okay, well only one guy to a Box unless you kids are on a Valentine's date and you want to make out for us!"

Soda grins at me. We both reach for the whiskey at the same time and touch hands instead, which makes us laugh nervously. "We're waiting!" the girls coo.

I must be drunk because I grab Soda by his black neck handkerchief and dive in. His kiss is hard and warm like the first sip of whiskey after a dry spell. When I pull away I can still smell him, mixed in with the dark musty smell of the cum-and-bleach infused Box floor. I remember that the girls are watching and I pull away from the intense eye lock I've got going on with Soda.

"Oooooh." The girls are all peering into the Box on their hands and knees, cooing and giggling at our make-out. One has her mouth gaping open like a wide-eyed fish. One looks like a girl I've seen at The Vine once or twice, like possibly she is wearing that fake-looking blond wig over her short dreads. Another looks oddly like Cruzer's first girlfriend from art school. I heard she'd moved to New York years ago. The one in the pageboy wig has joined them so that the rest of the room is empty of live nude girls, since they're all only in front of our window.

The girls have started whispering to each other.

"Is this how you *boys* spend Valentine's Day?" The girl with the blond wig says *boys* like she knows we're queers. I mean hadn't Nicki said that tons of dykes worked with her? I can't believe The Crew's never been here before. It's like the final frontier.

Soda is still wide-eyed, checking out all the T&A inches away from our faces. I take another swig off the whiskey and set our brown-bagged bottle down on the screen ledge. "Ohh. I want some of that," pageboy wig coos.

I pretend to try to pass the bottle through the glass. "Pesky glass here." I grin. If there weren't glass between this girl and me we would be getting married. First, I would track down and divorce crazy Zeena and then I would marry this gorgeous stripper. "What's your name?" I ask, as if that will reveal anything real about her.

"Page. You can visit me in the Fantasy Talk Box in an hour."

"I don't got an hour. How 'bout now?"

She giggles.

Soda sits down on the booth bench, which I worry isn't very sanitary. He puts his hand on the bulge of his jeans. He usually wears a soft pack but tonight it looks like he's packing something bigger. He bought that bendable dick that Luc had a few months ago. He let me try it on over my Jockeys the day he brought it home from Tiny's work. I wore it around his room for a while. I suddenly could tell why guys were always grabbing their dicks. I wanted to grab it all the time. It was in the most perfect reachable spot, so easy to hold, like a joystick or something. "Hey I want to jack off in here for real," Soda says. "Like with my cock. I want pretend I'm like a real regular customer, a married dude, or business guy coming in here after work. Can you go get your own booth? Because married dudes wouldn't bring their bro friend in and that kinda ruins my fantasy."

"Okay." I shrug. I'm a little hurt that Soda doesn't want to play married dude circle jerk but, whatever. "That's hot," I say, "but are you gonna steal my girlfriend?"

"Naw, I like the one with the cherries on her stockings."

I look onto the window for a last glimpse at my favorite, and she isn't on the stage anymore. *Bummer!*

"Meet me later in Number thirteen," Soda says before I leave him. That's the video booth that we ducked into when we first got to the Minxy and we couldn't figure out which of the gazillion numbered doors were connected to the Live Nude Girls Stage. We realized it was a video booth so we tried to figure out if we could watch the Paris Hilton porn, but then got bummed that the booth was already programmed to certain porn, so we ducked out to search for the real girls.

I wander around the dark hall for a minute wondering if I want to go back to the live booths, even though my favorite is gone. I start to get sort of creeped out by the guys straggling around the hall looking at me like they know that underneath all my layers of clothes I'm a girl, like they can smell some secret girl scent that I'm not even aware I exude. There's also this girl on a platform, in a red-lit box down the hall, who starts gesturing at me to come into her booth. I get nervous. I can see how this place is a porn labyrinth of whirling and buzzing windows and doors that make the dudes feel like they are in a confused daze and can only follow the direction where their hard dicks point.

I see the number thirteen with the green light on underneath and it's like a familiar beacon in a maze of halls and doors. I duck in and shut the door hard behind me. The booth is smaller than my bedroom closet. It's like a confessional, painted all shiny black, even the bench. I search my pockets for some more dollars, but I've only got a five-dollar bill. I think it might be my cab fare home that I'm about to feed into the bill collector. But, I'm not going to sit in the creepy coffin without the porn on so I give up my money. A dude comes on the screen with a huge dick that's getting sucked by one of those ugly blond fake porn-star looking girls. The camera is aimed down at her face, and she is looking right up into the screen with widened blue eyes. "I love to suck your cock," she says with her mouth full.

At first I'm just grossed out by the whole thing, the dick, the busted girl, and I want my money back. Then I start to get creeped out at how the girl is looking up, right at me. It feels like she is staring up at me because she is in between *my* legs, sucking *my* dick. *Whoa*, I can't help but start to get turned on. *Duh*, I'm sure that's the point of the porn. I even wish I had a dick like Soda's to play with. I wonder if I could cum like he can, with just the friction of the base of the cock rubbing my junk. I consider sticking my hands in my pants and rubbing one out, but I wonder if I could get pregnant just by sitting on the bench. I stay standing up and put my leg up on the bench, so I can get into my jeans a little bit.

Click. The doorknob turns.

I freeze. I think I might have a heart attack the way my heart is wailing against my ribcage. I yank my hands off the fly of my jeans just as the door comes creeping open. I can't believe I didn't lock the fucking door! *Dummy!* Pageboy wig comes in the booth and locks the door for me. "Your friend told me you wanted to meet me in here." She glances down at my unbuttoned pants.

*Thank you Jesus*, I think. "Ya, uh I don't have any money," I stutter

"Ha silly. It's not like that." She laughs hard. "I just want to make out with some cute girls on Valentine's Day but I'm stuck here at work! Nothing wrong with that huh? But quick I'm on my ten-minute break." She moves closer to me. I wish it weren't so dark in the black-walled room that I can only see the shadow of all her half-naked hotness. "Ten minutes and back to stage, looking pretty," she singsongs. She pushes me back on the booth, and I don't even care anymore about accidental pregnancy. I would deliver triplets in order to make out with this girl.

Page straddles me in her black silk kimono. She tastes like whiskey. I wonder if she just made out with Soda. *That snake.* The camera changes position on the porn so more light comes into the room and flickers over Page's face. I kiss her neck and she moans softly. She presses her entire body against mine and grinds her sequined booty-short-clad ass against my crotch.

How did my life all of a sudden get so good? I run my hands up and down Page's body as she bounces on my lap. She puts her hand on the crotch of my jeans. I get the feeling she thinks I'm packing like Soda. *Damn-it.* I put my hand there instead and rub the tight seam of the glittery shorts against her pussy.

The porn star girl moans on the screen behind Page's

wig. I see she's back to deep throating on the dick. "God this shit is so weird," Page says, turning and glancing at the video. "Sometimes, guys come into The fantasy Box and say, 'Hey will you stick your dildo in your mouth and say, I love to suck cock?' I mean they want to hear you choke on the words. And you sound like a fuckin' idiot, like you're saying, I Wuv to Wuck Wock." Page puts her hand in her mouth and demonstrates it to me. She laughs.

*Shoot.* Suddenly I feel bad for objectifying her. I take my hands off her body. In response Page leans in to kiss me and grinds her body harder on my lap. She shifts so her leg is now in between my legs and her tongue swims on mine. My crotch feels like it's about to explode.

But a loud buzzing noise explodes instead, and a red light flashes as the video screen goes black. My money has run out. "Time's up," Page laughs. She kisses me again, real quick, and then she's gone. I sit back, alone in the empty booth, staring at the black screen, and listening to the extra loud beating of my heart. I wonder if I just imagined the last five minutes. An image of Soda stroking his cock down the hall pops into my head and once again I unbutton my pants.

When I duck my head out of the booth, I sheepishly look down the empty hall at the surveillance camera above that seems to be pointed right at me. Can I get in trouble for the hands-on freebie? I wonder. I find Soda around the corner of the lobby, leaning over the front counter where the door guy is sitting reading a comic book. The girl who was wearing the cherry tights on stage, who looks like Cruzer's ex, is sitting on the stool next to him smoking a cigarette. When I'm up close to her I see it definitely is her. How could I forget the face of the crying girl in nearly two dozen huge photographs?

"This is Cherry," Soda says. And I want to say, *no* that is Bitchy Brenda, which was what Cruzer and I nicknamed her, but I keep my mouth shut.

"Hey Georgie." Cherry sucks on her cigarette all casual, as if it hasn't been three years since we've seen each other. Come to think of it, I haven't seen her since she threw all of Cruzer's stuff out on the street in front of the studio they shared downtown, around the corner from the fancy art school they both went to. "Soda and I were just discussing the incredible flow of our names combined." Cherry exhales.

"Yeah like how cute would our answering machine message be?" Soda says.

I nearly gag. They're so flirting and it's so not okay.

"Did Page show you a good time? She's so wild. Practically gets herself fired all the time."

I'm glad Cherry is changing the subject to something more crotch-warming. "Yeah. I'm in love with this place."

"Right. Soda just told me you want to work here. We're always desperate for new girls. I'm sort of a boss, technically a Mademoiselle not Madam, but whatever. How 'bout I write your name down for the amateur night in a few weeks and you can either show up, or not."

"Okay. But I don't think this is my line of work. But I'll try to come." I tug Soda's jacket towards the door because I don't like how he is grinning ridiculously at Bitchy Brenda. "I'll see you Friday night?" he says to her as we leave the club.

*What?* Did Soda invite her to Tiny's friend's party on Friday night? Not good.

In the cab I tell Soda that Cherry is off limits. "That's Cruzer's ex and I can't believe that by some bizarre circumstance you have never met her. But she is crazy and Cruzer would not like it, at all."

"That was soooo long ago. That girl is banging hot."

I groan. I drop it because Cherry probably won't come to the party anyways since she's obviously been hiding out all these years. Plus, I would rather tell Soda every single detail about Page grinding her pussy into my lap in the video booth.

By the time the cab pulls onto our street Soda and I have decided that we'd just had the best Valentine's ever, borderline the best night this year since it's sucked so bad so far.

"So you gonna audition now or what?" Soda teases. We drunkenly wobble up the windy Creamsickle stairs.

"Hell yeah. I'll become a stripper if I get to work with Page!

It can't be that hard."

"It sounds easier than skating off a roof for a girl." Soda laughs. "You just gotta shave your hairy legs and learn how to work a pole."

"Shave my legs?" I groan. "Aw, man, I'd rather jump off a roof."

That next week I start practicing wearing the stripper shoes all the time. Whenever I strap them on, I think about Page's hot red platform heels and I get turned on. Sometimes I don't even get to the practicing walking part because I fall back on my bed and rub one out instead.

After I accomplish walking and dancing in the shoes, I decide I should probably get comfortable in them around others, so I even try casually leaning around my kitchen and having conversations with Tiny, or whoever is at the house. I also think up other challenges, like doing pull-ups in the stripper shoes, and jumping down from the bar and practicing landing steady in them. Or, cleaning, so I have something to distract me from the shoes and make me act instinctual in them.

One day when no one is home I rock out to *Motley Crue* and dance around the kitchen while I sweep the floor in the platforms. Shelby, who I guess came home stealth-style, suddenly pops her head in the room. I'm so surprised that I jump like three feet and still land gracefully. I'm so excited about my dexterity in the shoes that I don't even care that Shelby is standing in the doorway looking at me with her mouth falling open. It's questionable as to whether or not she's more shocked about me wearing stripper shoes or that I'm actually cleaning our slummy house, which no one who lives here does.

I can't wait to impress Nicki with my lunging abilities. I wish she had just seen that jump! She would say, "Look how you can dart through the kitchen and can even be taken by surprise and miraculously stay standing tall in those four-inch heels! You're a natural born stripper, Georgie!"

Monday night I meet up with Cruzer for some pool at The Vine and when we're smoking out front Nicki comes up to us.

She's leaving with a bunch of hot girls who are standing near the street looking for a cab, one of them being her femme twin who she is juggling with Soda. Everyone has been talking about them lately, how they've been making out everywhere and causing feet traffic jams on dance floors all week long.

"I want to do your makeup tomorrow night," Nicki says to me. "I'm dying to."

"I dunno if I'm even gonna go to the audition." I shrug, because I haven't convinced myself yet, and plus Cruzer is listening. I'd mentioned the whole stripper career idea earlier and she had a field day teasing me.

"Sooo? *We* still want you to come over tomorrow night," Nicki coos. "Puh-lease?"

"Maybe." I can feel my cheeks turning red. Nicki is now leaning close to my face and squinting at it like it's a book she is trying to read in the dark. "I know just the colors I want to use on you," she purrs.

A cab pulls up to the curb, and Nicki and the hot girls pile in as Cruzer and I watch them and practically drool. One girl has a skirt so short she flashes us her panties. "Maybe this stripper thing is a good idea after all," Cruzer says wide-eyed. "Like what if those hot chicks are your future co-workers?"

Nicki lives in a tiny one-bedroom apartment with a balcony that she tells me makes the smallness of the place worth it because she likes to sunbathe nude. Her floor is covered with heels, makeup, wigs and sparkly things. There are also girls everywhere. "Everyone heard I was gonna give you a makeover, so they all begged to come watch," Nicki says. "I guess it will be like a slumber party."

Nicki's on-and-off-again sidekick (depending on if they hated each other or not because they're sisters), Veronica, is mixing drinks in the kitchen. Man, I love lesbian sisters. The only thing better is lesbian twins and those aren't as rare as you might think. Cello is reading a fashion magazine on Nicki's pink bed, and two of the girls who tell me their names are Lexy and Kitten are sitting cross-legged on the floor painting each other's nails. Full-on femme slumber party! I can't wait to tell Cruzer and Soda all about crashing one. They'll be so jealous.

Nicki is rigging up a bunch of bright lights because she told me while we were climbing her apartment's stairs that she wanted to videotape me getting madeup. It turned out that getting to film, as she put it, a "butch" in lipstick would be excellent for a project she was doing for her Gender and Sexuality Studies course. She said the theme was roughly about femme identity. "But, who is going to see it?" I protested.

"Just my professors and classmates. How're you gonna be a stripper if you don't even want to be videotaped with lipstick on?" she teased.

By the time Veronica hands me my third fancy mixed drink I get over the being filmed thing, even though the bright white light that's rigged up to shine right on my face is terribly annoying. The girls are in a semi-circle around me. They keep pinching my cheeks and holding colored sticks and tubes up to my face. I feel like I am fifteen again, when for at least a year my fashion magazine-obsessed sisters would try to corner me and make me give a fuck about my greasy hair and bushy eyebrows. That was before they gave up and just stuck to calling me mean names instead.

Of course, the first thing Nicki does is pluck my eyebrows. I hate that shit. I've had ex-girlfriends pluck them before. You can tell they get some sort of feeling of satisfaction from it. I don't want to sound like a baby, but I would rather take a dive off my skateboard than have those little tweezers fly at my eyes repeatedly like a stinging bee. But, what makes the experience almost pleasant this time is Nicki's sweet watermelon breath warm on my cheek, and how Veronica keeps refilling my gin and tonic, and Lexy is holding my hand, getting ready to paint my nails.

"You have a totally awesome makeup face, big eyelids and sharp cheekbones." Nicki starts smearing things onto my skin. "If you become a Minxy we will take you to Sephora."

"What's that?"

"It's a makeup paradise," Veronica sighs. Her eyes grow huge. "I hate it there because I want *everything*!"

"You're gonna see how much we pay to look hot!" Lexy says.

"Yeah, like see this eyeliner, it was like twenty bucks," Nicki wags a small pencil in my face.

"What? Can't you just use a colored pencil?" This makes all the girls crack up hysterically. I start to imagine all the easy ways I could steal a little pencil like that, or an inch-sized tube of lipstick. I stopped shoplifting years ago after the habit got completely out of control, but maybe this job was going to require some new forms of consumer ingenuity.

"You're starting to look hella pretty. But it still feels like I am putting makeup on my little brother." Nicki laughs.

A few minutes later I look in her little mirror and I decide I look more like a drag queen than one of the girls. I have to back up from the mirror because it's hard to get used to all the colors popping from my cartoon-looking face. Nicki takes the mirror from me and starts tugging a piece of my hair around a curling iron. Eventually, the girls exhaust every possible primping thing they could do to me. To my relief, they switch the focus to drinking and gossiping in front of the camera. Nicki asks questions like, *What does femme identity mean to you?*

I feel hot and sticky under the glaring light. I get my blue blocker sunglasses out of my backpack. "Why are you hiding your ingénue eyes," Nicki shrieks and snatches them off my face. She goes back to filming, but she's drunk so I question how good her film is going to come out. I entertain myself by checking out the hot pictures of Nicki and her sister in high school that are hanging around the room. High school pictures of my boi friends are always the opposite of cute, and so funny, their miserable butch faces under hairsprayed bangs and long braids, or pigtails.

My eyes itch, so reflex like, I rub them. My cheek tickles, so I scratch it. When I look down at my hands a minute later they have blue, red and white powdery streaks on them.

"What are you doing?" Nicki yells when she sees me inspecting the colors on my fingers. "I'm going to tie your hands behind your back."

I think she is joking but then she ducks under her bed and

emerges with a string of black rope. Obviously, she would have rope under her bed. It's of the variety that Tiny sells at the sex shop. All the girls giggle as Nicki really does tie my hands behind my back.

After that I just rub my cheeks on the folds of my hoody hood when they feel tickly. Since I'm tied up, I'm now hoping all the girls will leave, like on cue, so I can be all alone and tied up in Nicki's room, but they just sit around getting drunker and more loose-lipped with gossip. Especially, when Nicki shuts the camera off, and they start taking about my friends like they've forgotten I'm in the room.

"What should I do about Tiny?" Cello moans.

"Should I forget about Soda?" Nicki groans.

"Why do you guys like Soda anyways?" I pipe up. I slyly hide the fact that I've managed to wriggle one hand free when the girls weren't looking and now I can take gulps off my drink.

"Small hands," Nicki says without skipping a beat.

"The perfect size," Veronica readily agrees.

I forgot that Soda fucked both the sisters, on different occasions. That's so wild.

"I mean they just pop right in and it's like heaven between your legs," Nicki says.

"No one had ever fisted me until her," Veronica says, who is mostly straight.

"Ha, one thing about Soda though, is that I was always trying to play trashy with him, you know, trailer park girl or cowboy games in bed. But, he always wanted to play pirate or some shit! Like that's sexy! Oh you little bois and your Peter Pan complexes," Nicki giggles.

Then she says, "But man, that kid was hot as a concealed weapon." Nicki shakes her silky black hair and runs her finger over her lips.

"What about Cruzer?" I ask next.

"Hmmmf," Nicki says. "She's such an asshole, but she goes straight for the money. No fucking around. She'll eat pussy twenty-four/seven. It's got to be appreciated, that kind of dedication to pussy."

"Cruzer is a dickhead," Cello groans.

"Wait, are you gonna tell them all this shit?" Veronica cuts in.

"Yeah, 'cause if you double-cross your femmes we will get crazy on you," Nicki warns. Her feline eyes get mean and narrowed, like they so easily do.

I feel a little scared of the girls. They're a tough bunch of femmes with razor heels and sharp tongues. You had to be fierce girls to handle our neighborhood a lot of the time. So, I shut up. Also because that shit about Cruzer was kind of more than I needed to hear and when I'd tried to cover my ears I ended up just tugging the rope tighter instead.

The girls stop talking and decide to show me how to give a lap dance. Just when things are getting good, Kimi comes in the door. "Oh we've got a plaything!" she says when she sees me all madeup, and tied up. *Oh great*, this is totally going to ruin our barely started sex life. I have been refusing to let Kimi fuck me since day one. I can't get fucked till I'm over my exes. It's a pattern in my life that I'm coming to terms with, and here I am looking like a tied up little bottom, wearing lipstick to boot. It's weird that Kimi has even come over, because I thought she hated Nicki. Girls are so confusing. Most of the time when Nicki isn't around all the girls call her a whore, but now they're giggling into her lap.

Kimi is the one who eventually wipes the lipstick off for me. She does it because she wants to make out. I'm relieved that finally after all the abuse I get some action. I also decide that maybe if I stay over late enough the girls will start a game of spin the bottle or something. I mean, isn't that what girls do at slumber parties? That's how I made out with a good half of the cheerleading team at my suburban high school.

The next day I'm smoking a joint on the back porch with Soda and he wants to know all about the slumber party. "I got tied up by Nicki, and then Kimi came over, out of the blue, and cock blocked me from the other girls."

"Damn, maybe I should pretend to want to be a stripper and see how much ass it gets me!" Soda says.

"I really am dirt poor, dude."

"I know, I know. Hey, if you want to fuck Nicki, I don't care. I've always thought it might change your life and I'm not weird about that shit."

I wonder if Soda is just saying that to justify trying to get in Cruzer's ex's pants the other night at the Minxy.

"I dunno. I think Nicki is just obsessing over me so much right now because I'm a direct link to you, and she likes to make you jealous."

"Huh. Well I can't handle her games. I'm on the prowl for a new girlfriend, for sure. Maybe, a long-term one. Cruzer looks so happy and cozy lately it gets me jealous. You know what? I heard from Dixie that Cruzer might move to the East Coast if Topsy gets into school. She's probably too scared to tell us."

"Oh, she'll never leave," I say. "She loves it here. She thinks it's pussy paradise on earth. Plus she has never moved anywhere without me!"

I don't want to think about any possibility of Cruzer moving. I'm too stoned to trip out on sad shit like that.

"You should let me pluck your eyebrows. They're all crazy." I peer closely at Soda's face.

"What the fuck! You sound like one of my ex girlfriends. Go away."

On the subject of hair removal, last night Nicki told me that I should wax my bikini line before the audition. That seemed like a good idea because ever since seeing how naked the girls were at the Minxy, I've been stressing out, wondering whether my pussy could ever be ready for a big debut to the peepshow public. I think about how much I hated the eyebrow plucking. How I can even *think* about the bikini wax option?

Soda nudges me and passes me the joint. I trip out for a minute when I notice the girls are right. He has remarkably small hands.

The big party Friday night is at this house in the hills where some fag lives who Tiny works with, and some girls in a band. I see Kimi dancing in the living room when I walk in with Soda and Tiny. She comes over to me. "Here." She takes a plastic baggy from her pocket and pulls out a few brown stems. I swallow them down with a swig of beer. Kimi then spins away back to the dance floor. I'm glad because I can tell she's got a lot of crazy drug energy and I can't handle it. I'm already feeling anxiety about this party because I think there's a possibility one of the girls who lives here is Mia's new date.

I go out on the large back deck for a minute but there are so many people I get nervous so I duck back into the house and open one of the doors along the long hall. I don't know anyone in the first room so I move on to the second, then finally find my friends, Coby and Manno, sitting on a bed in the third room. "What's up dude?" Manno says when I come in the room and shut the door so the electronic beats from the DJ table fade away.

There's a laptop open on the floor and there are beautiful sounds coming out of it. It sounds so familiar. I sit on the floor next to the computer and feel sort of hypnotized. I lean back against the bed and close my eyes. "What are you listening to?" I ask even though I think I already know the answer.

"Mia's new CD. We're playing it on repeat."

"Oh." I wonder if this is Daisy's room, one of the girls who lives at the house who works at a recording studio that had once volunteered to help Mia record her new album back when we were dating. The girl that I've been speculating Mia is fucking. I mean, I don't have her new CD, so why does this person?

"Listen to it like this," Manno says. She puts a black and gold pair of padded headphones over my ears. The entire room is suddenly sucked out from around me, all the people talking, the dancing outside the door, the giggling girls, and a neighbor's dog howling at the party people. Mia's voice is all I hear, the nerve-tingling wails, and then a climatic crescendo when the energy of the song blows up like a huge balloon. A tightness in my chest that hasn't been around for weeks since the break-up comes back in full force. I can hear parts of lyrics that Mia has said to me, or said aloud when she was writing songs while sitting in my windowsill when we lived together. Every song has pieces of our love affair woven into it. She had bottled love, hurt, jealousy and sex into three-minute melodies.

*I wrote an entire album about you breaking my heart.*

I take the headphones off and stay sitting there listening to the music for what feels like a long time. Long enough for the mushrooms to kick in, at least. When I stare out the sliding glass doors of the room I can see a million different ways the buildings below are glowing, honey orange, with swimming colors flickering at the edges.

Halfway through the second time the CD plays on repeat I look up and there are a bunch of new people in the room hovering by the window, probably doing drugs. I feel like I should leave. The whole situation is weird, sitting in some random room listening to my ex's music that I'm no longer part of. What if my head is leaning back on the bed where she has sex with her new lover? *Ew.* I feel like I might puke up stems. I get up.

Manno is leaning forward with her head resting on the ball of her hands, knuckles up, one that reads *Stay* and the other that reads, *Gold*, a tattoo she got for Goldy right after she was killed. Her eyes are half-slits. Manno and Coby are always so fucked up that it's hard to ever speculate what they're on. Coby has her hand on Manno's lower back. Is she rubbing it or am I tripping? Sometimes I get thrown off for a second when the butch girls are fucking each other because they always do it undercover. But, the more I watch Coby and Manno interact I can tell they're so obviously fucking. It isn't just the mushrooms. They pass their cigarette back and forth with lingering gazes.

That's hot, I think. I want to go find Soda and whisper, "Coby and Manno are having a serious BROmance," in his ear. He would be so shocked, but into it at the same time. We both like to theorize that everyone is fucking each other. In secret, in the early dawn hours, butch on butch, femme on femme. "Let's All Love Each Other," as Zeena would put it.

I go out to the back balcony where I last saw Soda, plus I need some air to help me keep the stems down. I can't toss up the drugs because I need them to handle the night. Soda is sitting on the balcony talking about the apocalypse, which is a sure sign that he is wasted. He is describing his plan to build a ship, somewhat like Noah's Ark, when The End comes. He's convinced he will know how to build a pirate ship from scratch. Most of his friends get extremely bored with the *talky-apoc-y*, quick. They just stare into space and nod as he rambles on, like Tiny is doing right now. But Soda has a new excited audience because Cherry is sitting by him nodding eagerly. *Oh shit*. I didn't think she was going to show up. When I sit down, I hear how he's even broadened the subject to the best ways to commit suicide in an attempt to avoid the impending doom of the apocalypse.

"Bridge jumping," they both agree.

I want to cut in the conversation but the mushrooms seem to be making it hard to talk all of a sudden.

"I think it's fate that we met, Soda," Cherry says.

I almost choke on a piece of ice in my gin and tonic. Cherry and Soda are so not fate and if they were, Cruzer would kill them before they could ever confirm that theory. Soda scoots closer to Cherry. It looks like they're gonna kiss any second. I quickly debate some sort of cock blocking method, but this lasts only a second. I'm too high to mess with "fate" and I've completely given up on curtailing any drama in this city. What I've learned is that the queers are gonna fuck no matter what. No thought of ex-girlfriends' feelings, or best friends getting mad, ever actually stops anyone from getting messy with each other's hearts or ever stopped girls from doing it, even if the consequence might be a bitch slap or ruined friendship.

I turn around and head back into the safety of the inside.

Then, I see Mia.

She's sitting on a couch near the kitchen. I haven't seen her in nearly a month. She's cut her hair, shaved and undercut it on one side above her left ear. The other side is still long and almost to her shoulders. It looks insanely good. It makes my stomach lurch again. Now you can see her neck, my favorite part about her, with its caramel softness and that row of tiny freckle-like moles an inch above her collarbone, they always drove me crazy. I'd loved to pull her hair back and kiss them in the morning. Now, with her hair buzzed on one side the *whole* world can see her neck. Even the tattoo that used to be under her hair, old style script of a nickname her grandma used to call her, *Mouse*, is now half exposed. I want to run over to her and throw my hoody over her freckle-moles and tattoos. I want to pretend I'm still the only one who knows about them. I want to make her mine again. I can't stand the thought of someone else kissing her neck, knowing her nicknames and secrets. Probably the Daisy girl sitting next to her knows all of her.

I stumble back, away from the couch where Mia sits with her probable new lover. I look for Kimi. I find her spinning on the dance floor twirling colors from her hair. I tell her that I'm tripping out and want to go. "Oh I'll go too," she says.

*Shit*. I want her to just stay and dance. What the fuck! Are we girlfriends or something? Why are we leaving together? I'm so not ready to have a girlfriend. I remind myself that I need to break it off with Kimi. That it's okay to be alone. I know exactly what to say, "I'm not over my ex." Obviously. She can't argue that.

Do I know where her jacket is? Kimi is asking. She ducks her head out onto the balcony to look for it and when she pops back in, she hisses, "Oh my God! Soda is making out with Cherry!"

I grab Kimi's hand, go into the dancing room and toss around piles of jackets and bags. I finally find her jacket and grab her from the dance floor, shove through the sweaty mess of people to the door. "Cherry-Soda," Kimi slurs, all the way down the stairs. "Ha, ha, ha, ha, ha, ha! That's fucking funny! They could name their kids, Rum and Vodka. Mmmm, I love me a vodka soda, or a rum and cherry Coke, or how about a whiskey ginger with a cherry?" Kimi is tripping. She rambles on, her voice trailing off as I leave her in the stairwell and she stumbles after.

I feel super crazy today, skating away from the Triple P where I had Morning-After-The-Party-Breakfast with Dixie and Cello.

Everyone was talking about how Soda went home with Cherry and what Cruzer was going to do when she finds out. Cello thought she was going to give Soda a black eye. Not Soda's first black eye, for sure. Everyone was so caught up in that drama that I barely said a word about my crazy night. I just sank into the Triple P booth with my hoody pulled over my head, and the strings pulled tight so the sides of the fabric scrunched around my face. Everyone thought I was still tripping out from shrooming last night, so they kept just patting my head. In between all their gossiping, in the spaces between their sentences, I could hear the melodic beats of Mia's songs that had been pumped in my ear last night. The girls were going to Dolores Park, but I told them I wanted to skate. There was this tingling energy that was making my feet tap impatiently under the booth all through breakfast. I needed to skate out this anxiety. I glanced at my phone before slipping it into my back pocket. I was thinking maybe Kimi would call. Maybe I could change my mind about breaking it off with her, because I had no idea I would wake up feeling so alone.

Shrooming and walking down the Mission streets at three in the morning is not the best time to break up with someone. Kimi wanted to fuck one last time. She would try to push me into every doorway we passed. I couldn't even kiss her because her face kept looming at me in strange shapes. Who wants to fuck on mushrooms? I didn't. I wanted to get home and maybe attempt to jack off thinking about Mia's neck. I hate that I can't make myself like Kimi. I mean, there's nothing wrong with her. She's cute. She's a good fuck. She gives me drugs. Except for having to share my food stamps card with her, everything has been cool, and the best thing about her is that she's been distracting me from thinking about Mia.

I think about the hot girl at the strip club. I think about how I need to get a life. A hobby. A fucking *job*. Then I think about the Page girl some more. I stop skating and sit on my skateboard with my back up against the wall of the 24th Street mural.

I call up Nicki. "Hey, it's Georgie, uh I was wondering what I should do about my, you know?"

"Your what?" Nicki hollers. "I can't hear you sweetie."

There's this couple that has stopped right smack-dab in front of me, looking at some piece of paper, like a map, or something. I'm trying to stall so maybe they will walk away but they are stuck to the fucking concrete in front of me.

"Helllllloooow?"

"Uh yeah, I'm still here. I need to know what I should do

about my *pussy*?" I mumble into the phone.

Nicki laughs. "What do you mean?"

"I mean, it's *way* au naturelle." I can imagine Nicki biting her pretty red lips trapping a fit of giggles that she will let escape as soon as she hangs up, and relays the entire conversation to her cute sister. I can feel my ears start to get hot.

"Well, it sounds like you need some Pussy Confidence, Georgie-Porgie, if you want to land this job."

"Duh."

"Okay, well here's the deal. Get a pen."

I reach my hand back into my backpack's front pocket and grab my tagging Sharpie.

"Here's the address of this real cheap, cheap place on Russian Hill. I know how broke you are and how Soda has been your sugar daddy, so uncharacteristic of such an asshole, but anyway I'm sending you to the low budget stripper secret. This place is wild, it's only like ten bucks for a bikini wax, and that will for sure give you total Pussy Confidence which you totes need for your tryouts."

I write down the address she gives me on my forearm where I write important shit that I need to remember to do.

The next day Tiny and I are sitting on the outside benches of the hamburger joint on South Van Ness. "What are we doing today?" Tiny says, shoving french fries in her mouth.

"I'm thinking you could drive me to Russian Hill to get my pussy waxed," I announce.

Tiny looks worried and swallows hard. This really throws her off since usually we spend our days sitting around getting stoned or skating around the neighborhood lazily dropping off job applications. I'm also probably fucking with our bro-friend dynamic by mentioning my pussy because she looks like she wants to laugh, but upon seeing my serious face she sticks to just eating her fries.

I'm convinced getting my pussy waxed will be a sort of stripper portal that will make me feel like I can actually be a stripper. I have never waxed anything, ever. I don't even shave my legs or armpits, but secretly, there's another reason I want to get waxed. It's because ever since seeing Mia the other day I have been back on the dark train to numb town. Pain can be a great distraction from this kind of depressed existentialist attitude. After having my heart ripped out I'm pretty down with pain, like getting a huge goopy break-up tattoo, or being tossed extra-hard to the concrete daily on my skateboard. Getting hot wax slapped on my bikini line and the hair ripped out from the roots seems like a somewhat economical way to actually feel something today. Eventually, I talk Tiny into driving by telling her she will probably be able to hear me scream. "Plus there will be whiskey and Vicodin involved in this adventure," I add, to sweeten the deal.

First we go to the bar next door to *Nina's Nails and Wax* so I can prepare my body and mind by popping painkillers, and taking shots. I only have a few minutes to self-medicate because Tiny has to be somewhere in an hour, so unfortunately when I walk next door I'm still sober.

Nina, a stocky Asian woman with a no-nonsense face, takes me away into a small room made of plastic divider walls, like an office cubby. Tiny will for sure be able to hear my hair get ripped out since there isn't much between me and the waiting room where I left her to watch a row of hot babes getting pedicures.

Nina doesn't speak much English so the orders she gives me are in the form of short, sharp hand movements that mean things like, *Take your clothes off*, or *Lay on your back*. Suddenly I'm even more scared because I feel for sure, the way she is bossing me around, it's like she's an undercover dominatrix. Nina confirms this suspicion when she demands, "Spread 'em," while she waves her wax paddle at me.

I hope Tiny hasn't heard that.

After spreading 'em I don't hear anything at all. My whole body tingles with the pain and I start to feel like I'm floating. I decide I could be experiencing some sort of Bikini Wax Zen transcendence. My mouth is dry and my face is numb and tingly. Maybe I should have eaten more than just a milkshake earlier. It feels like I might pass out. Wait! I think, how awesome would it be to pass out? That way I could skip all the pain and wake up with a nice trim pussy, but then I think about how embarrassing it would be to pass out spread eagle! No way, especially in a room that's flimsy as an office cubicle. But, I don't pass out. I watch Nina working fast at ripping all my hair out. And she is really going for *all* of it, not just the bikini line. She keeps whipping her small paddle dripping orangey wax goo at my pussy and then yanking. Before I know it she's eliminated my entire muff in under three minutes. *Whoa.* Then she orders, "Turn over!"

Huh, what had I gotten into? Nicki didn't tell me about this part! I do what Nina says though, because she is wielding that hot wax whip and I feel too dazed to even question anything about this crazy situation. I flip over and Nina takes both of my hands and places one on each of my ass cheeks. "Spread 'em!" she orders.

I don't argue. I spread my ass cheeks and prepare for the hot wax to be slapped in.

"Too tight!" Nina says.

"Huh?"

"Too tight." Nina taps my ass cheek with her plastic gloves.

I realize my ass is clenched shut, just as tight as my eyes are as I'm silently praying that the whole process will be over with immediately, but I guess I'm so tense that Nina can't get her wax into place. I try to relax. I think about how Tiny is probably grinning ear-to-ear listening to the ripping noises. Afterwards, I slowly put my clothes back on, standing awkwardly due to my tingling crotch and butt. I feel stunned, transformed somehow by the experience.

In the car I joke about showing Tiny the results. She screeches, "Please, no!" I laugh. I'm feeling so proud of my new pussy or at least what I went through to get it that I want to show someone. I want to show off how tough I am that I had let some stranger drip hot wax in my goddamn ass and rip all my hair out! But it isn't like a new tattoo. I can't just show it to everyone.

Later I call Nicki, "You did not tell me they were gonna put hot wax in my ass!"

"What! You got a Brazilian? I said Bikini Wax not Brazilian!"

Nicki cracks up.

"How was I supposed to know? She didn't speak English!"

"Ha ha, they only spoke Brazzziiilllan, huh? The language of hoochie love!" She giggles some more. "Come over and show it to me."

"No way." I can feel my face turning red.

"Please," Nicki whispers all husky. I bet she is holding her old-fashioned pearly vintage telephone in one hand and a glass of white wine in the other. So hot.

"No," I say and hang up, cutting her off mid giggle. *Shit*. If I can't even handle the thought of showing my pussy to Nicki how am I going to show it to a room full of strippers and customers at the audition?

Cruzer offers to drive me to my Minxy audition in the truck since it's across town. I would go with Nicki but she has to work at her other job. I'm tired from staying up and partying last night so I get myself completely jacked up on coffee first.

I sit on the pink futon in the dressing room and jitter as I wait my turn. I'm completely naked except for Nicki's stripper shoes, because shoes only are the rules. I'm sitting next to two other naked stripper wannabes waiting for their turn to audition. Every ten minutes the Madams come out and call the next girl in line by her chosen dancer name, the one that would be theirs if they got hired. Earlier, back in the office, I had stared at the blank line on the thick application form that said, *Dancing Name* above it. I tapped my pen on the side of the paper for a few minutes. I was tapping it to the rhythm of the *Guns N' Roses* song that had come on the radio in Cruzer's truck. We'd blasted it loud and pretended to mosh.

*Dancing Name* _____

Tap, tap. Tap, tap.

I wrote down, *Axl Rose*.

I realize the excessive coffee was a terrible idea since it is making my nerves feel all twitchy. I fidget with my coffee cup. I jitter. I grind my teeth. I eye my jeans and baggy *Spitfire* T-shirt that are lying on the floor. I miss them desperately. They have never looked so good. I mean, everyone else is naked (from when I glanced around, before my eyes had became perma-glued to the lime green rug beneath my feet) and I should feel at one with them or something, but I feel extra-naked because of my super bare pussy. I cross my legs as tight as possible over my bald junk.

I think the girl who is sitting at the front of the couch is staring at me. "Hey, you're Georgie, huh?" a chirpy little voice comes from the staring girl. I look up and recognize her button nose and cupcake face. She's that girl in Santa Cruz who Cruzer had fucked the night I met Mia. She looks different from the last time I saw her, dancing on the empty diner tabletop. I mean, she's *only* wearing red cowboy boots right now, but her hair is different or something. I remember also that she's Mia's ex. *Fucking small world.* I hope she doesn't tell Mia she saw me here. If she hears that piece of gossip she'll think our break up caused me to have a mental breakdown.

"Oh hey," I mumble to the girl. "You live here now?"

"Yeah. Just moved a week ago. That's so interesting to run into you here."

I'm very aware of the interestingness of the situation. *Geez.* I cross my legs even tighter over my bare pussy and wait for the Madams to call my name.

"Dakota." The Madam in the cat-eye glasses comes into the room and Mia's ex pops up, and says excitedly, "Wish me luck."

Ten minutes later the Madam comes back and calls, Axl Rose. She doesn't seem to react to my name. *Whew.* When I had jotted that down I didn't think they were going to use it straightaway like that. If I get the job I'll think up a more serious stripper name. This girl in the dressing room earlier introduced herself as Panacea. *What's that mean? Greek Goddess of healing.*

*Oh.*

I'm so busy panicking about my shallow stripper name that I barely even notice that I've already skittishly balanced on Nicki's moon shoes all the way to the stage. The Madam introduces me but I barely hear her above the noise of my heart pounding in my chest. "Ladies, this is Axl Rose," she chuckles to the room of naked girls already dancing. I teeter into the middle of the rouge-lit room and I wait for something to happen for half a second, staring at the lit up mirrors like a deer in red headlights.

Suddenly small windows start to pop open from different sides of the circular stage. The wall of windows look kind of like the stalls of a shooting range, and I feel like the stunned naked target teetering near the mirrored back wall. I'm glad I've practiced surprise attacks in the shoes because I feel like the eyes come from all directions and are taking me off guard. Nicki told me that the main thing I had to concentrate on was making sure I spread my legs as much as possible and flashed the Money Shot. I try to be inventive with this so I start to climb on the clear sparkling poles that frame all the windows. I climb up and swing at the walls like a little monkey. I'm also so caffeinated that I'm sort of acrobatic in my leg kicks and straddling of each little window box. I make sure to flash each grinning head in each window.

After a few minutes of spastic movements I turn around and look at what the other *real* stripper girls are doing. *Ooopsy!* How slow they're moving! They look like lazy cats, the way they roll around playfully and stretch out on the red carpet. When they do curl open their legs, they do it teasingly, so it looks like a porn movie stuck on the slow motion setting. How embarrassing! I try to slow my body down to imitate the sphinxy Minxy cats. But all that coffee still makes me feel like a pinball, hurling at the windows like they are ten point goals. Right when I think my pounding heart will explode from my bare chest the Madam finally comes to get me. *Wow, that wasn't so bad.* It was actually sort of fun. I was so busy swinging from tiny glowing poles that I even forgot to check out the hot naked girls on stage with me.

The Madams tell me they will call me within the week. I call Cruzer who is waiting at the bar around the corner. She has a strange look on her face. "How was it?" she asks when I hop in her truck.

"I was like a monkey on crack in there. I don't think I'm meant to be a stripper," I say sadly.

"I coulda told you that."

We start to drive back to the Mission. We're both quiet. I'm bummed about my audition and Cruzer still has that weirdly serious look on her face.

She finally breaks the silence. "So Soda just called me and told me he wants to fuck my ex. I figure he already has and is just trying to break it to me."

*Shit*. Why now?

"Uh. I dunno. I've been so caught up in learning to walk in moon shoes, dipping my body parts in hot wax, and letting femmes put makeup on me, that I haven't been paying attention to what everyone else is doing."

"Right."

"You hate Bad News Brenda anyways," I remind her.

"Yeah, whatever. I told Soda I'm not coming home if he's gonna date her. I'll just move to Philly with Topsy if I ever see them together. Fuck Soda and his bullshit. He thinks he can make every last girl in this city fall in love with him!"

I know that Cruzer has been an asshole lately, but I don't want her to move. *Fucking Soda*. Why did he have to almost give her a real reason that I couldn't argue with?

In the morning I can't walk right, my upper thighs are so sore from all those spastic spread eagle squats. If I'm this sore after ten minutes how would I even work a whole shift? "You'll get your stripper muscles," Nicki says on the phone when she calls to see how my audition went. Even though I told her about my dance moves she still thinks I'll get a call back.

All day I lie around and watch TV since my body hurts too much to skate. Soda comes home and tries to talk about Cherry, but I tell him that he isn't allowed to talk about her to me. I don't want to hit rock bottom today thinking about the possibility of Cruzer moving.

My phone rings and we both jump up, excited.

"Oh it's just Kimi," I say.

I'd forgotten that she kept calling and the other day I told her I would get a Sunday night drink with her. She either wants closure, or she wants to try to get back in my pants. I should go meet up with her and get out of the house. I've been in the twilight zone lately. Plus my legs feel better so I want to try and skate again.

§

Kimi tries to seduce me but I'm good and trying not to get drunk enough to let her. Someone plays Mia's new CD on the jukebox and I cringe. Can't I go into my favorite bar and not hear all about my latest break-up crooning out of the jukebox! I decide to get drunk. *A shot of Jameson, please.* Later, I go in the bathroom and pull out my tagging Sharpie and tag over everything I've ever written for Mia on the great wall of bathroom graffiti. When I come out of the bathroom I run smack into Nicki. She's so attractive. I can't believe that if I get the job I will see her naked all the time. That and tons of other pretty girls. It's such a far-fetched idea that I don't think it can possibly happen. Nicki gives me a quick kiss on the lips and I see Kimi glare from across the bar. I can't handle any drama. I already broke up with her. I go back to where I was sitting next to her and tell her I have to go. "The new CDs they've added to the jukebox are really annoying," I say. She looks confused. I grab my deck from under the bar and go.

When I come home Cruzer is shoving everything from her drawers and off the floor of her room into black garbage bags.

"What the hell are you doing?"

"What the fuck Soda is fucking Cherry!" Cruzer yells like it's half-statement, half-question. She holds a pile of clothes stalled at the mouth of the open garbage bag.

"Uh."

"Fuck him!" Cruzer tosses the clothes the rest of the way in.

I stand in the hall with my mouth falling open. A heavy truck rolls by and The Creamsickle floor lurches to the left. I clutch the railing and it wobbles, too.

*Oh no.* Cruzer is my fucking foundation.

"I'm going to Philly with Topsy and Tiny is going to live in my room."

"Noooooo!" I howl.

"Fuck this winter. Soda is fucking my first love in front of my face. Girls are getting run over and killed by massive SUV's. Everyone is doing too many drugs, and it's way too fucking cold in this fucking house!" Cruzer is dragging the garbage bags to the back closet room.

"You can't leave me here," I stand in front of her and plead.

"Come with me then."

"I have no fucking money. I have like ten cents!" I shout. I empty my jeans pockets and tufts of lint, some girl's phone number, and assorted pink and blue pills scatter all over the wooden hallway floor. Cruzer ducks down to pick up the spilled contents of my life's wealth, which probably means she's just after my pills. While she's crawling on the floor I spin around and grab my skate that is leaning against the cream-colored wall. I run down the stairs with my legs aching. Fuck Cruzer and her fucking rich parents making it possible for her to just up and move just like that!

As I skate, I wonder who I will skate with, when Cruzer is gone, and Soda is dating that bitch Cherry. I wonder if the Minxy will call me and even if they do, could I even work there? I wonder how long it will take for my hair to grow back on my weird-looking pussy. I wonder if Mia's new girlfriend fucks her better than I did or loves her as hard. I wonder what Nicki sleeps in, naked or a lacy slip type thing. I wonder how quickly Cruzer will be back. I wonder if I can still bomb a steep ass hill with these jelly legs?

When I get to the top of Dolores Hill, I pause to make sure there aren't any cars. The streets make me so scared ever since Goldy died. My heart beats hard in my chest. I blink the fog out of my eyes, slap my board back onto the asphalt, and don't think about anything but flying.

# Chapter 15

The window I'm dancing in front of slides down and I pop my heel off the ledge right before the screen closes. It's a real practiced coordination knowing how many seconds it takes for every movement, something my months of working tons and tons of shifts at the Minxy has taught me. I look over at the other girls who are all plopped down on the floor, because when all the windows are closed, that's when we can lounge around for a minute without our legs spread at some impossible frozen angle.

Dakota is talking about how she has discovered this new trick of filling a soap dispenser up with lube so as to keep it readily accessible.

"That is fuckin' genius!" Lexy says. "Do you get it at like a bath store?"

"Yup, and it looks just like those pink cone-shaped ones in a public restroom. I had Jen install it on the wall right next to her bed, so we can fuck all day and not even bother with looking for the bottle. You just reach over and *pump, pump*, it's dripping into your hand, all the lube you want."

"I need that!" Lexy shrieks. "I hate when you're in a moment, and you can't find the dang bottle. Like when it's all-small and it falls down the crack of the bed, and you're like, c'mon don't pull your damn hand outta me to find that bottle! Grr!"

A window creaks open nearest to me so I sway towards it. I flip my belt skirt up, and shimmy down so my legs slowly spread wider as I check out the guy in the half of a second before his booth light switches off. Most the time all I see is a bobbing grinning head.

No matter how many months I've worked at The Minxy, when I look in the mirrors I still feel like my sexy moves look funny. I'm convinced that all the sexiness that girls seem to have inherently learned, by practicing in mirrors as teenagers, or rehearsing at slumber parties, or whatever they did, that just made it all come naturally, had completely escaped me. It's like when a camera is pointed on a Minxy dancer, and as a reflex she arches her back, sucks in her tummy, thrusts out her tits, and purses her lips in some sort of sexy smirk. Last month when I got my picture taken for The Fantasy Box, Madam Vivian had to practically coach me through every pose. In the first few I did my typical tough look for the camera; chin down, eyes narrowed, and lips smug. "Don't you have a *sexy* pose, dah-ling?" Madam Vivian asked, hesitating before snapping the shot.

If I were with Soda and Cruzer, we would have done the face I was doing, but with shoulders hunched, and holding our hands cupped like C's for the Crew.

"Um, I guess not," I said.

"You're not gonna get any Fantasy Box customers wanting to come see you if you look like you are gonna kick their asses," Madam Vivian said sweetly to me like she was a schoolteacher. A super, super hot schoolteacher.

"Sorry," I mumbled.

"I mean unless you want to learn more dominatrix stuff?" she suggested. "But then you are gonna have to get some new outfits. I would give you some, but I gave all my stuff away to the other pretty Babeez."

My current outfits consist of a bunch of pink frilly things that had been cheap at the ho store in the Haight. I bought them even though "cheap" just meant cheap for stripper clothes. On average it was like twenty dollars for a two-inch scrap of ruffled lace that was supposed to be a stripper "skirt." As soon as I had some time on my hands and wasn't always working, I planned to prove that you could get the same outfit by ripping the hem off a tutu at a thrift store, or cutting up some ugly sequined Eighties dress that would probably cost under a dollar. Fashion for the thrifty stripper.

Anyways, my pink ruffly and polka-dotted clothes worked for my image, since the madams tended to advertise me on The Fantasy Box hotline as "a young tattooed tart," or "a punk kitten nymphet." I wasn't bored yet with this alter ego. I imagined I was the underage punk rock girl who could only get into all-ages shows, and had a Gilman's membership card in her pink skull-and-crossbones wallet. I was the slutty drunk eighteen-year-old whose bra strap was held on with safety pins. I probably shopped at Hot Topic for my pirate bras and kitty cat lingerie. The Fantasy Box red lights helped me back this all up, with their insane power to make me look barely sixteen years old. The guys would constantly ask, "How old are you?" with eager eyes, and they didn't even listen for a response. They had already made up their minds. I was *young*. I think the line was just part of a fantasy and "How old are you?" was some excitingly dirty question. I never destroyed their fantasies and told them I was twenty-two, that seemed too old for the route they wanted to go. "Barely legal," was my answer because they liked it when I used terms they were familiar with.

Madam Vivian finally got at least one good picture of me; she got me to relax by giving me swigs of whiskey. She was such an enabler, for a boss.

She told me not to worry if I thought sexy didn't come natural, that it could be learned just like cooking, hand jobs or sewing. Yeah, she said hand jobs. Sounds random, but I think they were on her mind because earlier in the dressing room these girls, Sapphire and Ivy, were talking about learning dozens of new hand job techniques from instructional videos on handjobadvice.com. They were both planning to try out for a new massage parlor that was opening up.

"Have you tried the Two Finger Corkscrew?"

"No, but have you tried the Swizzle Stick?"

It went on and on. I listened as I got ready for my photo

shoot.

"What about Milking The Bull?"

I forced a chunk of my too-short hair around the curling iron. Yup, I was even curling my hair. Nicki would have been so proud. She had taken a special interest in all things involving what she referred to as "Breaking My Femme Cherry." Recently, she'd even left fashion magazines in The Creamsickle bathroom on top of the piles of *High Times, Skateboard Magazine*, and the well-worn copies of *Playboy*. First, I suspected Cherry was to blame, but later at work, Nicki said, "Did you see in that *Cosmo* how you are supposed to moisturize while you're still wet after a shower? I always thought you should be dry before lotion time so it can sink in, but apparently I was wrong!"

"I knew that," Sapphire said.

"Oh yeah, it locks in moisture," I said and nodded absentmindedly. And then I noticed Nicki smiling proudly at me, and I couldn't believe what had just popped out of my mouth. I had never applied head-to-toe lotion after a shower, or at any other time, but I had in fact been reading those silly magazines when I was on the toilet and apparently the information had been sinking in.

"If you want I can make you feel sexy," Madam Vivian said as she printed out the digital picture of me.

What? Had my boss just said that?

"Uh, I feel sexy but not in the way a *girl* feels sexy," I said.

"Yeah, but you could act like those Babeez you fuck, like a sort of, *What Would Jesus Do?* You could ask yourself, *What Would a Babee I Was Fucking Do?* How do they play and seduce you? I bet they twirl their hair, lick their lips, give you wide fuck-me eyes, huh?" Madam Vivian demonstrated all these moves while she made copies of the printed-out digital photo of me on the photocopier, against which she was pressed very closely in her tight black pencil skirt.

Madam Vivian's mind lived in a completely different era. I have never seen her wearing anything but vintage Twenties clothing, pillbox hats, lacy gloves, and top-notch absolute vintage glamour. I had seen her on stage dancing only once, and she wore authentically vintage lingerie, as if she had borrowed it directly from Betty Paige.

Madam Vivian was an insomniac and she officially kept ridiculously late office hours. I would peek in on my breaks and see the yellow desk lamp illuminating half her face, like a private detective in an office decorated as an old brothel. Like she was a P.I. who worked strictly for johns and harlots. When she got elected to the Madam position she immediately gave the old boring office a complete makeover: she hung peacock feathers, vintage bathing suits, decadent scarves and Parisian flapper-style posters all over the walls, and even some in the dressing-room bathrooms. She brought in a plush vintage armchair for girls to relax in when she met with them. When dancers needed to schedule a meeting with her, or if Madam Millie and The Mademoiselle, who had normal office hours, were busy or out of town, then Madam Vivian would try to schedule the girl for a "Midnight Meeting."

"I feel we can communicate best at this hour," she would argue with the dancer. It was rumored she only fired girls at midnight too.

"If Madam Vivian calls you at midnight then you are through," Lexy had warned me my first week on the job. Whenever midnight rolled around for a while, back in the beginning when I wasn't sure I was faking out the Minxy that I looked like a girl and could strip, every time I was at home and my cell hit midnight I would panic until the minute changed. When Madam Vivian scheduled my Fantasy Box photo shoot, I had to haggle her down to eleven p.m, arguing that at two in the morning I wouldn't look my most awake. Once Madam Vivian caught me sleeping on the couch in the dressing room before my shift, and she offered me a line of coke. Bijou and I joked about it onstage. "Just want to keep my Babeez up and alert!" we mimicked, using her rolling accent.

Madam Vivian finished copying my photo and was cutting the edges off so they were perfect squares to fit in the window in the hall, and the display in front of The Fantasy Box. I peeked over at the picture. I looked super hot, red lips and liquid eyeliner wings on my eyes, like Nicki had taught me, red and black push-up bra giving me tits, a phony ponytail curling in one fat ringlet, and the rest of my hair in those baby curls I had spent so long working on. I knew it would get me a lot of new customers, but still I felt completely disconnected from the girl in the picture.

All made up, lounging around The Fantasy Box and waiting for a customer I usually felt like a boy in drag. One night I got super excited because these drunk thugs in the hall discovered my alter ego. They tapped on the window and one said, "Hey, are you a man?" and then started laughing to his friend. I nodded eagerly and smiled huge. I grabbed the little black microphone that projected my voice into the hall, that I was supposed to talk sexy into in order to lure guys into the Box, and I said in a really fake voice, "Well, yes I am big daddy." They thought that was pretty funny so they cracked up some more. After my shift I told Dakota that story in the dressing room and she said young stupid guys asked her and a lot of the other girls that all the time. "They can't handle it if strippers don't have bleach blond hair and huge fake tits."

"Your three-month evaluation is coming up and I think you will have no problem passing and becoming a permanent and bona fide Minxy," Madam Vivian said as she handed me my copy of my stripper glamour shot.

I grinned. I guess I had gotten pretty good at "faking sexy." I had perfected the art of holding a "fuck-me" facial expression for an extended period of time while gyrating on the stage, even if mostly my thoughts had drifted to thinking about wherever I wanted to skate downtown when I got off work. Getting off work and being so close to downtown was one of the great things about my new job: there was a whole new world of skate spots.

Onstage Dakota and Lexy are still talking about The Lube Dispenser invention. It takes a long time to finish a conversation sometimes because the girls, who follow the rules, *hush up when the windows are up*. Right now there is only one window up and Bijou has it covered. It's the lull between one a.m and two a.m. when only two or three guys come in. At two a.m. the booths get crowded with drunks who have just left the surrounding bars, and they usually stay till three, trying to get their whiskey dicks hard.

"My guy can't get his eyes off your booty," Bijou tells me, and backs up from a window so we can trade spots. I'd figured out early on that the big butt I'd been hiding under baggy skate pants all these years is now my best asset. I can hypnotize men for a good twenty minutes just wiggling each cheek in a timed manner. My first shift, Sapphire asked me, "Are you sure you're all Caucasian? That ass is off the hook."

And then she taught me some moves that she called her "Shakin' Rump Ass" and "Slappy Ass" moves.

Besides shaking my ass, the other thing I'm pretty stellar at doing at my new job is working the stripper pole. My first day I was practically doing upside down sommersaults off it. I like to charge up to the top and do a death drop going face down. I'm like a dinosaur on the pole. It rattles as I charge it. The other dancers gasp every time I come crashing down onto the red carpet. For weeks and weeks after practicing on the pole I had bruises spreading like the Great Lakes across my inner thighs and calves. Now, I clean off the pole with rubbing alcohol so I can practice my death drop as I listen to the girls gossip.

"What happened to that Wild Card you were fuckin?" Bijou asks Lexy.

"Wild Card?" Gypsy Rose laughs from the other end of the stage, which is not very far away because the stage is like smaller than my living room. "What's that?"

"It's a girl that you think you know what you're getting into when you fuck 'em but you really don't. I mean if they are gonna wanna top or vanilla or whatever but then they just pull the exact opposite, like a Wild Card, on you," Bijou explains.

"Over it. She's a rabbit humper. All she does is grind my leg for forty-five minutes. She doesn't know what she wants. My hipbones were actually sore from an overdose of lesbian fuckin' frottage. What the fuck!" Lexy laughs. She lifts her leg, and bends down till she can press her hands flat on the red rug. Her eyes flick down, examining her chipped nail polish, as she kills the few seconds left before the eight turns to the nine, signaling that it's her next break. I'm so aware of Lexy's breaktime because mine follows hers, and I'm dying for a cigarette. Or if I get Bacci the door guy, to let me upstairs I can take a few puffs off a joint. Getting stoned on the late-night shift makes everything more interesting. I could ask Bijou to borrow a few of her minutes, since even though we get a lot of breaks they are short. *Ten minute break and back to stage looking pretty.* Page's singsong that night in the video booth rings in my ear whenever I'm rushing around on my break.

The great thing about break is that it follows a strict time code, so a lot of the time you get to walk away from the customer, who is completely absorbed in jacking off to you. I used to think this was mean, but that was before, when I was new and I actually gave a fuck. Now, I understand that pussy is pussy, and it's completely legitimate peep-show customer service to switch one out for the other. They are paying for a pussy puppet show, not an individual relationship.

After Lexy is gone on break Bijou says, "I wonder if I should get on her leftovers. That girl she's talking about is way cute."

On my break I clunk down to the dressing room. It's late-night-empty and silent, except for the soft beat of the stage music, and the faint moans of pornos behind the walls from the private video booths on the other side. It is almost midnight and we go till three a.m., the world falling asleep at some point but we Minxies floating in a nude girl spaceship, with pussies wide awake and smiling on a time clock.

I quickly roll down my tube top so it's a makeshift skirt, throw on a shirt, and trade my three-inch heels for my checkered slip-on Vans, then go through this portal-like door that separates the girls' back room, an underground clamshell of hot pink walls, shiny lights and glittery everything, from the dark smutty halls that smell like cum and cologne. From the other side, admission to the downstairs requires a girl to smile up at a ceiling camera to get a buzz open. The Minxy is like a fun house with all these little rooms divided up by locks, buzzers and permission slip lights that control the opening and closing of doors as the customers play a constant game of jack-off musical chairs.

I still think the dudes look dizzy as I skirt around them in the hall for my smoke break. They look like they are shuffling through a fun house of mirrors trying to decipher between fantasy and reality. From work break pussy jerk off to going home later to their wives. They switch things off and on in their heads so much I figure it's hard for them to compartmentalize their fetishes. I smoke a quick cigarette behind the front desk, hiding from the hooting and hollering outside by the Friday night bar trollers. I know there's a ruckus out there because coming into work earlier the frat boy crowds had me tucking my skateboard, with its wheels hooked to my arm, against my body so's not to smack their drunk swayin' legs as I pushed past. Funny thing is, they thought I was just some little boy but fifteen minutes later some of them probably jerked off to my madeup pretty face and pushed up tits.

I rush back inside after my break because I need the last minute to do an uplift on my outfit before going back on stage. I need to center my wig—it gets all lopsided sometimes when I roll on the floor—and pull up the thigh highs so they stay high and snug right under my ass. Sometimes my unshaved leg hair pokes out of the thin fabric of my tights and I have to tug them up so it goes back to being hidden.

Since becoming a Minxy I've learned some tricks for how to sideswipe a lot of girl maintenance shit. My most genius discovery was when Nicki first took me to the cheap stripper store in the Haight and said, okay, buy some tights, and thigh highs, especially black ones for those in-between waxing days–or you know, those days you might forget to shave."

Forget to shave, *duh*. That was every friggin' day.

Even for all the trauma I went through for that pussy waxing, it seemed like in no time at all the hair started to grow back in a somewhat unattractive, uneven, bristly fashion. I decided that there was no way I was going to relive the trauma of that experience and go visit Nina's Nails and Wax again. I didn't care if Nicki made fun of what she called "my low tolerance for pain."

"What? I've got tons of tattoos," I argued with her. "But that hot-wax-in-your-ass business is messed up!"

So, I stick to the simple routine of shaving my bikini line, which means that I often find myself ducking into a friend's bathroom and shaving quick-style if I'm hanging out and don't want to rush home before leaving for work. I keep the pink disposable razors in a small pouch that used to hold my pipe in the front pocket of my backpack. But legs, that's a bigger commitment, and so time-consuming. I had never shaved except once after an attack from my sisters who waved my mom's *Victoria Secret* catalog in my face and said, "Don't you want to be pretty like her?" jabbing their fingers at the image of Cindy Crawford's long, smooth legs." Hmm, no. But can I borrow that magazine after you're done with it?

I also have scars on my legs, quarter-inch ones on my shins from slamming into the sides of concrete planters, circular red ones on my knees from eating shit a million times when dropping in half pipes or bowls, and small nicks on my ankles from my board flying back at me from the top of a ramp.

One day I walked into the dressing room to see Bijou with one leg up holding a small aerosol can spray-painting her thigh and I made her show me her trick. She taught me about a fun product called Air Brush Legs. The stuff is awesome, you can just spray on a thick coat of Cindy Crawford legs, just like that. "You can even cover up bruises," she said. Bijou's a burlesque dancer but she is also a super-duper klutz, so she's always falling and bruising her legs. It was okay at The Minxy to have bruises, but usually only if they looked sexual, like bite marks on your tits, or needle-play scars, stuff that got the customers thinking about how kinky you were. But, it didn't go over too well trying to wrangle money in The Red Box if you had bruises on your calves and knees like a homeless squatter kid. That's why I got the darkest can of Airbrush Legs available at the Walgreens by my house. I didn't care that it was designed for African-American women. I wanted to cover up my skateboard battle scars and bruises. I figured it would look like I was wearing super dark nylons.

I emptied a can pretty fast. I quickly found out that the one problem with Airbrush Legs was they started to rub off halfway through my shift since I rolled around on the floor so much. I also got in trouble for leaving smudges of my Barbie legs on the metal stools in the dressing room. It was so sad learning how eager my faux pantyhose were to get away from me.

Staring at the wall of colorful tights in the stripper store with Nicki, I realized that tights were a lifesaving accessory. Camouflage for the lazy shaver! I grabbed about six pairs, old-fashioned black thigh highs, the kind with the seam up the back, hot pink houndstooth, pink ones with ribbons, black and gold glittery ones, and a few other varieties of dark-colored ones. "You need that many?" Nicki asked with raised eyebrows when she came out of the dressing room wearing a pleather mini dress. Dude, shopping with strippers is so fun.

"I get extra physical when I dance," I said with a very serious look on my face. "I'm worried about getting runs."

The trick with the tights is that I had to remember to constantly tug 'em up off my skin when I was onstage since sometimes hair poked through the fabric. I never know how much the dudes can see though, so maybe it's not that obvious. Another great thing about the tights is that they totally hide slapdash toenail paint jobs. I read in one of Nicki's strategically placed beauty mags that there's nothing that screams "unkempt woman" more than a foregone pedicure. *Whoa*, who knew? I guess Nicki did because she made me get a pedicure before she would train me for The Fantasy Box. Of course I agreed. Nicki training me for the Box meant that I got to make out with her, and have her teach me how to talk dirty, and watch her fuck herself, all while getting paid to be at work. Mani-Pedi date? No problem.

Nicki must love torturing me because she took us to a nail place that was right on Valencia, the street that usually guaranteed a run-in with a friend, ex-girlfriend or possible next ex. *Great.* The place even has huge windows that everyone can look in as they walk by. I sat back in the massage chair next to Nicki, placed my feet in the bubbling water, and cocked my baseball cap low so it hid as much of my face as possible.

Nicki practically pissed her skirt laughing at me when I got a huge case of the giggles from how the bubbles coming from the foot jets tickled the bottoms of my feet. I got stoned before meeting her, so the day might be more fun, and now I couldn't stop giggling. The ladies who worked at the place laughed at me too. They knew Nicki by name. "Your little brother?" they asked her about me, as they rolled up the scruffy pant leg of my skate jeans. I couldn't tell if they were joking. My giggle fest turned into a feeling of anxiety though after the ladies started clipping, digging, scrubbing, trimming and polishing away at me. One lady had my foot and was digging a tool under my toenail while the other was applying clear nail polish to my fingernails. It felt just plain weird to be picked at in this manner. How much were these women getting paid to clean people's toenails! I justified the whole thing by thinking that my new fancy feet would be doing some sort of service to the public when I did foot worship shows in The Fantasy Box.

Nicki thought I looked so amusingly uncomfortable about the whole thing that she took a phone picture of me in the pedicure chair and group texted it to Lexy, Cello and Veronica. I didn't care, that was minor compared to my fear that Mia and her girlfriend Daisy would walk by and think I was Nicki's bitch boi, or something. *Nicki's Bois for Hire, they will even accompany you to your mani-pedis!* I could just see the updated slogan in my head.

I chose Strawberry Margarita for my polish color. I chose by name, not shade. It was close to happy hour and I would have rather been at the Mexican restaurant around the corner where you can order a pitcher of margaritas for fewer than ten bucks. Nicki got a French Manicure. She kept looking down at her fingers as we walked to the bar and exclaimed, "I love this shit. It reminds me of when I was in Catholic school and how all the snobs I would fantasize about making out with had French Tips."

The glossy berry color on my nails only lasted a few days because the next time I went skating the grip tape scraped all the color from the tips. The toes lasted longer though, so I ended up getting a pedicure again, since it was also a good way to bond with the other Minxy girls and get in on the gossip. I had plenty of time for random femme primping outings since Cruzer was long gone, and Soda was always with Cherry.

My new Minxy posse was the new scene I needed to get me out of the self-loathing rut I had been in post-Mia break up. Right before starting to work The Fantasy Box I stopped by Tiny's work and loaded up on new sex toys. "Somebody's got a new girlfriend," Tiny's co-worker, our friend Skeeter sing-songed as she rang me up for a pink sparkly vibrator, ass dildo, ass lube and purple leopard print handcuffs. I almost explained that I was in training to fuck myself at work, but then I just nodded. It really was like my new job was as exciting as a new rebound relationship. Soda told me that Mia had cornered her one night at The Vine and demanded the name of who I was shacked up with. Everyone thought since I had dropped out of the scene I was in hibernation with a new lover. Really, I was just spending all my time at the Minxy. I'd even started to leave my toothbrush and pajamas there and spending the night when I worked the late night. We were totally U-Haul.

Since I worked the late-night shift every weekend, a requirement of a new girl, I never went out. The Minxy was like AA, for how well it kept me away from the bars, and off The Creamsickle couch drinking and doing drugs all night. When I did try to go to the girl bar with Soda I would get bored because all the girls had their clothes on. At work I was completely over-stimulated with eye candy. There was always a new girl to check out. Hundreds of girls were on call, and only worked once a month to keep their membership and new girls were always coming through, usually crazy fireflies that burned out by the end of the night and never came back.

The night I went out with Soda I just watched the bubbles pop in my beer and didn't even look around to check out what he called all the new hotties emerging from post-winter hibernation break-ups. "You're totally pussy-jaded!" Soda shouted. It was true. I had just finished telling her how earlier today, Lolita, wearing a little tie and argyle knee-high socks like a prep school girl, suddenly bent over to touch her toes in front of me before rushing to stage and hollered, *Tampon string check please!* And I hadn't even blinked an eyelash.

"I bet you could draw a dozen types of anatomically correct pussies," Soda said, tossing bar napkins at me. "I mean even most girls aren't completely sure what pussies look like, right? I mean, what does a dick got to hide? Everyone can draw a dick if there was a dick-drawing contest but a real legit pussy, that's more complicated."

"A dick drawing contest?" I laughed.

Soda was drinking so much lately, depressed over Cruzer hating him, Nicki hating him, Cherry stalking him, and me being so busy with work that I never hung out. He was slurring worse than the drunk man who stood on the corner of our block every night, swaying and always hollering and slurring at us, *Hey Rascals, hook me up with that girl in them rattlesnake heels!* The other night he hit on me. It's like men can smell the stripper on me now. The other day I left work without wiping off my lipstick and damn, the bus driver shrugged at my expired transfer and the same liquor store clerks who usually glare at me suspiciously when I come in with my board were smiling all big at me.

"You're a fucking pussy aficionado, my friend," Soda said and sloppily clunked his glass into mine.

It was true. After a month at the Minxy I knew how pussy looked from every angle, bending over, spread eagle, and pussy popping on a handstand. I didn't need to chase girls. There were naked girls all around me. And plus if I was gonna hook up with anyone it would be Page, my teasing co-worker. *Damn* she's unreal. I never get scheduled with her because she works the day shift since the girls who are part of the co-op get pick of the good schedules. But I see her between shifts. She snuck into the office and got my locker combination and leaves me whiskey and treats.

At the work meeting where we all got drunk at The Motorcycle Club, she cornered me near the bathrooms. She said that she would never date a co-worker. "Minxy romances are the subject of legend and also the swift downfall of many notorious dancers' careers." She set her drink on the seat of a vintage motorcycle that was part of the museum display and adjusted my tie. I'd decided to dress nicely for the meeting because there was a film crew from France shooting for a TV segment on the club. "But, we should do a double trouble in The Fantasy Box sometime," Page murmured. "My regulars would love that."

Later Bijou came up to me. "Page is a total tranny-chaser. You'll never get it. She's just teasing you. What she's best at."

I didn't care if it was true that Page only dated trans guys. Flirting with her was fun enough. Plus, I knew Bijou wanted to fuck me, she was always trying to talk me into to making porn with her for her amateur porn company, so probably she was just jealous.

After getting my outfit in order, I go quickly, down the narrow hall back to stage. I rub the alcohol on my shoes and can already hear the music good and loud in my ears making my body move. Dakota has next break so I shimmy towards her spot. She looks up from her hands and knees and smiles. I say, "Breaktime doll face." She grabs her leopard print ass coaster and snaps her heels by me and I replace her in front of a large man with his dick in his hand. His expression doesn't change when he looks up at the new girl in front of him. His hand doesn't miss a single beat as it pumps away.

At three a.m. when we're done, I take the stripper shoes off during the thirty-second walk down the teeny hall from the stage to the dressing room, so that they are already clicking their chunky plastic parts together as they dangle from my hand by the time I get to my locker. I press my bare feet hard into the floor, stretching out the aching parts and making them learn to walk normal again. I shove the shoes in my locker. The lockers cover two walls of the dressing room. They're the only relief from the other walls that are painted a blindly hot pink with bright lime green trim. Everyone has their lockers decorated with stickers, Sharpied names, sex workers' rights stickers, pictures and magazine cutouts. On mine there is a picture of Bob Burnquist doing a sick ass grab over a hip at one of those crazy gnarly-looking Brazilian skate parks. My grand plan is to save up enough money from dancing to go on a crazy South American skate adventure, and visit Lucia, check out real live versions of the skate parks I've only seen in the magazines, oh and, of course, to hang out with beautiful Brazilian girls.

Madam Vivian comes in the dressing room, wide-awake and smiling coyly in the late night hour. She looks around at all of us changing back into our street clothes. "I just recorded the hotline message pretty Babeez. Bijou, I called you a busty glamour girl whose voluptuous good looks, and sexy giggle will leave you weak in the knees."

"Good. I hope I get hella big titty loving guys tomorrow," Bijou giggles.

"My absolute favorite thing is when I am at home at three a.m. and I record the message and think of all My Pretty Babeez, while smoking out my bedroom window."

I can imagine Madam Vivian smoking in her vintage decorated bedroom with her gold-tipped, black cigarette holder extender in one hand, and an old-fashioned phone in the other. She personifies the dark vixen woman on the cover of a Fifties lesbian pulp novel. She would be the willowy one in a dark dress, back in the shadows, with her hands on the shoulders of a curvy blonde she's luring over to the dark side.

"Nice skivvies." Madam Vivian checks out my boy's Jockeys before she twirls out of the room with her silk scarves flapping behind her.

Sometimes being at the Minxy in the early hours of the morning, high off dancing for hours, I feel like I'm in an alternate universe. I don't even feel like going home to bed, I just want to laugh longer with the other girls. All our private jokes about the customers, we have all kinds of nicknames for the regulars. I get that same feeling I used to get when Cruzer, Molly and I were seventeen and would take crazy skate road trips, like to L.A., or even once we jumped in the car and drove two days straight to Canada for Slam City Jam. It's the, *I've been trapped in the car for hours on end with these girls and we are all high and loopy off each other* feeling. That's what the Minxy does but we are trapped in that glowing red spaceship of a mirrored stage instead. Maybe, that is why a lot of times I just end up crashing in the dressing room after the late night shift. If I leave the safety of the cozy naked girl spaceship then I have to deal with getting home on those cold, crackhead filled, three a.m. city streets. If a few girls I'm dancing with are all from my neighborhood then I can afford to split a cab, but that is rare. A cab by myself is an hour of wages. Skating is sometimes cool because the streets are so beautiful and careless, except for the city workers with huge whirling trucks that hose down Market Street every night. But still, it is the prime hour for the police and the homeless. I can expect to be hollered at and harassed by drug dealers who think the reason I'm out at the odd hour is to buy drugs. One time a cop even jumped in front of me and practically gave me a heart attack. Plus the skate takes nearly forty-five minutes so by the time I get home the sun is about to come up.

Once I got home at that hour and Soda was still up, high as hell and watching the sunrise. Soda is so messed up lately. It's depressing to come home, too. I don't know how to help him and it sucks so it's easier just to sleep on the fold-out futon, nestled up in the pink clamshell dressing room and take the BART when it starts back up again in the morning. Dakota and Lexy also stay over a lot. We are usually able to sleep until at least eleven a.m. the next day because the dressing room is underground so it stays pitch black, like my room in the Cave house did.

In the morning the dressing room phone wakes me up before the dancers coming in for the morning shift at eleven a.m. do. It's Sapphire calling in sick for the morning shift. "Can you work for me?" she begs. I look over at Lexy sleeping next to me. We stayed up late reading the trashy tabloid magazines lying around the dressing room, and playing the "Which star would you rather fuck?" game. This was fun because Lexy is a bisexual, so it was always a surprise what gender she would chose. I could ask Lexy if she wants the shift, but she has been here like every day this week, and I feel bad.

I decide since I'm already at the Minxy and getting here from my house, which is across town, is half the battle, I should just work the shift. I glance at the picture on my locker of Bob doing the grab in Brazil and say, "Sure." This is how I end up *living* at my job. I won't even know what the outside weather is like until I go for a cigarette break. It feels like it's hot though. The dressing room is so hot and stuffy. There are no windows so Lexy and I had the huge fan pointed at our futon bed all night. It made me dream I was in a huge whirling red ball of a spaceship hovering above the city.

I finally get off work at three p.m. I drag my feet down to the dressing room and plop down on the futon. I'm so tired. I start to lazily roll off my thigh highs. Cherry is in the dressing room getting ready for the afternoon shift. She's pulling off a tight blue jean dress that reminds me it's a fluke hot spring tease of a day outside of the dark room. I'd enjoyed some of the sunshine on my hurried smoke breaks.

"Hi punk," Cherry says, completely naked now. She sits down on one of the stools directly across from me and leans into the long vanity counter that is always cluttered with all kinds of girl tools, makeup, hair clips, hair curlers, a straightening iron, blow-dryer and assorted skin creams. She peers into the wall of mirrors, her face lit up by the row of big round lightbulbs above, and starts doing her makeup fast, in a flurry of white powder, blue shimmer and red smudges.

Cherry is called Cherry not because she has red fruit-colored hair or even any sort of a sweet disposition, but because she has two V-shaped cherries tattooed on the nape of her neck that she got during a teenage Rockabilly phase. No one else could see her name's source tucked under her hair, unless you danced with her and she leaned her head to the floor. Besides us, probably only Soda sees it since to everyone's shock, he was actually in a monogamous LTR with her. Soda became monog with Cherry after she supposedly saved his life. He had been on a bender since back when Nicki first started coming over with all the drugs. Then, it got worse when Cruzer left and I checked out. I would come home from work and Soda would be asleep in a different place every time. He wandered around the house in the middle of the night dragging his blanket behind him, falling asleep in a different place every few hours. He would never sleep in his own bed. He slept in Cruzer's bed when Tiny wasn't there. He slept in my bed if I wasn't home. He curled up in the vagabond library in the spare room. One night I found him passed out on a pile of couch pillows stacked up in the claw foot bathtub.

When I wasn't working I tried to look after Soda. I would go to bars and bring him home. One night I found him at The Vine and he was dressed awful, looking like a complete wreck. He'd lost his jacket the night before so he started dressing straight out of The Vine's lost and found box that was in the basement. "That is the gayest jacket I have ever seen." I made fun of Soda. as I walked him home, about the corporate lesbian style sports coat. That's when you know you have to stage an intervention. When your friend starts dressing out of the lost and found.

The next week, skating home from the Cat Fight, Soda fell off his board drunk and chipped a tooth. I was at work till late but Cherry swooped in and scooped up Soda. He had been blowing her off because he was still in love with Nicki, and he felt bad about Cruzer but then from that night on, things changed. Cherry bought Soda a fake gold tooth to go over his chipped one.

The next week Cherry apparently saved Soda's life again when she came into the house using the key that used to be the random hook up key that Cherry had now confiscated and claimed as hers. She found Soda passed out on the floor of his room with a purple bruise on his forehead. Soda had finally tossed himself from the deck of the Pirate Ship.

The next day when I came home, cranky from sleeping on the fold-out futon in the dressing room and taking BART with my stale makeup on, there was Cherry, hysterically telling me how she saved Soda from dying.

"Drowning," I corrected her, but she was talking so loud she didn't hear me.

That was three weeks ago, the drowning incident, and ever since then, Soda and Cherry have been joined at the hip. So much so that I have only seen Soda once since then. He told me that he wasn't dying that night, he was just dreaming of oceans. He'd been so happy that he hadn't even realized he had fallen off the ship and his head was throbbing until Cherry was shaking him and screaming and crying in this hysterical way a girl in love with Soda would do.

"That's how Ol' Dirty Bastard died," Cherry yelled at him.

He said Cherry was trying to make him go to rehab, or at least an AA meeting, but he wouldn't. "I'm not a quitter," he joked.

They would fight about it for hours until the girl subletting Cruzer's room, who was in school, threatened to move out if people kept screaming all the time.

I was glad Cherry was watching over Soda but why did she have to keep him locked inside her house? I missed him. Not only did Cherry live on the other side of the city where there weren't any bus lines, she also never let Soda drive her car. So if I even saw them, they usually were stuck together like conjoined twins. Unfortunately, I saw Cherry all the time at work and got to hear what Soda was up to from her. She seemed to get a sort of satisfaction from telling me how good Soda was doing. She liked to say it in front of any other queer Minxies who might be onstage or in the dressing room. She liked to brag, like she had tamed the wild beast that was Soda. Like Soda had been this old car sitting out back for as long as anyone could remember and she'd fixed it up and made it run, smooth and dependable again.

The other night onstage Cherry told me that she and Soda were fate. That over the last two years Soda's name had been whispered into her ear nearly a dozen times before they met. She said sometimes it was just because some friend would grab her at a club or bar and whisper, "That is that kid Soda," in that giggly way meant to try to hurl her in Soda's direction, but she would roll her eyes because she didn't want to get involved in her ex's scene. She claimed that Soda said the same about her. That a certain bartender at The Vine who saw and knew everything would occasionally say, "You should meet that girl Cherry, and she was just in here a second before you walked in." Then she would chuckle, "Aw, Cherry and Soda, now that would be perfect."

"And then we finally met after all those years of trifling whispers." Cherry smiled and wiggled her tits in front of an open window.

I see something sparkly in the free bin so I get up from the futon to check it out. I'm always scoping out the free bin because I'm so cheap about buying new stripper outfits. I only wear that shit at work so it isn't like it has a dual purpose, like most of the girls who wear their stuff out to clubs or whatever.

Lolita bounds down the stairs and starts talking about a panty party she just had in the Red Box. "I want a panty party!" Cherry says.

I have to lean over Cherry to grab the sparkly thing from the free bin.

"What's that?" She points at a polka dot scarf, so I hand it to her. She pulls her dark hair up and tucks a scarf under and ties it into a knot. She has that stiff-straightened sort of hair that shags over her face, hiding her mean-looking arced eyebrows.

"I think that was Betty Lou's." Lolita looks over. Betty Lou got pregnant so she isn't coming back, although there have been a few pregnant girls who have danced till they were almost ready to pop.

"I can re-accessorize my entire outfit out of that bin sometimes," Cherry says.

I'm busy trying to see if I can make the sparkly top fit me, if I need to go to the Madam's office, get the scissors and make the right snips to make it work.

"Soda's going to the bar tonight. You should go hang out with him, he misses you," Cherry says as she puts some candy-smelling goo in her hair.

*God*, I hate how the only way I get any news about my friend is to hear it from this chick who has him on a leash. I feel sick. I haven't eaten all shift, except for doughnuts Madam Millie brought in this morning. Cherry is just adding to this nausea. I toss down the sparkly top and decide the scissor snipping will have to wait. I gotta get out of the dressing room and get some fresh air. The small room is overcrowded with all the other dancers waiting for the next shift. Lolita continues to describe her panty fetish customer's particular quirks, Dakota speaks loudly into her pink cell phone to talk over Lolita, and this new girl, Sunshine, is arguing club politics with Madam Millie. I shove the rest of my stuff into my locker, yank my jeans over my briefs, put on my skate shoes, zip up my backpack, wipe off my lipstick on the black sleeve of my hoody, grab my skate from under the futon, and go through the portal door that spits me back into the outside world.

I like to skate to BART down Montgomery because if I slow down at the right spots I can catch all the lights since they are designed especially for all the business pedestrians. I put my hoody hood up, knowing that some of the suits I skate past are probably some of today's customers.

I must be completely insane because even though I'm dead tired I pass up BART and skate a few blocks over to the Embarcadero. I just can't handle the thought of going home and being indoors after I have been cooped up for the last twenty-four hours. Even though years ago they tore down the best skate stuff at the Embarcadero and restructured it to be totally un-skate friendly, there are still some small ledges that I like to fuck around on.

I skate until I'm so tried that my legs feel like jelly. Then I eat shit. I shove my hands out quickly to guard my face before it flies to the concrete. I realize right then that I can't try things like I used to, or be a crazy daredevil because now my body is my income. I can't make money at work with a busted face, and I can't dance with a busted ankle. Is this what growing up means? My skateboard will gather dust in the corner so I can eliminate all risks and make sure I pay the bills? How depressing.

I leave the Embarcadero and skate to the Montgomery BART. I can't wait to get home and crawl into my bed. I don't have to work for the next three days, and I just want to curl up under my purple comforter and sleep the entire time. That's the only good thing about having The Creamsickle practically all to myself lately. I can work nights for three days straight and then sleep the rest of the week away, undisturbed.

I call Soda a few days later when he still hasn't come home to see if he'll go skating with me. "I've gone sober," he says. "It's messed up and I don't even want to go outside. I just sit in the house and Cherry's cats glare at me like I'm a loser."

"Shit. 'Cause Cherry made you?"

"Naw. It's 'cause I found out The Doc is a narc. I feel so betrayed."

Yeah right, I think. Soda *would* use that as an excuse. And what! The Doc is a narc? Soda tells me the whole story. What happened was that Katie, the bartender at The Vine, had been dating an undercover narcotics officer. I knew this too because months ago when she started dating the cop I was at the bar with Soda and Dixie on Bloody Mary Sunday and Soda was being super funny and paranoid about Katie.

"She could be wired," he whispered to us. "The cop could be dating her as an undercover sting operation on Lesbian Drug Use! The cop is probably not even a lesbian but on an undercover assignment disguised as one!"

"A Lesbian Drug Use Sting Operation. Yeah right, because that's so necessary!" Dixie laughed so hard that she practically choked on an olive.

"Shhhhh." Soda grinned. "From now on whenever Katie is lurking around and anyone wants to talk about drugs we all need to start talking in code."

Soda explained that the code was that we had to quickly change the subject to computers. She even demonstrated the new code when Katie came over to make Dixie another Bloody Mary. Soda said, very loud and obvious, "Okay, well, what kind of programs are you running?"

Dixie and I were laughing and Katie looked at us like we were on drugs anyways, so Soda's plan wasn't working too well. It was such a random code topic that I figured Soda just wanted to sound smart in front of Katie because he was hot for her, even if everyone was skeptical about her dating habits. He'd been trying to get with her for years.

"She's never going to hit it with you because you're not a baller," Dixie told him. Soda usually pretended to forget what he was ordering when she leaned her rack over the bar.

"A Pabst, duh?" Katie would roll her eyes.

"You're so fine. It makes me forget everything," he would say.

That's why Soda got so excited a few days ago when Katie said, "I have to tell you something!" He thought she was going to make out with him because a lot of times that's what happened in the back room. But instead Katie said, "So the other day my date was talking about The Doc and she said he's a narc!"

"No. Way." Soda was so sad to hear this.

"That's why he's out there sitting in broad daylight hustling all day long. The cops don't care about all the hipster kids buying pills off him. They've got him out there to rat out the heroin pushers and heavy drug dealers."

Soda felt stupid in that moment. He thought about how The Doc sat in his wheelchair all day long on the corner gazing out into the street. He thought about the constant black eyes that The Doc always said he got from other drug dealers, and the time he had up and disappeared for weeks with no explanation. It was so obvious!

"But it's not like The Doc will narc on you," I tell Soda on the phone. Not that I'm trying to be supportive of his drug habit. I was just pointing out that The Doc loved Soda. They'd become so close in the last year that Soda talked about him like he was an old friend or family member.

"I'm not supporting a narc!" Soda exclaims. "That's fucked up! A narc is the worst thing. I don't even want to walk around the neighborhood now because I'm associated with him!"

I remember a story Soda told me once when I first moved into The Creamsickle and we used to stay up all night in the Pirate Bed talking, about how growing up he had been screwed over twice by snitches. The first time was when he was thirteen and he got so crushed out on an older Christian girl at his high school that he actually became a Christian for her. The girl came over to his house and made him throw out all his CDs and any stuff that she deemed un-Christian. Then he spent months fundraising to go on a group Christian camping trip with the girl, figuring that would be his one chance to be alone with her. Then his heart was crushed when the girl went behind his back and told the Christian camp counselors about Soda having what he called "a tiny piece of pot" in his hiking pack. Soda got sent back home that day on the bus and lost all the money he had raised for the trip. The girl never talked to him again.

The second time was a year later when he was escorted straight out of school by two policemen and shipped to a juvenile correction facility for a month. That was when he was selling weed, and working under this bigger drug dealer who he thought was his friend. He had even fucked him to insure the trust, but he still turned Soda in to save his own ass.

"I hate narcs," Soda says on the phone. "It's the lowest fucking betrayal. I will miss The Doc though. If I ever see him I might have to kick his wheelchair, like that one lady did, *ha* remember that?"

"So what now?" I ask Soda. "Why no skating? It's a perfect sober activity."

"Can't right now. Cherry got me an appointment with her therapist. I hear she's good. I want to try and work my shit out. You know, the last few months I would get wasted and then when I was falling asleep I would think about Cello's friend who died, you know, Goldy. She was so young and had her whole life ahead of her and I would just freak out because I felt like it was so unfair. She was so *good*. Why her? I mean, why not me? I would think, here I am, so worthless compared to that girl. I can't even handle love. I was born into the wrong body, and I'm miserable in it. I waste my life popping pills, but I thought... maybe if I died I could be reincarnated as a bio boy. That's fucked up right?"

I would give anything in the world to be able to hug Soda right now. I wish I'd been able to talk to him the last few months about trans stuff but I seriously had no reference point. I mean, of course I'd read *Stone Butch Blues*. We all had. But Soda needed more than a book. He needed a real person to talk to who knew about what he was feeling, maybe like Luc had done for a minute. I'm glad Cherry got him a therapist. Dixie told me the other day that lots of bois were starting to transition. I hadn't gone out in so long but Dixie always filled me in. She'd said, "That kid Denny is on T, and Chad goes by 'he' now, and that kid Theo, and Manno is like this whole new person."

"Maybe you should talk to Denny or Manno about transitioning?" I tell Soda.

"Yeah. But just thinking about it freaks me out. All the 'what if's' run through my head all the time. Like, what if my parents disown me more than they already have? What if I turn into that kind of awful meathead dude that I can't stand? What if girls, like Nicki, don't want to date me any more 'cause I'm a real man? What if I can't afford to transition? What if I can't do it by myself? I just get scared, Georgie, every time I think about it, and not much scares me. It's such a huge deal."

"It's just that you're talking about Goldy's life being cut short, and you know you might be happier if you took this other path, so what's life if you don't take that risk?"

After I hang up. I grab my board and decide to go try to kick flip that three stair at the Embarcadero that I chickened out on the other day after work.

# Chapter 16

There's this mandatory work meeting today to plan Minxy Mania at Vesuvius, this bar around the corner from the club that dancers like to go to on break, or after shift for a shot of boozy. Minxy Mania is this party the Minxy has every year in the spring to celebrate the birthday of the club becoming worker-owned. It's a day when everyone can play and do whatever they want, and come out from behind the glass to do lap dances and topless shoe shines. Of course, it's also the day when all the girls make out with each other, so I'm sure I'll be getting in some debauchery with Page. I can't wait.

When I get to the bar, Bijou, Lexy, Nicki, Page, Lolita and Dakota are already piled into The Topless Lady Psychiatrists booth drinking cocktails. I guess they went early to snag their favorite perch. I squeeze in next to Lexy and she tells me that Bijou is buying rounds because she's in a fantastically good mood. "I think she is finally having good sex with the Wild Card."

It's past the time the meeting is scheduled to start but Madam Vivian, who had called the meeting, isn't even here yet. Most of the other Minxies aren't either. They're rolling into the bar slowly though, in a fashionably late way that's typical of Minxies. The club is enveloped in an air of lackadaisical lateness and meetings tend to start at least a half hour late. "I love Minxy Mania," Nicki squeals. "One year I passed out onstage with

Sapphire and woke up completely covered in lube and feathers in the morning."

"I can't believe we're getting paid to roll around in whipped cream with each other," Bijou says. It was her idea to plan a human sundae girl-pile.

Madam Vivian finally arrives and she orders a drink, then leisurely starts talking to "The Misfit Girls" like she forgot there's even a meeting. The Misfit Girls are a group of Minxies who are all models on this soft-core porn site that is hipster-famous for featuring alternative and punk rock models.

Cherry comes rushing up the stairs thinking she's late, but really no one cares. When she slumps into the booth I see that her eyes are all puffy, like she's been crying. Her perfect shag hair is rumpled, and her high arcing eyebrows that usually look like they are airbrushed onto her forehead are smeared, like the rest of the makeup on her face. The first thing I think is that for sure Soda has cheated on her since it is hard for me to have faith in Soda being monogamous. Cherry just got off shift so the other girls immediately think maybe she is having a sexwork-burnout type meltdown. "Have you been working too much, sweetie?" Bijou asks.

"No, it's not that," Cherry blurts out. "It's that Soda is gonna shoot T! Like real soon. We were fighting in the car, and then just before he drops me off in front of the club he says, 'By the way, I'm gonna start shooting next week.' Like that's any way to tell me something major! And then I was this big crying mess all my shift!"

It's actually pretty easy to cry while working at the Minxy. You could cry all you want, tears spilling down your cheeks that disappear under the red light. And the guys in the boxes won't notice as long as you didn't lean over and give them a face shot, which I usually only do if I am in a good mood. Then you go on your break and think, *Oh great, now I'm this crying stripper girl! How awful!* I went through that my first few weeks on the job when I kept having small nervous breakdowns about my life, stressing out about things like Soda's self-destructive drinking, or the mind fuck involved with going femme for pay. It was easy to lose it onstage when I was really tired and still in complete culture shock about the nature of the job in general.

Everyone tries to comfort Cherry. "Soda is just gonna get hotter," Bijou assures her.

"It's not that," Cherry says. "It's just that I can't believe he didn't want to talk more about it with me. I want to be part of his transition."

Page, who had been quietly reading in the corner nook of the booth (damn she's hot *and* smart) pulls her long lashes out of her book, and slides over until her hips press right into Cherry's. She whispers something into Cherry's ear that brings a smile to her sad face. If anyone can console Cherry, it's Page. "Of course Page knows *all* about the T Boys," Bijou says to me, but I ignore her. I'm busy watching Page move her hands excitedly as she whispers to Cherry, the motion making her small breasts slip out of the too big fabric of her scoop neck vintage dress. Page catches my eye and gives me a flirty smile as she whispers to Cherry. She's always on seduction mode.

"I don't get dating a transboy. I mean what's the difference from a man?" Lexy asks. She's bi but she doesn't ever hang out in the queer scene. Page, who has been busy with her mouth half pressed against Cherry's ear while giving me sex eyes, suddenly pulls away from Cherry. "Oh girl! Sucking tranny cock is so hot," she says as she bites her rougey lip. I imagine that she's also squeezing her thighs together under the table. "Tranny cock is so different than even a dyke with a strap on cock," Page continues dreamily. "Those boys know how to work it. They know what is up."

"You know it girl," Bijou says.

"I don't care about any of that." Cherry's voice is a small explosion from her huddle in the corner of the booth. "What if he doesn't smell the same? What if my Soda's pheromones change and it's not the same love? Or what if his pheromones change and he doesn't like me anymore?"

Until that moment I didn't really understand why Cherry was upset about Soda going on T. I thought she was so proud of him for sobering up, going to therapy, and now finally trying to figure himself out. To me, it seemed like the right thing for Soda and that he'd been moving in that direction for a while now.

But now that Cherry brought up the pheromones thing, it did sound like a legitimate concern. Would I still be secretly longing for Mia if I pressed my face into her neck and she smelled like nothing to me? Like if you fell in love with someone for their smell, or whatever organic process love is, deep within your cells, then I guess you would want them to stay exactly the same, right?

"Plus, what if he wants to only fuck other tranny boys?" Cherry howls.

Bijou, who left the table a second ago, comes back and puts a shot of syrupy Jaeger in front of Cherry. She whips it down, her long tangled hair flying in front of her grimacing face.

"It's true plenty of boys fag out once they go on T," Page says, even though she probably shouldn't be perpetuating Cherry's fears. I would love to tell her that Soda has already "fagged" out, so to speak, with me and a few other bois in the past so it isn't like T is going to change anything, but I keep my mouth shut because I've seen an entire art show dedicated to this girl's tears and I know how hard it is to stop them. Instead I say, "Yeah but we all know that Soda *loooooves* girls."

"Well it's like that kid Theo," Bijou says. "I've been trying to get the attention of him for weeks now and he won't even look at me."

"Maybe he just doesn't like her," Lexy whispers in my ear. She's mad at Bijou, because she had just been elected to Junior Mademoiselle in charge of the schedule and she'd scheduled Lexy for the worst dancing shifts last week.

"So what's up with Theo? Is he a fag?" Bijou asks Page specifically. "I think he is because I was all over him, like lotsa girls are always all over him and then nothing! At the end of the night he just left with that boi Cody."

Page rolls her eyes and laughs. "I dunno, you never know if they like a girly-girl or a faggy-boy. Tranny boys are the ultimate Wild Cards."

"Back when I dated that kid Jo he wasn't on T yet and he said he would never make out with a boi or dude and then the next summer when he was in New York he totally got with this bio guy," Dakota says.

The conversation is making Cherry start to sniffle again.

"Who's Theo?" Bijou asks, trying to change the subject.

"Remember that one boy at Kitten's party that night who I said was asking me about you?"

"Oh I remember him. It was freezing outside but he kept taking his shirt off."

"Well if you couldn't take your shirt off in public for twenty or so years then you could, you would be doing it all the time," I say.

"Yeah, I think like three times he took his shirt off and I had no idea he wasn't born a dude. Wow it works really well," Lexy says.

Cherry sniffles louder.

"Well no matter if Soda was gonna turn into a fag, what fag could even resist Hot Cherry?" Bijou strokes Cherry's shiny hair. "You even turn the peepshow fags straight and get their dollars."

Everyone agrees. Cherry throws back another shot and then Page takes her to the bathroom and when they come back she looks better. I go in there after them to call Soda on my cell, and there's crumpled up tissue all over the counter that Page had used to clean up the pools of makeup from under Cherry's eyes. I want to make sure Soda is okay. If I get a hold of him I would easily ditch this meeting to go hang out with him. Soda doesn't pick up my calls so I head back to the booth.

*Clack, Clack, Clack.* Madam Vivian is tapping the side of her vintage metal cigarette case on a booth tabletop. All the Minxies gradually turn to her direction, moving slowly, like lounging cats. "Okay, down to business my pretty Babeez," Vivian says. She slaps down the clipboard with the sign-up sheet for Minxy Mania attached. "Pass this around. So far we've got a wrestling show. We need a whistle for that. Lexy is doing a girl pile human sundae. Lexy, dahling, remember you need to bring plastic to lay down for that, don't want any chocolate sauce on the new dancing rug. Cinnamon is doing a speculum show and needs volunteers. Sapphire is doing body shots. Dakota is organizing girl fights, Bijou is doing burlesque and wants back-up dancers, and I, of course, am doing my famed *Valley Of The Dolls* show.

Also, we need more volunteers for topless shoe shines. And ladies, ladies, *ladies* no hair pulling, there is always enough debauchery to go around."

I share a cab home with Cherry, Bijou and Nicki since we all live in the same twelve-block radius across town from the Minxy and Cherry is coming back to The Creamsickle to look for Soda. We are the last stop so for a few blocks it's just the two of us. She's drunk off all the shots everyone bought her to make her feel better.

"You know I always knew that Soda wanted to be a boy," she tells me. "One night back when we first started dating, we were drunk and I begged him to let me fuck him and he broke down. He lost it, cried for hours in the locked bathroom. That was when I talked him into going to therapy."

I give Cherry a weak hug. It's the first time we've ever been nice to each other and partially it's only because she is drunk and I'm buzzed and feel sorry for her endless crying.

"I feel like I could tell you that because you're Soda's best friend," Cherry says.

*Am I?* Then why isn't he calling me back? And where the fuck is he?

When Soda does finally call me it's much later that night when Cherry's already asleep in his bed. I can tell right away from his voice that Soda has been drinking. Even before he says, "Meet me at the Photo Booth Bar." He also wants to know if Cherry is at our house. "Well I don't want to see her, so don't tell her where I am. I can't deal with that girl right now."

I skate to the Photo Booth. I walk into the smell of cigarette smoke and sulfur. The bar is the last one in the city that people can smoke in, and the back wall is lined with four photo booths that are always broken. After a night at the Photo Booth Bar, your entire outfit smells like cigarette smoke and photo developer. You had to finally wash that hoody that you probably only washed every once in a while. Soda is crouched over a little round table with a red candle burning in the center. He looks much better than he did when he was drinking away his days and snorting away his nights a few months ago at The Creamsickle. The circles are gone from under his eyes and his skin is back to being rosy and glowing. His dirty blond curls are tucked up in a styly fedora with a small red feather on one side. He's ashing his cigarette on the floor along with everyone else, and takes a small sip off his beer when I slide into the empty seat next to him. "I knew you couldn't be completely dry. Dixie said people call you Sober Soda and it sounded like an oxymoron!"

Soda laughs and admits this isn't the first time he's had a drink or two. "Sometimes it's the only thing I can do that is secret from Cherry."

"I don't know how you deal with her."

"I love her, I think, so I deal with her." Soda shrugs. "But she drives me crazy. Trying to make me into her stay-home houseboy or some shit."

"She's totally upset."

"She's just mad 'cause I didn't run this shit by her," Soda says. "But it's my decision and I know I'll be happier if I feel right about who I am. All my life I've wanted to run away from myself. I don't want to anymore."

"Yeah but she's talking all crazy about pheromones and stuff."

"Whatever, she switches up her perfume every other week but I still want her." Soda laughs. Then he gets a serious look on his face and raises his pint glass. "I'm gonna be a boy."

I haven't seen him look so happy and sure of something in a really long time.

A few weeks later I come home from work and Soda scares the shit out of me when he jumps out from behind the kitchen door. I got sort of used to pretending like I live alone, since no one is ever home except Shelby, or maybe Tiny every once in a while who is now subletting Cruzer's room, so Soda makes me jump like ten feet. Soda laughs so hard at me. "I'm back for good," he announces. "I just wrangled myself out of lockdown."

I glance at the Femme Fetish Calendar hanging in the kitchen. The date indicated that the live-in honeymoon was officially over. "Is she still your girl?" I ask.

"Yeah, but I need major space. I'm going through some shit where I need to concentrate on myself, be selfish. She's pissed I'm not staying with her but she will get over it. She's just gonna have to sleep over here for once." Cherry once told Soda she didn't like sleeping at The Creamsickle because she thought it was a slum house.

"Let's go skate!" I say. "I mean after I take a shower."

Soda grins. "Yeah, I need to unpack and shit, then we will go shred."

# Chapter 17

I have to get better in The Fantasy Box. Nicki tells me that I'm not good at it because I'm too nervous and need to get control over the customers. "They're like dogs. They can smell your fear," she says in this spooky voice. She suggests I start watching porn and copying the one-liners the girls say. "Just get used to the classics like, '*Ohhh* fuck me harder. I love to suck your huge cock. Fuck my tight pussy.' Stuff like that."

After my shift one day I ask Bacci if I can borrow from the club's extensive porn stock. I'll bring the porn home to watch with Soda, who needs entertainment since he's so bored lately being booze-free. He's not drinking or doing pills or blow so instead he smokes like three times as much pot. Instead of going to the bars every night, he stays home and gets stoned and watches TV, or gets stoned and skates, or gets stoned and hangs out in his room with Cherry, or gets stoned and paints shit on the bottoms of old skateboard decks. The painting skateboard decks is his newest manic I've-got-too-much-sober-time-on-my-hands art project. It started when Ed gave him a huge stack of decks that were in the basement of his house, since all Ed's roommates are pro-skaters and they get new decks all the time and just toss aside the old ones. It took Soda two arms loaded-up trips to get all the decks home. When I came home from work there were at least twenty decks laid out on Soda's floor.

Every day Soda comes home from work, smokes a joint, and then starts painting on the decks. Cherry comes over and watches him. "Make one for me," she says in her overly excited voice, because she's extra supportive of anything Soda does that doesn't involve drinking. Soda collects stuff from around the house to glue on the decks so each one has themes. Potter, who only really stops by anymore to collect the rent, emerged from his room to give Soda some random trinkets one night, and another night he had some packaged syringes from Shelby who volunteers at the Needle Exchange. When he ran out of scraps from the house he started going to the Alemany Flea Market every Sunday morning and coming back with tons of cool finds. "When you don't drink there's this entirely undiscovered Sunday morning waiting for you," he announced. One Sunday I went with him, and found a bunch of old-school sunglasses for Cruzer's collection.

We both miss Cruzer terribly. She calls me once or twice a week, but she hasn't talked to Soda once since she moved. Whenever she asks about Soda she makes snarky comments about him and it pisses me off. "Soda still painting those boards?" she asked once. "What a waste, people could skate those." Another time I hung up on her because she said, "Oh Soda's going to transition? What are you guys, poster kids for gender queer San Francisco or something?" She pisses me off but I know she's just jealous because she feels left out. Once when she was drunk she asked me a million questions about Soda's transition and then she'd mumbled, "It's messed up. It's like I don't even know my Crew anymore."

It's so hot skating home from work. My backpack is extra heavy because it's stuffed to the brim with porn videos. Bacci wouldn't let me borrow the DVDs, just the VHS tapes. I skate extra careful because I keep imagining falling into the street, my backpack flying open so videos with titles like *Horny Young College Sluts* and *Ass Hungry Ladies* go scattering across the intersection.

By the time I climb The Creamsickle staircase I'm uncomfortably hot and sweaty. I holler *hello* to the house and my voice echoes back at me as I yank off the baseball cap that I tuck my hair up into when I skate, its brim damp with sweat. My hair's so long now that when it's not tucked up in my cap I can feel it tickling the lower part of my neck, almost my shoulders. It's a sensation I haven't felt since before the second grade when I first got my hair cut short and never went back to long hair again. Bijou told me to take prenatal pills, pumped with iron to make it grow faster and I think they worked overnight. I'm growing my hair out because it sucks wearing my itchy sweaty wig at work. I wouldn't care so much if I hadn't noticed that I made more money the day I wore a long flowing wig instead of trying to hustle with my short shaggy cropped mop in The Fantasy Box.

I don't think anyone is home, that's why I walk into the living room with my T-shirt tucked up like a belly shirt so I probably look like a twinkie fag at a nightclub, big mess of skate-sweat hair, and arms full of porn. That's what Soda sees when his eyes blink open. He was asleep on the couch in front of the open bay windows, head perched on the ledge so scraps of clouds are backdropping the hat skewed on his head, the one Cruzer scrawled *Eat Organic Pussy* on under the bill. The sun is hitting Soda's face and he kinda looks like an angel, eyes bluer than the sky behind him, blinking at me like they don't know who I am.

"What's up dude? No school today?" I start stacking the tapes on the table.

"Dude? You're looking hot," Soda says slowly, squinting and grinning and fully checking me out.

"Shut up." I yank my T-shirt down.

"If we weren't best friends..." Soda mutters, lights up a cigarette and continues squinting at me as he smokes. "You walked in here and I didn't even know you were my roommate, looked like a dream hottie coming over to deliver me porn."

"Dream on. I don't have sober sex," I joke and flop onto the couch in front of the breezy window.

Soda laughs. He grabs a skate deck off the floor. "Check it out." The deck is painted a swarmy blue and green and has stenciled outlines of ships along the side, the beginnings of what looks like a mermaid's fin on the tail end. I'm impressed. I never knew Soda could paint, but it makes sense because he's such a good tagger.

"Whoa. You should start trying to sell this shit at the art galleries in Hayes Valley. Those hipster yuppies would totally shell out." I get up and pop in one of the porn videos into the VCR. "Gotta do some homework."

"Like what? Figuring out what Elephant Dick is?" Soda cracks up. He loves to make fun of me. When I first started working at the Minxy I was confused about some things, so I would come home to a drunk Soda after work and tell him elaborately raunchy stories. One night I said, "Some guys have dicks that look like elephant trunks."

"Eww what's that?"

"Dicks that have like a floppy doughnut 'round the top and are weird and floppy."

Soda started laughing hysterically. "Oh my God those dicks are just uncircumcised!"

I guess since Soda had fucked a lot of his drug dealers when he was in high school he'd seen plenty of dicks. Me, I had only seen like one, and that was in the dark when I was fifteen in the back shed behind my mom's house and I was drunk off a forty of King Cobra. Of course I had seen dicks in porn magazines and movies or whatever but it really wasn't till my first shift at the Minxy that I saw a dozen real live dicks in all shapes and sizes, including elephant style, in my first half hour of work. I went on dick overload and my head nearly exploded that day. I went to sleep that night and my dreams were full of dicks. Not sexual, more like I was skating and doing a front side 50/50 on what I thought was a ledge and then I looked down and it was really the side of a huge dick.

Even though Soda made fun of me all the time about the Elephant Dick incident, I was so glad I had only told him about it instead of my brand-new stripper friends. *That* would have been embarrassing.

Three hours later we are still glued to the TV watching porn. We've discovered the superhero that is Jenna Jameson, and we're obsessed. Our mouths hang open for a few minutes while we watch her fuck two girls at the same time who are lying above her, one with each hand. "That's what I call *hella* multi-tasking!" Soda exclaims while we replay that scene for the third time.

A few weeks later and I can accredit Jenna J. for improving my income. I got so much better in The Fantasy Box after I started channeling her. I also start copying exactly what one guy tells me to do and use it on the next customer. Like if Fantasy Box Customer number one says, "Lay on your back and say, 'Cum on my face.'" Then I do the exact same thing to Customer number two and he goes wild for it. In this way the guys are really just having sex with each other, because they have watched way more porn, and read way more magazines than I ever have, so they know better than I do what guys like.

"I can't believe you said that, you are such a dirty girl," Customer number two says and I think, *Well I didn't really. That man you just saw walking out came up with it.* They think I'm this sex obsessed little cock slut, but actually I'm just a well-trained parrot.

One day this guy says, "You're like the ultimate sex goddess girl, huh?" and I nearly start cracking up. Still, I'm glad to hear I'm good at my job. It's like if at the coffee shop a customer had said, "You make a damn good Iced Vanilla Soy Latte." Now, I can say I give a damn good fake BJ through a pane of glass.

The mystery of pussy is what makes the whole world go round. Guys are both obsessed and utterly confused by it, the way they slide money into the cash box and then just stare between my spread legs, mesmerized, eyes unblinking, like they've never seen anything like it. They probably haven't. The way the awful, unattainable beauty standards of society have made girls so insecure that they'd just rather fuck with the lights out.

But at the Minxy the lights were on, spotlights even, shining on my pussy and making the guys get on their knees, bowing down to get a closer look. One customer asks me to tell him exactly how to make his girlfriend come. Another asks me if I know how to squirt? How can he make his wife ejaculate next time they have sex?

I smile and give a detailed demonstration. I even give him an extra minute for free just to make sure he understands the technique. To make sure he'll never forget where the clit is, even in the dark. I give him every possible angle, kicking my legs up towards the spotlights on the mirrored ceiling like a synchronized swimmer, and thinking that some straight girl should be thanking me for her next orgasm.

"Who's that?" Soda would mumble from his couch whenever we're watching TV and my phone beeps. Sober Soda is always all up in my business, because he doesn't have any. Sadly, none of our alcoholic friends call him much, and since he's got a girlfriend, girls don't call him all the time anymore.

Most of the time when my phone beeps at night, it's not even that exciting. It's usually a text or call from a Minxy girl who wants her shift covered. "The naked girls are always calling me," I brag to Soda.

"*Hmmm*. Lucky, lucky you." The blanket tucked over his head muffles his stoner laugh.

The naked girls, the Sapphires, Candys and Lulus, always have a zillion great excuses for why they can't make it to work. At three a.m. on a Saturday night, someone is certain to suddenly have a family member at the hospital, or sudden debilitating flu-like symptoms. There are endless reasons why they can't possibly dance.

*Beep. Beep.*

"More naked girls?" Soda asks hopefully. "From now on whenever your phone beeps I'm gonna imagine a Minxy lounging in the nude on her black leather couch, or ruffly pink bedspread, and calling you."

"Don't fantasize about their sick calls, Jerk. They're just a bunch of lying babes."

Soda laughs. I reach for my phone. It isn't a Minxy this time. It's a missed call from Mia. I haven't seen or heard from her in months.

"Something big happened and I've told everyone but you but then I realized you're the only person I care about knowing…" she says in her message.

I go in my room to call her back since Soda is more paranoid than chill now that he's a stoner instead of an alcoholic. I know he would tell me not to call Mia back, and he would say something with a dark apocalyptic vibe, like that it was a Pandora's Box situation, or something.

On the phone Mia's voice doesn't have the heart-wrenching effect on me it would have had three months ago. She tells me about how Bijou put one of their collaborative songs on her band's Web page, and how this electro-pop band listened to it and tracked her down because they wanted her to be their vocalist. So then they flew her to Seattle to record and all of a sudden she gets this call that they are getting a record deal and a promotional budget, including a paid national tour.

I knew Mia had recorded with Bijou because one day at work Bijou was telling everyone on stage that she was so tired because she'd been up all night recording songs with Mia in Starla's basement. "Her voice is so amazing! I've been trying to get her to start a side project with me forever and now that we are doing it, it's so genius," she gushed. I was annoyed that Bijou was talking about Mia in front of me but also, I could imagine that their collaboration would be really good. Bijou made electro feminist pop on beat machines and Mia did more of an indie rock, guitar thing so the combination could sound dope. I told Bijou I was jealous she got to hang out with Mia so much, "We still haven't got to the stage of breaking up where being friends is okay."

"Yeah that doesn't happen till you're totally over someone," Bijou said.

"You think she's not over me, too?" I asked, although I knew I was pressing for too much info.

"Duh," Bijou said and turned around to focus all her attention on the customer in the booth in front of her, so I knew that was all I was going to get out of her.

"I'm so proud of you!" I say now to Mia on the phone. I can't help but think of her as a PYT, pretty young thing, smoking on that patio at sunrise outside of the shut down Seaside Diner with the sun rising behind her head and saying to Dixie, "I'm moving for my music," with that look of fierce determination in her intense eyes.

"You know, when I heard, you were the one person I wanted to tell," Mia says on the phone, "and it was so hard to not call you, went a whole week sitting on my hands and staring at my cell phone and then I just couldn't help it."

"I'm stoked you did. I miss you," I say awkwardly. And the conversation is silent for a whole minute.

"One more thing. When you disappeared at the end of winter I thought you were all shacked up and in love, and I was so jealous, but then I ran into Dakota the other day and she said you're spending all your time dancing at the Minxy? What the fuck! Is that true? I mean, I can't even imagine you in a skirt!"

"Yeah. It keeps me busy and makin' money."

"Does it feel weird to show your twat to the enemy?" she asks.

"Naw. I don't even think about it. Except if I'm having a shitty day or something. I mostly just think about the money. I'm saving to go travel."

"So weird, I can't imagine you doing that." She laughs. I remember how much I love her laugh. I wonder what she even looks like now. I feel like I've changed so much.

"I'm leaving for L.A. tomorrow to sign the contracts and meet the record execs, but maybe when I get back we can get a drink or something?"

"Totally."

When I go back in the living room, I sit very close to Soda on the couch and stare at him. "What? You're making me paranoid!" He tries to look over my head at the five-some going on in the porn video.

"Do I look different?" I ask.

"I'm the one on T I should be asking you that!"

"We always talk about that," I say. I mean, I didn't mind, the other night he read me the entire FTM handout from Dimensions, the Castro-Mission Health Center, and I learned all the changes that were permanent and the changes that were reversible if you stopped taking T, and so on. We also joked for a while about whether it was actually possible for Soda's sex drive to increase when it was already at the maximum setting.

"I guess, you do." Soda squints at me since it's now past sunset and we hadn't turned the light on because we've been so absorbed in Jenna Jameson for the last three hours. "I mean you're hot, but I always thought that."

"Do you think Mia would think I looked different?"

"Why you thinking about Mia?"

I don't answer that.

"Yeah, Mia might kick herself that you weren't handy with the eyeliner when you guys dated and you didn't do her make-up for her."

I sock Soda hard on his arm.

"Ow." He rubs the spot I hit. "You certainly don't hit like a girl."

"*Ooooh*, my new Minxy Mafia friends would hate you. Remember? All The Sexy Naked Girls? They're also Hot Third-Wave Feminists!" I tease Soda.

"That's cool, girls that hate you hard usually want to fuck you twice as hard. Funny how that works, eh?"

I laugh.

"And I bet Mia still kind of hates you so you've got it made."

# Chapter 18

I stare at a poster taped to the Minxy dressing room door. *How to cope with sex worker burnout*, it reads. *Get a massage. Treat yourself.* What? I don't have any money for this shit. *Take a vacation* is the one on the list that jumps out at me.

I need a break. I scowl at the men who walk by me lately when I'm in The Fantasy Box, the smell of the club makes my stomach twist in knots, and worst of all, Page isn't working for a few months. She was smart and escaped the foggy half-ass summer of San Francisco. She went home to the East Coast, where there are true sticky hot summers, where she told me she would be wearing tiny cut-off shorts and tube tops all summer long while sipping iced tea on wide porches. Before she left she wrote in The Fantasy Box employee notebook that everyone reads when they're bored in the box, *Axl Rose, I'll miss you. I'll think of you in the middle of the night.* Man, she's such a tease. I didn't feel that special because she wrote a few flirty lines to some of the other Minxies. Everyone was always flirting with each other in that book, saying they wanted to fuck each other and stuff, once a dancer even wrote, "*Candy, will you do a double Box with me? Circle Yes, or No.*"

Burnout.

It has been nearly six months of hardcore engrossment in the Minxy. All the shit that used to be exciting to me, the stories

of crazy fetishes in The Fantasy Box, the naked girls, even the
late nights at Vesuvius were starting to get old. I tell this to
Sapphire and she tells me that I just need to take it to the next
level. "The Peepshow is just a gateway drug."

She's right. A lot of girls who start off at the Minxy later
start doing print work, Internet porn, queer porn films, bachelor
parties, outcall sex work or dominatrix work. Page could afford
to go away all summer because she did a queer porn last month,
one that I already made up my mind I wouldn't watch because I
didn't want to ruin the surprise. "You gotta leave something to
the imagination," I explained to Soda one night when he insisted
we ask Tiny to bring the newly released porn home from her
work. There was a waiting list for the movie but since Tiny was
a manager we could bypass it.

"What? You see the girl naked almost every day!" Soda had
whined, "What's even left? You're ruining my night."

"Watch it with Cherry!"

"Dude, I hate watching local porn with her because she gets
all jealous if I look at a chick too long, because she thinks it's
one of my ex-girlfriends, or future ex-girlfriends, and she gets
all crazy about it."

Another good reason for sex worker burnout is the strange
rash on the back of my thigh. It's from the Minxy rugs, and
it's not rug burn, it's something way more traumatizing. I can't
even tell you what the traumatizing thing is because I don't have
health insurance, so I don't know. When I get sick, I do what all
my friends do, and wait at General for like six hours. It's always
an adventure, that waiting room. One time, when Mia had the
flu, this guy who was doubled over in pain with blood on his
white shirt, like he had a stab wound, kept hitting on her. He
was across the room and he was making the whole waiting room
of people uncomfortable because he kept yelling, "Hey girl!"
and making these hissing, cat-call type noises at her.

Most of the time when anything weird and health-related
happens to me, my first response is to try to ignore it for a
while. *Please go away, I do not wanna go to General, or the Haight
Street Free Clinic, or whatever*. If it doesn't leave, then I call my
friends for advice. When I showed Tiny my rash she insisted I

had scabies. "The medicine is eighty dollars without insurance," Tiny said. "If you get a nice pharmacist you can maybe get away with lying and saying it's for crabs, and get it for free, since the city covers that sort of thing, but most the time you will not get a nice pharmacist."

"I don't have eighty bucks," I whined.

"I heard Jo's house had scabies last month. You should call them and see if they have any medicine."

I didn't want to call Jo. I don't even like him because one time he stole a girlfriend from me, but I also didn't want to think that I might have bugs living in my skin, so I called Jo. I explained my rash and he insisted that it was so not scabies, that scabies itched like a motherfucker. My rash didn't itch. I was so mad that I had to call my sort-of enemy and tell him about my embarrassing infliction for nothing.

The next Wednesday I went to St. James Infirmary, the sex worker's heath clinic, during the drop-in hours. I sat in the waiting room sandwiched in between a gorgeous Brazilian transvestite prostitute named Za-Za, who called me Sweetness, and a gutter punk girl who kept scowling at me. Later, when we were smoking out front, Za-Za told me the gutter punk girl was only scowling at me because she wanted to jump my bones. Za-Za was so optimistic, I knew that if the girl jumped me it would be to kick my ass and steal the less than five dollars in my pocket. There was free food at the clinic that everyone scrambled for, and wow, they even gave free massages.

It turned out my rash was a pretty harmless thing. It was definitely from the Minxy rugs though. I told Madam Vivian about it and the next day she made these fancy felt tip marker style signs that said, "*Summer Solstice cleaning! Time to clean out your lockers and wash all your things, towels, ass coasters, blankets. Refresh for the summer!*" Dakota said that if they actually told anyone you could get a rash from the rug then Minxies would quit by the dozens and the theater would have to shut down for good. "This place is held together by a thin thread. The cookie could crumble at any second." You could tell some of the older Minxies knew that the place was harboring skin rashes, like Marla, who always wore satin gloves up to her elbows, even on hot days, or Claudette, who scowled at you if your stripper heels so much as accidentally grazed her arm when you were doing a leg twirl.

I kept my mouth shut, out of loyalty to the co-op. But, I made sure that my furry leopard-print ass coaster was always between me and the rug when I did floor shows.

I got the fabric for my ass coaster off Cherry. At the beginning of summer she came over to The Creamsickle with a bag full of colorful material and announced that she was going to redecorate. When Soda stopped staying at her house and she realized she had to slum it at The Creamsickle, she told Soda that she was going to spruce up the place.

Cherry did incredibly tacky things to the decor. She hung lace curtains in the usually curtain-bare living room. She shined the floors. She put a doily-looking tablecloth on the nasty table. She even tried to take down some of Cruzer's photos one day to replace them with strange muted paintings of triangles and squares but I stopped her.

"Cruzer will kill you," I threatened, and since she'd dated Cruzer and knew firsthand that she was crazy, she believed me and stopped trying to pull the masking tape off the sides of the huge photo strips. I knew that Cherry just wanted to take down some of the photos in particular because they were of her. Cherry, during her eighteen-year-old, art school, freshly out of the closet fashion phase, complete with double pierced eyebrows, a septum piercing, spiky Manic Panic dyed hair, and a tribal tattoo on her chest that had since been covered up with a huge wingspread eagle.

"What, like Cruzer is ever coming back," Cherry huffed.

"Oh she'll be back, as soon as you and Soda break up," I hissed at her. That was pretty harsh. It made Cherry slam down her scissors and box of nails and stomp back into Soda's room.

Cruzer was actually closer than that to coming back. The other day when I called her she said, "I just had a mental breakdown. My horseshoe ring broke on the way to work and it was totally symbolic. I miss you guys so much."

I twirled my horseshoe ring around on my hand. I was surprised I had never lost it, since the only finger it fit on was on my fucking hand. That meant many a time I had to take it off in the heat of the moment and toss it into my sheets, or those of the person I was fucking. If I still had my jeans on I would always manage to slip it into my pocket, but when I forgot I lost it for a minute. It always came back to me though. Once, I took it off to fuck a girl in the back of a rental car, and when I realized it was gone, I called the company and this lady said, "I just almost sucked that thing up with the vacuum, lucky you." Another time I left it on a one-night stand's dresser and a week later her girlfriend, who she was non-monog with, handed it to me at The Vine with a smirk on her face.

Cruzer told me she was getting her ring fixed at a shop. She also said that she and Topsy were fighting all the time.

"Come home," I begged.

*Take a vacation.* The last line of the *Do You Have Sex Worker Burnout?* poster keeps repeating in my head while I lay in The Fantasy Box. A usual lurker who wears a blue apron and cooks in one of the restaurants nearby walks by for the third time in ten minutes to get a quick freebie shot of my ass and titties in my little outfit. Never, ever, have I seen him spend a penny in the place but he is always lurking around for sneak peeks. I think about my meager South America skate trip savings. I would have more but I feel like whenever I get an extra fat paycheck, I have to spend it on new stripper shoes because mine have been worn down, or a new dildo, or new makeup, or whatever. Maybe I should just go visit Cruzer, I think.

This regular guy comes in the Box clutching a plastic bag that I know is full of panties. "Another pair of panties please," he will want me to say at least five thousand times during the next three minutes. He will also try to argue about the price, by insisting that since I don't have to take all my clothes off, he should pay half price. Why are fetish dudes so cheap when obviously this is the only club that a dancer will tailor her act directly to their needs? I reluctantly click the buzzer on.

Potter comes by the house later, which is weird because he never comes around lately except to deal with bills and leave.

When I see him down the hall I think for a minute it's already the first of the month and I forgot rent. He comes into the living room.

His hand shakes slightly around the heavy jug of Carlo Rossi wine he is holding by the neck. "They're selling the house."

Soda lets one of the small weights he's lifting drop to the floor with a heavy clunk. The ground rattles. "What does that mean exactly?"

"It means we may have to move out. If that is what the new owner wants, which, knowing this street, he probably will."

Potter is referring to how it seems like every month a new house on our slanted street is getting gutted, and re-rented for a much higher profit. I would tick them off one by one when I skate by. *Another one taken by the man!* Our house was on the edge of historic Liberty Hill, a hot spot for revamped million dollar homes.

"Any day now there could be an eviction letter on our door. You never know," Potter tells us.

"Where the fuck would we move?" I think about how rents have been skyrocketing lately in the neighborhood. I stare at the incredible view out our living room windows. I have to push Cherry's lace curtains aside. How sad that The Creamsickle just got a lacy-esque makeover and now it may be done for.

I immediately call Cruzer and inform her of the possibility of tragedy.

"What the fuck, again?" she gasps.

She says *again* because when we lived in Chicago we had to move out of a house that we loved hard. I tell Cruzer she has to come home to help save our house. I barely have to persuade her.

"Shit, Topsy is going to be *sooo* mad at me. And how will I get all my stuff on the stupid plane?" Cruzer whines.

"I'll come get you," I say suddenly. "But, only if you take me to skate *Love Park* and *Philly Side*."

# Chapter 19

I follow the tail of Cruzer's board as she leads us down a Philadelphia street. I love skating a new terrain, not thinking about where we are going. I pay attention to the unfamiliar concrete, the smooth parts I want ride, and the potholes, cracks, and divots I swerve around or Ollie over. I just have to follow the tail of Cruzer's board. She is leading us to the bus stop so we can go check out the famous renegade FDR Skate Park. That's our second stop. We just got chased out of *Love Park* when a security guard came running after us, but we got a good twenty minutes of skating in before that, so it was worth it.

I've been in Philly a week and I'm staying the whole month. Cruzer had to put in a month's notice at her job and she lured me into staying as long as possible with the promise of free booze from the bar she works at and new skate adventures every day.

It's hot. A sticky hot that makes my toes feel squishy in my black-and-white-checkered slip-on Vans. I can feel the sweat trickle down my back. I got this gray pilot's utility jumper at the vintage store Topsy works at my first day here, and then by the afternoon I'd cut off the legs and arms. I've been wearing it since but it still feels like I'm wearing too much.

A huge truck honks loudly as Cruzer and I go through an intersection, and two guys leer out the window. What the fuck? In Philly I get so much car hollers and honks, it's insane. No one ever paid attention to me skating in SF, but here it's like I am skating in a bikini or something. It's not like the baggy jumper is even that revealing. I think it's more about looking like an obvious chick on my board, instead of usually being pretty incognito in my pulled up hoody and sagging jeans. An annoying thing about a dude shouting from a car is that it seems like such a cheap move. It's equivalent to a sucker punch, they get you from your blindside with a whistle or holler and then run away like little bitches. It's not like you want to even bother shouting back because they're gone by the time you spit out a *fuck you*. The whole thing reminds me of being fifteen, back when girls didn't skate at all, so every male in a car that went by had something to say about it. A lot of times cruising down the street on your way somewhere felt like being on a stage.

*Do a trick!*
*What else can you ride?*
*Hey, girlie do an Ollie for me.*
*I'll give you something even bigger to ride.*
*Heeeeeeey, Betty.*

Riding a skateboard can be similar to having a visible tattoo, it's an excuse for any stupid dude to try and talk to you. A good thing about being on a board though is that you can always skate quick-style away from lame dudes. Also, sometimes the sound of the wheels on the asphalt drowns out the car hollerers, so they just end up looking like dumb dogs with their heads flopping out the window, mouths hanging open like they're ready to catch bugs. I can relate to wanting to check out a girl or whatever, I mean, when I'm skating in the middle of the road, I like to check out the ladies. But I don't have to holler at them, or give 'em a sucker punch holler from a semi. They smile at me anyways, when I cruise by.

"Hey Pigtails," this guy yells from the doorway of a liquor store when we're stopped in the street waiting for traffic to slow down so we can cross over to the bus stop. Cruzer hops off her board, pulls off her ball cap and tosses it at me. She rolls her eyes. Even though my hair is sweating and I'm too hot to wanna wear her cap, I put it on my head, and tuck my two little ponytails underneath the lid as we walk across the street to the bus stop. I look at my super blurry reflection in the bus shelter scratched up plastic wall. Besides the street comments, overall I've been having an awesome time not thinking about my body. I can forget I even have a body. For the first time in six months, I don't have to make sure I have those pesky razors in the front zipper of my backpack. I don't give a fuck if I get a fatty bruise, or a zit on my face. I don't give a fuck if my hair is all greasy, tucked up into the cap, or if my clothes smell sweaty from skating all day. I don't put any makeup on or anything. I am extra dirty-style and I love it.

Cruzer tells me while we wait for the bus, "My friend told me never to call the *FDR Park*, *Philly Side*. And we have to be on our best behavior because the locals built the park themselves from the ground up, like *Burnside*, so there's blood sweat and tears in those walls and they are territorial, so they aren't too nice about sharing the park with beginners."

After rolling around at *FDR Park* for a while, we buy sandwiches and sodas and sit on our boards on the side street. There's stuff to skate on the side street that is actually more fun for me than the actual park. Inside the park there are a lot of burly locals zipping around that had come pretty close to bulldozing me a few times. "Look Geo, it looks like I'm getting barreled," Cruzer says as she rolls through a half tunnel made by a rusty metal fence that is curling over at the top. It starts higher on one side then curls tighter like a wave. She puts her hand out like a surfer. Cruzer sits down on her board and lights up a cigarette. "Topsy wants me to stay so bad."

"I know. I think she might handcuff you to the bed when we try to leave next week."

"Ya know, I like it here. I'm stoked I've got a bartending job, and Topsy's rad, but I feel so lonely without my friends... my Bro Crew."

I can't believe Cruzer is talking about her feelings. The only time this has ever happened before was when we were like sixteen and tried acid for the first time, and got a ride to the beach with all these hippies who hit a deer with their car and then did a ceremony in the street to say goodbye to the deer's soul, which completely made Cruzer and me freak out. Then later, sitting on the beach in the foggy night, Cruzer unloaded all this shit about not knowing her real dad and that she would be ashamed to meet him anyways since she didn't even speak Spanish or know anything about her real Mexican family, and how her mom marrying a rich white dude and suddenly getting money made her into even more of a stranger and her past even more distant and how she didn't like boys and hoped she wasn't a lesbian since the lesbians at school had such awful fashion. But that was a long time ago. Now the only way to know what was going on in Cruzer's head was to read between the glossy pages of her scrapbook, to read her small scribbled handwriting in the margins, or crammed into the small empty spaces between the photographs.

"I never thought I would miss my queer family this much," Cruzer continues, "and now thinking about how they are going to take The Creamsickle from us, it totally blows. I'm not ready to not see you and Soda in the living room. I mean, I know Soda can be a motherfucker, but dude, I miss him. And to think he's transitioning and gonna have a new name soon, and voice, and all that shit. I remember his first day in town. I was at that party when Mandy sat on his lap and first nicknamed him Soda, back when he was just a kid."

"He still is," I say. "A kid."

"I want to get back to The Creamsickle before I miss out on everything."

There's a moment of silence. Cruzer is looking out at the people skating the park across the street. Then in the silence she sniffs out the sentimental moment coming on, and so she quickly slugs my shoulder. "Also I gotta get back because you do completely mental things when I'm not around, like turn into a fucking girl, and I don't want to know what's next. You'd probably fall in love with Soda, or something equally ridiculous."

I laugh. "Fall in love with Soda, as if."

The sentence rolls out of my mouth a little strange and Cruzer gives me a sharp look. She snaps her board and starts walking towards the dusty red buildings. I scramble up to follow her because without her I have no idea which sharp turns and rough streets lead home.

Cruzer and Topsy live in a small apartment right above the bar where Cruzer works. To get in their house you even have to walk through the bar. It's so loud that when I try to fall asleep before two a.m., I listen to Mia's new demo on repeat until I fall asleep.

Bijou gave it to me right before I left. We were in the dressing room and she said, "Here's something to listen to on the plane. It's going to give you a heart attack." The demo is like nothing Mia has ever done before. They set her melodic voice, and guitar riffs to electronic beats.

The other day I let Cruzer share my earphones. "That girl is going to be famous," she said.

I had been trying to get a hold of Soda most of the month I was in Philly, and then he finally calls me back during my last week there. I'm excited because I've been dying to tell him this story about this straight girl that I've been fucking. She's a regular at Cruzer's bar so it's been convenient going home with her the last three nights.

Soda's voice is a bit raspy, like it's lingering in the middle of the road waiting for the next shot of T to take it farther down the vocal scale. He explains that he lost his cell phone during a fight with Cherry, during which his phone fell into her cocktail glass. "It was a highly suspicious accident," he says. "Since she was pissed that I started selling weed again and she kept telling me to stop, so of course I need my cell phone to sell, and next thing you know, it's floating in pink-tinted vodka. She can't stop me from slinging. That shit's profitable and I'm trying to save money for top surgery."

The best news is that Soda says that things aren't going well with Cherry. "She nearly dumped me the other day when I asked her if I could check out doing male escort work. I don't know if I care anymore if she dumps me. I want to focus completely on my transition."

Dixie picks us up from the airport. I had missed Dixie. Her big brown eyes and her southern charm are so comforting. She's the one that always takes such good care of everyone. Whenever anyone is sick at The Creamsickle she comes over and makes them tea, and brings them movies. The little dog is sitting on her lap while she drives. It has this funny snarl on its face as it stares at Cruzer in the front seat. The dog trips me out, as if someday it's going to attack and get revenge for Viva Vendetta.

Dixie and Cruzer are flirting in the front seat and I can tell Cruzer is making her nervous. Cruzer slid into the front seat of Dixie's car wearing her reflective sunglasses, her hair bigger than I've ever seen it, her clothes all styley from having the first pick of Topsy's vintage store for the last six months, a red bandanna around her neck and the white cumberbund she wore at her marriage to Dixie slung around her jeans. But I don't think it's just that Cruzer looks good that's winning Dixie over. It's that Cruzer actually moved across the country for love. It made Dixie see Cruzer in a different way. The whole time Cruzer was away whenever her name came up, Dixie would get a sad look on her face, chew her bottom lip. "I miss her," she would admit. Shoot, girls always want what they can't have.

Dixie says she's jealous of our tans. "You guys have to check out Soda's arms," Dixie says. "Whoa, he has been working out. It's crazy how T is bulking him up! Oh and Soda and Cherry broke up. I heard Cherry tried to flush his weed!"

"Finally," Cruzer sighs. She has the windows rolled down and her hand is dancing on the warm air as we fly down the freeway towards home.

Lugging my stuff up the old familiar Creamsickle stairs all I can think about is now that summer is almost over it probably means that it is the last Creamsickle summer, and we didn't even know it till too late. I wonder how long do we have left?

Cruzer runs up the stairs behind me but just drops off her bag in the hall and then heads back down to Dixie's waiting car. "We're gonna go get a Bloody Mary."

I can tell by the look she gives me that she doesn't want me to come with them and be a cockblock. I drag Cruzer's bags into her room, check that no one is home and collapse on my bed. Sleeping on a floor for a month in a hot sticky room above a rowdy bar will make you really miss your own bed.

I wake up to the sound of someone dragging a skateboard behind them up the stairs and tapping the tail against each stair. *Tap. Tap. Tap.* And then Soda is jumping on my bed. He grins down at me, on all fours, arms making walls around my head, his dirty blond hair falling in front of his electric blue eyes. "Oy mate." Soda's voice is different, has a gravelly tweak to it. His face is different too, just slightly, in a way only his close friends might notice. Might be his jawline, more square, maybe.

The afternoon sun is coming through my windows and splitting it right down the center, like a dividing line. Funny that when I was living with him I didn't notice him changing, but it's like it took going away and forgetting what someone looks like to come back and see all the ways they might not be how you remembered them. I missed him so much I want to grab him and kiss him, and for a minute it looks like he's thinking the same thing, the way he's looking at me like he's about to pounce. The air is charged, my heart beating hard. There are beads of sweat on Soda's dirtstache. How could he have gotten even hotter?

Soda jumps up all of a sudden breaking the moment like snapping a twig in silence. "Is Cruzer here? Does she still hate me?"

I roll from my side onto my back and stare at the ceiling, start to breathe normal again. "Naw. She's with Dixie." I get up and go in the bathroom, wash my face with cold water to get the plane funk off me and cool down.

Soda follows. "Is it gonna be weird?"

"Nope. She brought you presents." I saw all the peace offerings she got for Soda when we were packing last night, the caps he liked, fitted 59FIFTY fitted caps in styles that hadn't even made it out to the West Coast yet, skate decks and smuggled top shelf liquor since she got so excited when she heard Soda was drinking again.

The presents and a shared joint is all it takes for The Crew to be best buds again. That night the three of us are sitting on the back porch, just like old times, smoking the killer weed that Soda has been slinging. *Kush.* Soda grinned while licking the rolling paper. *It gets ya all kushed out.* The city looks like a huge mouth splitting open beneath our feet and hands that are hanging through the wood railing slats and dangling over the edge. "Nicki called earlier. The girls want me to come over and sell 'em some weed, and they want us to check out their new pad," Soda says. "Maybe they have Internet we could use."

The other day Potter had told Soda to look up the The San Francisco Tenants Union Web site, and read up on the renters' rights, the fourteen just causes for eviction. Which lucky number would they use on us? It sounds depressing, seeing Nicki's new house that she had just moved into with a bunch of other girls including her hot sister and Cello, when we're getting evicted, but I sure missed the ladeez. Boring-ass Philly girls had left me craving the San Francisco femmes, rocker hair, fierce smiles and fuck-me eyes.

"A Victorian full of vixen princesses, let's go." Cruzer hops up from the porch and I stumble up after, so stoned that the streets below now have little white teeth on them instead of houses.

The living room of The Vixen Victorian is full of cigarette smoke, empty wine bottles, a skinny fag wearing blue wing-tipped eyeliner, and a handful of dark-haired girls lounging on the couch. The last girl in the couch lineup is Mia. She's curled up so small it's like she is trying to make herself disappear, black skinny pants into the black velvet couch cushions, a faint apologetic smile at me through a wall of smoke. I shrug at her apology even though I feel like I've been set up, stoned and so not prepared to see her. Nicki could have given a warning!

I plop down across the room from Mia on a recliner and try to act casual, pretend that my head isn't tripping. I try to keep my eyes focused on the old Eighties music videos flashing on the TV. The girls are jumping all over Cruzer, since she's been gone so long, and she brought them presents, more thrifted treasures. Meanwhile, Soda is trying to collect the money for the weed but no one is listening. The girls start huffing and talking about how Soda owes them.

"You chicks are gonna put me out of business. All my friends acting like I'm a weed givin' tree or somethin'."

"Wait! Are you on T?" This girl Tammy perks up on the couch, peers through the smoke at Soda. "You totally have T voice."

"Yeah."

"It's crazy that people don't even tell their friends about it. All these kids on T lately and you don't even know until their voice cracks or something," Tammy complains.

"What are we 'sposed to do? Send out a mass email announcement?" Soda shrugs.

Nicki is pulling on Soda's arm. She announces that she wants to give us bois a tour. Halfway through the tour, Soda and Nicki disappear, the tour ending in her bed.

I go back in the living room where Cruzer is smoking weed on the couch, sandwiched between Veronica and another girl, her eyes half slits. "Man, I shouldn't have smoked more of that weed. I'm beyond Kushed out. I'm on Kush planet with no spaceship."

Tammy pumps up the electro music coming out of a laptop on the table. I think about how I should use that computer to check up on the renters' rights but Mia is on that side of the room so no way. "Listen to this, Bijou and me stayed up all night making this beat." The gay boy and Tammy start dancing around the living room. My head spins. The whole room is now hot boxed. Mia keeps trying to make eye contact with me until it finally sticks. There's no avoiding those goddamn eyes. Her chin is nodding towards the back hallway. Her eyes are tricking me again, making me follow her.

Mia and I slump against the hallway wall and she passes me swigs off a warmish beer. Soda and Nicki come tumbling out of Nicki's room. Nicki is yelling at Veronica and Cello on the couch, "He just called our house a femme princess pad!"

"I hope you're not inferring anything about pillow princesses," Veronica says and tosses a couch pillow at Soda's head. "I've bent over half the bois in this town over my knee and fucked the daylight outta them."

"C'mon, how you gonna say you're not a pillow princess with those nails?" Soda laughs, referring to Nicki's long bright pink acrylic tips.

"Cotton balls and some gloves!" Veronica shouts. "Easy."

"Right." Soda laughs.

"Jenna Jameson does it!" I holler into the living room.

Nicki shrugs. "Call our house whatever you want. We call your house the *Stink*cicle."

"That's not nice. We're probably getting evicted," Soda says sadly.

"What!" all the girls yelp. "What is wrong with this neighborhood? Manno's house just got evicted last month. Everyone's rent is getting raised! Promise you guys won't move away like all my friends have been doing!"

"Where are you guys gonna go?" Mia turns her sweet, dark eyes on me.

"I dunno." I don't even know how much time we have left. I wonder who I would even want to live with if I couldn't live with Soda and Cruzer.

The yelling in the living room tapers off and Mia has started telling me a story, a really long story about a girl with an aching heart, or maybe the Kush is just slowing down time. Somewhere in the story I learn that Mia and the music producer girl broke up. Mia ended it. *I wasn't feeling it*, she mumbles. *Are you dating anyone?*

I close my eyes a second. I see Page naked, back arched against a full wall of mirrors, a platform heels covered in shiny rhinestones, kicking invisible kisses in my direction.

"Kinda."

Mia's bow-lipped mouth sags at the edges. My immediate reaction is to want to make her laugh, to make her smile again, but then I remember how much she hurt me. I shoot her my best poker face, and lie through my gritted teeth, "I'm really, really happy." I watch the rest of her face follow the downward direction of her mouth, drooping down, down, down like the walls of The Creamiscle.

# Chapter 20

By the tail end of summer a series of luxury cars start to park outside our house and realtors point their fingers up at our windows, with their excited hands drawing big plans in the air.

We watch them. We sit defiantly in the front windowsills and smoke our cigarettes, till day turns to evening, to late night. We're like tree sitters. We want the property investors to know that we come with the transaction, that we're stuck on the house like barnacles on a whale, and that they might have to pry us off the furniture with their forklifts. After we smoke our cigarettes, we flick the butts down at the cars. The people who own them are busy inspecting the empty bottom flat. They see green money lining the dirty old walls like wallpaper. Our cigarette butts thud dully off the shiny sides of the cars, falling limply to the sidewalk, like useless featherweight missiles.

Then one evening I come home from work, during my first week back at the club, tired from a long day of grinding the pole and flashing my pussy, and Cruzer is standing at the top of our creaky stairs, waving a white piece of paper at me. "Bad, bad news."

The Creamsickle had officially got its eviction letter. We had known it was coming, last week Potter had stopped by and announced the deal had been closed, shaking his head and sighing, *Any day now*. Every time I came home I expected a white piece of paper to be tacked to our door that read SCREWED in big red block letters.

But just now when I came to the door I had forgot all about that. My head was filled with other worries, my shitty day at work, how I wasn't sure I could do it anymore. How hard it was to try and snap back into the mindset of hustling, after such a nice long break. I didn't want to think about my body again, shaving it, shaking it, or just simply depending on it again to pay the bills. Also today Lexy said that Page had fallen in love, probably with some jerk face boi who wasn't good enough for her, and that she might not be coming back to dance. What was working at the Minxy without Page leaving whiskey and flirty notes in my locker? And why the fuck did I blow Mia off when she was trying to pour her heart out to me? Happy? Pfttt. I want to scream I AM NOT HAPPY off the back porch and hope it reaches Mia's house. This city isn't that big.

We have to be out of the house by the end of next month, a week and thirty days from now. The news is ten times heavier reading it all official on the typed up lawyer's letterhead. It's like this final trigger for me—a tear sneaks out, rolls down my face and splatters onto the paper. Cruzer, panicked by any display of emotion, takes the opportunity to quickly bum some tip money off me, and flee down the stairs to buy a twelve-pack. When she comes back we slump onto the couch in silence, drink Pabst, and stare at the walls of the house we love.

At some point Cruzer goes and drags out the slide projector that has been collecting dust in the back room for ages, and rigs it up on the coffee table. We sink deeper into the funky couches that are sinking into the sagging floor, and watch the flickering wall, sinking sadly into the deep dark bottoms of our beer cans. Cruzer's colorful photographs of the last few years are putting us into a nostalgic coma.

That's how Soda finds us when he comes home from work. "It's official?" he asks even though he knows the answer just by looking at our drooping faces. He plops down next to us, hand diving into the twelve-pack on the floor in the same motion. "So what now?"

The thirty-day countdown has officially begun. There are

things we've said we were gonna do two hundred times that now *really* need to be done. Like, I need to for sure prove that I could spit off the back porch farther than Soda, and there was that pull-ups contest showdown we needed to have, there are rooms I'd never had sex in, and art installations in dusty corners of the house that we'd been collecting pieces for. Now everything is on a deadline. "Oh this house!" Cruzer howls.

Soda suggests throwing a party but gets bored grunts in response. We're too depressed to party. He disappears out to the back porch for a while, and when he comes back he says, "Get your asses off the couch. I'm taking you guys to Kings Diner for milkshakes."

He sounds like he's our dad, like we are moping children, pouting on the couch all night, Cruzer scribbling in her scrapbooks furiously with colored pens, and me distracting myself from harsh reality by staring at the glowing orb of the projector. We blink up at Soda. I don't really want to leave, Cruzer looks scared about leaving too, like we think if we leave, even for a second, when we come back the house will be gone, a black hole in its place.

We bike to the diner, Soda on his BMX, me on a beat-up cruiser Scwhinn that someone left in the spare room, and Cruzer behind us on her skate, grabbing onto our bike seats so she can keep up.

At the diner we each stir our milkshakes in a gloomy silence.

"Maybe this is our fate, saying goodbye to doomed houses," Cruzer mumbles.

Doomed houses. Houses that kids like us will never live in again. This is Cruzer's and my second dead-end house. Evicted House number one was a beautiful old brownstone on the edges of Wicker Park, a Chicago neighborhood fastly going from hipster to yupster. We loved that house, it was our first house, having just driven halfway across America in order to get as far away from our parents as possible. The house was dirty and huge, and dangerously all ours, for a minute, until the landlord spoke of tearing the place down. We got phone calls and threatening letters in the mail, but we were young and naïve then and we didn't know those weren't enough to legally push us from our beds.

I was the one who went back to Chicago, a year later to see about a girl. I walked down our old street and saw that the entire house was gone, all three brick stories of it, demolished. A black hole. I stood on the sidewalk in front of it and called Cruzer in San Francisco to make sure the house had even existed. It felt like those weeks during that hot summer when heatwaves blacked out the power in entire sections of the Chicago grid, so our block faded to black and we couldn't find our way home from the bars. Also we had been like eighteen and nearly blackout drunk most the time so there was a lack of proof. But like any good blackout we had lingering flashbacks, how our rent was even cheaper than at The Creamsickle, how there weren't any doors on the rooms or glass in some of the windows, how the splintering floorboards caught on our skateboard wheels when we rolled through the wide rooms, and how the cold wind came hard through the cracked windows, so we clung tight to whatever girl we could.

Stirring my milkshake I tell Soda how we heard later that the black hole turned into brand-new sparkling condos. But, that's not the way I remember it. I remember it in all its decrepit, peeling paint glory, groaning floorboards burned into my mind, like a rock star who died young. "The Creamsickle would be the Kurt Cobain of doomed houses," I say.

"It's the James Dean," Soda says.

"Naw it's the Marilyn Monroe," Cruzer says.

Soda sighs. "I've lived in so, so many houses, left houses, short-lived houses, rooms ditched in a hurry, but seriously guys, this is the only one, ever, that felt like home."

We are all silent again. The milkshakes are sitting there, melting, dejected, we've given up slurping on them, silly to think they could cure this gloom.

I watch the waitress, who earlier had ID'd Soda for his beer. He had grinned at her flirtatiously as he flipped open his wallet and handed over his ID with his legal girl name printed on it. It's funny how being on testosterone is making Soda look even more like a teenage heartthrob. The waitress's cheeks had flushed as she locked eyes with him and handed back his ID, turning quickly to hide how his smile made her nervous. We'd all watched her walk away. And now I check her out again, walking through the yellow swinging doors to the back kitchen. She's got these tight blue jeans on, really nice ass, and slinky way of moving across the yellowy glare of the linoleum floor. The floor reminds me of the first time I kissed Mia, her shirt crumpled up on the linoleum in that seaside diner bathroom, the way I watched that shirt slide right off her, looked down and could see the smeared reflection of us in the shiny floor, legs puzzled together, a hand tugging a head back by the hair, and her mouth parted. A beautiful black hole.

Maybe I have the same attraction to dead-end houses as I do girls, like Hurricane with her skin all scrawled upon with all those shaky lines, like the walls of an evicted house. Those broken windowpanes for eyeballs luring me in, and wanting me to fix her up. Mia with her hair tangled like miles of knots left clotted in a bath drain, eyes hung with a dark fringe of draping old curtain-eyelashes. How had Mia managed to creep into my thoughts again? I want so badly to move on. But now she's back, like her heart itself is a dead-end house, so clearly a temporary arrangement, but so achingly hard to abandon.

"Let's go out with a bang!" Cruzer's head suddenly pops up from where it was slumped over her milkshake. Her hair is electric, springing up like a dark-colored Koosh ball against the background of the bright yellow diner booth behind her. "We gotta make something good outta this shitty situation. We gotta make some fucking art about it!"

"Like an art party?" Soda looks confused.

I know what Cruzer means though. She always tells me that whenever her life gets shitty, she always knows she can at least get a good photo or two out of it, like when Cherry was breaking up with her, throwing her stuff out into the street in front of their studio, that was the month she took all the best pictures of Cherry crying. The ones that were blown up huge as the sky and sold for hundreds of dollars, the ones that became the art show that got her written up in the Weekly, her career surfing the wake of that show ever since.

"Yeah. It could be a party. I mean The Creamsickle has this long-standing reputation. It's legend, and now here we are the last ones to kiss its ass goodbye. We need to call up everyone who has ever hung out there and make something outta this, something that people can come over and add to. Soda you can hang your decks, and I'll hang my photos, and you guys can tag on the walls, and it will be like Warhol's fuckin' factory or something!"

"I can tag *on* the walls?" Soda asks.

"Why not? They're gonna paint the whole thing anyways, tear up the floor, knock down some walls. I mean look what they've already done to the bottom flats. Gutted."

"We should have a show," I say. "So anyone can come over and check it out."

"Okay. Georgie, you be in charge of that part," Cruzer says, always the bossy one.

Soda, so excited about the idea of tagging up his own house, jumps up, nearly knocks over his chocolate milkshake, and slaps some cash on the table.

As we leave I scan the diner for one last eyeful of the waitress. She smiles at me, the kind of smile that ruins lives. I will never ever fall in love with another doomed house, I will never fall in love with another doomed girl, I think, as I grab my u-lock from the table, shove it into my back pocket, and follow The Crew out the door.

Cruzer slips her skate through her backpack loops and jumps on the back of Soda's BMX pegs so we can get home faster.

Then at home we clean The Creamsickle from top to bottom. We make the glass coffee table shine again, scrub off the layers of cigarette ash, beer circles and garbage. We lug huge bags of trash down the stairs. Then we start making phone calls. "We want people to come over and make art on our walls and all over the house," Cruzer says to each person she calls. "*A what? A papier mache pony? Okay. Sure. Bring it over.*"

# Chapter 21

"You guys *know* we have to have one last contest," Cruzer says one evening while we are drinking on the couch. Living in an evicted house is a real roller coaster of emotion. Some nights we sit around depressed for hours and other nights the house is full of people working on their art projects. This last week The Creamsickle has been transformed into a circus. Soda usually has all of his skateboards laid out, spray paint cans in all colors forming ant lines down the hall. Tiny has been collecting beer cans from all over the house and putting them into piles for her beer castle installation. Cruzer had started a weird paint by numbers style drawing on the wall, big hollows numbered one, two and three, but the other night the drunker she got the more the painting started to spread all over all walls, and even into Dixie's hair. That started a huge paint fight. Paint splattering everywhere. The next night Dixie brought over pies and decorated Cruzer's hair with cherries, which of course led to a food fight. Cherries and paint everywhere.

Tonight I'm not working on my art project. I'm feeling kind of bummed. Bijou was over hanging photos and she told me that Mia had left on her month-long tour. I had thought for sure she would be at the Evicted House Art Opening we were having this Friday, and I would get another chance to be real with her, tell her how I really feel. So I'm not thinking about last contests.

I'm thinking about sex and how long it's been since I've had it. I'm thinking about having sex with Mia even though she's probably having sex with some cute starry-eyed groupie right this second.

"What kind of contest? I feel like we've done everything," Soda mutters. Cruzer and Soda are very quiet like they are thinking hard.

I mutter out loud what's on my mind. "Sex."

"Yeah," Cruzer agrees. Then everyone is quiet again.

"Threesomes," Soda finally breaks the silence. "We have never had a three-some."

Cruzer's face screws up into an *ew* expression.

"No, no, not us three," Soda laughs. "I mean like an orgy, or something. This place is hook up central and there's never been any crazy sex shit during our term in office."

"Yeah, an orgy! Don't lesbians have orgies anymore?" Cruzer asks.

"That seems so basic," I agree.

Soda looks especially confused. It's like we are all wondering if everyone else is having threesomes except for us. It actually does seem so basic. What if we weren't doing everything to make sure The Creamsickle was living up to its reputation? Cruzer grabs a forty-bottle wrapping-sized paper bag off the floor and writes on it with a black Sharpie. "Reasons why we have never had a threesome." She looks at Soda and me for answers.

#1. Uh, we know all our friends so it would be weird.

#2. We don't want to do it with each other.

#3. Not enough femmes except for each other's exes, which is hella drama.

#4. Don't do ecstasy enough! (That was Soda's suggestion.)

Cruzer tacks the paper bag on the wall so we all can be reminded of our inadequacies for the next thirty days. "The last Creamsickle Contest: The first one to score a threesome gets first pick of the house record collection," she announces.

*Whoa.* The house record collection consists of a half dozen crates of records people have left over the years. It's similar to the Vagabond Library in the pantry, except it's completely off limits for anyone to borrow the records. There are too many exceptional treasures, like bands that are now defunct who had stayed at the house and left a seven-inch, or even some stuff left over from Potter's era.

"It's on," Soda and I agree. We butt our fists cupped in the shape of C's to seal the deal.

The doorbell rings. It's Lucia and Tiny with a case of beer ready to work on their art projects. Cruzer nods over at Lucia. "No way, she is way too sweet to have a threesome," I whisper. The doorbell rings again. It's Dixie and Cello. Cruzer grins at me and all I can do is laugh.

A few hours later, everyone is so busy working away on their projects that no one really notices when Potter walks into the living room. We'd been wondering where the hell he's been. He hasn't came by all week, even though we left him a voice mail about the eviction letter. I'd been afraid he was suicidal. Now Potter is looking around the room with a sad smile on his face. He looks at the paintings on the walls, the papier mache pony swinging from the doorway in front of his face, the graffiti wall in the kitchen, the beer can castle of Pabst on the floor that Tiny is hovering over armed with a tube of superglue, and the collage of "home" pictures Lucia is making above the blue couch. I wonder if Potter is going to be mad but instead after he is done taking in the bizarre scene he simply says, "Well, how much do we get?"

We look up at him blankly. *Huh?*

"I told you guys to look up the renter's rights!" Potter says. "If you did your homework assignment you would know that they are paying us off."

"Money for being evicted? Yeah right!" Cruzer scoffs. She's thinking of the empty pockets we went away with in the past.

"Where's the letter?" Potter wants to know.

*Hmm.* I guess Cruzer and I hadn't got past the thirty-day notice part of the letter when we had read it last week. We hadn't even bothered to read the other legal documents stuffed into the fat envelope.

Soda pushes around all the stuff on the cluttered coffee table and finds the letter. It looks like it's been used as a coaster for pop cans, beer cans and pizza slices, so it's no wonder none of us noticed the money symbols at the bottom of the second page. Soda even has to squint to read the words, spotted with inky spots from my tears that have nearly blurred the sum that is to be divided amongst us. "Well, no fuckin' shit. That's some money!" his face brightens up for the first time in a while. "Almost enough to get rid of my rack! If I go work at the shipyards this summer I will have enough!" Potter grabs the paper from Soda and jumps up and down excitedly. "I'm going to Australia to see Tim!"

Although we'll need most of the money to rent new houses in this expensive city, everyone gets quiet for a minute like we're counting bills in our heads. All of a sudden the room feels so overcrowded with everyone's dreams that it becomes suffocating. Tiny shouts out that she would use that money to fix her motorcycle, and then everyone else starts saying what *they* would do if they had that amount of money. Nicki says she wants Chanel jewels and designer clothes, Dixie wants to pay off her mama's debt, I want to live an endless skate summer in Brazil, and Cruzer punches some numbers into her cell phone calculator and announces that with that amount of cash she could get one thousand six hundred and eighty Vicodins.

When Shelby comes home, she leaps up and down about the news. She'd wanted to move to New York for the last year, but has never been able to save enough cash. "I'm moving out next week," she announces dramatically. "An evicted house is like a dead rat. No one wants to be around it."

Even after everyone has gone home or gone to sleep, Potter lurks around the house slugging off his jug of red wine. He wanders through the rooms muttering, "This house has so many memories." He stands in front of the living room windows and shouts loudly, "Oh the people who have lived here!"

The next day Shelby starts clearing out her room and the many hall closets, huge piles of clothes and leftover junk mixed with treasures start forming in piles on the living room floor, and people stop by to look through the freebies.

Dixie stops by on Monday morning and tries on things from a pile of girls's clothes. "What's up with Cruzer talking about threesomes everywhere? It's embarrassing. Cello's dad was in town last night and came to this art show and then out of the blue Cruzer goes, 'Cello what do you think of threesomes?' Like practically right in front of him."

I laugh. Cruzer has been drinking extra recklessly to drown her sorrows of losing The Creamsickle so she probably hasn't been using the best tactics. Dixie describes how Cruzer had been suggesting all casual to her friends or other pretty girls at the bar, "Hey wanna have a threesome?" like barely after saying hello. It was as if she thought the only reason she hadn't had a million threesomes before was because she just hadn't suggested it.

"So, do you think she's gonna find someone to have a threesome with?" I ask Dixie, trying to make sure I say it in a confused way, like I wouldn't know why Cruzer would suddenly be so concerned with the art of ménage a trois.

"No, everyone just laughs at her and I've turned her down a zillion times!" Dixie says as she inspects the inside of a junked up Picture-O-Vatic that is so rusty I think it is permanently stuck on one picture.

The next morning Tiny comes over to look through the free boxes of video games, tapes and records. "What's up with Cruzer not shutting up about threesomes lately?" she says as she stacks tapes up in a pile. "Last night was hilarious. We go to this after party at some girl's house and we're hanging out with these three chicks and all of a sudden Cruzer disappears for like ever. And then I want to leave and I find her in the bathroom, wasted, with her shoes and socks off and trying to wash her feet in the tub. So I'm like what the hell are you doing? Let's go! And she says, man these girls totally wanna have a threesome so I'm washing my feet."

I start cracking up when I get a mental image of Cruzer with her jeans rolled up and her feet in the tub.

"Yeah," Tiny continues, "I had to drag her out of there. I was like, 'Cruzer, dude, those girls are not gonna have a threesome with you, put your shoes on. We're going home.' The girl who was all over her was offended that she even wanted to throw her friend in the mix." Tiny shakes her head.

When Cruzer finally wakes up I have a talk with her about all the gossip about her that's been delivered to our doorstep the last few days. She agrees that maybe last night was a little embarrassing and she will give up on the threesome thing. "I was real close though. Those girls were totally down."

The day after Shelby moves out I notice the paper bag list has even mysteriously disappeared, or got torn down. Did Cruzer forfeit? Or did Shelby take it along with everything else? Shelby took most of the furniture, the couch and the kitchen table. She took the dishes and the toilet paper. She took the silverware and half the books from the Vagabond's Library in the spare room. She even made off with the Eileen Myles Chapbook I had stashed long ago.

I stomp around the house mad about Shelby's book thievery for a while. I notice that I can hear the echo of my footsteps in the hall. The Creamsickle is suddenly incredibly empty. I look in Shelby's room and it's gloriously huge and bare. I drag the coffee table into her room and start skating it. When Soda comes home he joins me. We try to skate the wall and basically crash into it so hard every time that the windows make noises like shaking maracas. It defies the laws of gravity to skate a wall, but they do it on skate videos so we keep trying. I stop only when I start to worry that I might crash through the wall and into a lair of dead rats.

Cruzer comes home from Dolores Park where she was all afternoon with Napoleon, and we invent a game of hybrid style skate-dodge ball. Napoleon runs in crazy circles around the perimeter of the room, barking at the flying kickball. I can already feel aching bruises forming on my arm where Soda had repeatedly tagged me in the same fucking spot. The fun comes to an abrupt halt when the front door slams. It can only be Potter since Shelby is already in a van driving east. We all rush into the living room as Potter walks up the stairs, so he finds us flopped down on the couches, sweaty and breathing heavy with streaks of Creamsickle dust on our faces.

"Hey kids," he says as we struggle to hold in our laughter.

"I'm going to rent Shelby's old room out for this last month."

What? I've already been plotting other things we could do in the empty room. Soda had an idea about inviting the hot Roller Derby Girls over for a house match, rollers vs. skaters. And plus, is Potter in denial that we're all moving out real soon, like less than a month?

The next morning I wake up to Cruzer standing over me on my bed, waving around a white piece of paper and hollering. *Ow, my head hurts.* I guess I passed out on top of the covers with all my clothes on after I came back from the party last night. I blink sleepily at Cruzer who looks extra wild with her hair in a huge ratty mess and her eyes popping from her head. I debate whether she's still on some sort of drugs but then I remember she didn't come out with me and Soda last night because she said she was "busy working on my paint by numbers, and scrap project." Right. Everyone knew she was just hiding out because she was still embarrassed about the feet-washing-bathtub-threesome incident.

Cruzer straddles me and holds the paper she's been waving in front of my face so I can see that it's a check for four thousand five hundred dollars made out to Miracruz Gonzales. "I need you to cash this. I just went to Bank of America and they said I had to open a bank account to cash this shit and man, I owe those assholes a bunch of money so they will take it. I mean, I think they've already got their dogs on me 'cause right after I left there all these weird numbers have been calling. Creditors, man, they know what I've got and they want it!"

I reach for the huge jug of water that is usually next to my bed but it isn't there. My mouth is so dry I can't swallow. Cruzer can tell what I'm looking for so she rushes over to the other side of my room and thrusts the water jug at me. "Wait, what exactly do you want?" I finally manage to say.

"Will you put this in your bank?" Cruzer pleads and shakes the check at me.

"Just take it to a check cashing place," Tiny groans from next to me on the bed, where she's passed out with all her clothes on too, even her shoes.

"Okay let's go!" Cruzer yells, hurting my head again. "There's breakfast in it for all of you bitches."

In the living room Soda is also hollering about his check and running around the room. He is waving the check in Tiny's face. He even dangles it in front of Nicki and Veronica. Too excited that he didn't even care about trying to hide his feminine birth name. "Baby girl, where's the most expensive place I can take you to breakfast?" He grins at Nicki.

After breakfast Cruzer announces she wants to split up from all of our friends. She suddenly begins referring to them in a hiss under her breath as, "potential freeloaders." We hop on the bus and go to the skate shop on Market St. and pick out brand-new decks. I get a new Toy Machine board, and Cruzer buys a new deck, skate cap, hoody and shoes. I'm jealous that since I didn't live at The Creamsickle as long as her I got a lot less money, and I have to watch what I spend so I will have money to rent a new room. Soda says he's not even going to spend any of his money. He's putting it into a top surgery savings account that he isn't allowed to touch. He's smart. He thinks the eviction is a sign that it's time to get his ass out of the Mission and go fulfill his dream of working on the ships in Alaska. Last night while we were smoking cigarettes outside this party he told me he was leaving for sure. I was sad but also excited for him.

Cruzer isn't as good with money. "I'm gonna need to hide this in your room," she says when we are heading home, about the fat stack of rolled bills she has bulging out of the pocket of her jeans.

Back at the house Cruzer takes Polaroids of us holding four thousand dollars cash in all one hundred dollar bills. It feels delirious, that much money. After that she puts a grand in her bag and puts the rest in a tin can in my room.

The next day Cruzer is already rattling my door in the morning wanting to scoop from the tin can. She says she's taking Soda and Cherry to race go-carts at the miniature golf place and then maybe head over to a shooting range. It sucks that I have to work today. Soda has already quit his job to get ready for his Alaska trip he's leaving for in two weeks.

Cruzer is muttering about Cherry. "So of course me and Soda's evil ex would pop back up after we both get rich! At least she's gonna look super hot racing cars and shooting guns."

I suggest Cherry as Cruzer and Soda's missing link for winning the threesome contest. "You could both tie for first," I joke.

Cruzer groans. It's funny that with all the crazy money spending action, and missing paper bag reminder, no one had mentioned the threesome contest in a while. "When all my friends come tonight from L.A. the contest will be back on!" Cruzer says. "We just need fresh meat around here."

A carload of skater girls that Cruzer used to skate with in L.A. is headed to The Creamsickle right this second to come to the Evicted House Art Show, knowing that it's their last chance to stay at the infamous house.

The next day when I come home from work, there are dicks all over the house. Dildos of all shapes and sizes, piles of them on the couch, windowsills, coffee table and floors. Everywhere. Tiny had suggested Soda and the L.A. kids come visit her at work, for a tour of the dildo-making factory, where she slaved all day manipulating silicone into pleasurable shapes. During the tour they passed by a big box of dildos and Tiny explained that there was this new cock being patented and they were trying all these testers and the dildos had packaging flaws. "Take as many of those as you want." Cruzer's friends found themselves in free dildo heaven and they stuffed their hoody, pockets and arms with every size and shade.

That night we're all sitting around smoking and drinking in Shelby's empty room and people are tossing around dildos like a game of hot potato. There are also dildos lined up in front of the door, like a row of small missiles lined up for take off. I have to hopscotch over them when Cruzer and I go to buy liquor.

The visiting girls are super excited about their bounty. Sly says, "This looks like the beginning of a porn, *ha ha*," and then there's an uncomfortable silence because no one is drunk yet. The girls throw the dildos in the middle of the circle like a fire pit. Someone just needs to light a match.

"Let's call Nicki," Cruzer says. We all know the match would be Nicki. Her red mouth alone is a three-alarm fire. The L.A. girls met her the night before at The Vine. A few of them wanted to make out with her because out-of-town girls always fall in love with Nicki because they don't know what a train wreck she is.

"Nicki is on her way," Cruzer says as she snaps shut her phone.

When the doorbell rings I go to get the door but when I swing it open Nicki has been replaced with an outdoorsy looking brunette wearing khakis. "Hi, I'm here to look at the room," she smiles cheerfully.

*Oh shit*, a Craigslist room seeker. Fucking Potter didn't tell us he was showing the room tonight. Or did we forget? Well it can't be that hard. I decide to get it over with so I bring Khaki up the stairs. *Okay here's the huge cheap house, bathroom, living room. Blah, blah, blah.* In the living room Khaki wants to chat about the details of the living arrangements. "So how long exactly is the sub-?"

She stops talking mid-sentence because she went to sit on the couch but then stopped. We both look down at the couch and I see that it's literally covered in dildos! And these aren't the brightly colored obvious plastic toys, they are a new series of incredibly realistic-looking cocks in neutral shades of tan and beige, complete with bulging veins and realistic style balls attached.

"Oh! So many dildos," Khaki says.

I hurry to shove the dildos to the floor to make room for her to sit but then I stop myself because I realize the full extent of the situation. I'm suddenly aware that I'm drunk and being put in this awkward scenario, which makes this fact seem debilitating instead of fun. *Buzz Kill.* Secondly, I'm wearing bizarre articles of clothing such as a mink wrap because lately when I'm drinking my outfits come straight out of the found items piles on The Creamsickle floor. Earlier we found a fake pregnancy belly, once someone's Halloween prop, and took turns pretending it was a beer gut, but thank God I had passed that torch to Soda. Thirdly, The Creamsickle is strangely dark and quiet with everyone behind Shelby's old room's shut door so I'm really fending for myself. I can already see this woman's Craigslist commentary post on this situation. I can even imagine her calling her friends as soon as she gets down our stairs. "Okay you've heard of crazy cat ladies, now how about a crazy dildo lady? Living all alone in a sad empty house full of realistic looking cocks."

But then Khaki does something shocking. She reaches over and picks up a lint-covered cock. She picks up a couple, even, and balances them in her palms like she is comparing avocados at the supermarket. *Oh wow.* I wonder if she is the missing link for a threesome? How porn-esque would that be? What a plot, random khaki-wearing woman comes over and wants to play!

I figure my best bet is to introduce her to everyone, to at least show her that I actually have friends. I open Shelby's door and smoke billows out. Everyone is sitting on the floor in a circle like the bottle of Jack Daniels in the middle is a fire pit. "Hey guys this is Melinda. She's here to look at the room." No one pays any attention to me.

"Hey Melly, what's up." Cruzer smiles and hands her a shot glass of whiskey. Melinda takes the shot. I'm relieved that she doesn't think I'm a crazy dildo cat lady but I doubt she will want to live in our rundown evicted house for the last few weeks. Potter is so crazy trying to rent that room out. When I go to let Khaki out the door Nicki is standing on the porch. She slinks up to me in the stairwell. Her voice is a gargle of pretty teeth. "Heya sweets." I'm actually much more excited than usual to see her. I tug her up the stairs by her piles of slippery silver bracelets.

Immediately upon rejoining the circle around the dildo campfire, Sly pulls something out of her bag and Cruzer inhales it and then puts it under my nose. I inhale it, too. That's just my natural reaction. I'm such a sucker for peer pressure. A second later my ears start burning up. I look around and I love everyone. They're smiling at me and they look like laughing clowns. I feel like my head is burning hot and I'm embarrassed that everyone is looking at me. I turn my head to Sly who is sitting next to me and shove my face in her chest. Everyone cracks up. "What. Was. That?" I ask slowly when my head stops buzzing and I pull it out of Sly's T-shirt.

"Poppers," Cruzer says. "It's the only drug John Waters will even bother to do."

"Oh. They're fun." I never thought of trying poppers before. I knew that customers at my work did poppers while I did shows for them. The guys were the best customers because the Box was pay by the minute and the poppers would completely slow them down so they paid more, plus they always put all the money in first so they could keep their free hand cupped over their mouths, huffing. They talked slow and smiled a lot, and they were so easy to please.

"Why did you stick your head in Sly's chest!" Soda laughs.

"I dunno I was just thinking her tits looked warm, and safe!"

Everyone laughs harder.

Nicki inhales the poppers next. She giggles. She picks up one of the dildos off the floor and shakes it back and forth, and everyone turns to her like she's holding a microphone. "Wouldn't it be nice if you knew exactly what size you loved the best?" she says. "Like you just knew which one was the one?"

I raise my eyebrows to Cruzer. "Ummmm." The poppers are the gasoline and Nicki has just lit the match with her mouth.

"How 'bout a game," Cruzer says. "Everyone tries them out tonight and whatever one is the best Nicki can keep."

"Let's place bets on the winner," Soda says. "I'm betting on the girthy one."

All at once a half dozen sweaty hands shove into pockets and pull out crumpled one-dollar bills and lint-covered quarters. Everyone places bets, the long john, the girthy one, or the big black cock. Soda pushes the money pile into the center of the fire pit, next to the bottle of tequila. The air is charged with all the potential of sex.

"Hey Cruzer, better go wash your feet," I holler across the circle.

The next morning I wake up in a collapsed twister type formation with Abby and Sly in my bed. *Oh shit.* There are dildos all over my floor and a spilled bottle of poppers on my bedside table. I have this flashback of Abby tipped back over the bed when we fucked and Sly trying to give her a breath of the poppers and how she whipped her head up at the wrong time and the poppers splattering into her mouth. *Oh shit*, it was such a freak out. Sly poured a bottle of water in Abby's mouth and when she popped up, her eyes slits, she spat the water all over my chest. It was pretty hot. Poppers and sex go really well together. The poppers slow everything down for a minute and it's like moving underwater. I wonder if for the first time I've finally won one of Cruzer's damn contests. As long as Soda or Cruzer haven't tied me! There was so much drunken debauchery going on last night. I pull on some boxers and a tank top and pad down the hall. Soda's room is cracked open and I can see him passed out curled around Nicki. The rest of the L.A. kids are scattered around the living room asleep on the couches. How is it possible that I scored?  Maybe they all let me win. I'm so excited that Cruzer has to take me out to breakfast, and then when I get home I'm going to sift through the records and make all the best ones mine.

# Chapter 22

Standing on the docks and waving goodbye to Soda, Napoleon nearly flings me into the choppy water when he tries to leap after the looming ship. Cruzer yelps and grabs part of the leash from me and firmly plants her feet on the concrete to get leverage in the tug-of-war with the dog. A group of cute Japanese tourist girls standing next to us start giggling loudly at our struggle. I can just bet that Soda is probably also laughing at us from up on that ship dock railing. Cruzer took a Polaroid of Soda, looking so happy, standing in front of the huge ship with his anchor tattoo on his arm making him look like an authentic sailor.

Soda left Cruzer in charge of Napoleon because she's the only one who has already found a new house to move into. My queer family has broken up, and I'm still indecisive about what I want to do or where I want to move, or if I can afford to go on my epic skate trip. Cruzer has already offered up her couch in her new place till I figure my shit out.

The Creamsickle is extra empty and depressing when Cruzer and I get home. The partying stopped weeks ago when we got this new roommate, a small timid girl from Italy who's doing an internship program and has to wake up early. And then Soda started packing and everything just felt so terribly sad. "It's so quiet I can hear the ghosts walking all over the house," Cruzer said one night, which made me start to sleep in her room. It's also so cold in an empty house with no people to use as economical heaters.

I decide to hide for a while. I crawl under a cave of blankets on my bed and put on my fat headphones, listen to all my new records. I think about how Soda is sleeping on bunk beds on a ship, being rocked to sleep. I bet he's so happy. I miss him so much already.

Later I go into Cruzer's room where she is working on her scrapbook project. "Mia wants to come over tonight. She needs me to take a press photo of her," she says.

I watch the paper soaking up red Sharpie ink beneath her hand. I had known that Mia was in town for a few days. That her band was passing back through San Francisco having finished touring the Pacific Northwest and now heading south. I had seen the flyers for her show tomorrow night plastered all over The Vine and wondered if I should go. Wondered if there was something I could do to get her attention again. But now Mia was coming to me. Did she really need Cruzer specifically to take her picture or had the lonely road made her miss me?

We're out on the back porch because Mia asked Cruzer to take her picture with the glow of the city lights beneath her. The big fancy recording company that had just signed her band wants her to email them promotional headshots. They are spending a bunch of money to market her and want to know what they are working with.

It's one of those beautiful, nearly fall nights when the trees are blowing tattered leaves into the air. Mia brought a bottle of champagne as an eviction gift.

She takes off her leather jacket for the photos because she's worried the record execs will think she will look too butch to be marketable. "Whatever, look at Joan Jett!" Cruzer argues.

"They just want to see you're pretty. Your clothes don't matter," I say.

"I don't want to be a gay musician," Mia whines. "I want to make money!"

Even though Mia has just gotten signed, she's still dirt poor since they still haven't sent her the fat check they promised. They just sent her on a national tour, but in reality she and the band are still eating Top Ramen dinners every night. Mia is still wearing the same tattered black boots as when I first met her in Santa Cruz so long ago, and now they're extra ratty with soles held on with black masking tape.

Mia and I stay outside after Cruzer is done taking the photos. We pass the bottle of champagne back and forth. The house rattles underneath our feet when a Muni bus goes by. "It could all fall down," Mia says dramatically, flinging her hand that's holding the champagne towards the clouds.

I figure that's a good time to kiss her.

Back in the creepily quiet and empty house, Mia lights votive candles in every windowsill like it's Día de los Muertos. She says she wrote the house a new song called *Queer Castle in the Sky* and she sings it to me as she scrawls the lyrics with a purple pen onto the wall underneath her favorite window in my room.

Champagne sleepy we eventually fall asleep, leaving the house full of a hundred small fire hazards. When I wake up in the middle of the night I can hear rain heavy on the windowpane above the mattress and I'm surprised to find Mia's body wrapped around me, tight as a little kid's fist clenched around a lemon drop. I kiss her eyes open. I fuck her awake. We fuck while the world sleeps.

"I forgot about sex like that," Mia gasps afterward. She is naked, smiling down at me and I feel like my body was just plugged into an electrical outlet. I'm tingling, with weak knees and a nearly exploding heart. I so agree with her. *Having sex like that makes you feel like you've been sleepwalking through a whole year.*

"You'll come to my show?" Mia mumbles when we are falling back asleep, her voice sleepy and sex-dazed.

"Tomorrow night. Yeah, of course. At The Parkside."

"Naw," she mumbles, the pillowcase and the noisy rain swallow up her words. "The one in Lexington, Kentucky."

"What?"

She doesn't answer. Her long eyelashes are closed curtains over her eyes. She's sleeping. I light up a cigarette and wonder what it would be like if she was mine again. I wonder if she really said Lexington, what I imagined I heard. I wonder if she is joking. Funny though how she used to always tell me that there was a gay bar named Mia's there, and that she wanted to go there someday with me and put Dolly on the jukebox.

During our last week at The Creamsickle, Cruzer comes into my room and gets me out of bed by handing me a jumbo-sized coffee. "Stop moping! Remember, we're getting evicted in style!" I try to pull the covers back over my head, but Cruzer nudges my limp body with her skate shoe. "Get up. Mia's gone. Get over it. The house will be gone soon. Get over it! Now get up we're going to move into the living room!"

"What about the new roommate? She's gonna trip out!"

"What can she do? She's gonna come back from work and we'll have done it."

I drag myself out of bed and suck down the coffee. It's this kind of coffee that's brewed one cup at a time and makes you tackle insane projects. I dive into the massive job of lugging half of each of our rooms down the hall and into the living room. Cruzer puts her huge spray-painted gold bed under the windows and stacks our mattresses so they teeter into the windowsills and hang over the edge of the city like a raft over a cliff edge.

We don't leave the house for days and days. We're like squatters, living off whatever leftover food is on the pantry shelves, beans, rice, pasta and frozen things. We even find two big bottles of coconut Malibu rum behind a large bag of rice in the pantry. I get dressed out of piles of stuff on the floor, clothes that we find in the old closets, dresses and old dusty suits. I wear a buffalo hat all the time because it's so cold. We blast the stereo loud through the empty house.

I decide I can't possibly go to work. I keep giving my shifts away to the other naked girls, so I can smoke as many cigarettes as possible in the raft bed, leaning out the window. Mostly we just lie in the teetering bed all day, tell stories, and watch the weather change outside the window. It's October and every half hour the sky changes from black clouds to hail, to pink sun, to sunset, to black with the skyline crisp like a cutout against a black screen. I think that it's okay that I don't want to leave the house. I think it's enough that I can hear the world when I open the windows to lean out and smoke. The far-off sound of honking cars, police sirens, the noise of a drum circle in the park, kids shouting and snatches of sidewalk conversations. Cruzer says during the war protests, each morning she could hear every little shout, siren and click of handcuffs.

Cruzer is usually scrapping. She is taking down all the pieces of the art projects and photo collages and trying to glue and squeeze them into her bulging scrapbook, Polaroids, photo strips, phone numbers, scraps of wallpaper, scribbled stories and drawings.

Potter stops by every day and carries one single armload of stuff from his dusty room out of the house. He seems to be moving one book or sweater at a time, like he's slowly saying goodbye. Other people stop by that we don't even know. Old friends of Potter's, maybe. A lady with some kids who we let jump on our bed and gape out the window. An old queen brings over stale cake and tells us stories. Some other kids stop by who lived here just before Cruzer moved in three years ago. They tell us stories. We tell them stories. This kid James stops by, and says he had lived at The Creamsickle once, back when he was in between things, in between cities and houses, in between identities, back when his name was different than it is now. The kind of name boy-girls have when they first move to the city and have girl names, like Tiffany, Lauren or Isabelle, before they change their names. Before the city gives them a new one. He writes his new name on the wall before he leaves.

The last night of the month Cruzer makes us chilaquiles from the last of the food in the cupboards. When Potter was cleaning everything out she'd said, "Wait, I need those stale chips for dinner."

We get drunk off the found Malibu rum. I run around the house trailing my hands along all The Creamsickle walls and then eventually lay on the raft bed and watch Cruzer take down all her huge photos and pack them up in boxes. She won't let me help because they are her babies. She pulls down huge pictures of Nicki, Mia, Soda, Hurricane, crying girls, girls dancing on top of taxicabs.

She turns up the country song that's playing on the record player so it echoes through the whole house. It makes me think of Lexington, Kentucky where Mia's band is playing next week. I still don't know if I should show up there, but maybe Cruzer is trying to tell me something by putting this record on, or she just doesn't want me sleeping on the couch next month at her new house. Above my head the windows are wide open, I notice the sky has shifted to another shade, entirely different from one I have ever seen before.

## About the Author

Rhiannon Argo was born in a tipi in Moonshine Meadow, California. Her writing has appeared in numerous publications and anthologies including *Baby Remember My Name: New Queer Girl Writing, Lowdown Highway, ArtXX* and *Spread Magazine*. She has toured and performed her work nationally with Sister Spit: the Next Generation. She lives in San Francisco.